GIANT DAYS™

EXTRA CREDIT

VOLUME ONE

DISCARDED

P9-DGV-255

BOOM! BOX™

ROSS RICHIE	CEO + FOUNDER
MATT GAGNON	EDITOR-IN-CHIEF
FILIP SABLIK	PRESIDENT OF PUBLISHING + MARKETING
STEPHEN CHRISTY	PRESIDENT OF DEVELOPMENT
LANCE KREITER	VP OF LICENSING + MERCHANDISING
PHIL BARBARO	VP OF FINANCE
ARUNE SINGH	VP OF MARKETING
BRYCE CARLSON	MANAGING EDITOR
SCOTT NEWMAN	PRODUCTION DESIGN MANAGER
KATE HENNING	OPERATIONS MANAGER
SIERRA HAHN	SENIOR EDITOR
DAFNA PLEBAN	EDITOR, TALENT DEVELOPMENT
SHANNON WATTERS	EDITOR
ERIC HARBURN	EDITOR
WHITNEY LEOPARD	EDITOR
CAMERON CHITTOCK	EDITOR
CHRIS ROSA	ASSOCIATE EDITOR
MATTHEW LEVINE	ASSOCIATE EDITOR
SOPHIE PHILIPS-ROBERTS	ASSISTANT EDITOR
GAVIN GRONENTHAL	ASSISTANT EDITOR
MICHAEL MOCCIO	ASSISTANT EDITOR
AMANDA LaFRANCO	EXECUTIVE ASSISTANT
KATALINA HOLLAND	EDITORIAL ADMINISTRATIVE ASSISTANT
JILLIAN CRAB	DESIGN COORDINATOR
MICHELLE ANKLEY	DESIGN COORDINATOR
KARA LEOPARD	PRODUCTION DESIGNER
MARIE KRUPINA	PRODUCTION DESIGNER
GRACE PARK	PRODUCTION DESIGN ASSISTANT
CHELSEA ROBERTS	PRODUCTION DESIGN ASSISTANT
ELIZABETH LOUGHRIDGE	ACCOUNTING COORDINATOR
STEPHANIE HOCUTT	SOCIAL MEDIA COORDINATOR
JOSÉ MEZA	EVENT COORDINATOR
HOLLY AITCHISON	OPERATIONS COORDINATOR
MEGAN CHRISTOPHER	OPERATIONS ASSISTANT
RODRIGO HERNANDEZ	MAILROOM ASSISTANT
MORGAN PERRY	DIRECT MARKET REPRESENTATIVE
CAT O'GRADY	MARKETING ASSISTANT
LIZ ALMENDAREZ	ACCOUNTING ADMINISTRATIVE ASSISTANT
CORNELIA TZANA	ADMINISTRATIVE ASSISTANT

BOOM! BOX™

GIANT DAYS EXTRA CREDIT Volume One, June 2018. Published by BOOM! Box, a division of Boom Entertainment, Inc. Giant Days is ™ & © 2018 John Allison. Originally published in single magazine form as BOOM! Box 2015 Mix Tape, BOOM! Box 2016 Mix Tape, Giant Days 2016 Holiday Special No. 1, Giant Days 2017 Special No. 1 & Scary Go Round ™ & © 2015-2017 John Allison. All rights reserved. BOOM! Box™ and the BOOM! Box logo are trademarks of Boom Entertainment, Inc., registered in various countries and categories. All characters, events, and institutions depicted herein are fictional. Any similarity between any of the names, characters, persons, events, and/or institutions in this publication to actual names, characters, and persons, whether living or dead, events, and/or institutions is unintended and purely coincidental. BOOM! Box does not read or accept unsolicited submissions of ideas, stories, or artwork.

BOOM! Studios, 5670 Wilshire Boulevard, Suite 400, Los Angeles, CA 90036-5679. Printed in China. First Printing.

ISBN: 978-1-68415-222-3, eISBN: 978-1-64144-088-2

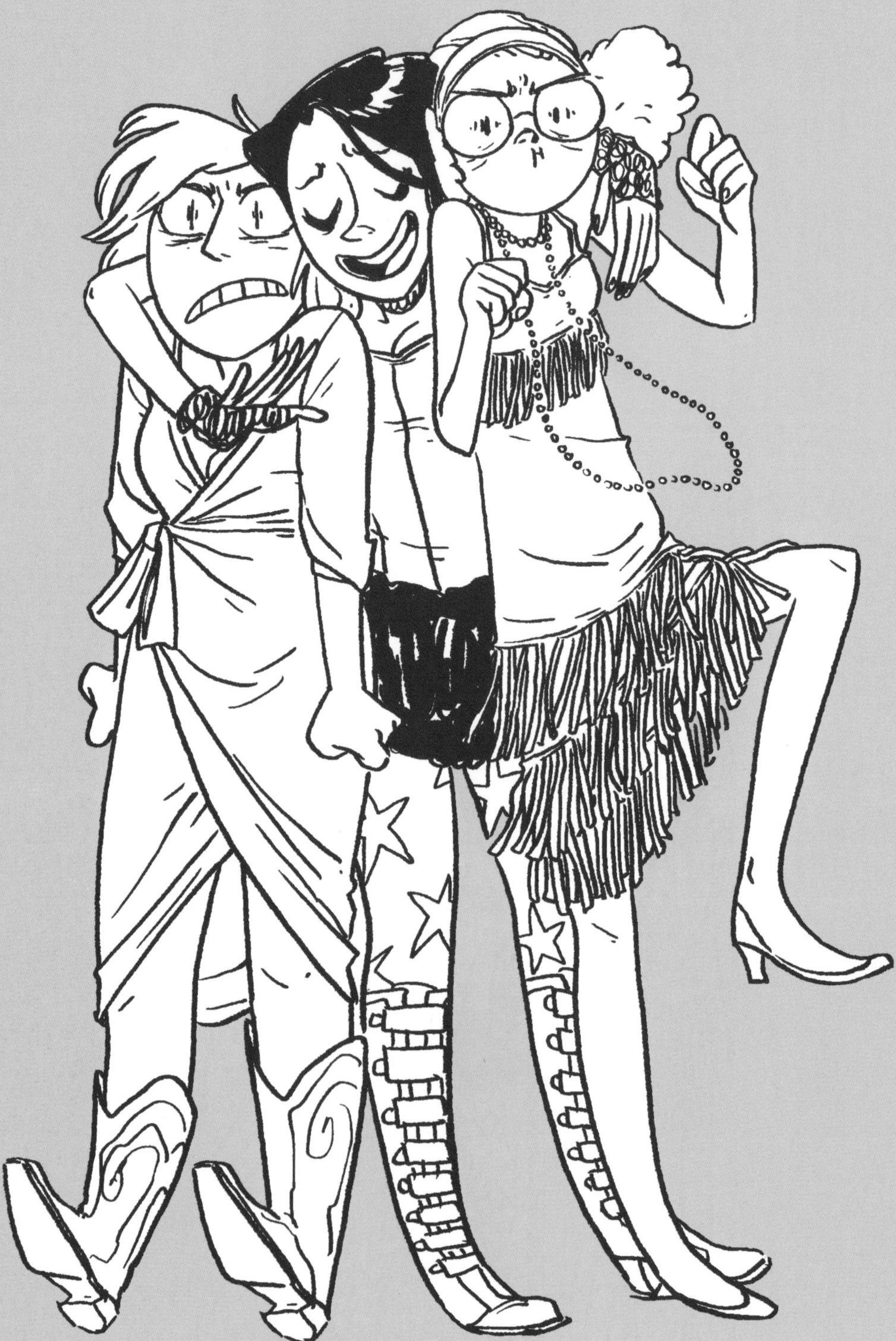

GIANT DAYS™

EXTRA CREDIT

VOLUME ONE

CREATED + WRITTEN BY

JOHN ALLISON

"WHAT WOULD HAVE HAPPENED IF ESTHER, DAISY AND SUSAN
HADN'T BECOME FRIENDS (AND IT WAS CHRISTMAS)?"

| ILLUSTRATED BY | COLORED BY | LETTERED BY |
| LISSA TREIMAN | SARAH STERN | JIM CAMPBELL |

"HOW THE FISHMAN DESPOILED CHRISTMAS"

| ILLUSTRATED BY | COLORED BY | LETTERED BY |
| CAANAN GRALL | JEREMY LAWSON | JIM CAMPBELL |

"LOVE? ACK, SHELLY!"

| ILLUSTRATED BY | COLORED BY | LETTERED BY |
| JENN ST-ONGE | SARAH STERN | JIM CAMPBELL |

"FRIDGE RAIDER" + "MUSIC IS IMPORTANT" + "DESTROY HISTORY"

BY

JOHN ALLISON

| COVER BY | DESIGNERS | ASSISTANT EDITOR | EDITOR |
| LISSA TREIMAN | JILLIAN CRAB + KARA LEOPARD | SOPHIE PHILIPS-ROBERTS | SHANNON WATTERS |

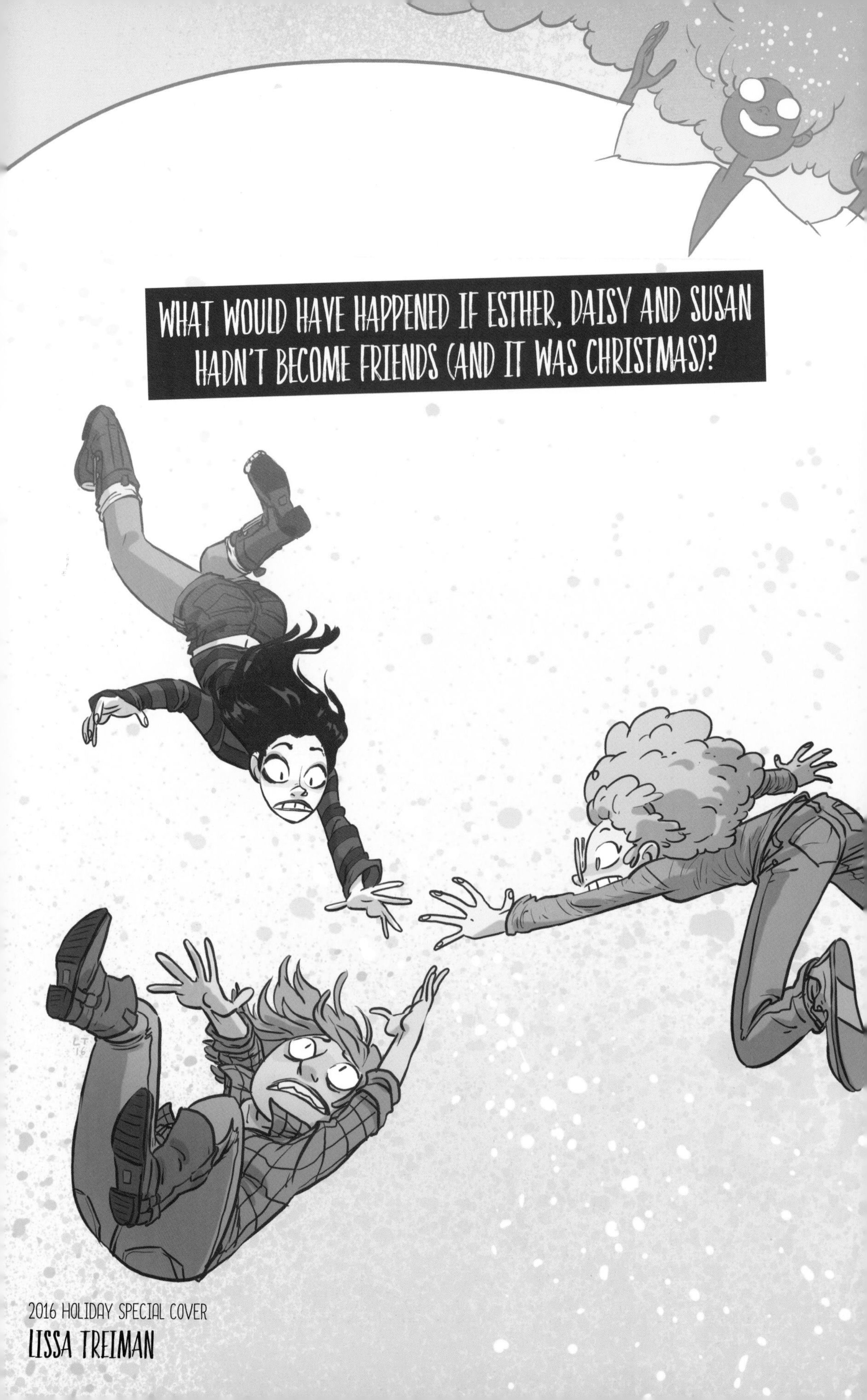
WHAT WOULD HAVE HAPPENED IF ESTHER, DAISY AND SUSAN HADN'T BECOME FRIENDS (AND IT WAS CHRISTMAS)?

2016 HOLIDAY SPECIAL COVER

LISSA TREIMAN

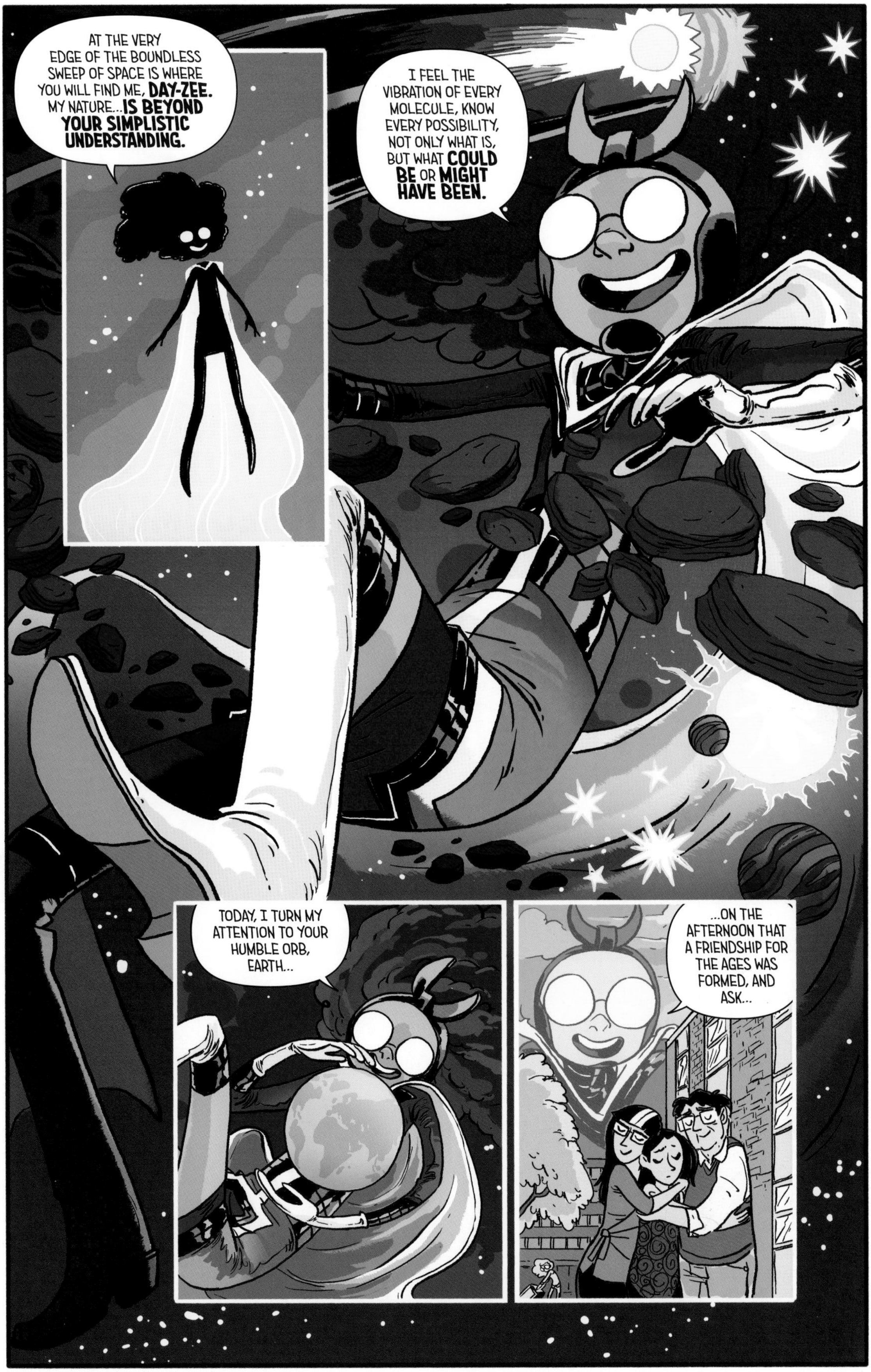
AT THE VERY EDGE OF THE BOUNDLESS SWEEP OF SPACE IS WHERE YOU WILL FIND ME, DAY-ZEE. MY NATURE...IS BEYOND YOUR SIMPLISTIC UNDERSTANDING.
I FEEL THE VIBRATION OF EVERY MOLECULE, KNOW EVERY POSSIBILITY, NOT ONLY WHAT IS, BUT WHAT COULD BE OR MIGHT HAVE BEEN.
TODAY, I TURN MY ATTENTION TO YOUR HUMBLE ORB, EARTH...
...ON THE AFTERNOON THAT A FRIENDSHIP FOR THE AGES WAS FORMED, AND ASK...

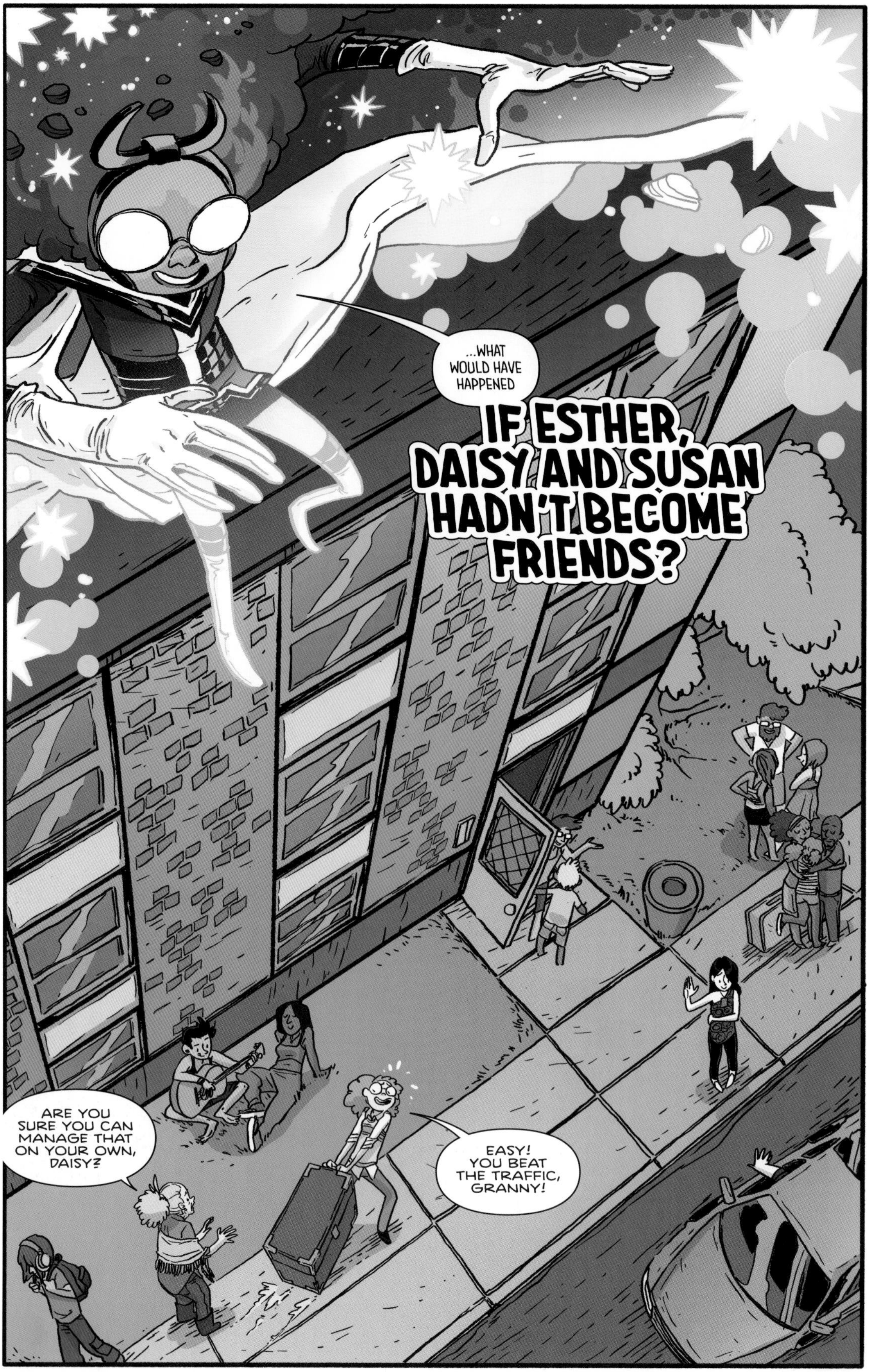
...WHAT WOULD HAVE HAPPENED
IF ESTHER, DAISY AND SUSAN HADN'T BECOME FRIENDS?
ARE YOU SURE YOU CAN MANAGE THAT ON YOUR OWN, DAISY?
EASY! YOU BEAT THE TRAFFIC, GRANNY!

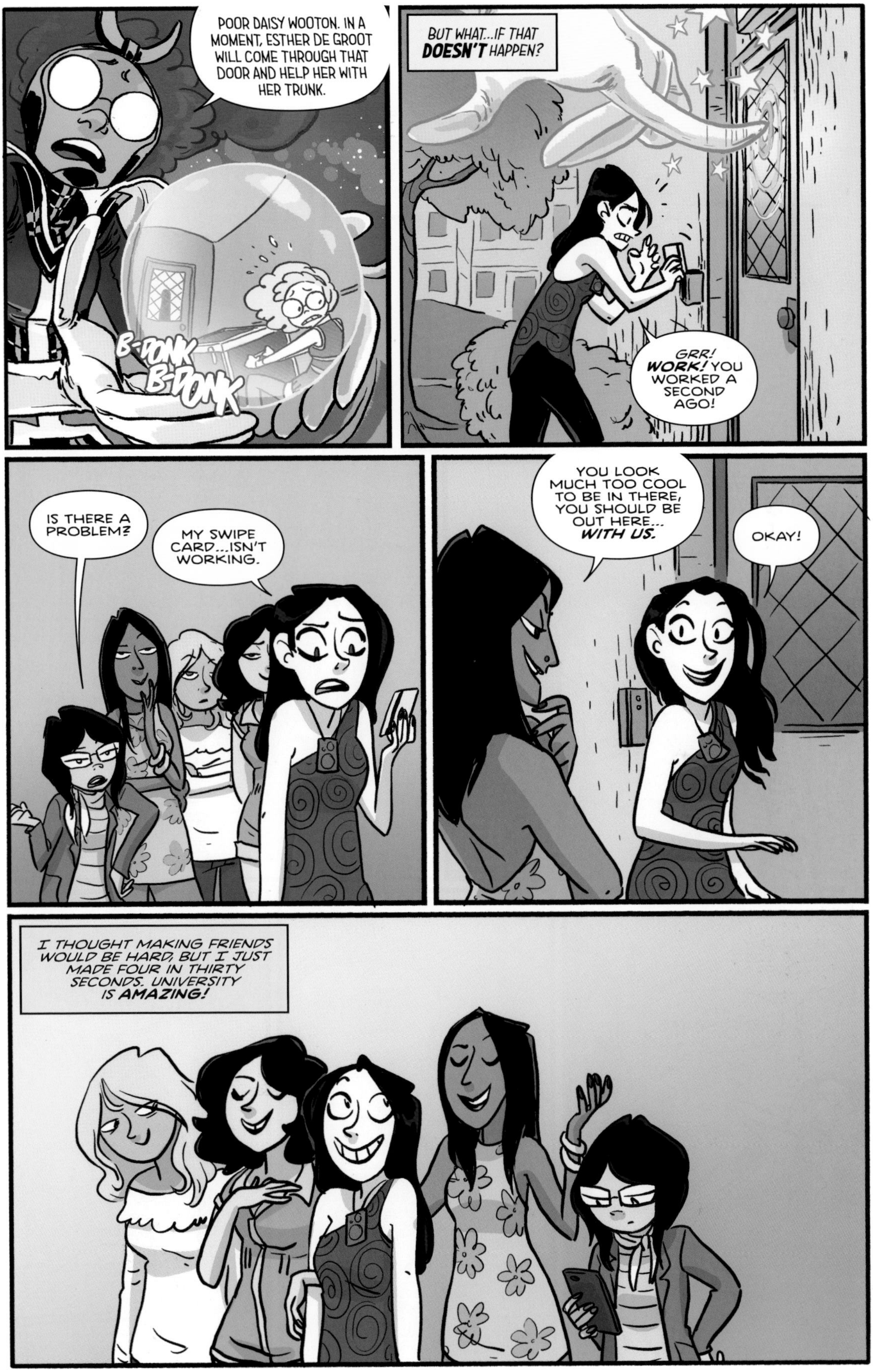
POOR DAISY WOOTON. IN A MOMENT, ESTHER DE GROOT WILL COME THROUGH THAT DOOR AND HELP HER WITH HER TRUNK.
B-DONK
B-DONK
BUT WHAT...IF THAT DOESN'T HAPPEN?
GRR! WORK! YOU WORKED A SECOND AGO!
IS THERE A PROBLEM?
MY SWIPE CARD...ISN'T WORKING.
YOU LOOK MUCH TOO COOL TO BE IN THERE, YOU SHOULD BE OUT HERE... WITH US.
OKAY!
I THOUGHT MAKING FRIENDS WOULD BE HARD, BUT I JUST MADE FOUR IN THIRTY SECONDS. UNIVERSITY IS AMAZING!

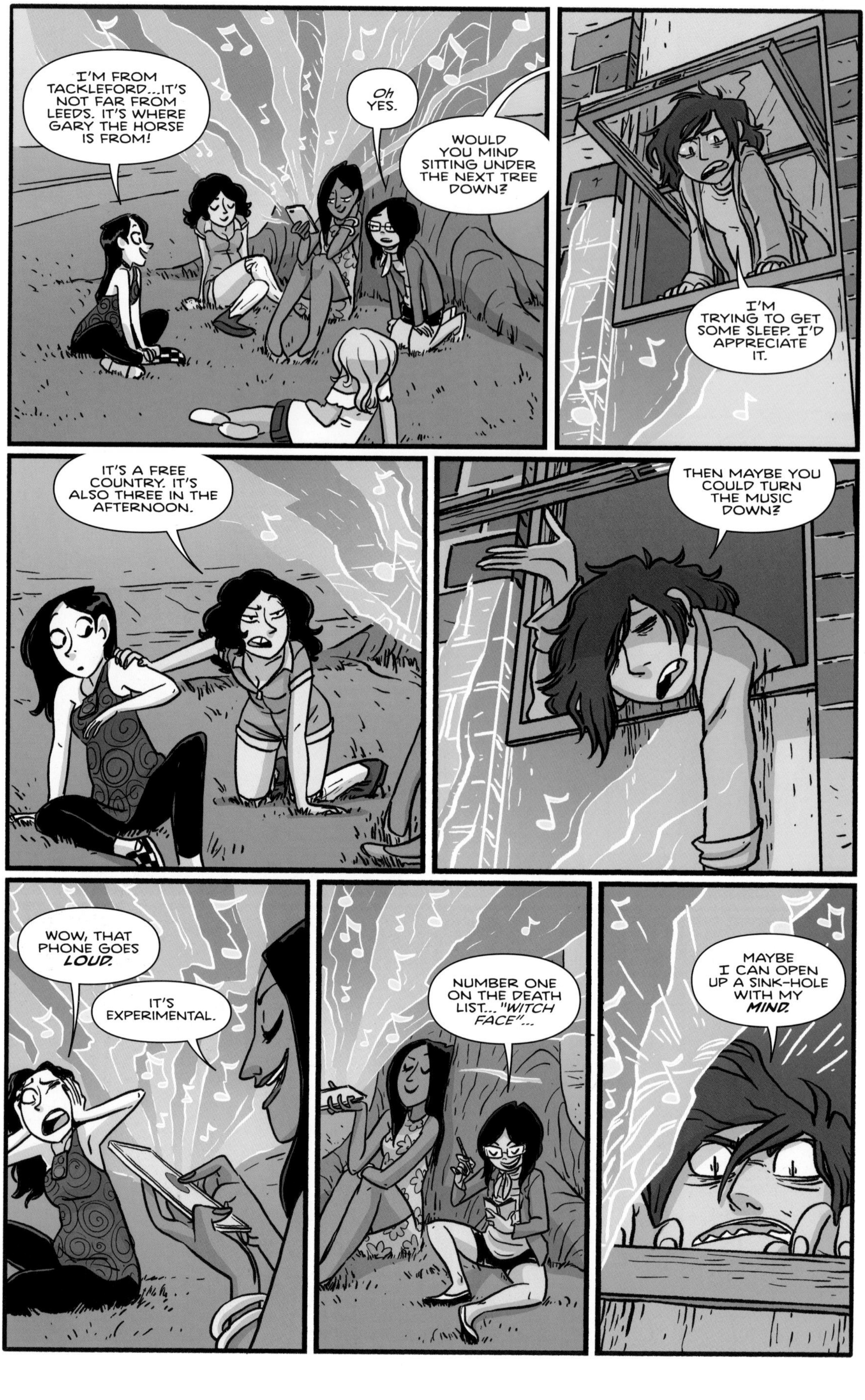
I'M FROM TACKLEFORD...IT'S NOT FAR FROM LEEDS. IT'S WHERE GARY THE HORSE IS FROM!
Oh YES.
WOULD YOU MIND SITTING UNDER THE NEXT TREE DOWN?
I'M TRYING TO GET SOME SLEEP. I'D APPRECIATE IT.
IT'S A FREE COUNTRY. IT'S ALSO THREE IN THE AFTERNOON.
THEN MAYBE YOU COULD TURN THE MUSIC DOWN?
WOW, THAT PHONE GOES ***LOUD.***
IT'S EXPERIMENTAL.
NUMBER ONE ON THE DEATH LIST... *"WITCH FACE"...*
MAYBE I CAN OPEN UP A SINK-HOLE WITH MY ***MIND.***

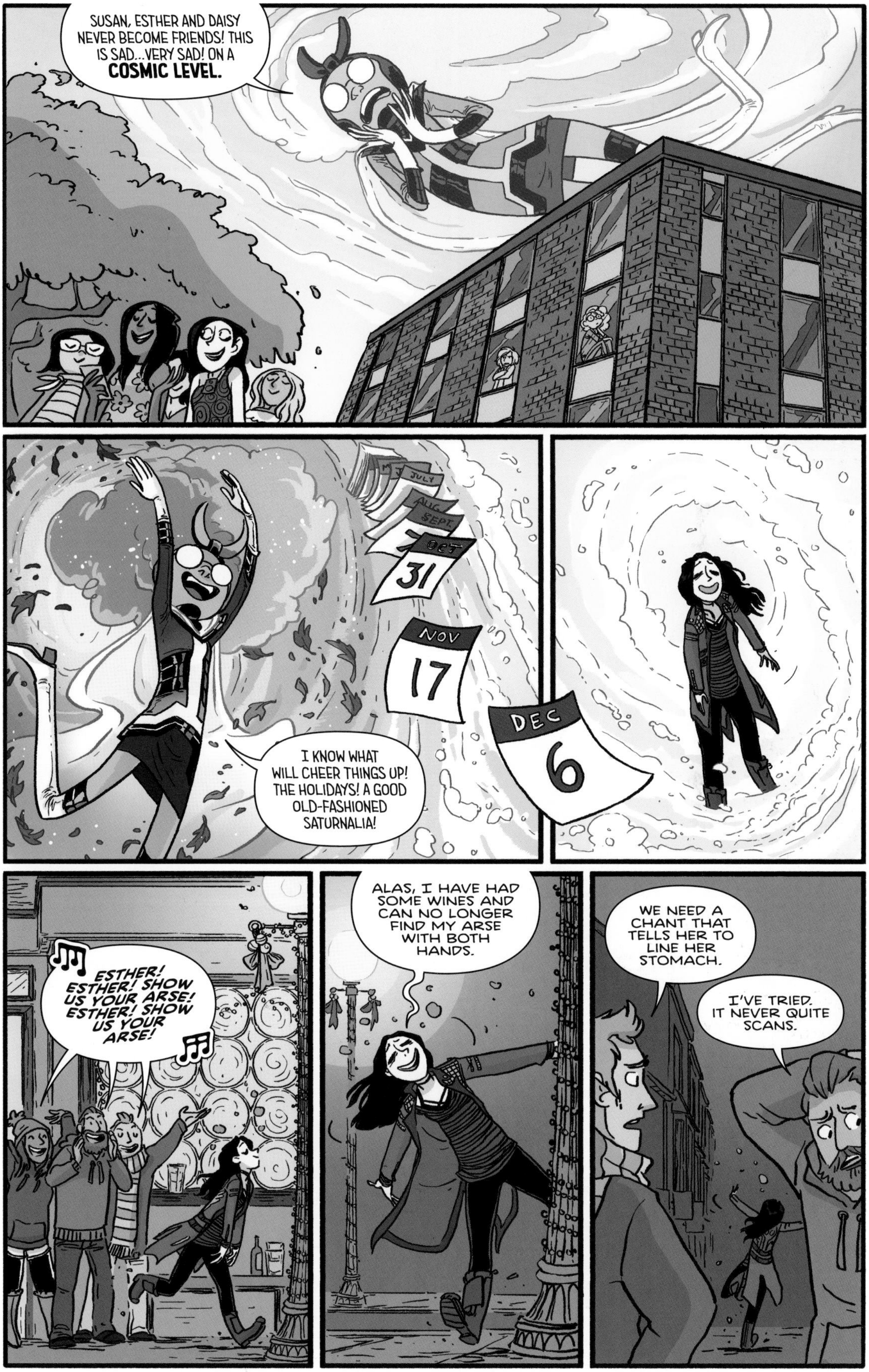
SUSAN, ESTHER AND DAISY NEVER BECOME FRIENDS! THIS IS SAD...VERY SAD! ON A COSMIC LEVEL.
JULY
AUG
SEPT
OCT
31
NOV
17
DEC
6
I KNOW WHAT WILL CHEER THINGS UP! THE HOLIDAYS! A GOOD OLD-FASHIONED SATURNALIA!
ESTHER! ESTHER! SHOW US YOUR ARSE! ESTHER! SHOW US YOUR ARSE!
ALAS, I HAVE HAD SOME WINES AND CAN NO LONGER FIND MY ARSE WITH BOTH HANDS.
WE NEED A CHANT THAT TELLS HER TO LINE HER STOMACH.
I'VE TRIED. IT NEVER QUITE SCANS.

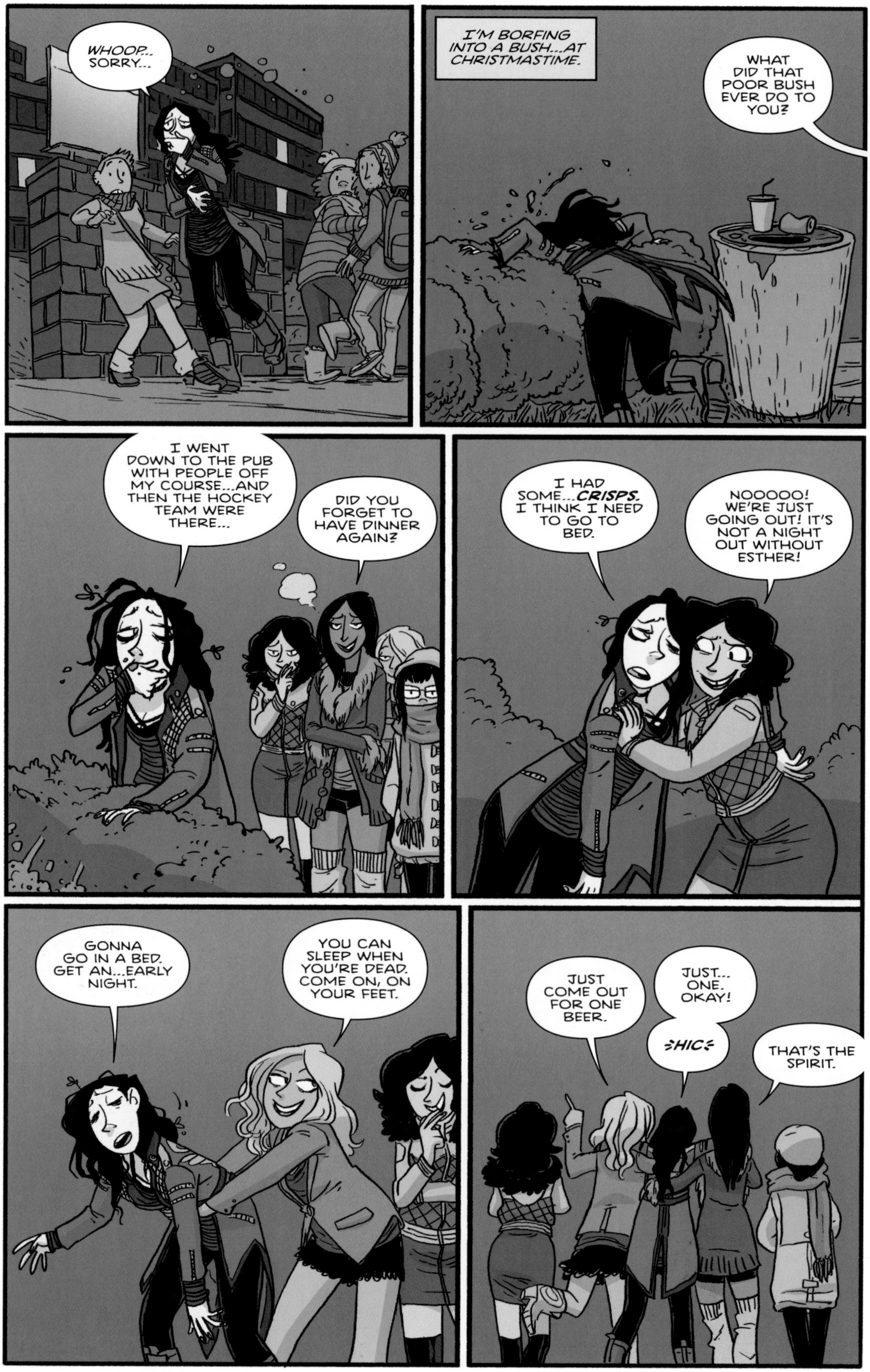
WHOOP... SORRY...
I'M BORFING INTO A BUSH...AT CHRISTMASTIME.
WHAT DID THAT POOR BUSH EVER DO TO YOU?
I WENT DOWN TO THE PUB WITH PEOPLE OFF MY COURSE...AND THEN THE HOCKEY TEAM WERE THERE...
DID YOU FORGET TO HAVE DINNER AGAIN?
I HAD SOME... CRISPS. I THINK I NEED TO GO TO BED.
NOOOOO! WE'RE JUST GOING OUT! IT'S NOT A NIGHT OUT WITHOUT ESTHER!
GONNA GO IN A BED. GET AN...EARLY NIGHT.
YOU CAN SLEEP WHEN YOU'RE DEAD. COME ON, ON YOUR FEET.
JUST COME OUT FOR ONE BEER.
JUST... ONE. OKAY!
HIC
THAT'S THE SPIRIT.

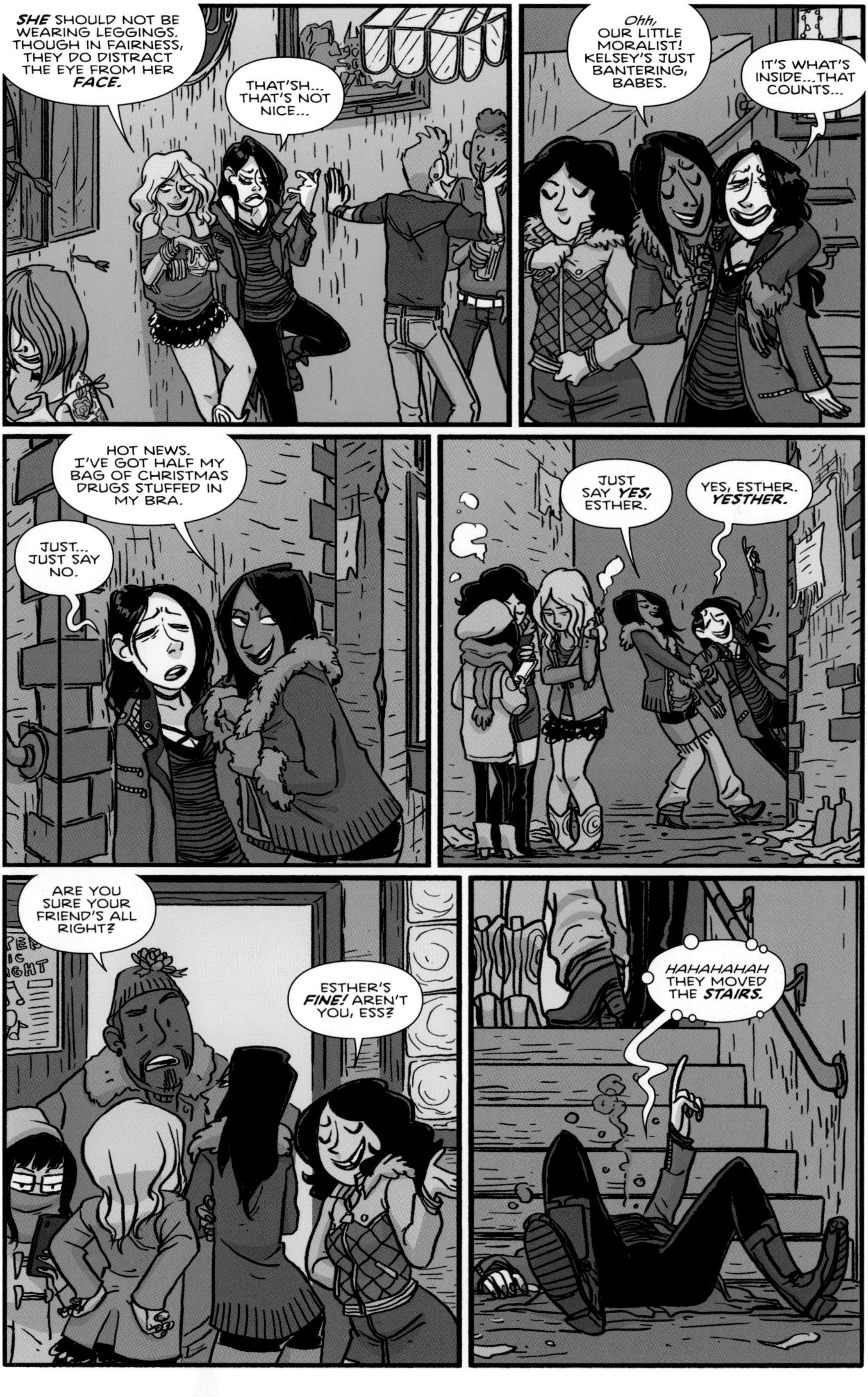
SHE SHOULD NOT BE WEARING LEGGINGS. THOUGH IN FAIRNESS, THEY DO DISTRACT THE EYE FROM HER FACE.
THAT'SH... THAT'S NOT NICE...
Ohh, OUR LITTLE MORALIST! KELSEY'S JUST BANTERING, BABES.
IT'S WHAT'S INSIDE... THAT COUNTS...
HOT NEWS. I'VE GOT HALF MY BAG OF CHRISTMAS DRUGS STUFFED IN MY BRA.
JUST... JUST SAY NO.
JUST SAY YES, ESTHER.
YES, ESTHER. YESTHER.
ARE YOU SURE YOUR FRIEND'S ALL RIGHT?
ESTHER'S FINE! AREN'T YOU, ESS?
HAHAHAHAH THEY MOVED THE STAIRS.

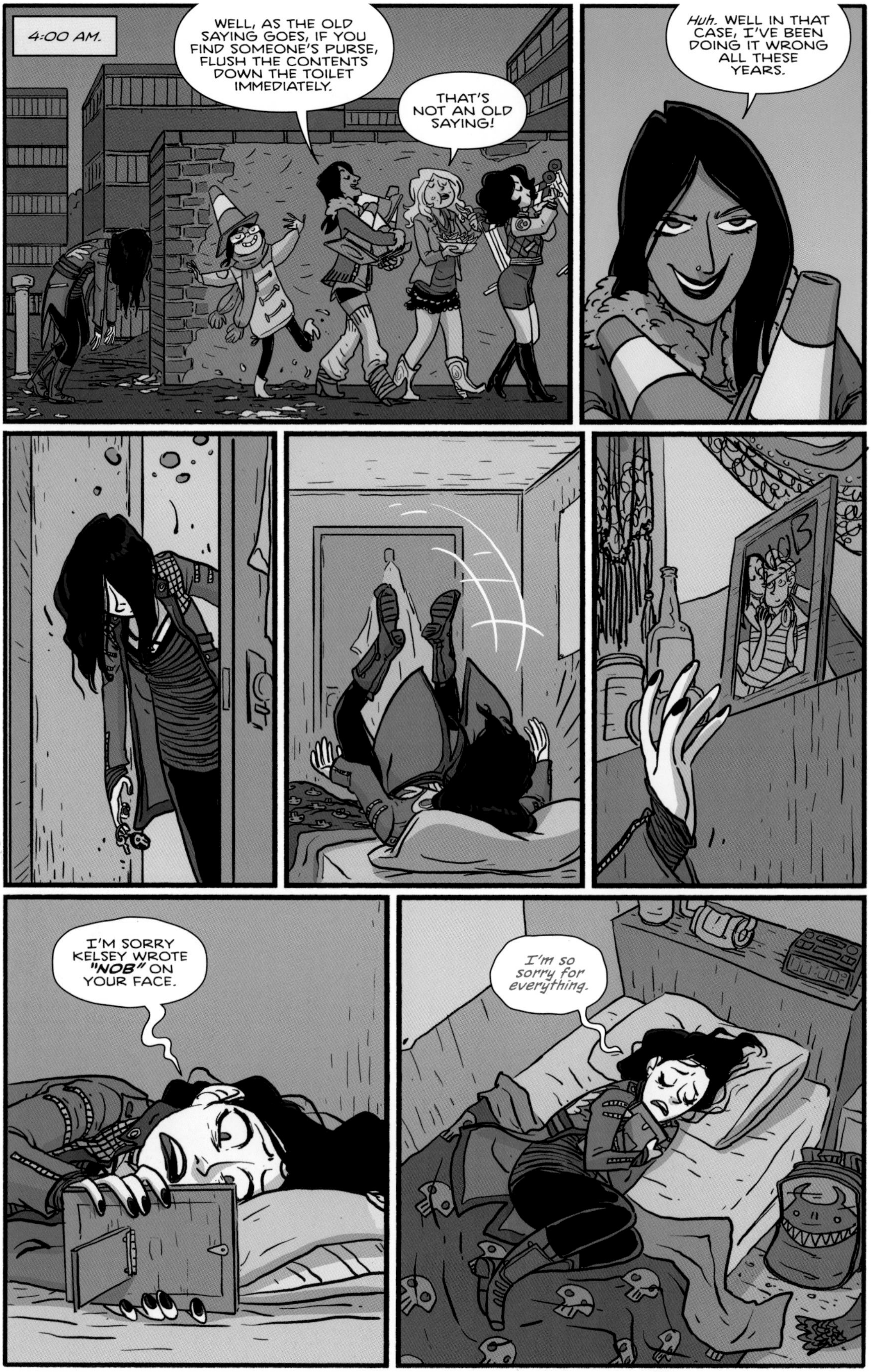
4:00 AM.
WELL, AS THE OLD SAYING GOES, IF YOU FIND SOMEONE'S PURSE, FLUSH THE CONTENTS DOWN THE TOILET IMMEDIATELY.
THAT'S NOT AN OLD SAYING!
Huh. WELL IN THAT CASE, I'VE BEEN DOING IT WRONG ALL THESE YEARS.
I'M SORRY KELSEY WROTE "NOB" ON YOUR FACE.
I'm so sorry for everything.

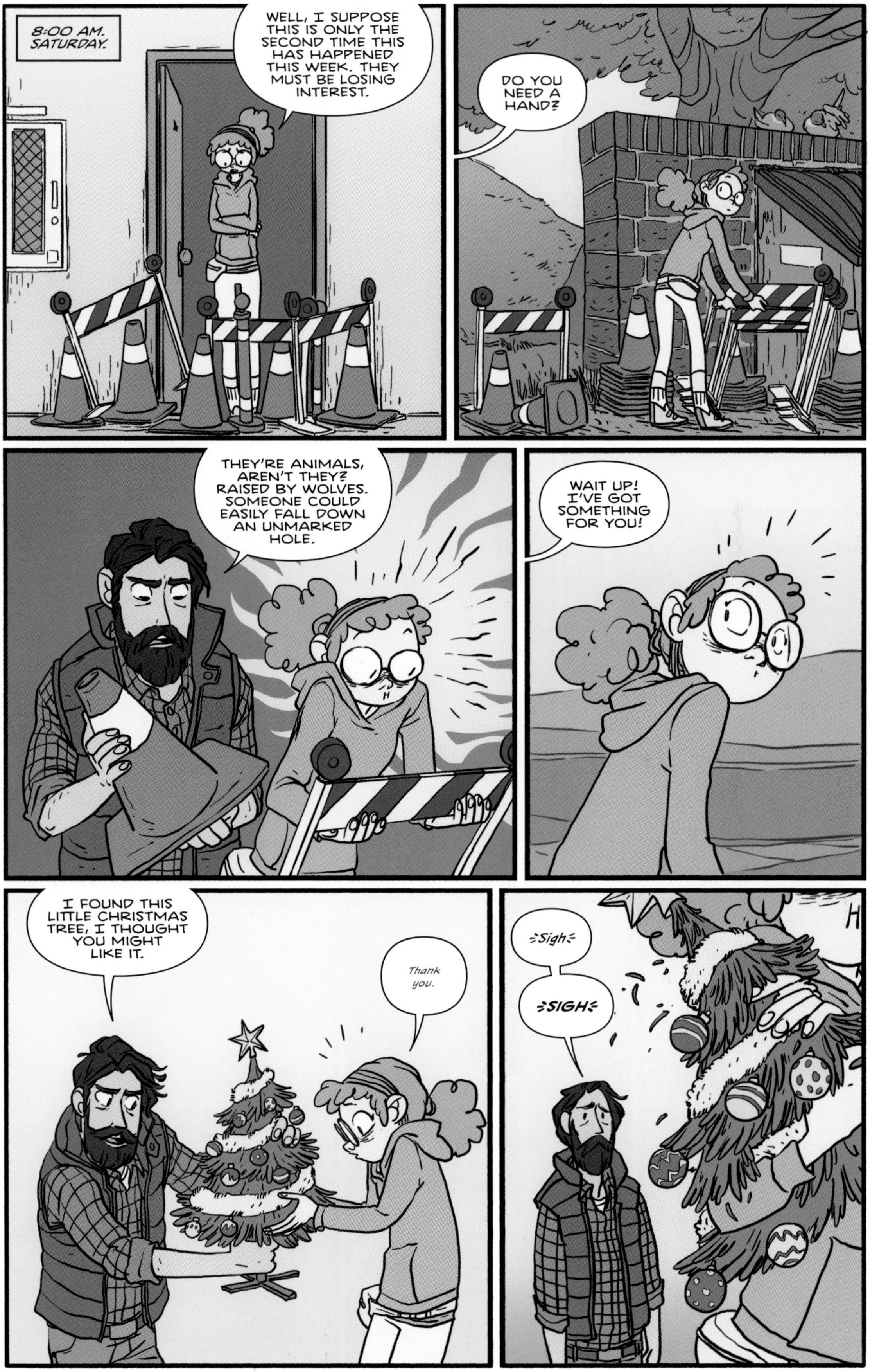
8:00 AM. SATURDAY.
WELL, I SUPPOSE THIS IS ONLY THE SECOND TIME THIS HAS HAPPENED THIS WEEK. THEY MUST BE LOSING INTEREST.
DO YOU NEED A HAND?
THEY'RE ANIMALS, AREN'T THEY? RAISED BY WOLVES. SOMEONE COULD EASILY FALL DOWN AN UNMARKED HOLE.
WAIT UP! I'VE GOT SOMETHING FOR YOU!
I FOUND THIS LITTLE CHRISTMAS TREE, I THOUGHT YOU MIGHT LIKE IT.
Thank you.
Sigh
SIGH

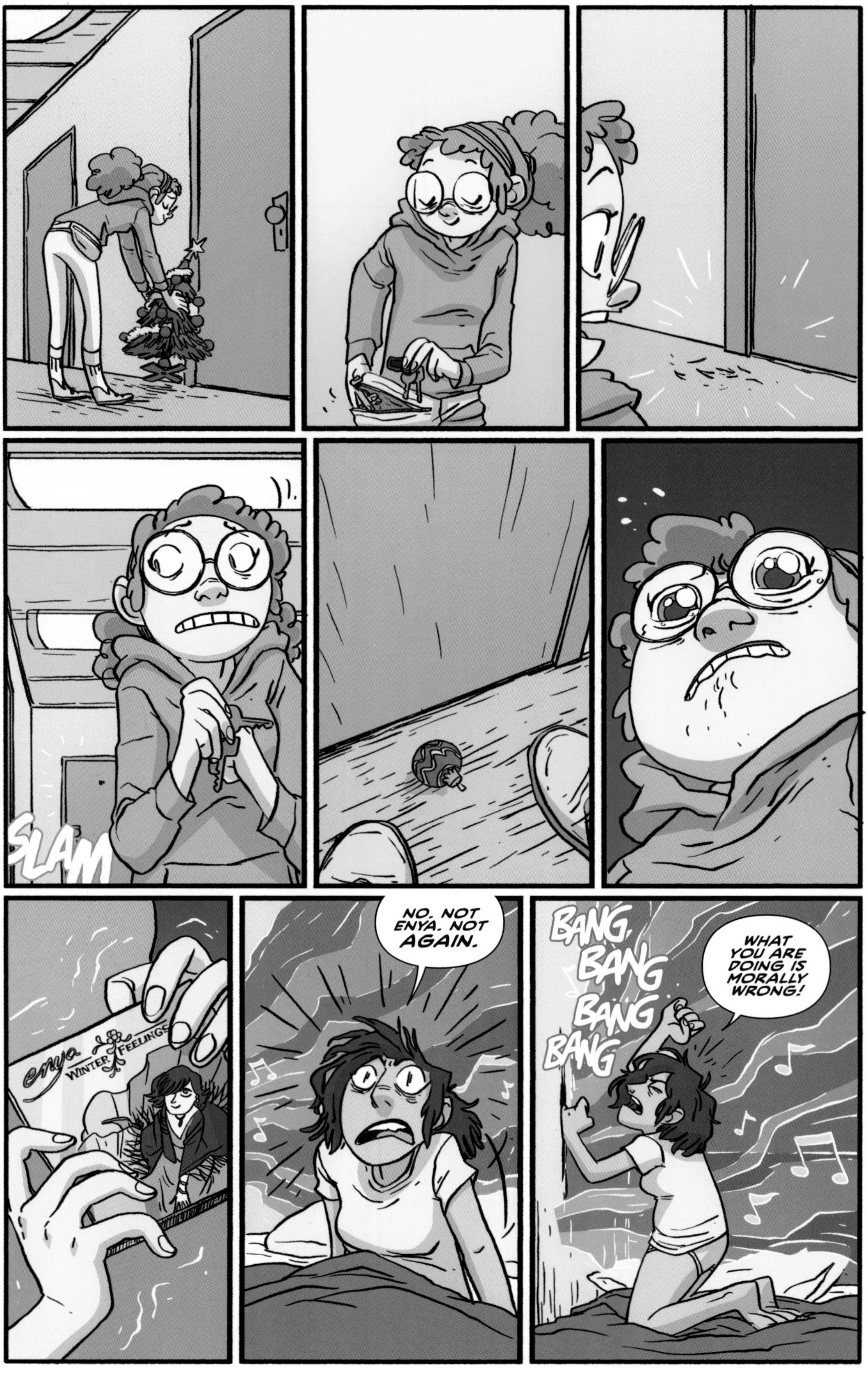
SLAM
enya WINTER FEELINGS
NO. NOT ENYA. NOT AGAIN.
BANG BANG BANG BANG
WHAT YOU ARE DOING IS MORALLY WRONG!

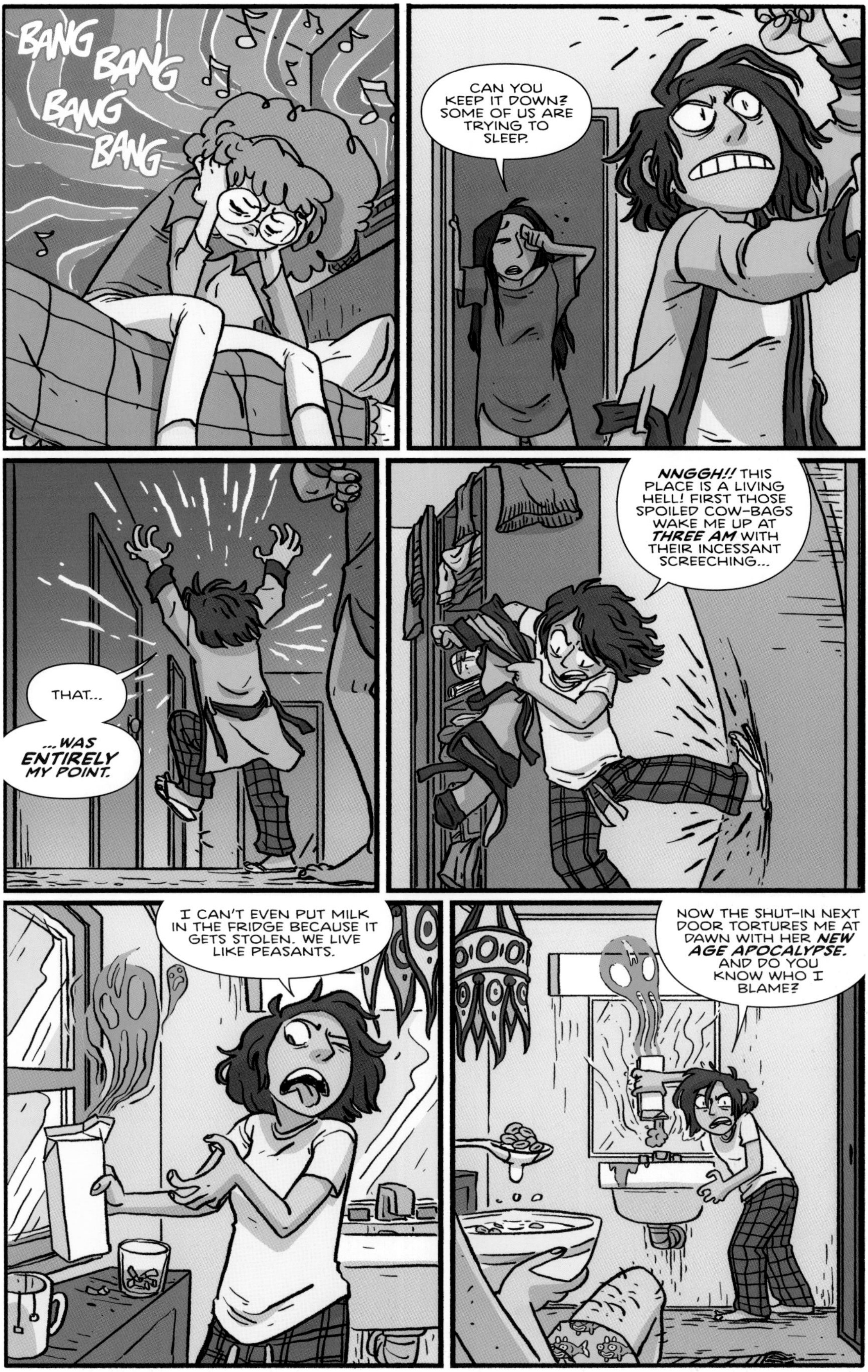
BANG BANG BANG BANG
CAN YOU KEEP IT DOWN? SOME OF US ARE TRYING TO SLEEP.
THAT...
...WAS ENTIRELY MY POINT.
NNGGH!! THIS PLACE IS A LIVING HELL! FIRST THOSE SPOILED COW-BAGS WAKE ME UP AT THREE AM WITH THEIR INCESSANT SCREECHING...
I CAN'T EVEN PUT MILK IN THE FRIDGE BECAUSE IT GETS STOLEN. WE LIVE LIKE PEASANTS.
NOW THE SHUT-IN NEXT DOOR TORTURES ME AT DAWN WITH HER NEW AGE APOCALYPSE. AND DO YOU KNOW WHO I BLAME?

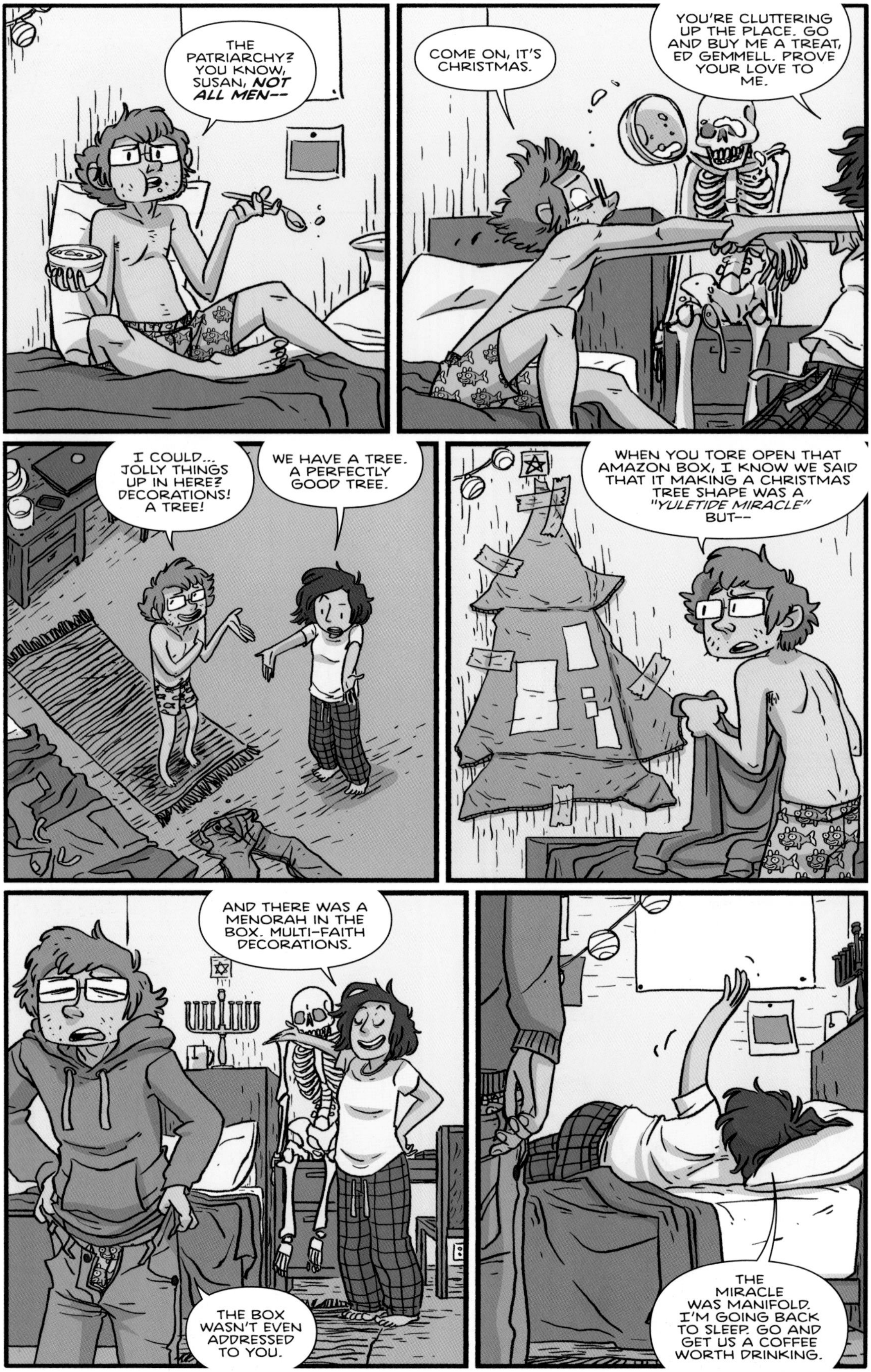
THE PATRIARCHY? YOU KNOW, SUSAN, NOT ALL MEN--
COME ON, IT'S CHRISTMAS.
YOU'RE CLUTTERING UP THE PLACE. GO AND BUY ME A TREAT, ED GEMMELL. PROVE YOUR LOVE TO ME.
I COULD... JOLLY THINGS UP IN HERE? DECORATIONS! A TREE!
WE HAVE A TREE. A PERFECTLY GOOD TREE.
WHEN YOU TORE OPEN THAT AMAZON BOX, I KNOW WE SAID THAT IT MAKING A CHRISTMAS TREE SHAPE WAS A "YULETIDE MIRACLE" BUT--
AND THERE WAS A MENORAH IN THE BOX. MULTI-FAITH DECORATIONS.
THE BOX WASN'T EVEN ADDRESSED TO YOU.
THE MIRACLE WAS MANIFOLD. I'M GOING BACK TO SLEEP. GO AND GET US A COFFEE WORTH DRINKING.

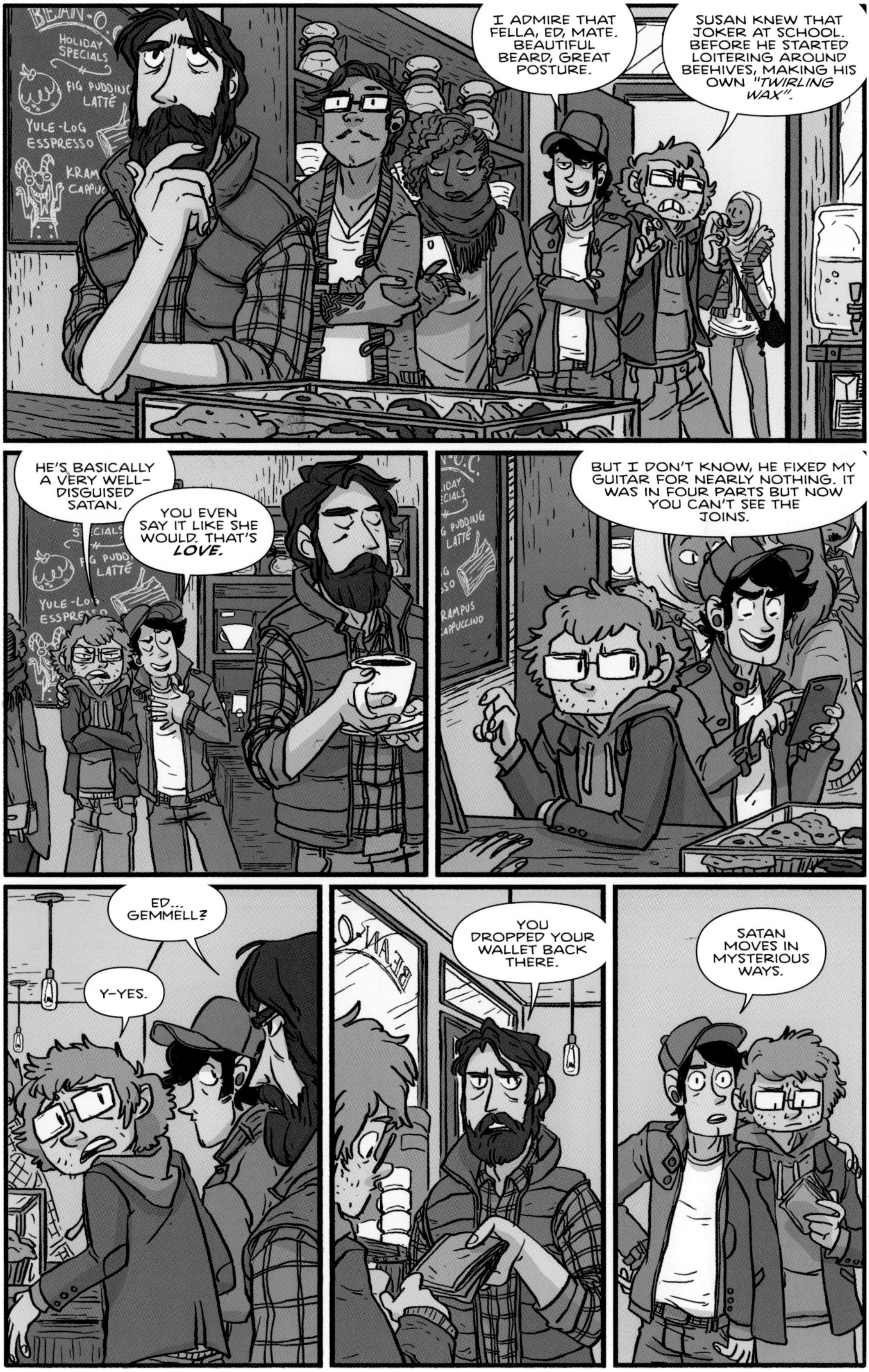
BEAN-O-C
HOLIDAY SPECIALS
FIG PUDDING LATTÉ
YULE-LOG ESSPRESSO
I ADMIRE THAT FELLA, ED, MATE. BEAUTIFUL BEARD, GREAT POSTURE.
SUSAN KNEW THAT JOKER AT SCHOOL. BEFORE HE STARTED LOITERING AROUND BEEHIVES, MAKING HIS OWN "TWIRLING WAX".
HE'S BASICALLY A VERY WELL-DISGUISED SATAN.
YOU EVEN SAY IT LIKE SHE WOULD. THAT'S LOVE.
BUT I DON'T KNOW, HE FIXED MY GUITAR FOR NEARLY NOTHING. IT WAS IN FOUR PARTS BUT NOW YOU CAN'T SEE THE JOINS.
KRAMPUS CAPPUCCINO
ED... GEMMELL?
Y-YES.
YOU DROPPED YOUR WALLET BACK THERE.
SATAN MOVES IN MYSTERIOUS WAYS.

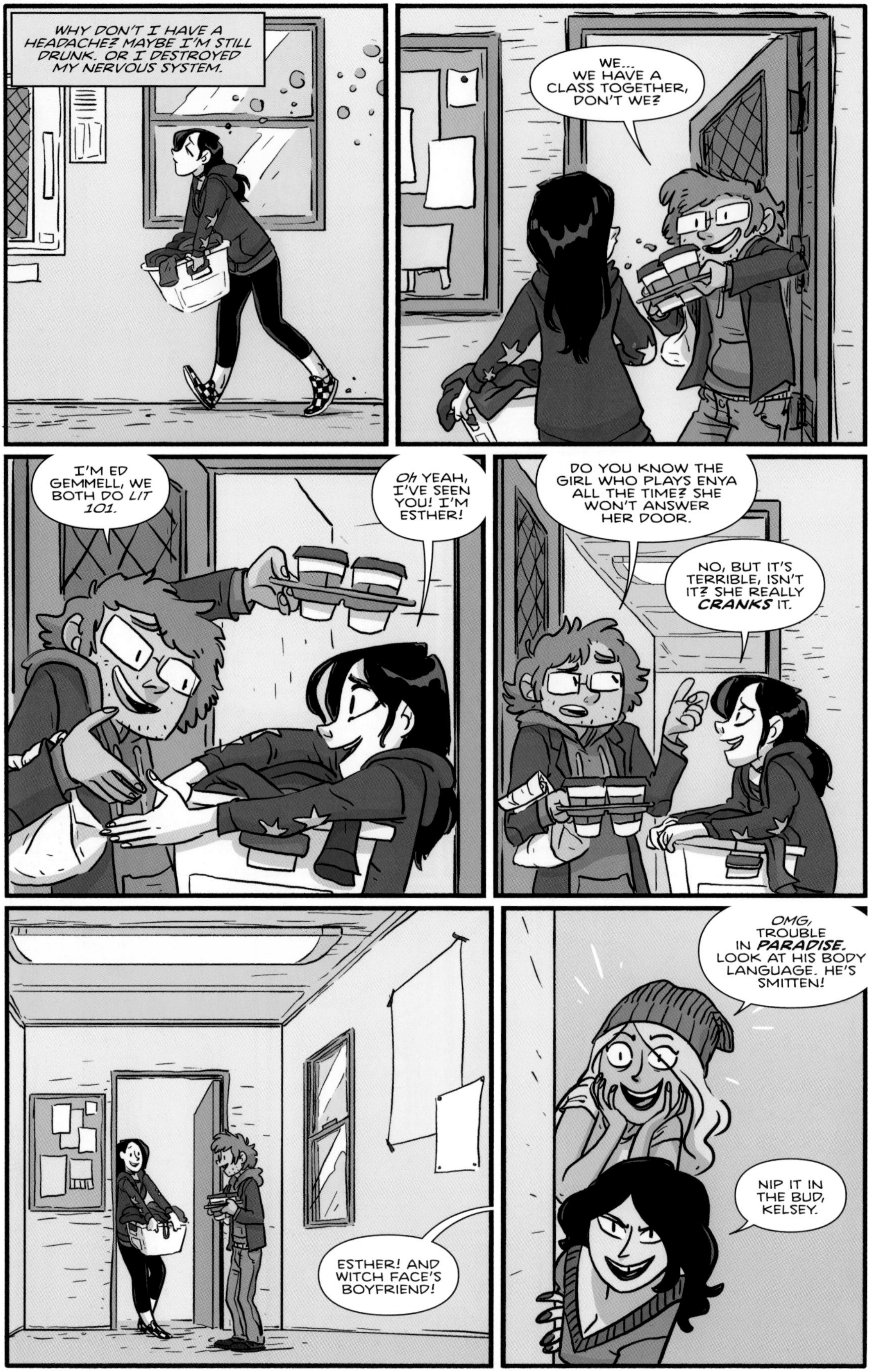
WHY DON'T I HAVE A HEADACHE? MAYBE I'M STILL DRUNK. OR I DESTROYED MY NERVOUS SYSTEM.
WE... WE HAVE A CLASS TOGETHER, DON'T WE?
I'M ED GEMMELL, WE BOTH DO LIT 101.
Oh YEAH, I'VE SEEN YOU! I'M ESTHER!
DO YOU KNOW THE GIRL WHO PLAYS ENYA ALL THE TIME? SHE WON'T ANSWER HER DOOR.
NO, BUT IT'S TERRIBLE, ISN'T IT? SHE REALLY CRANKS IT.
ESTHER! AND WITCH FACE'S BOYFRIEND!
OMG, TROUBLE IN PARADISE. LOOK AT HIS BODY LANGUAGE. HE'S SMITTEN!
NIP IT IN THE BUD, KELSEY.

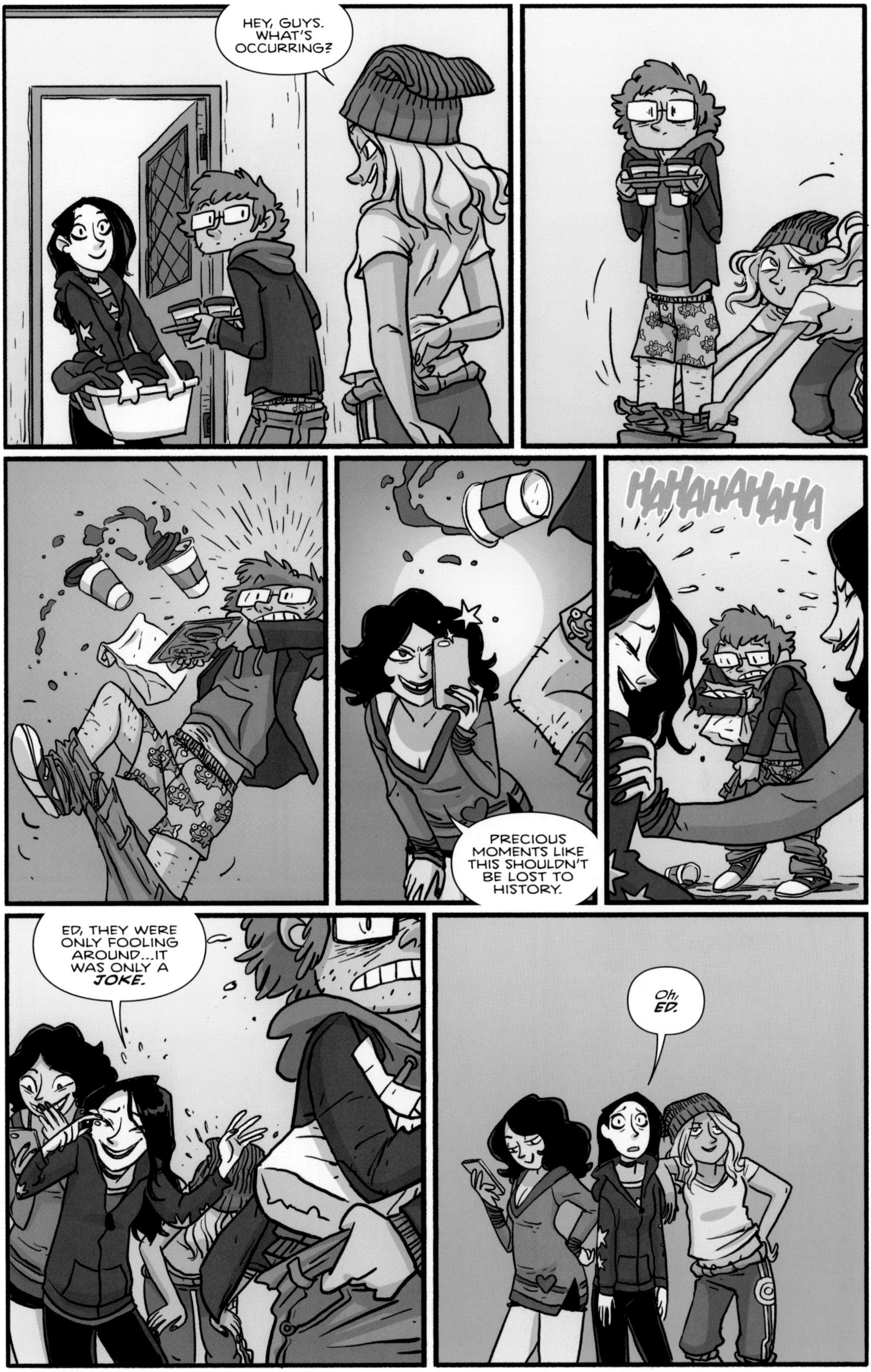
HEY, GUYS. WHAT'S OCCURRING?
HAHAHAHAHA
PRECIOUS MOMENTS LIKE THIS SHOULDN'T BE LOST TO HISTORY.
ED, THEY WERE ONLY FOOLING AROUND...IT WAS ONLY A *JOKE.*
Oh, ED.

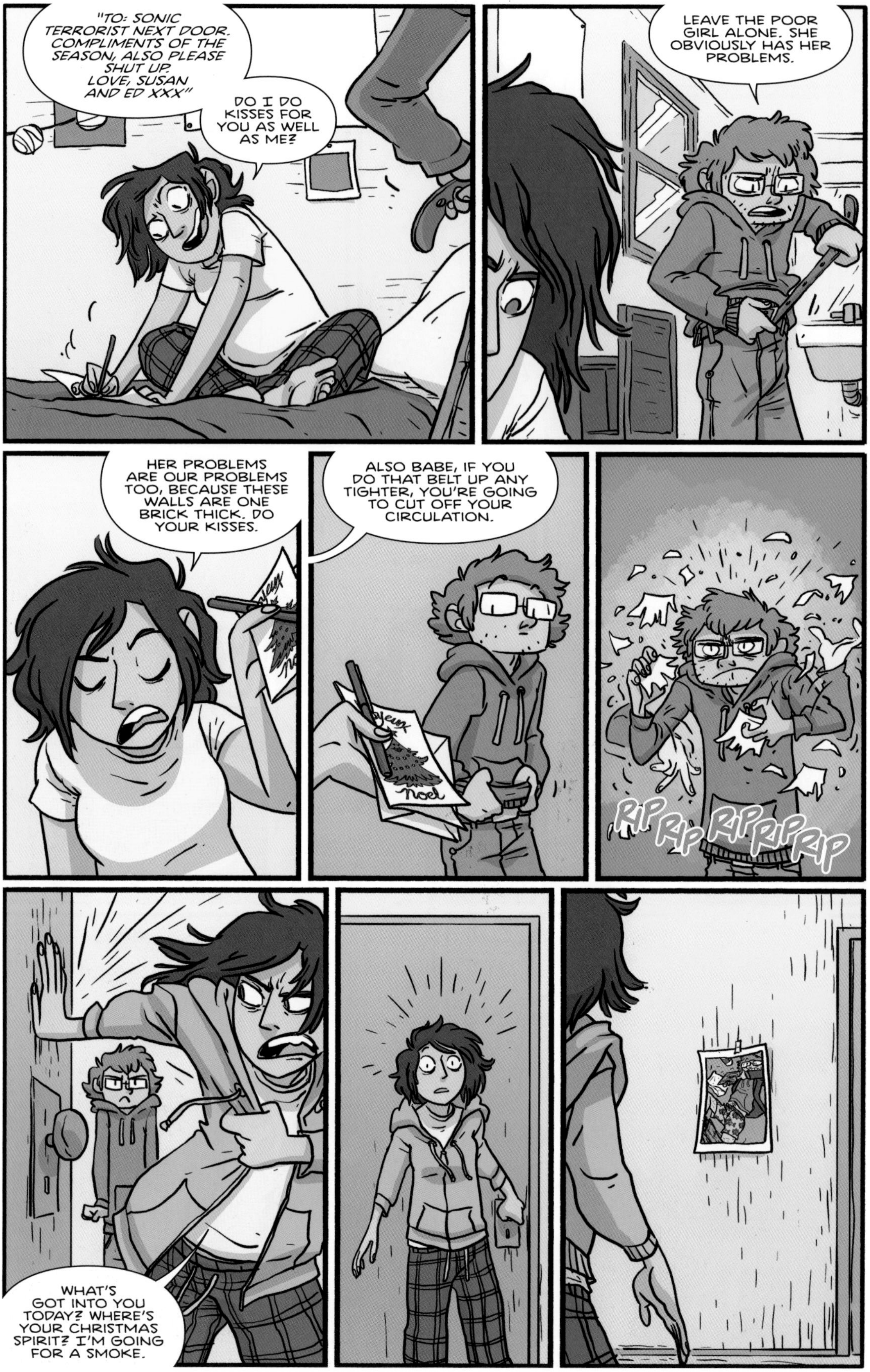
"TO: SONIC TERRORIST NEXT DOOR. COMPLIMENTS OF THE SEASON, ALSO PLEASE SHUT UP. LOVE, SUSAN AND ED XXX"
DO I DO KISSES FOR YOU AS WELL AS ME?
LEAVE THE POOR GIRL ALONE. SHE OBVIOUSLY HAS HER PROBLEMS.
HER PROBLEMS ARE OUR PROBLEMS TOO, BECAUSE THESE WALLS ARE ONE BRICK THICK. DO YOUR KISSES.
ALSO BABE, IF YOU DO THAT BELT UP ANY TIGHTER, YOU'RE GOING TO CUT OFF YOUR CIRCULATION.
Noel
RIP RIP RIP RIP RIP
WHAT'S GOT INTO YOU TODAY? WHERE'S YOUR CHRISTMAS SPIRIT? I'M GOING FOR A SMOKE.

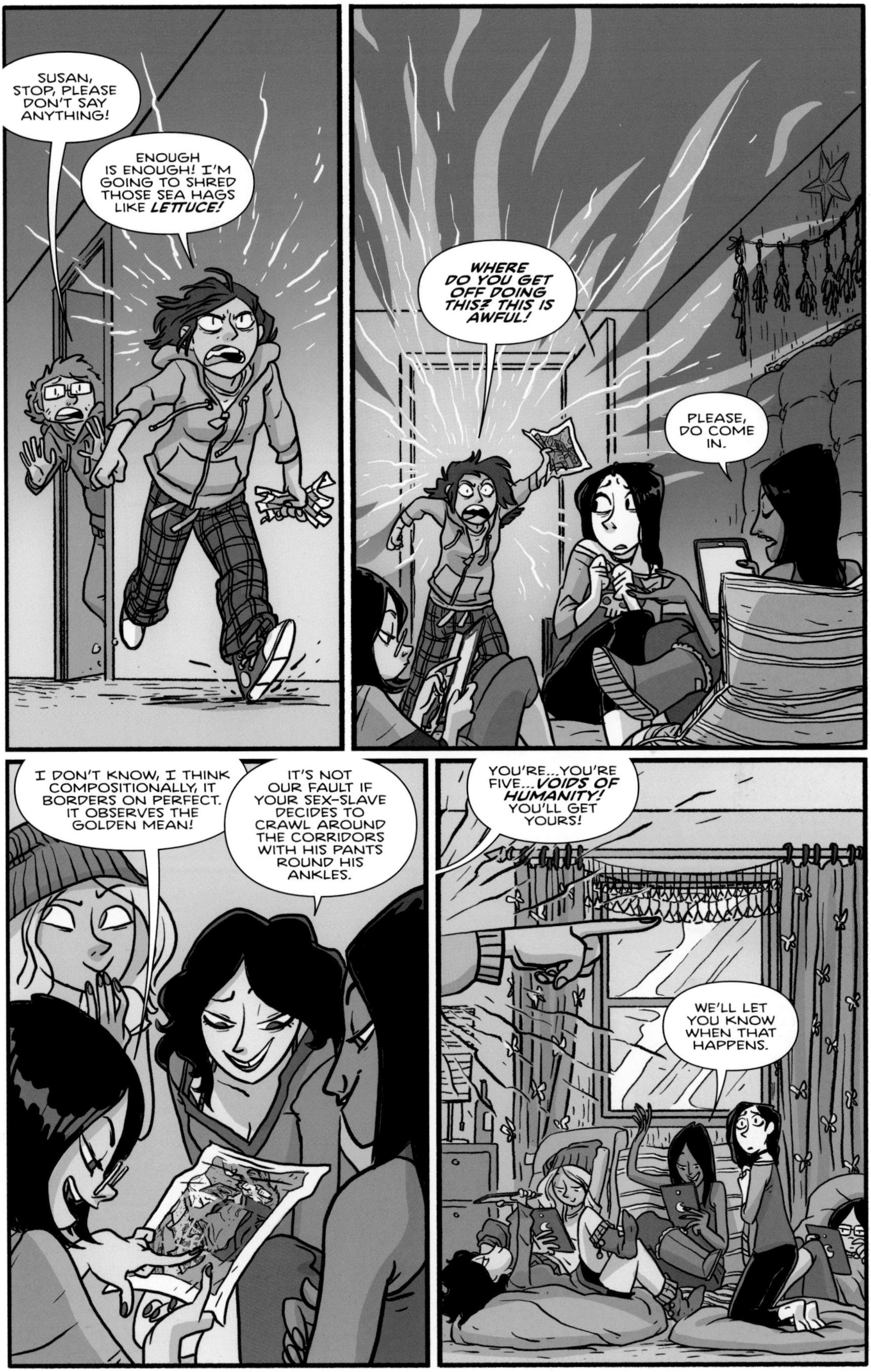
SUSAN, STOP, PLEASE DON'T SAY ANYTHING!
ENOUGH IS ENOUGH! I'M GOING TO SHRED THOSE SEA HAGS LIKE *LETTUCE!*
WHERE DO YOU GET OFF DOING THIS? THIS IS AWFUL!
PLEASE, DO COME IN.
I DON'T KNOW, I THINK COMPOSITIONALLY, IT BORDERS ON PERFECT. IT OBSERVES THE GOLDEN MEAN!
IT'S NOT OUR FAULT IF YOUR SEX-SLAVE DECIDES TO CRAWL AROUND THE CORRIDORS WITH HIS PANTS ROUND HIS ANKLES.
YOU'RE...YOU'RE FIVE...*VOIDS OF HUMANITY!* YOU'LL GET YOURS!
WE'LL LET YOU KNOW WHEN THAT HAPPENS.

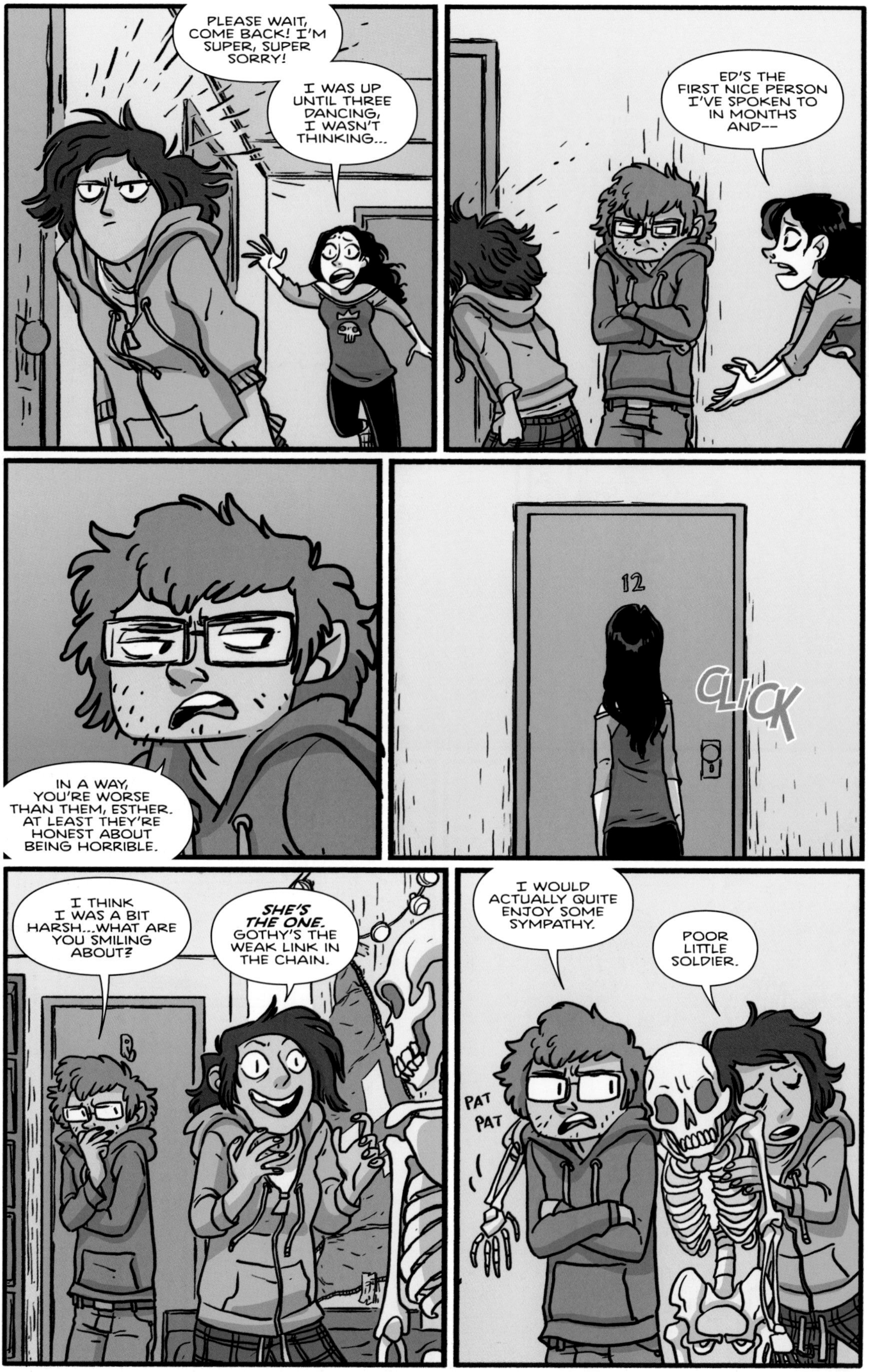
PLEASE WAIT, COME BACK! I'M SUPER, SUPER SORRY!
I WAS UP UNTIL THREE DANCING, I WASN'T THINKING...
ED'S THE FIRST NICE PERSON I'VE SPOKEN TO IN MONTHS AND--
IN A WAY, YOU'RE WORSE THAN THEM, ESTHER. AT LEAST THEY'RE HONEST ABOUT BEING HORRIBLE.
12
CLICK
I THINK I WAS A BIT HARSH...WHAT ARE YOU SMILING ABOUT?
SHE'S THE ONE. GOTHY'S THE WEAK LINK IN THE CHAIN.
I WOULD ACTUALLY QUITE ENJOY SOME SYMPATHY.
POOR LITTLE SOLDIER.
PAT PAT

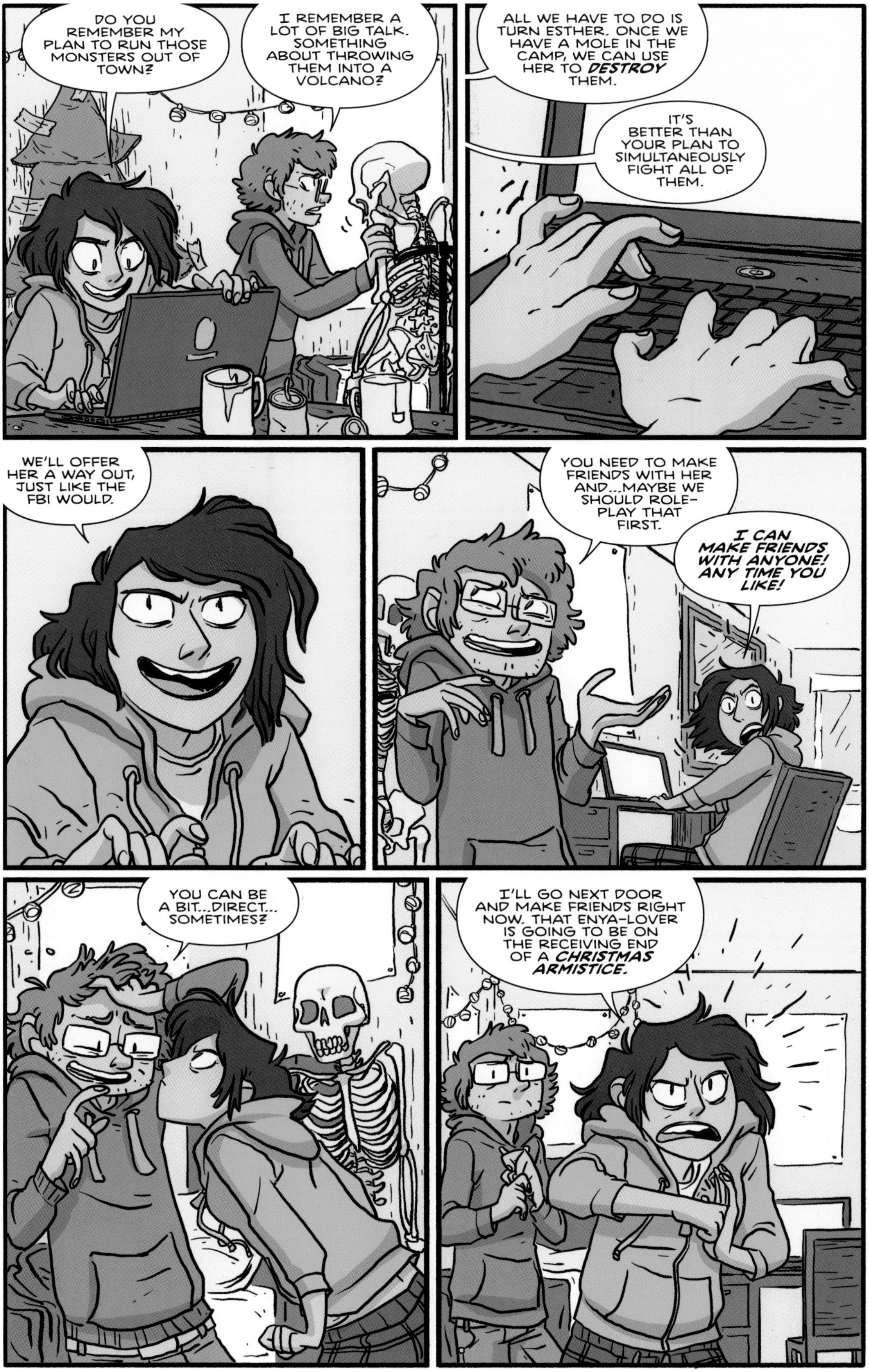
DO YOU REMEMBER MY PLAN TO RUN THOSE MONSTERS OUT OF TOWN?
I REMEMBER A LOT OF BIG TALK. SOMETHING ABOUT THROWING THEM INTO A VOLCANO?
ALL WE HAVE TO DO IS TURN ESTHER. ONCE WE HAVE A MOLE IN THE CAMP, WE CAN USE HER TO DESTROY THEM.
IT'S BETTER THAN YOUR PLAN TO SIMULTANEOUSLY FIGHT ALL OF THEM.
WE'LL OFFER HER A WAY OUT, JUST LIKE THE FBI WOULD.
YOU NEED TO MAKE FRIENDS WITH HER AND...MAYBE WE SHOULD ROLE-PLAY THAT FIRST.
I CAN MAKE FRIENDS WITH ANYONE! ANY TIME YOU LIKE!
YOU CAN BE A BIT...DIRECT... SOMETIMES?
I'LL GO NEXT DOOR AND MAKE FRIENDS RIGHT NOW. THAT ENYA-LOVER IS GOING TO BE ON THE RECEIVING END OF A CHRISTMAS ARMISTICE.

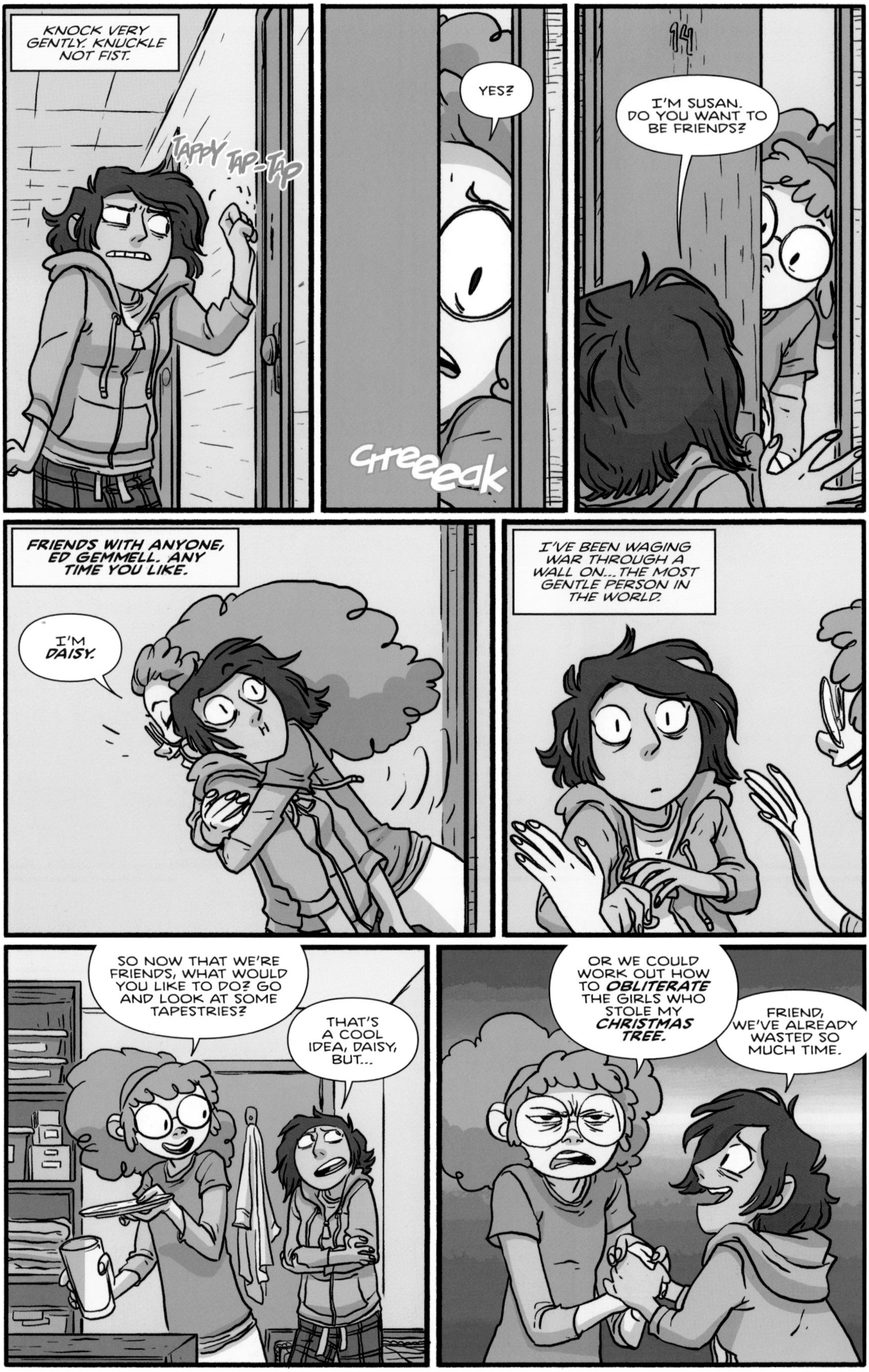
KNOCK VERY GENTLY. KNUCKLE NOT FIST.
TAPPY TAP-TAP
YES?
CREEEAK
I'M SUSAN. DO YOU WANT TO BE FRIENDS?
FRIENDS WITH ANYONE, ED GEMMELL. ANY TIME YOU LIKE.
I'M DAISY.
I'VE BEEN WAGING WAR THROUGH A WALL ON...THE MOST GENTLE PERSON IN THE WORLD.
SO NOW THAT WE'RE FRIENDS, WHAT WOULD YOU LIKE TO DO? GO AND LOOK AT SOME TAPESTRIES?
THAT'S A COOL IDEA, DAISY, BUT...
OR WE COULD WORK OUT HOW TO OBLITERATE THE GIRLS WHO STOLE MY CHRISTMAS TREE.
FRIEND, WE'VE ALREADY WASTED SO MUCH TIME.

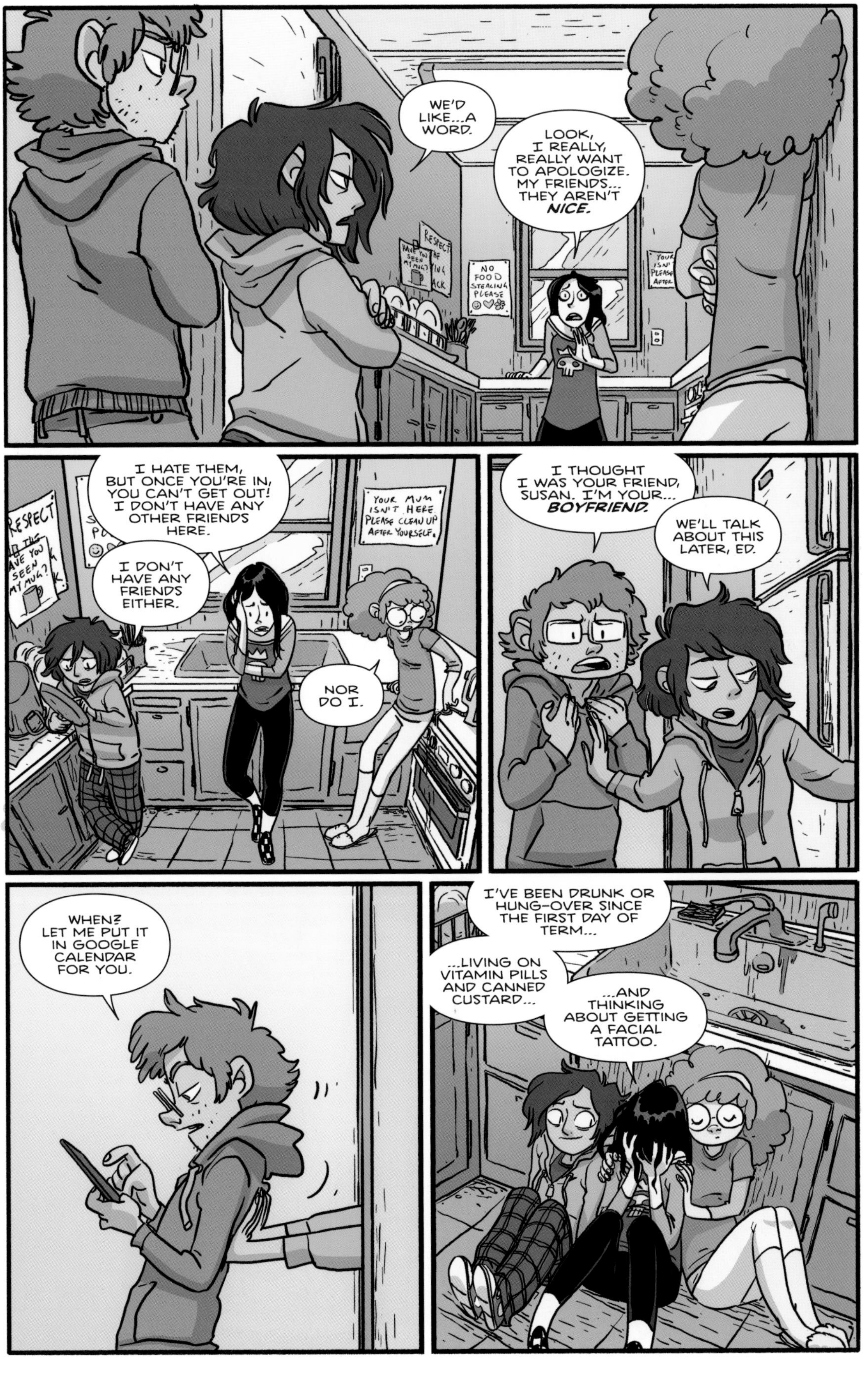
WE'D LIKE...A WORD.
LOOK, I REALLY, REALLY WANT TO APOLOGIZE. MY FRIENDS... THEY AREN'T NICE.
NO FOOD STEALING PLEASE
I HATE THEM, BUT ONCE YOU'RE IN, YOU CAN'T GET OUT! I DON'T HAVE ANY OTHER FRIENDS HERE.
YOUR MUM ISN'T HERE PLEASE CLEAN UP AFTER YOURSELF.
I DON'T HAVE ANY FRIENDS EITHER.
NOR DO I.
I THOUGHT I WAS YOUR FRIEND, SUSAN. I'M YOUR... BOYFRIEND.
WE'LL TALK ABOUT THIS LATER, ED.
WHEN? LET ME PUT IT IN GOOGLE CALENDAR FOR YOU.
I'VE BEEN DRUNK OR HUNG-OVER SINCE THE FIRST DAY OF TERM...
...LIVING ON VITAMIN PILLS AND CANNED CUSTARD...
...AND THINKING ABOUT GETTING A FACIAL TATTOO.

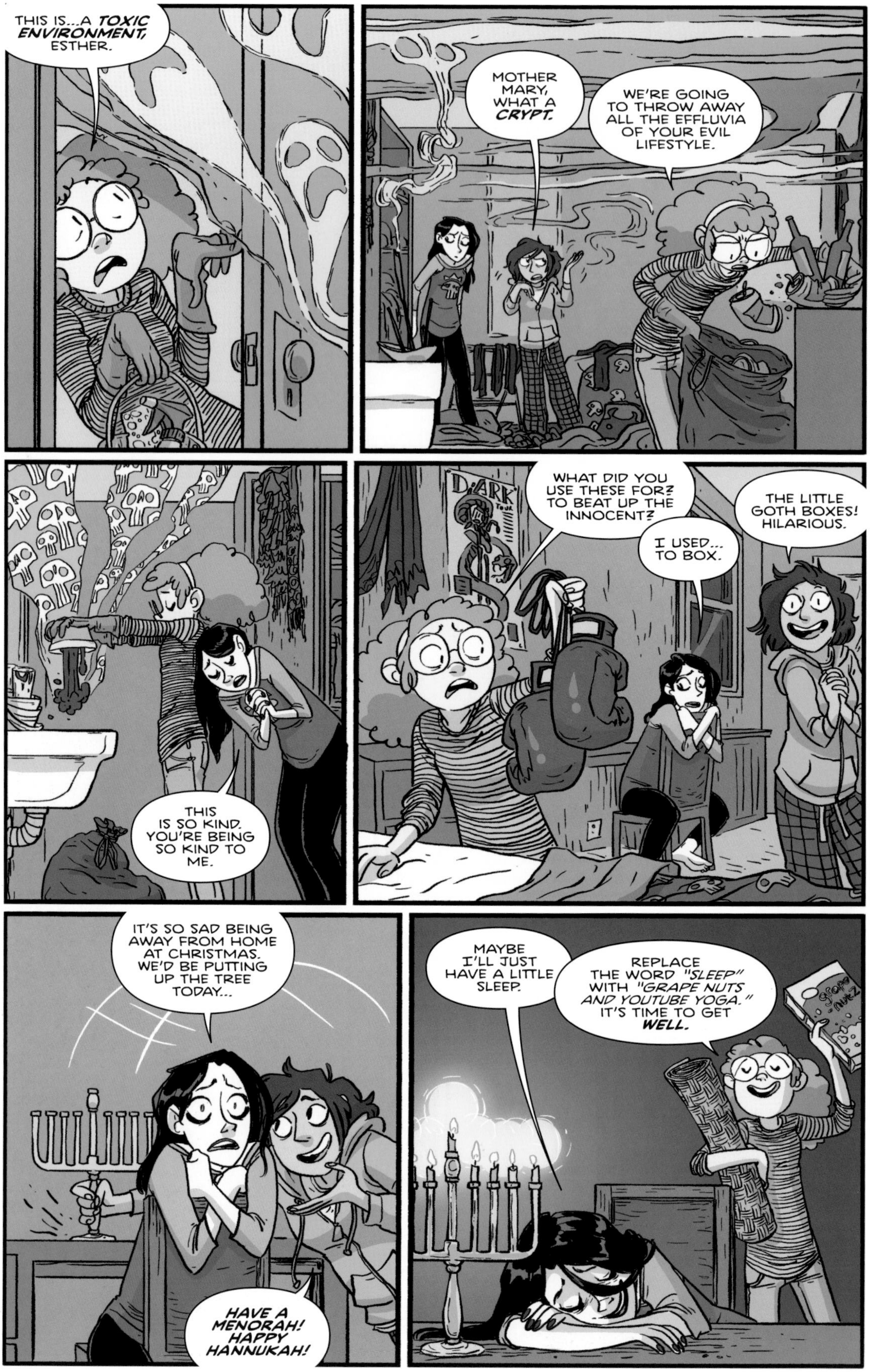
THIS IS...A *TOXIC ENVIRONMENT,* ESTHER.
MOTHER MARY, WHAT A ***CRYPT.***
WE'RE GOING TO THROW AWAY ALL THE EFFLUVIA OF YOUR EVIL LIFESTYLE.
THIS IS SO KIND. YOU'RE BEING SO KIND TO ME.
D'ARK
WHAT DID YOU USE THESE FOR? TO BEAT UP THE INNOCENT?
I USED... TO BOX.
THE LITTLE GOTH BOXES! HILARIOUS.
IT'S SO SAD BEING AWAY FROM HOME AT CHRISTMAS. WE'D BE PUTTING UP THE TREE TODAY...
HAVE A MENORAH! HAPPY HANNUKAH!
MAYBE I'LL JUST HAVE A LITTLE SLEEP.
REPLACE THE WORD *"SLEEP"* WITH *"GRAPE NUTS AND YOUTUBE YOGA."* IT'S TIME TO GET ***WELL.***

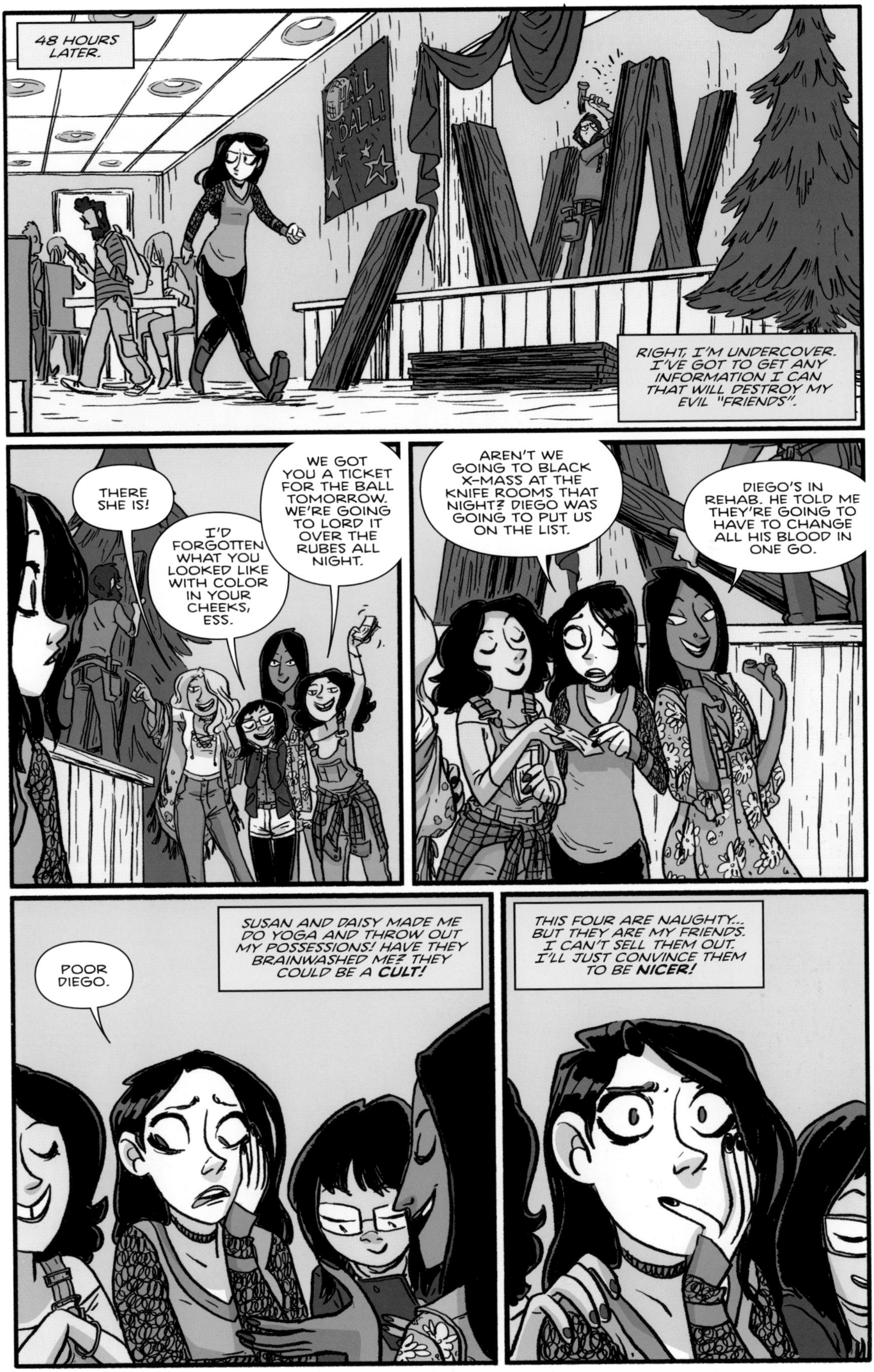
48 HOURS LATER.
HALL BALL!
RIGHT, I'M UNDERCOVER. I'VE GOT TO GET ANY INFORMATION I CAN THAT WILL DESTROY MY EVIL "FRIENDS".
THERE SHE IS!
I'D FORGOTTEN WHAT YOU LOOKED LIKE WITH COLOR IN YOUR CHEEKS, ESS.
WE GOT YOU A TICKET FOR THE BALL TOMORROW. WE'RE GOING TO LORD IT OVER THE RUBES ALL NIGHT.
AREN'T WE GOING TO BLACK X-MASS AT THE KNIFE ROOMS THAT NIGHT? DIEGO WAS GOING TO PUT US ON THE LIST.
DIEGO'S IN REHAB. HE TOLD ME THEY'RE GOING TO HAVE TO CHANGE ALL HIS BLOOD IN ONE GO.
POOR DIEGO.
SUSAN AND DAISY MADE ME DO YOGA AND THROW OUT MY POSSESSIONS! HAVE THEY BRAINWASHED ME? THEY COULD BE A CULT!
THIS FOUR ARE NAUGHTY... BUT THEY ARE MY FRIENDS. I CAN'T SELL THEM OUT. I'LL JUST CONVINCE THEM TO BE NICER!

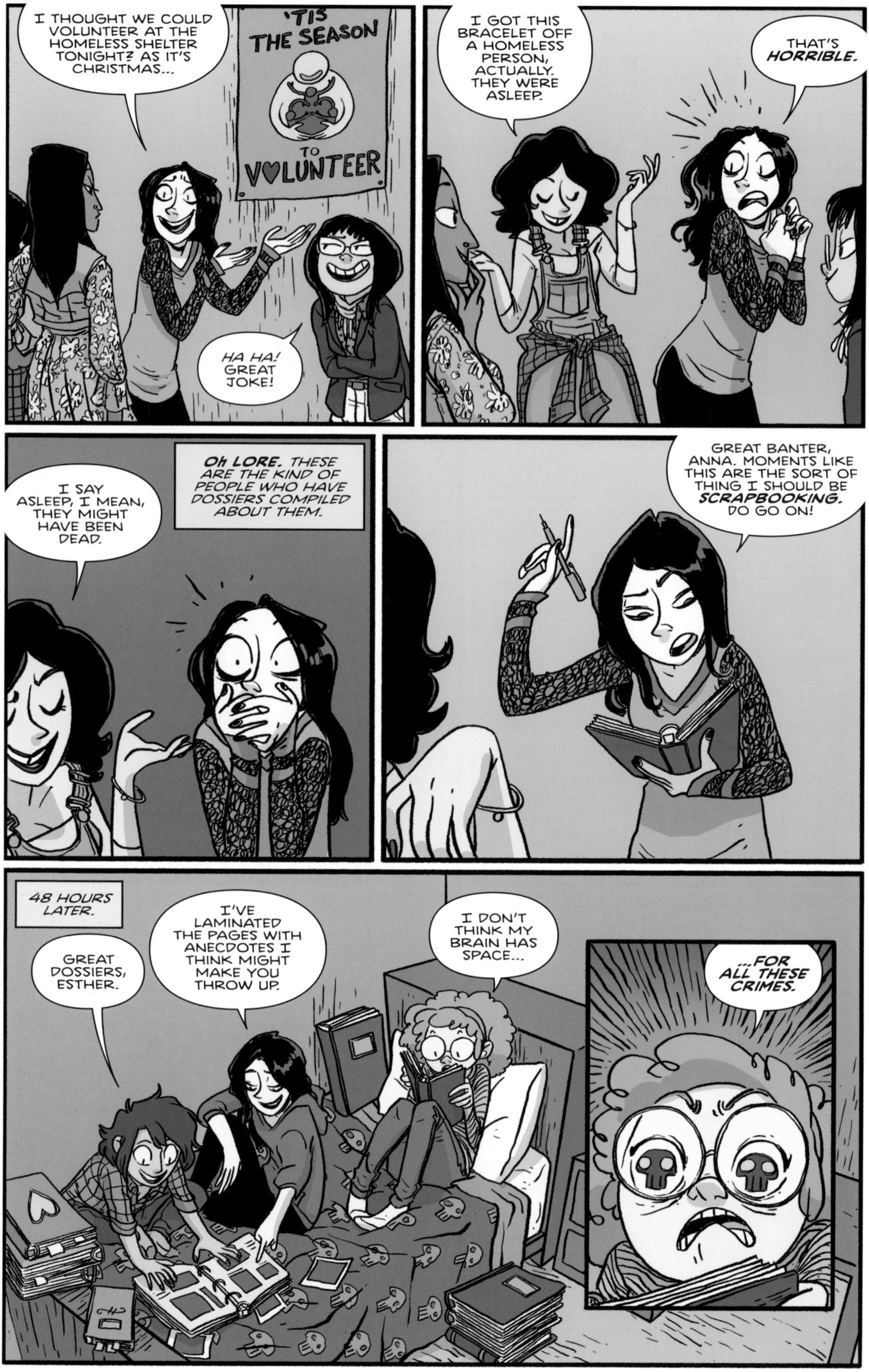

I THOUGHT WE COULD VOLUNTEER AT THE HOMELESS SHELTER TONIGHT? AS IT'S CHRISTMAS...
'TIS THE SEASON TO VOLUNTEER
HA HA! GREAT JOKE!
I GOT THIS BRACELET OFF A HOMELESS PERSON, ACTUALLY. THEY WERE ASLEEP.
THAT'S *HORRIBLE.*
I SAY ASLEEP, I MEAN, THEY MIGHT HAVE BEEN DEAD.
Oh LORE. THESE ARE THE KIND OF PEOPLE WHO HAVE DOSSIERS COMPILED ABOUT THEM.
GREAT BANTER, ANNA. MOMENTS LIKE THIS ARE THE SORT OF THING I SHOULD BE *SCRAPBOOKING.* DO GO ON!
48 HOURS LATER.
GREAT DOSSIERS, ESTHER.
I'VE LAMINATED THE PAGES WITH ANECDOTES I THINK MIGHT MAKE YOU THROW UP.
I DON'T THINK MY BRAIN HAS SPACE...
...FOR ALL THESE CRIMES.

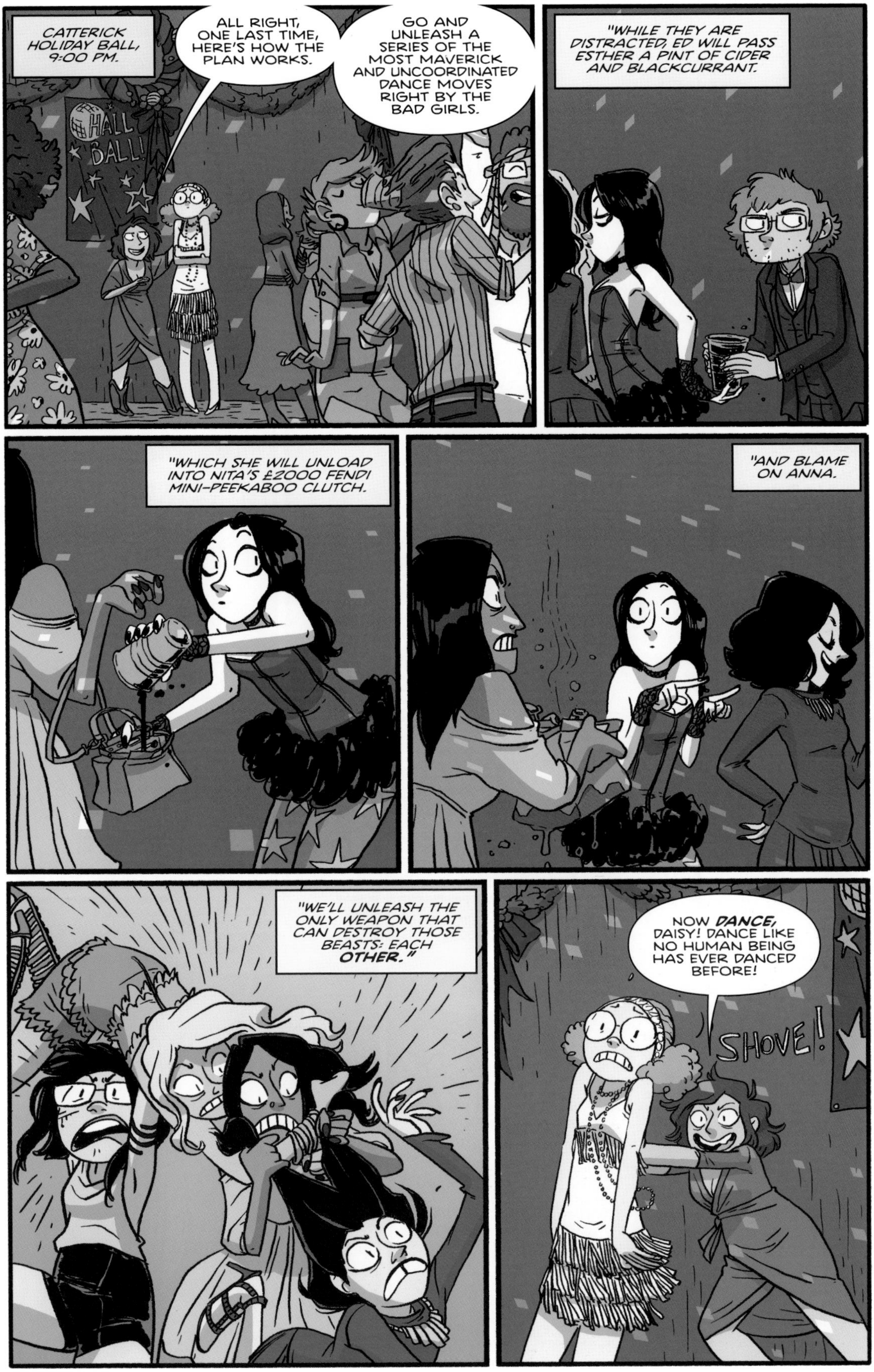
CATTERICK HOLIDAY BALL, 9:00 PM.
ALL RIGHT, ONE LAST TIME, HERE'S HOW THE PLAN WORKS.
GO AND UNLEASH A SERIES OF THE MOST MAVERICK AND UNCOORDINATED DANCE MOVES RIGHT BY THE BAD GIRLS.
HALL BALL!
"WHILE THEY ARE DISTRACTED, ED WILL PASS ESTHER A PINT OF CIDER AND BLACKCURRANT.
"WHICH SHE WILL UNLOAD INTO NITA'S £2000 FENDI MINI-PEEKABOO CLUTCH.
"AND BLAME ON ANNA.
"WE'LL UNLEASH THE ONLY WEAPON THAT CAN DESTROY THOSE BEASTS: EACH **OTHER.**"
NOW **DANCE,** DAISY! DANCE LIKE NO HUMAN BEING HAS EVER DANCED BEFORE!
SHOVE!

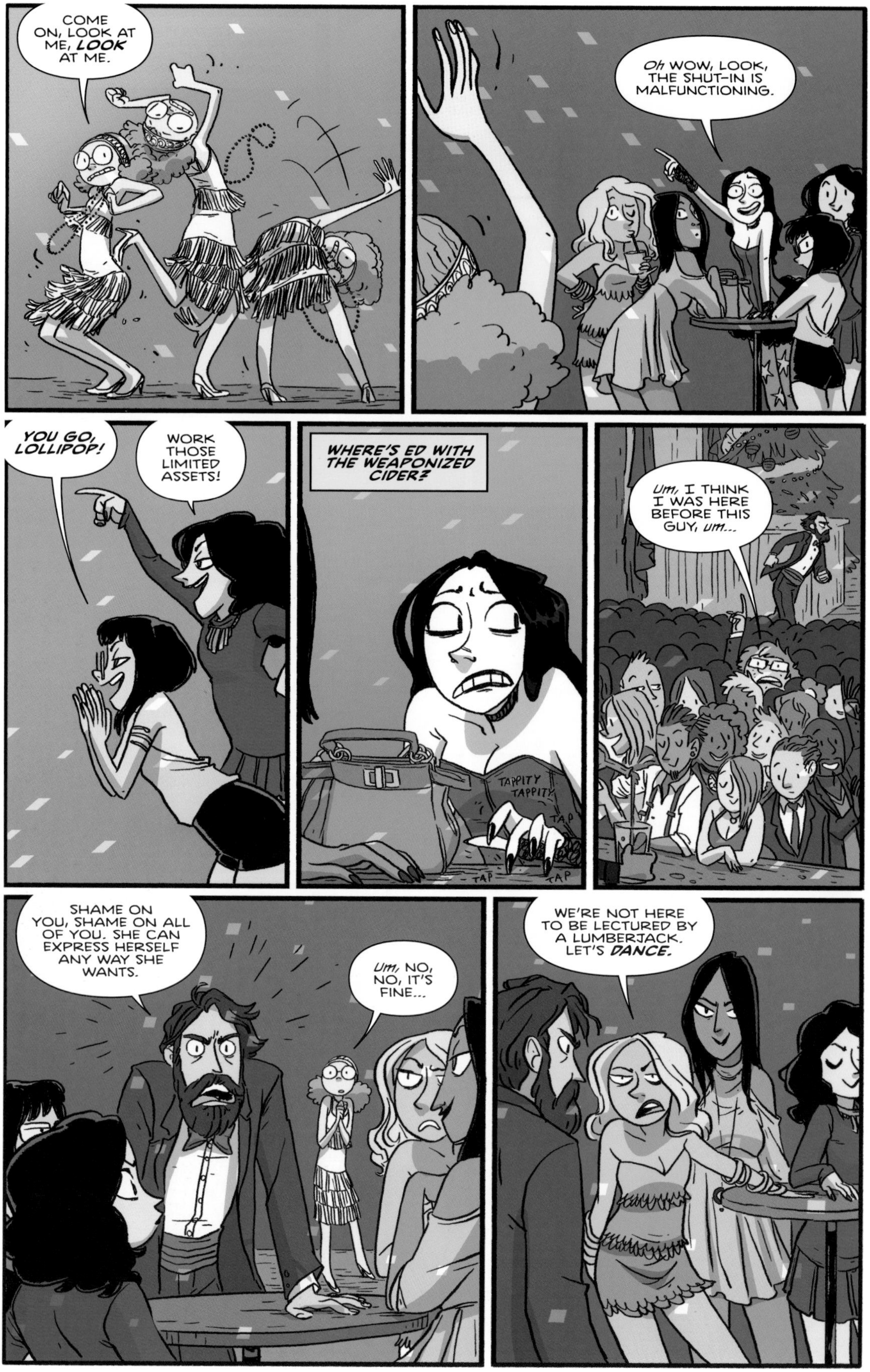

COME ON, LOOK AT ME, LOOK AT ME.
Oh WOW, LOOK, THE SHUT-IN IS MALFUNCTIONING.
YOU GO, LOLLIPOP!
WORK THOSE LIMITED ASSETS!
WHERE'S ED WITH THE WEAPONIZED CIDER?
TAPPITY TAPPITY
TAP
TAP
TAP
Um, I THINK I WAS HERE BEFORE THIS GUY, um...
SHAME ON YOU, SHAME ON ALL OF YOU. SHE CAN EXPRESS HERSELF ANY WAY SHE WANTS.
Um, NO, NO, IT'S FINE...
WE'RE NOT HERE TO BE LECTURED BY A LUMBERJACK. LET'S DANCE.

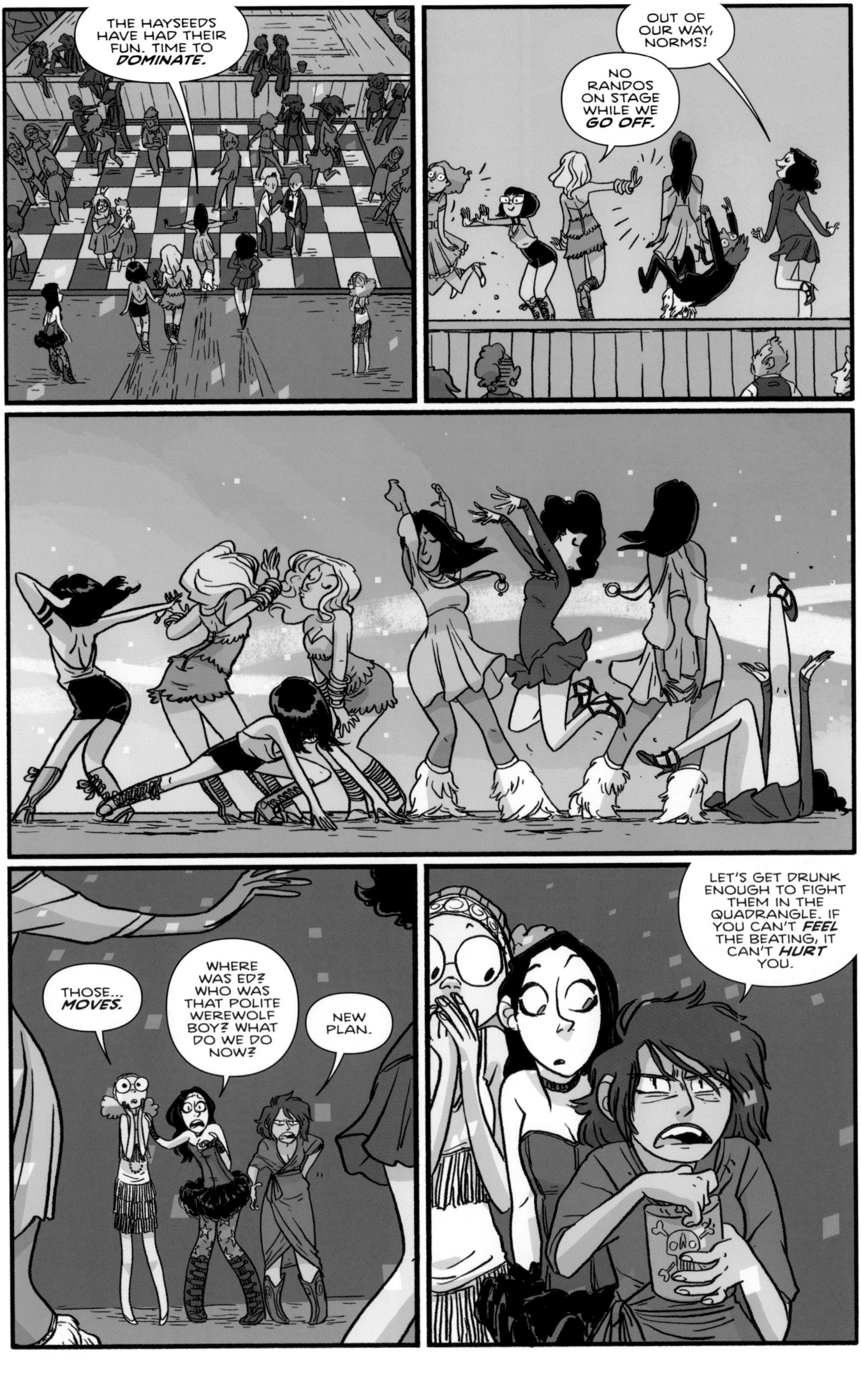
THE HAYSEEDS HAVE HAD THEIR FUN. TIME TO *DOMINATE.*
OUT OF OUR WAY, NORMS!
NO RANDOS ON STAGE WHILE WE *GO OFF.*
THOSE... *MOVES.*
WHERE WAS ED? WHO WAS THAT POLITE WEREWOLF BOY? WHAT DO WE DO NOW?
NEW PLAN.
LET'S GET DRUNK ENOUGH TO FIGHT THEM IN THE QUADRANGLE. IF YOU CAN'T *FEEL* THE BEATING, IT CAN'T *HURT* YOU.

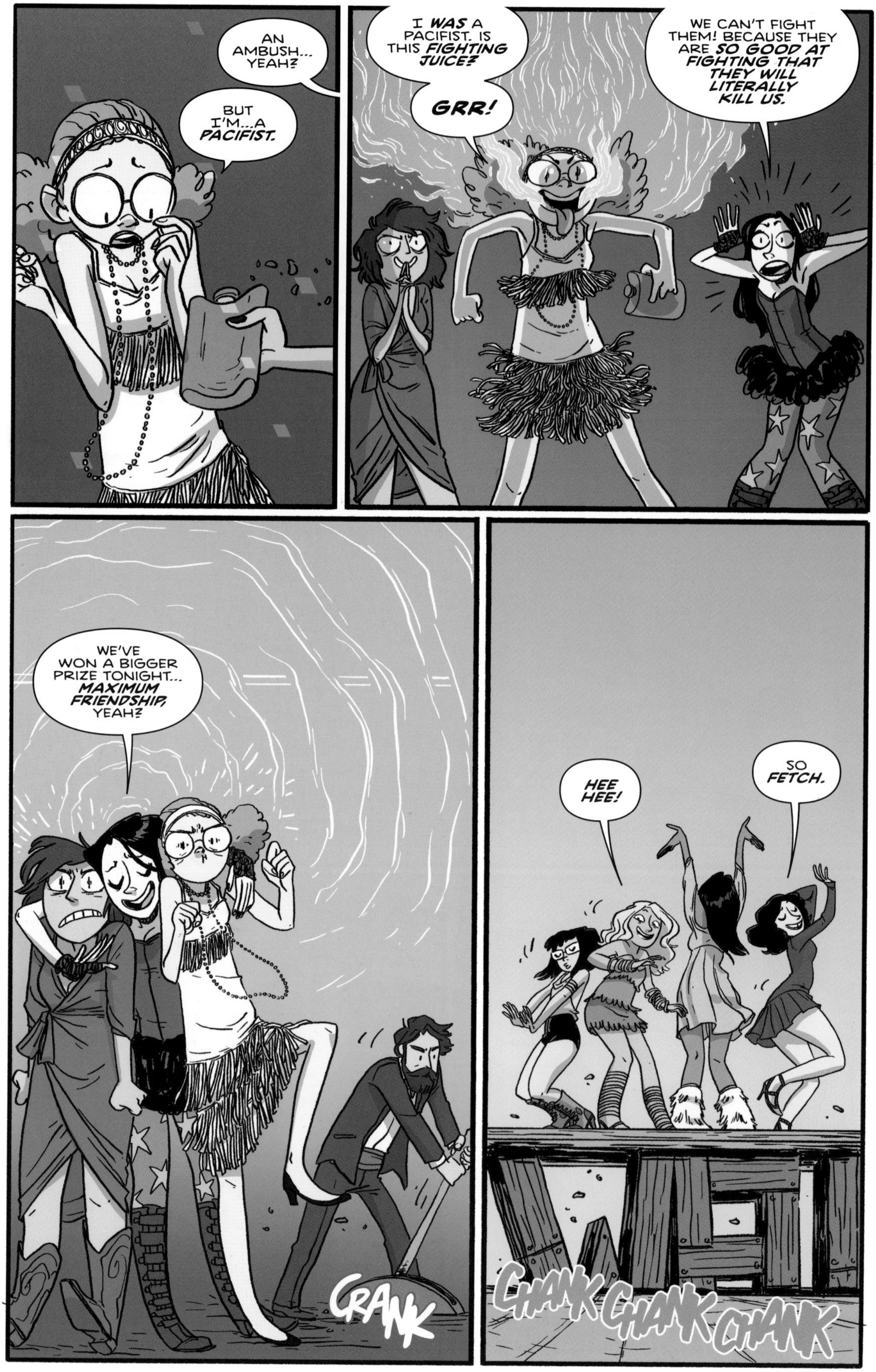
AN AMBUSH... YEAH?
BUT I'M...A PACIFIST.
I WAS A PACIFIST. IS THIS FIGHTING JUICE?
GRR!
WE CAN'T FIGHT THEM! BECAUSE THEY ARE SO GOOD AT FIGHTING THAT THEY WILL LITERALLY KILL US.
WE'VE WON A BIGGER PRIZE TONIGHT... MAXIMUM FRIENDSHIP, YEAH?
CRANK
HEE HEE!
SO FETCH.
CHANK CHANK CHANK

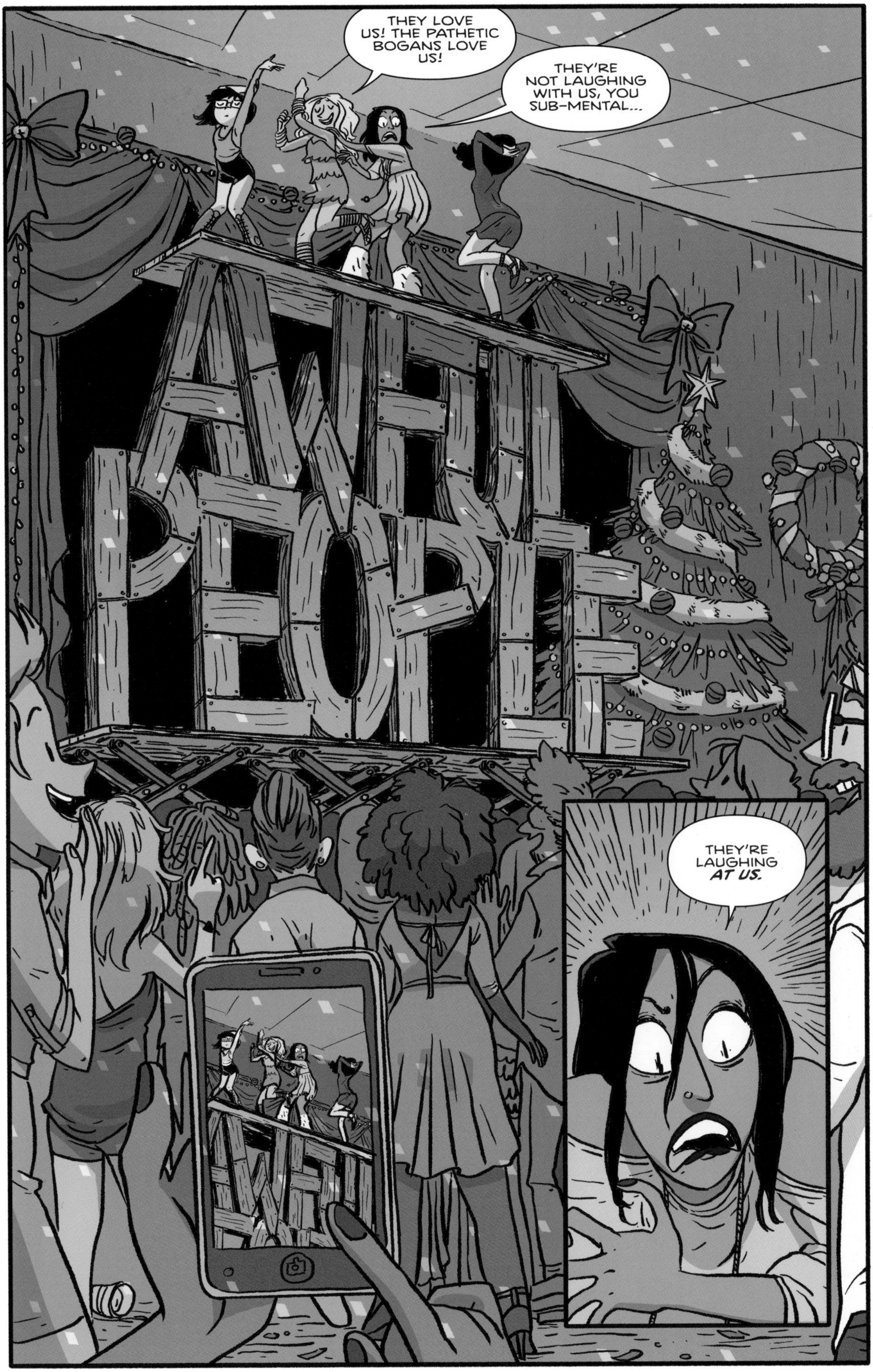
THEY LOVE US! THE PATHETIC BOGANS LOVE US!
THEY'RE NOT LAUGHING WITH US, YOU SUB-MENTAL...
THEY'RE LAUGHING *AT US.*

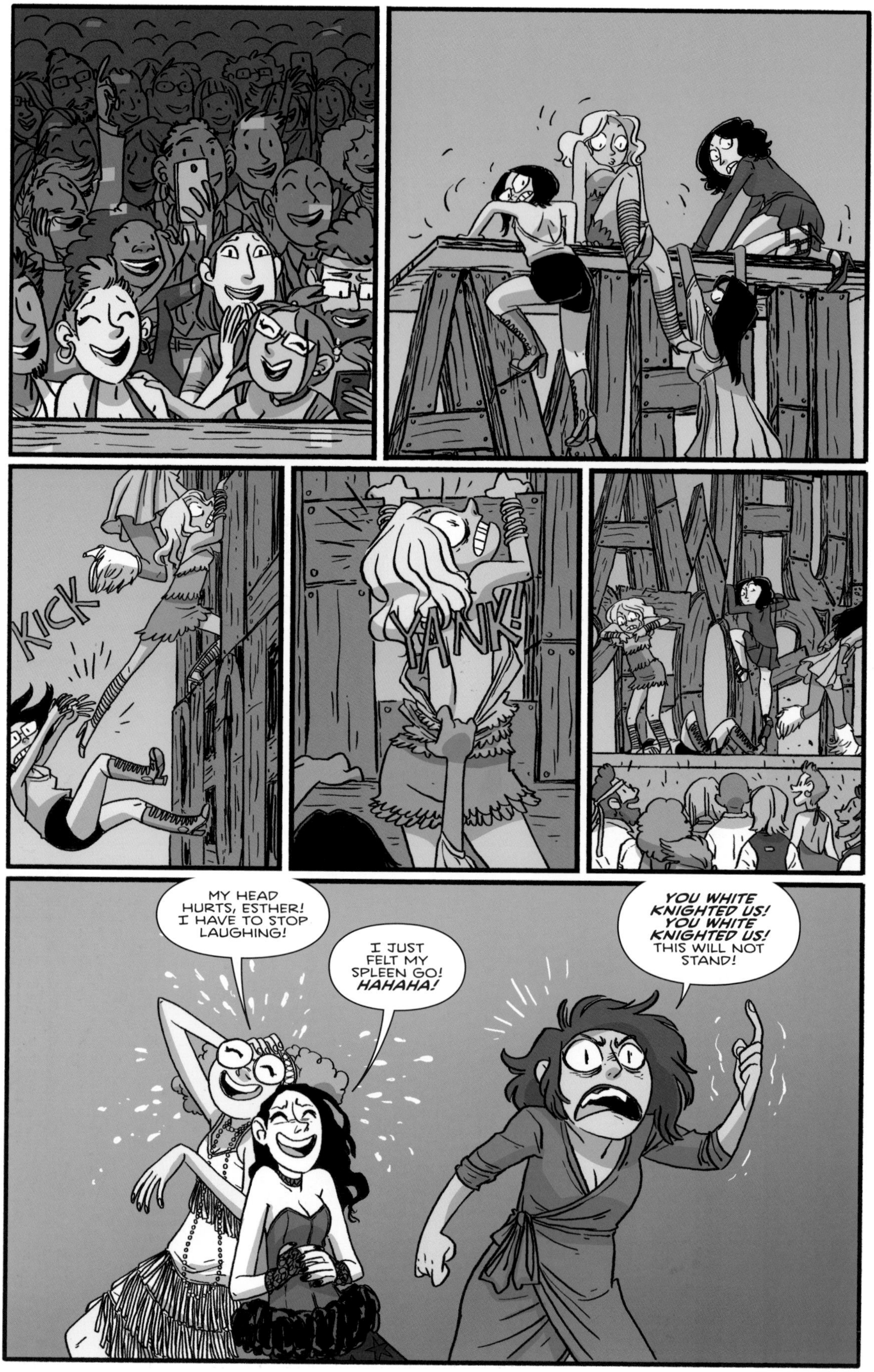
KICK
YANK!
MY HEAD HURTS, ESTHER! I HAVE TO STOP LAUGHING!
I JUST FELT MY SPLEEN GO! HAHAHA!
YOU WHITE KNIGHTED US! YOU WHITE KNIGHTED US! THIS WILL NOT STAND!

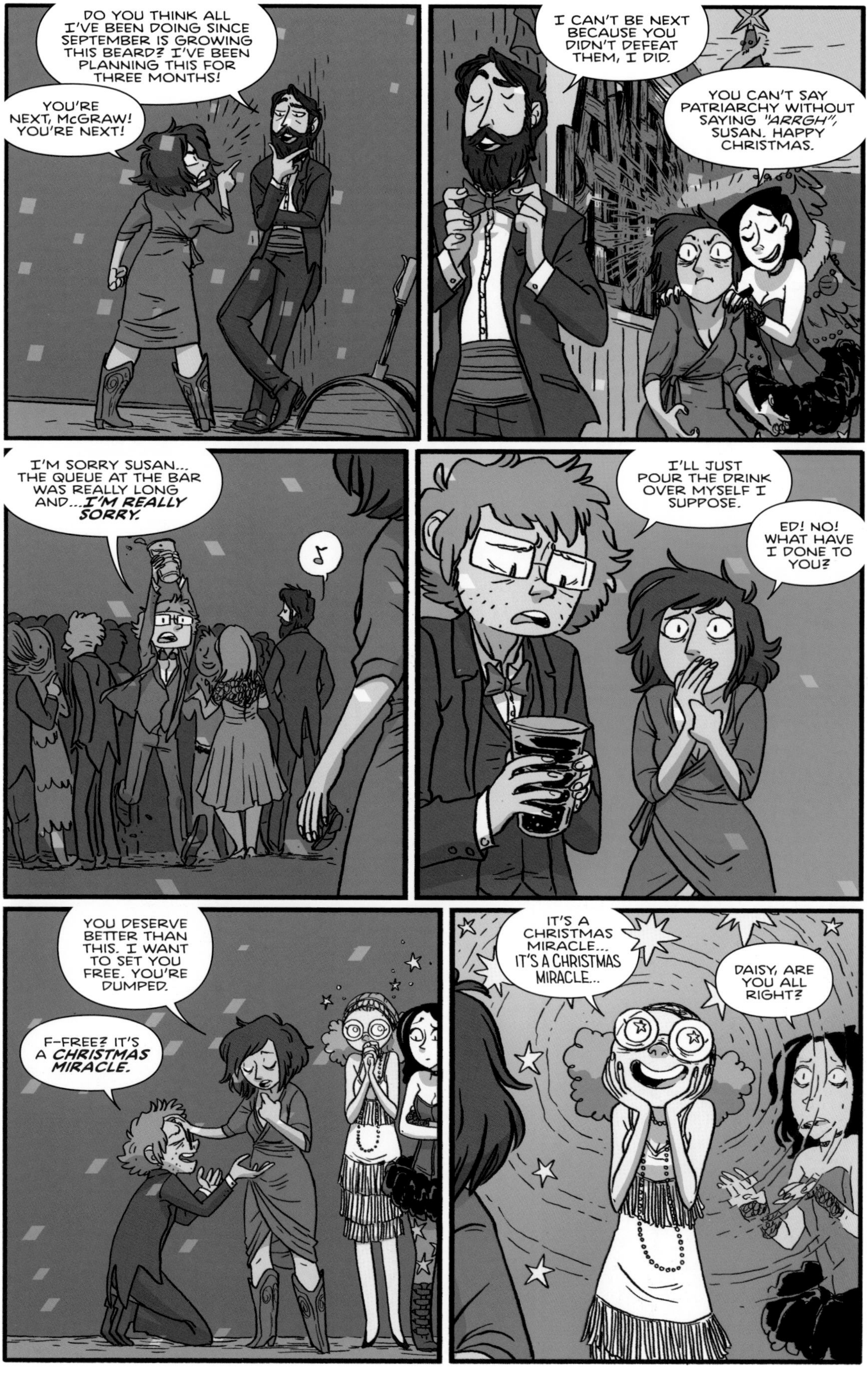
DO YOU THINK ALL I'VE BEEN DOING SINCE SEPTEMBER IS GROWING THIS BEARD? I'VE BEEN PLANNING THIS FOR THREE MONTHS!
YOU'RE NEXT, McGRAW! YOU'RE NEXT!
I CAN'T BE NEXT BECAUSE YOU DIDN'T DEFEAT THEM, I DID.
YOU CAN'T SAY PATRIARCHY WITHOUT SAYING "ARRGH", SUSAN. HAPPY CHRISTMAS.
I'M SORRY SUSAN... THE QUEUE AT THE BAR WAS REALLY LONG AND... I'M REALLY SORRY.
I'LL JUST POUR THE DRINK OVER MYSELF I SUPPOSE.
ED! NO! WHAT HAVE I DONE TO YOU?
YOU DESERVE BETTER THAN THIS. I WANT TO SET YOU FREE. YOU'RE DUMPED.
F-FREE? IT'S A CHRISTMAS MIRACLE.
IT'S A CHRISTMAS MIRACLE... IT'S A CHRISTMAS MIRACLE...
DAISY, ARE YOU ALL RIGHT?

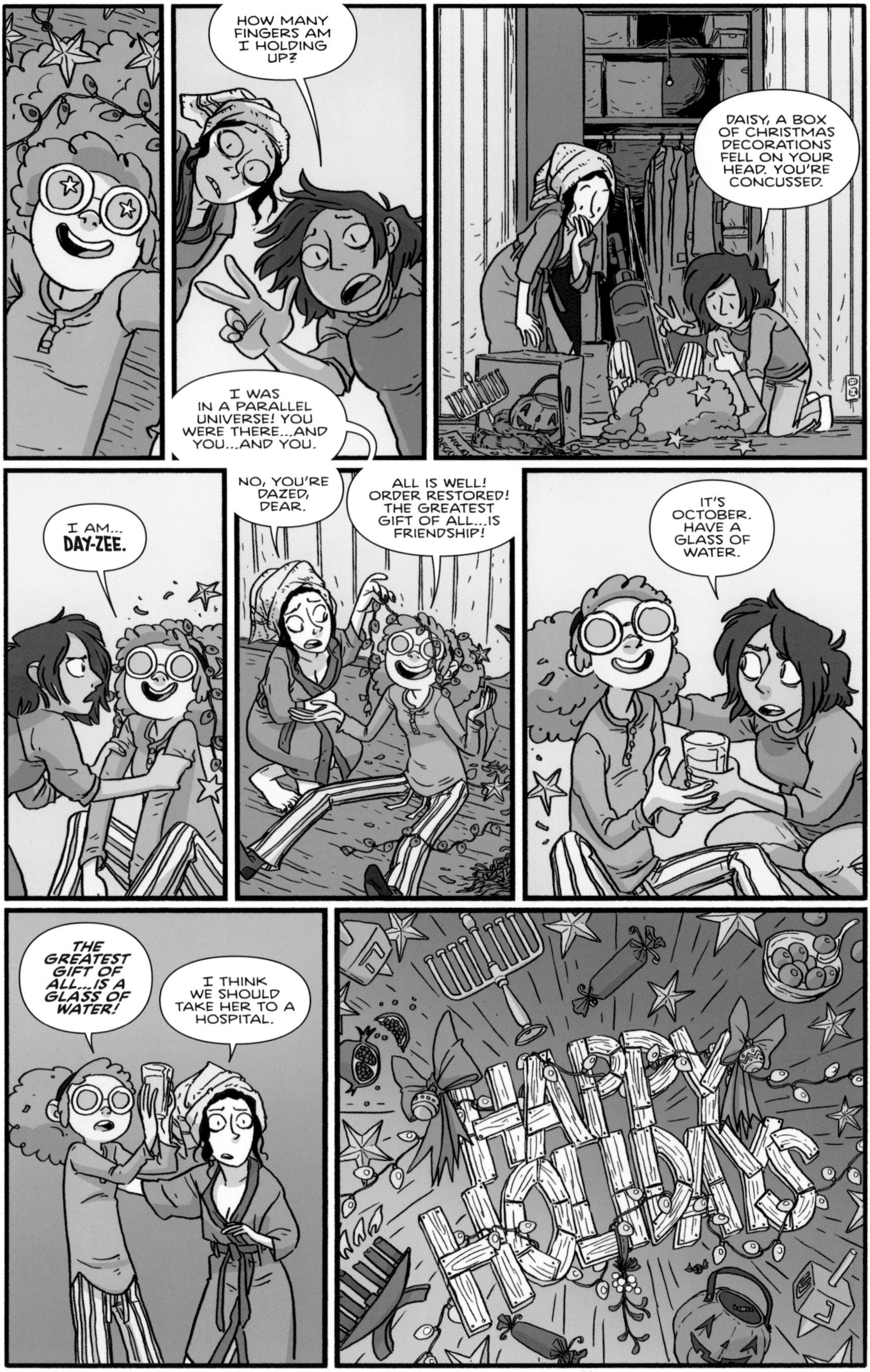
HOW MANY FINGERS AM I HOLDING UP?
I WAS IN A PARALLEL UNIVERSE! YOU WERE THERE...AND YOU...AND YOU.
DAISY, A BOX OF CHRISTMAS DECORATIONS FELL ON YOUR HEAD. YOU'RE CONCUSSED.
I AM... DAY-ZEE.
NO, YOU'RE DAZED, DEAR.
ALL IS WELL! ORDER RESTORED! THE GREATEST GIFT OF ALL...IS FRIENDSHIP!
IT'S OCTOBER. HAVE A GLASS OF WATER.
THE GREATEST GIFT OF ALL...IS A GLASS OF WATER!
I THINK WE SHOULD TAKE HER TO A HOSPITAL.
HAPPY HOLIDAYS

THE END

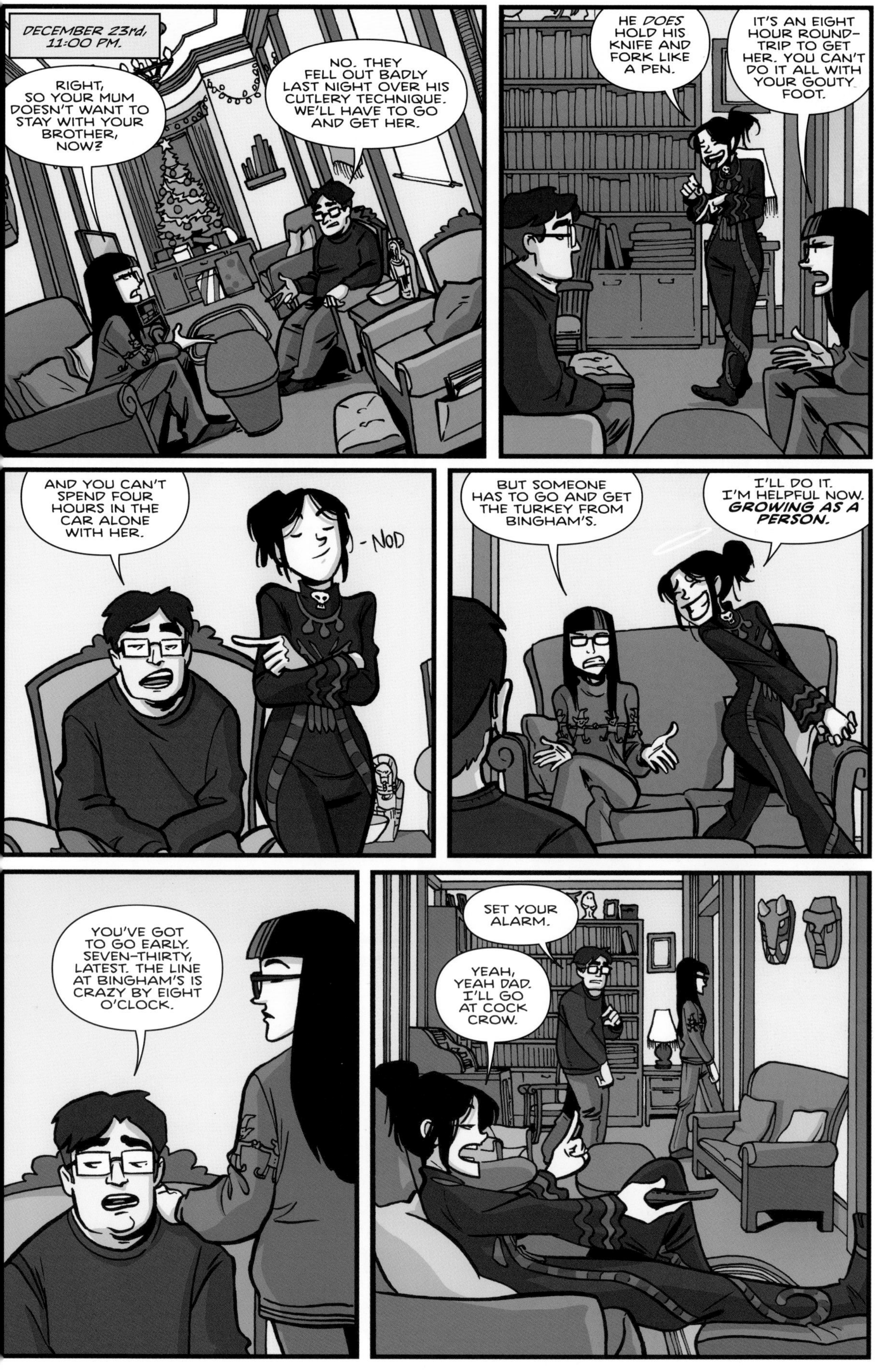
DECEMBER 23rd, 11:00 PM.
RIGHT, SO YOUR MUM DOESN'T WANT TO STAY WITH YOUR BROTHER, NOW?
NO. THEY FELL OUT BADLY LAST NIGHT OVER HIS CUTLERY TECHNIQUE. WE'LL HAVE TO GO AND GET HER.
HE *DOES* HOLD HIS KNIFE AND FORK LIKE A PEN.
IT'S AN EIGHT HOUR ROUND-TRIP TO GET HER. YOU CAN'T DO IT ALL WITH YOUR GOUTY FOOT.
AND YOU CAN'T SPEND FOUR HOURS IN THE CAR ALONE WITH HER.
-NOD
BUT SOMEONE HAS TO GO AND GET THE TURKEY FROM BINGHAM'S.
I'LL DO IT. I'M HELPFUL NOW. ***GROWING AS A PERSON.***
YOU'VE GOT TO GO EARLY. SEVEN-THIRTY, LATEST. THE LINE AT BINGHAM'S IS CRAZY BY EIGHT O'CLOCK.
SET YOUR ALARM.
YEAH, YEAH DAD. I'LL GO AT COCK CROW.

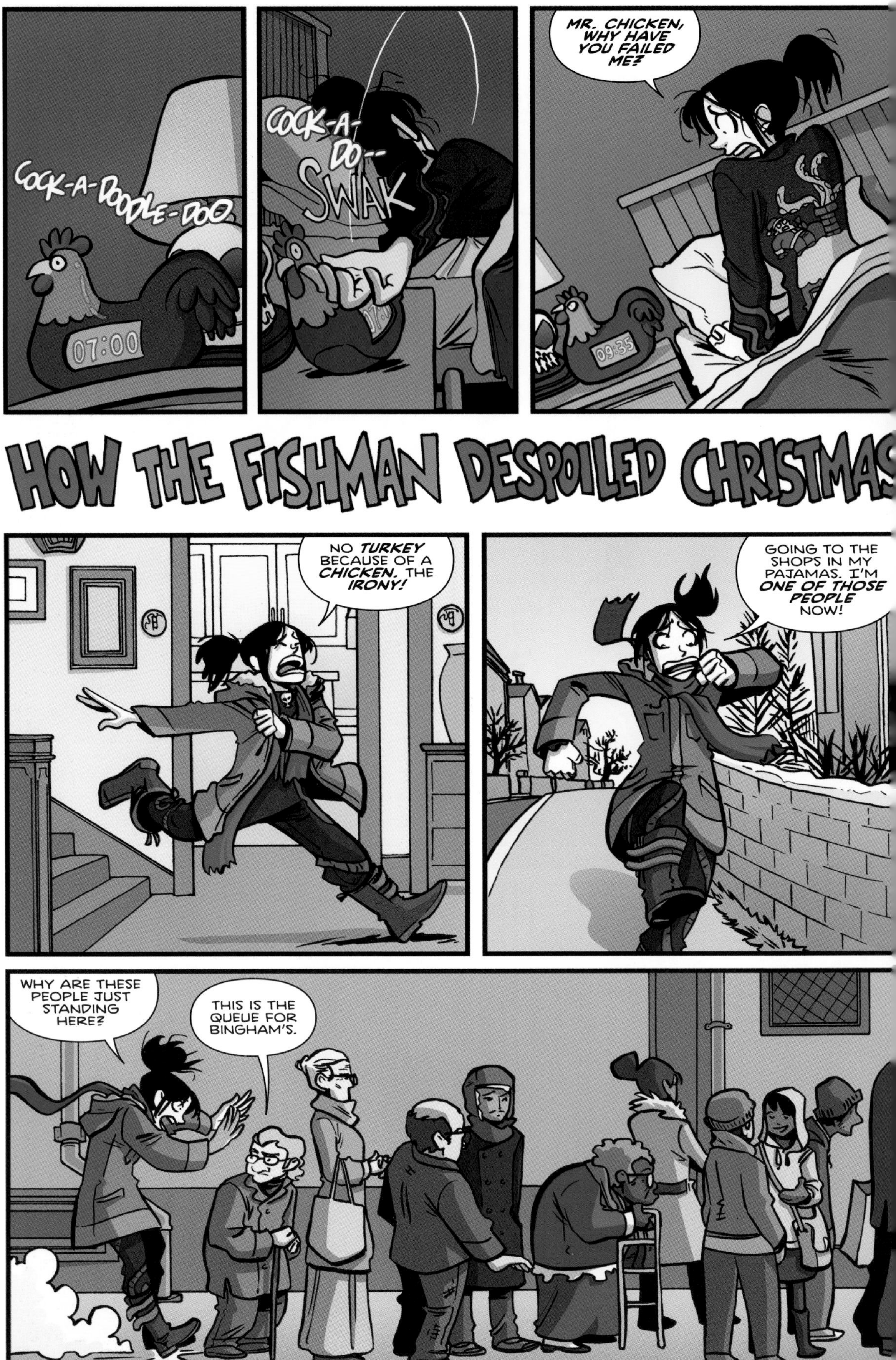
COCK-A-DOODLE-DOO
07:00
COCK-A-DO--
SWAK
MR. CHICKEN, WHY HAVE YOU FAILED ME?
09:35
HOW THE FISHMAN DESPOILED CHRISTMAS
NO TURKEY BECAUSE OF A CHICKEN. THE IRONY!
GOING TO THE SHOPS IN MY PAJAMAS. I'M ONE OF THOSE PEOPLE NOW!
WHY ARE THESE PEOPLE JUST STANDING HERE?
THIS IS THE QUEUE FOR BINGHAM'S.

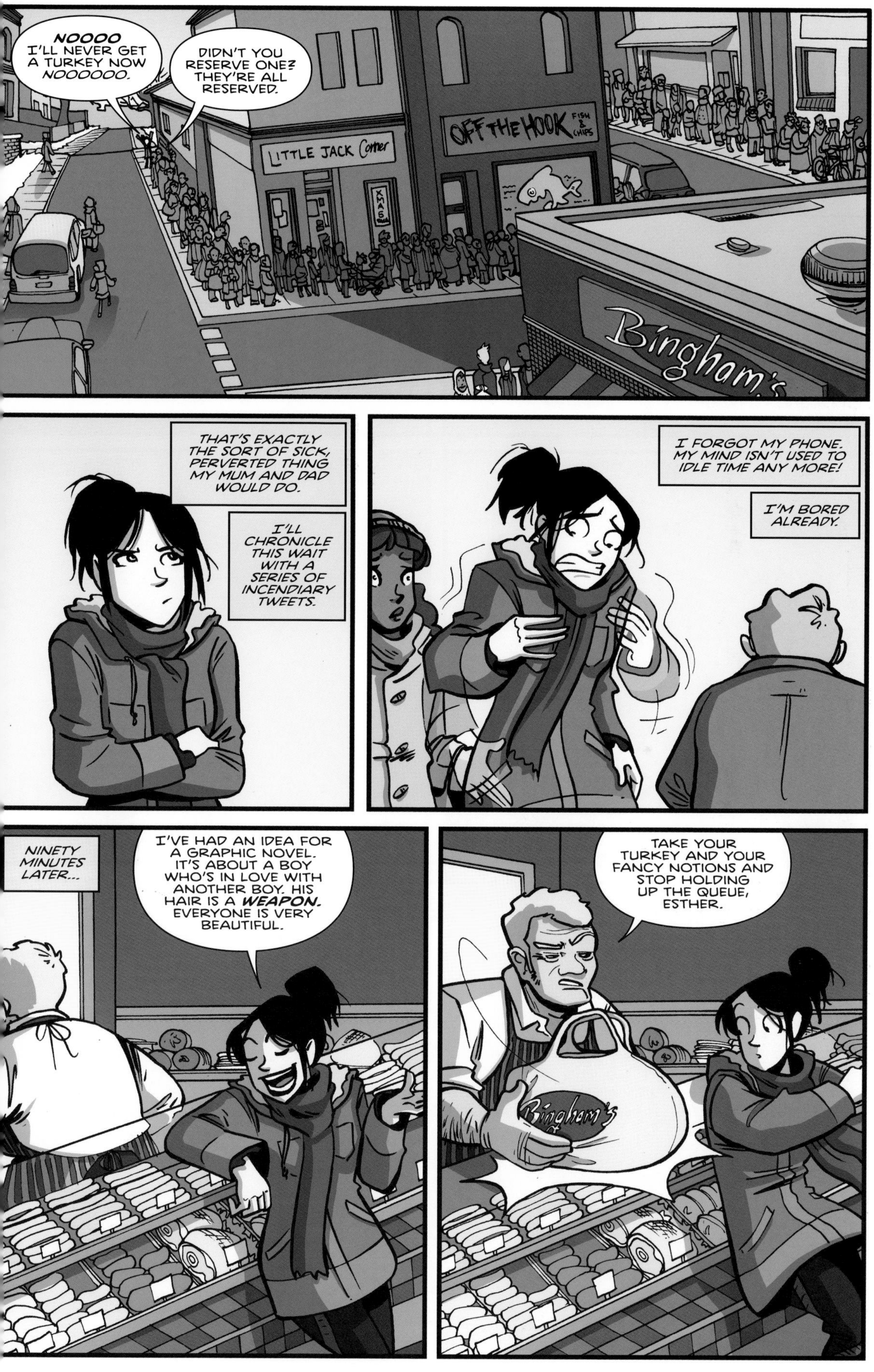
NOOOO I'LL NEVER GET A TURKEY NOW NOOOOOO.
DIDN'T YOU RESERVE ONE? THEY'RE ALL RESERVED.
LITTLE JACK Corner
OFF THE HOOK FISH & CHIPS
Bingham's
THAT'S EXACTLY THE SORT OF SICK, PERVERTED THING MY MUM AND DAD WOULD DO.
I'LL CHRONICLE THIS WAIT WITH A SERIES OF INCENDIARY TWEETS.
I FORGOT MY PHONE. MY MIND ISN'T USED TO IDLE TIME ANY MORE!
I'M BORED ALREADY.
NINETY MINUTES LATER...
I'VE HAD AN IDEA FOR A GRAPHIC NOVEL. IT'S ABOUT A BOY WHO'S IN LOVE WITH ANOTHER BOY. HIS HAIR IS A WEAPON. EVERYONE IS VERY BEAUTIFUL.
TAKE YOUR TURKEY AND YOUR FANCY NOTIONS AND STOP HOLDING UP THE QUEUE, ESTHER.
Bingham's

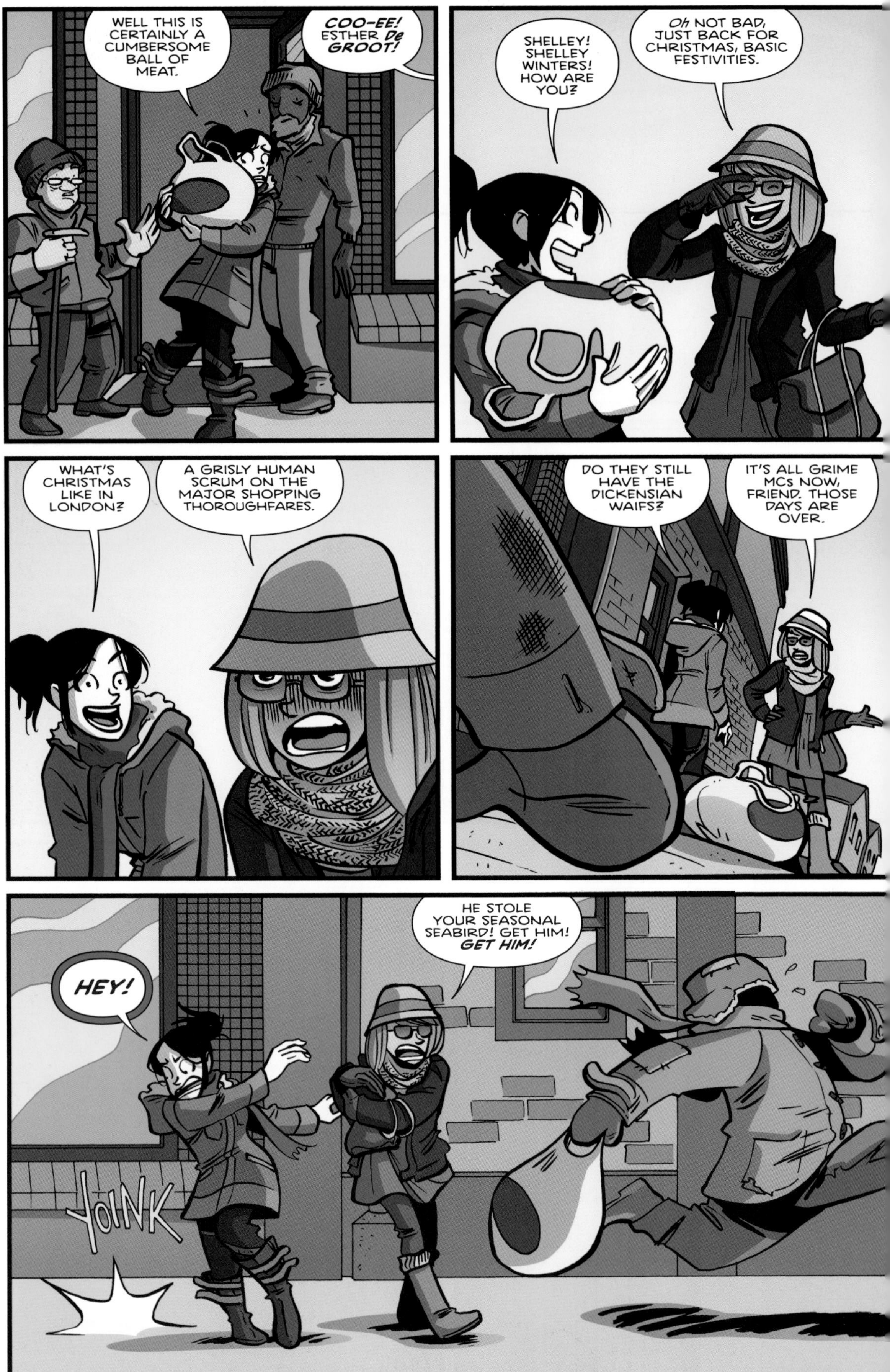
WELL THIS IS CERTAINLY A CUMBERSOME BALL OF MEAT.
COO-EE! ESTHER De GROOT!
SHELLEY! SHELLEY WINTERS! HOW ARE YOU?
Oh NOT BAD, JUST BACK FOR CHRISTMAS, BASIC FESTIVITIES.
WHAT'S CHRISTMAS LIKE IN LONDON?
A GRISLY HUMAN SCRUM ON THE MAJOR SHOPPING THOROUGHFARES.
DO THEY STILL HAVE THE DICKENSIAN WAIFS?
IT'S ALL GRIME MCs NOW, FRIEND. THOSE DAYS ARE OVER.
HEY!
HE STOLE YOUR SEASONAL SEABIRD! GET HIM! GET HIM!
YOINK

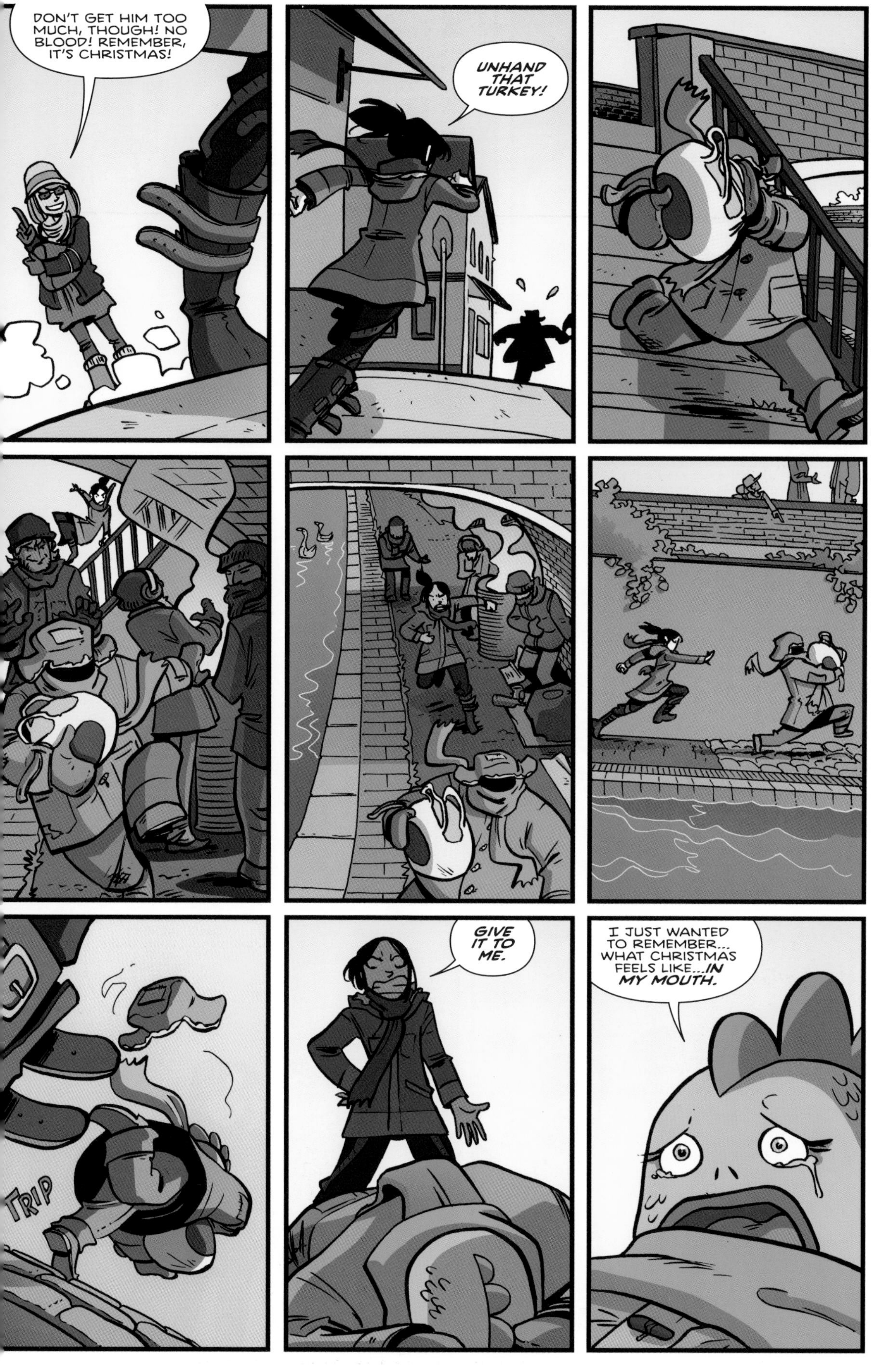
DON'T GET HIM TOO MUCH, THOUGH! NO BLOOD! REMEMBER, IT'S CHRISTMAS!
UNHAND THAT TURKEY!
TRIP
GIVE IT TO ME.
I JUST WANTED TO REMEMBER... WHAT CHRISTMAS FEELS LIKE... IN MY MOUTH.

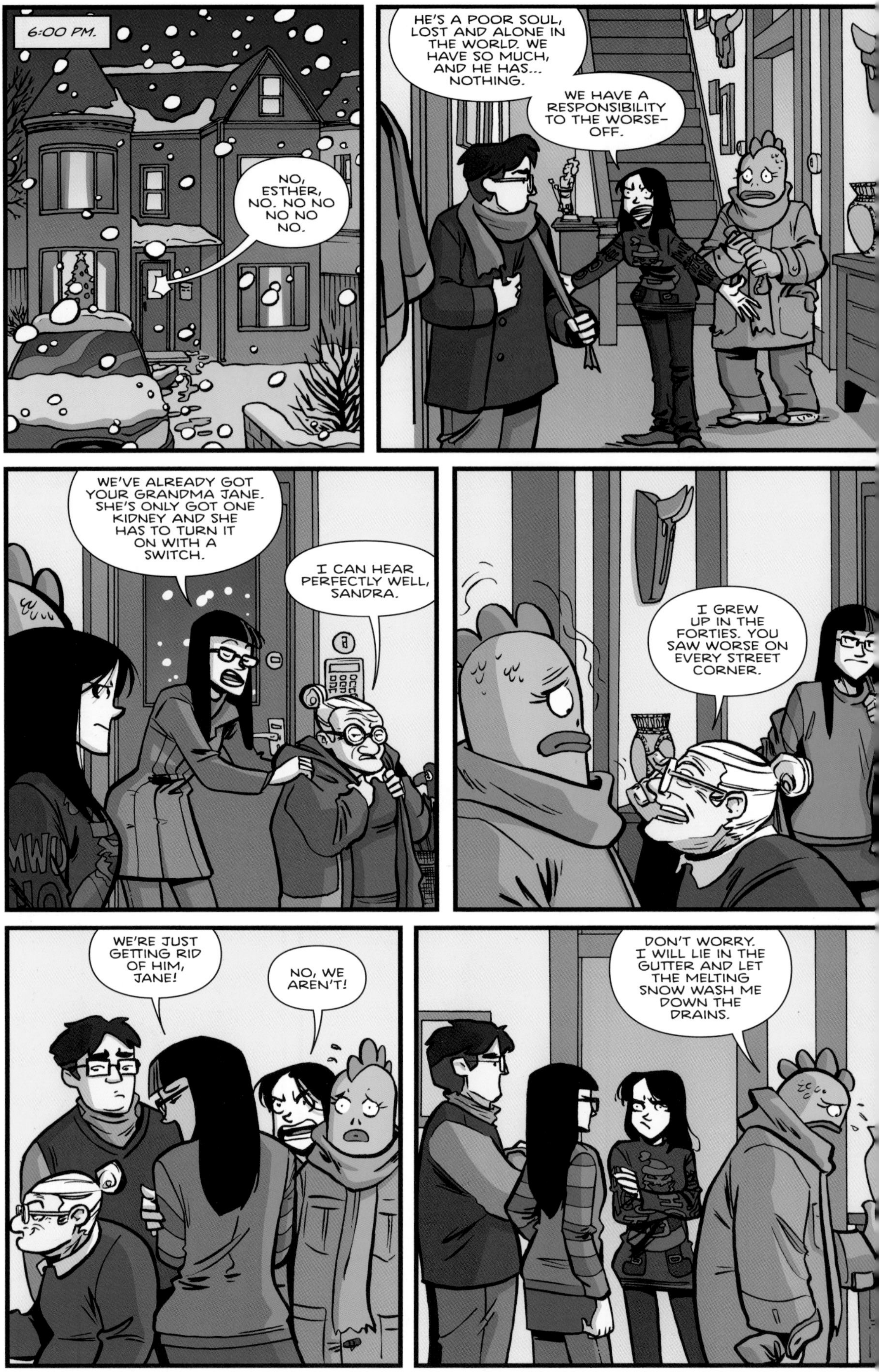
6:00 PM.
NO, ESTHER, NO. NO NO NO NO NO.
HE'S A POOR SOUL, LOST AND ALONE IN THE WORLD. WE HAVE SO MUCH, AND HE HAS... NOTHING.
WE HAVE A RESPONSIBILITY TO THE WORSE-OFF.
WE'VE ALREADY GOT YOUR GRANDMA JANE. SHE'S ONLY GOT ONE KIDNEY AND SHE HAS TO TURN IT ON WITH A SWITCH.
I CAN HEAR PERFECTLY WELL, SANDRA.
I GREW UP IN THE FORTIES. YOU SAW WORSE ON EVERY STREET CORNER.
WE'RE JUST GETTING RID OF HIM, JANE!
NO, WE AREN'T!
DON'T WORRY. I WILL LIE IN THE GUTTER AND LET THE MELTING SNOW WASH ME DOWN THE DRAINS.

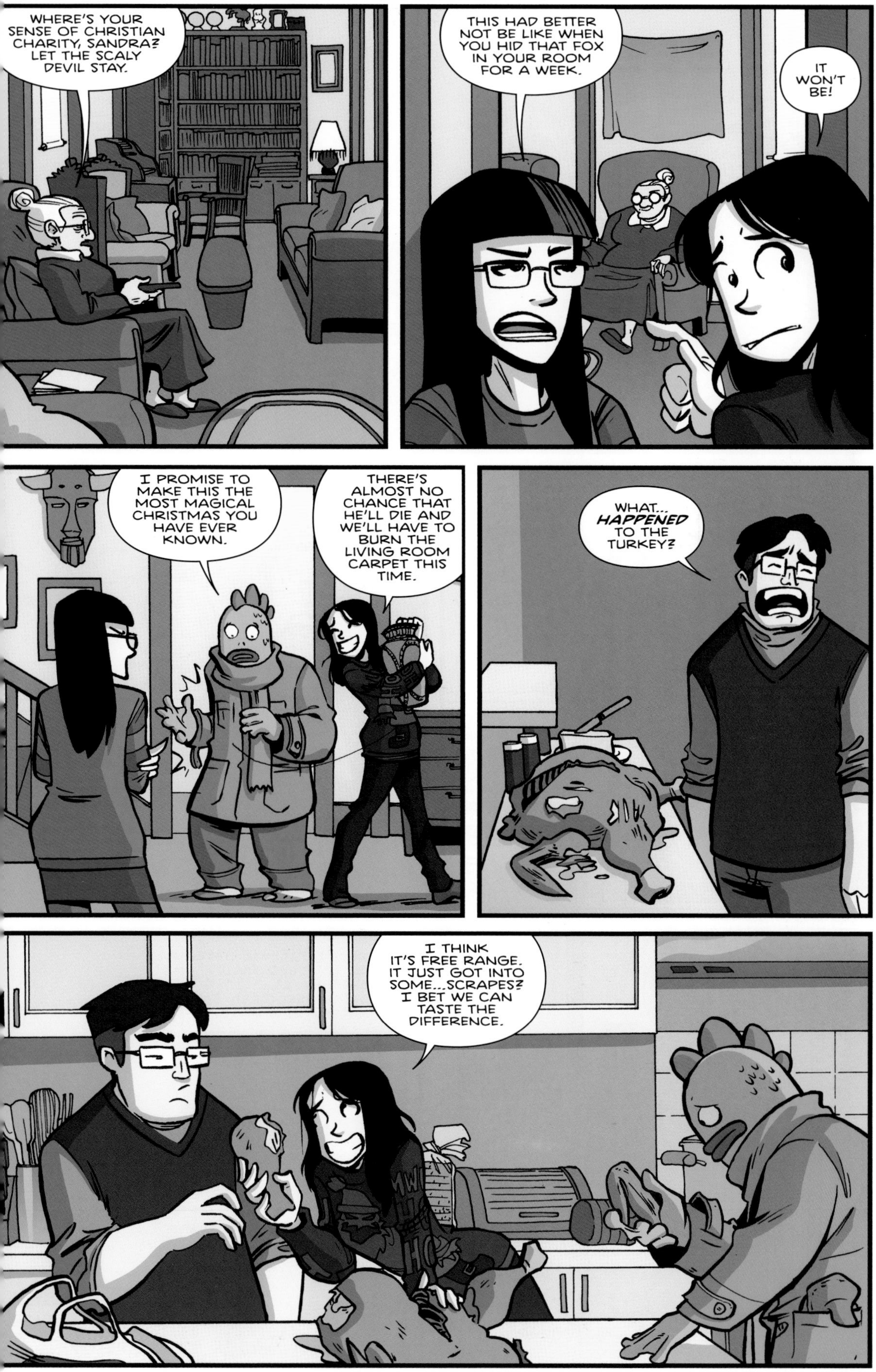
WHERE'S YOUR SENSE OF CHRISTIAN CHARITY, SANDRA? LET THE SCALY DEVIL STAY.
THIS HAD BETTER NOT BE LIKE WHEN YOU HID THAT FOX IN YOUR ROOM FOR A WEEK.
IT WON'T BE!
I PROMISE TO MAKE THIS THE MOST MAGICAL CHRISTMAS YOU HAVE EVER KNOWN.
THERE'S ALMOST NO CHANCE THAT HE'LL DIE AND WE'LL HAVE TO BURN THE LIVING ROOM CARPET THIS TIME.
WHAT... *HAPPENED* TO THE TURKEY?
I THINK IT'S FREE RANGE. IT JUST GOT INTO SOME... SCRAPES? I BET WE CAN TASTE THE DIFFERENCE.

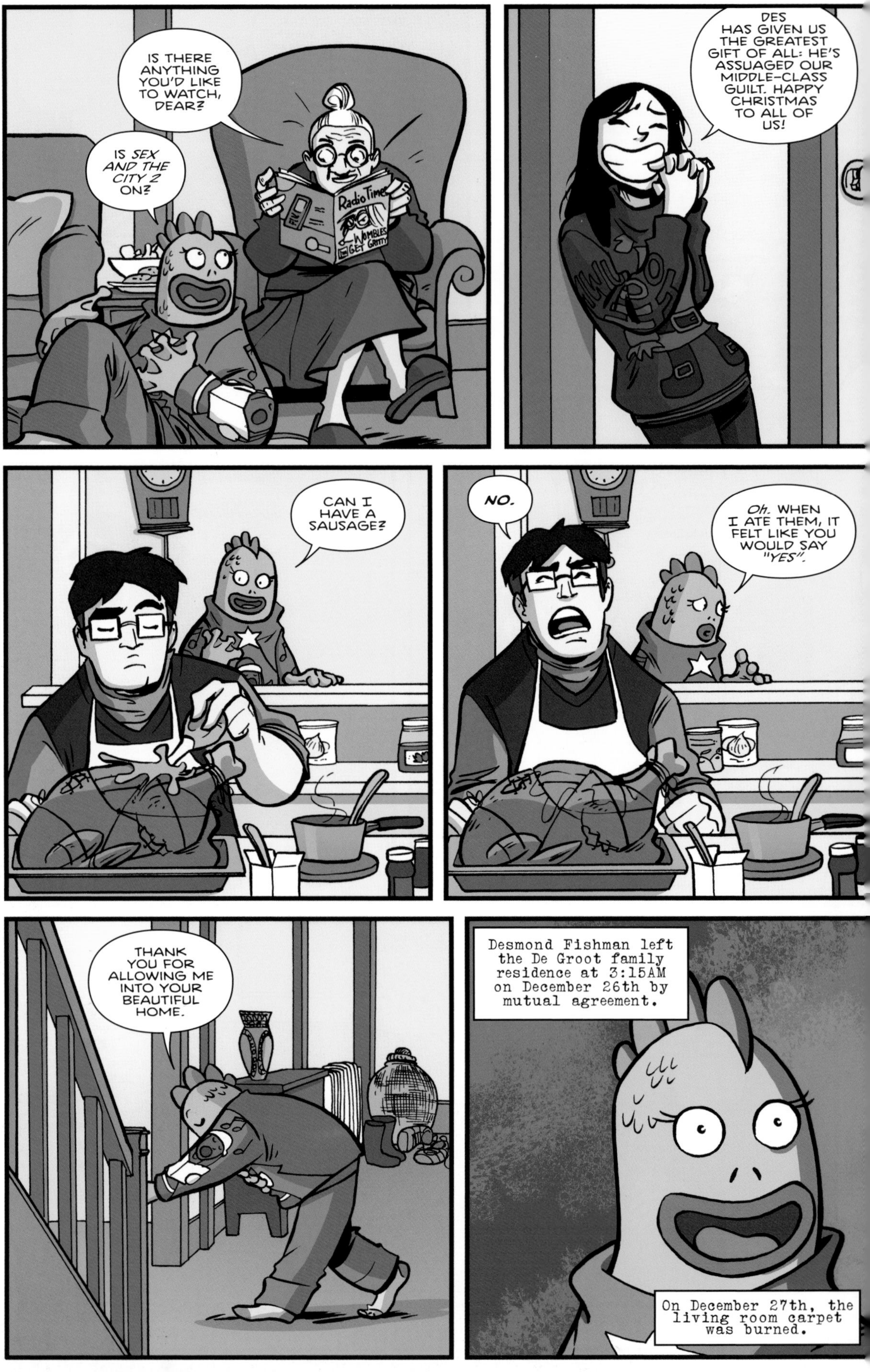
IS THERE ANYTHING YOU'D LIKE TO WATCH, DEAR?
IS *SEX AND THE CITY 2* ON?
Radio Times
WOMBLES GET GRITTY
DES HAS GIVEN US THE GREATEST GIFT OF ALL: HE'S ASSUAGED OUR MIDDLE-CLASS GUILT. HAPPY CHRISTMAS TO ALL OF US!
CAN I HAVE A SAUSAGE?
NO.
Oh. WHEN I ATE THEM, IT FELT LIKE YOU WOULD SAY *"YES"*.
THANK YOU FOR ALLOWING ME INTO YOUR BEAUTIFUL HOME.
Desmond Fishman left the De Groot family residence at 3:15AM on December 26th by mutual agreement.
On December 27th, the living room carpet was burned.

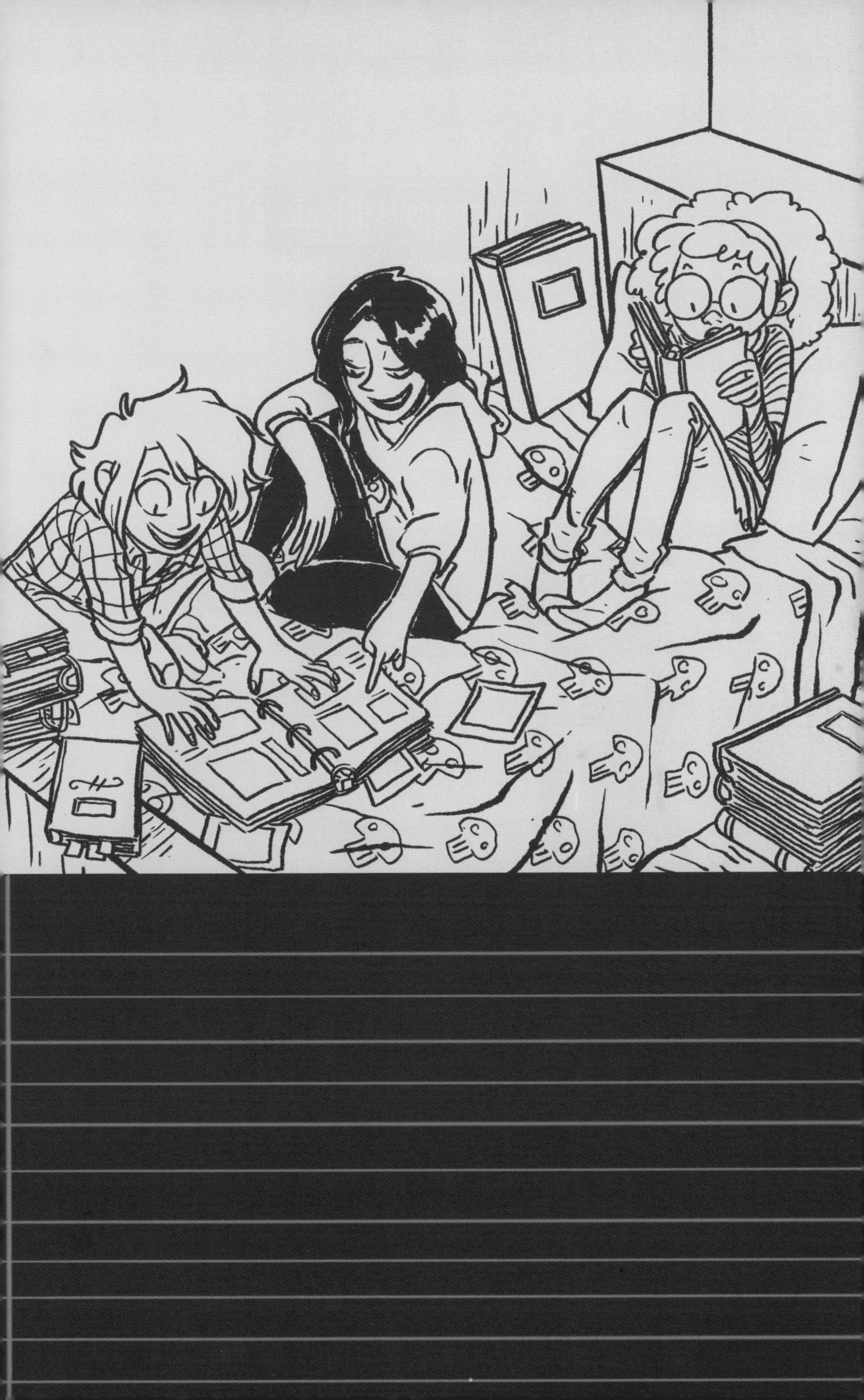

LOVE? ACK, SHELLY!

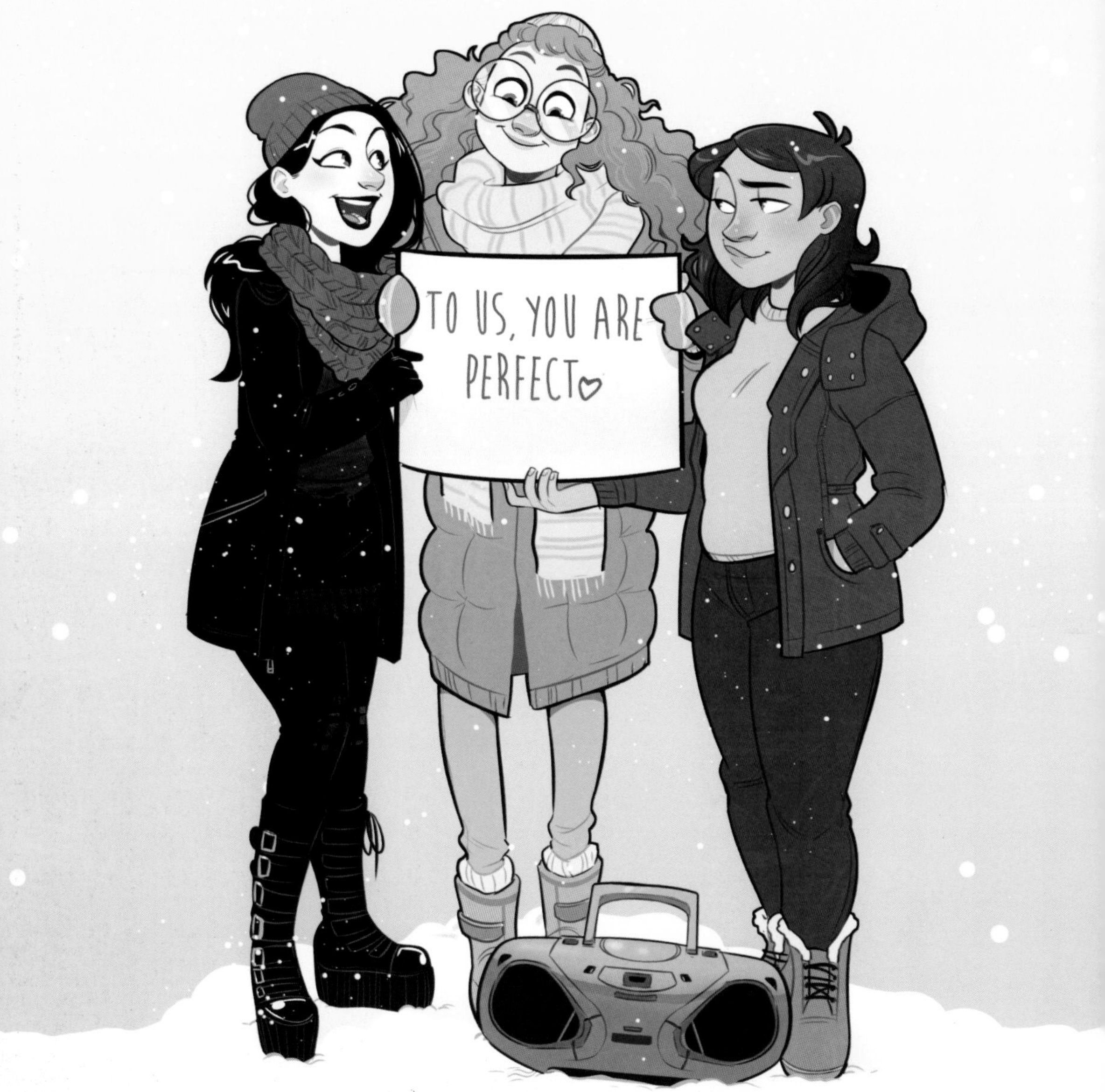
TO US, YOU ARE PERFECT

2017 HOLIDAY SPECIAL COVER

JENN ST-ONGE

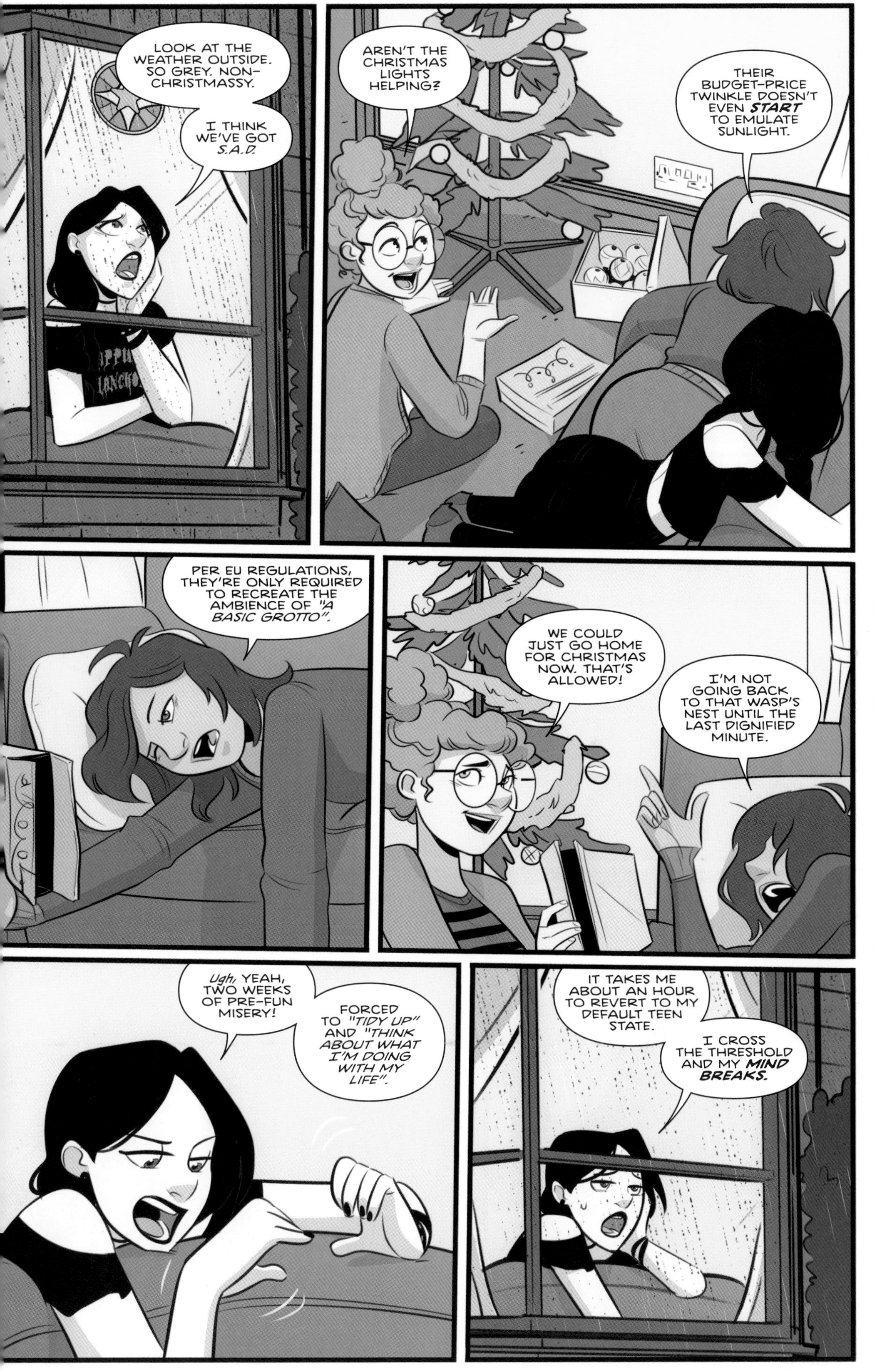
LOOK AT THE WEATHER OUTSIDE. SO GREY. NON-CHRISTMASSY.
I THINK WE'VE GOT *S.A.D.*
AREN'T THE CHRISTMAS LIGHTS HELPING?
THEIR BUDGET-PRICE TWINKLE DOESN'T EVEN ***START*** TO EMULATE SUNLIGHT.
PER EU REGULATIONS, THEY'RE ONLY REQUIRED TO RECREATE THE AMBIENCE OF *"A BASIC GROTTO"*.
WE COULD JUST GO HOME FOR CHRISTMAS NOW. THAT'S ALLOWED!
I'M NOT GOING BACK TO THAT WASP'S NEST UNTIL THE LAST DIGNIFIED MINUTE.
Ugh, YEAH, TWO WEEKS OF PRE-FUN MISERY!
FORCED TO *"TIDY UP"* AND *"THINK ABOUT WHAT I'M DOING WITH MY LIFE"*.
IT TAKES ME ABOUT AN HOUR TO REVERT TO MY DEFAULT TEEN STATE.
I CROSS THE THRESHOLD AND MY ***MIND BREAKS.***

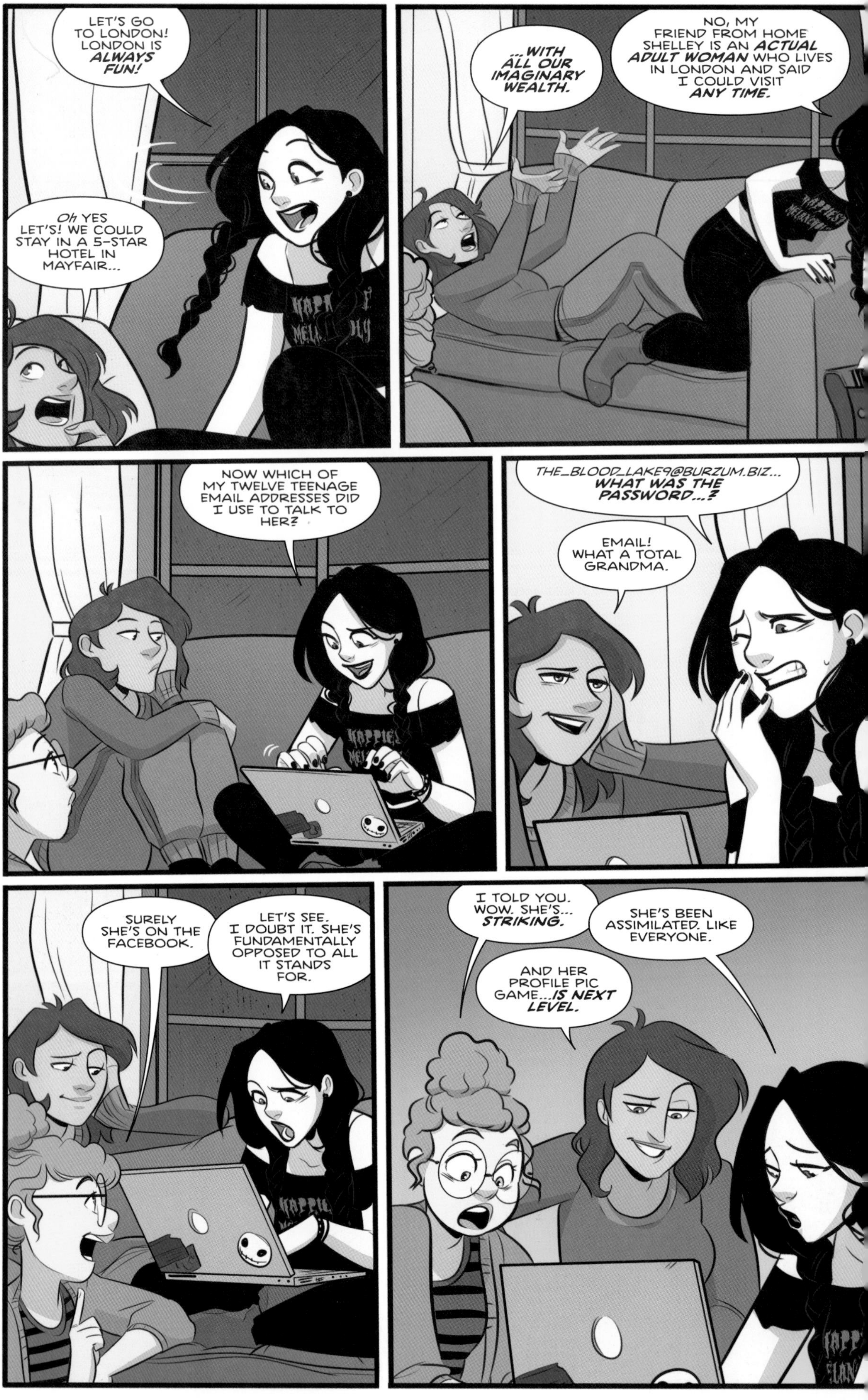
LET'S GO TO LONDON! LONDON IS *ALWAYS FUN!*
Oh YES LET'S! WE COULD STAY IN A 5-STAR HOTEL IN MAYFAIR...
...WITH ALL OUR IMAGINARY WEALTH.
NO, MY FRIEND FROM HOME SHELLEY IS AN *ACTUAL ADULT WOMAN* WHO LIVES IN LONDON AND SAID I COULD VISIT *ANY TIME.*
NOW WHICH OF MY TWELVE TEENAGE EMAIL ADDRESSES DID I USE TO TALK TO HER?
THE_BLOOD_LAKE9@BURZUM.BIZ... *WHAT WAS THE PASSWORD...?*
EMAIL! WHAT A TOTAL GRANDMA.
SURELY SHE'S ON THE FACEBOOK.
LET'S SEE. I DOUBT IT. SHE'S FUNDAMENTALLY OPPOSED TO ALL IT STANDS FOR.
I TOLD YOU. WOW. SHE'S... *STRIKING.*
SHE'S BEEN ASSIMILATED. LIKE EVERYONE.
AND HER PROFILE PIC GAME... *IS NEXT LEVEL.*

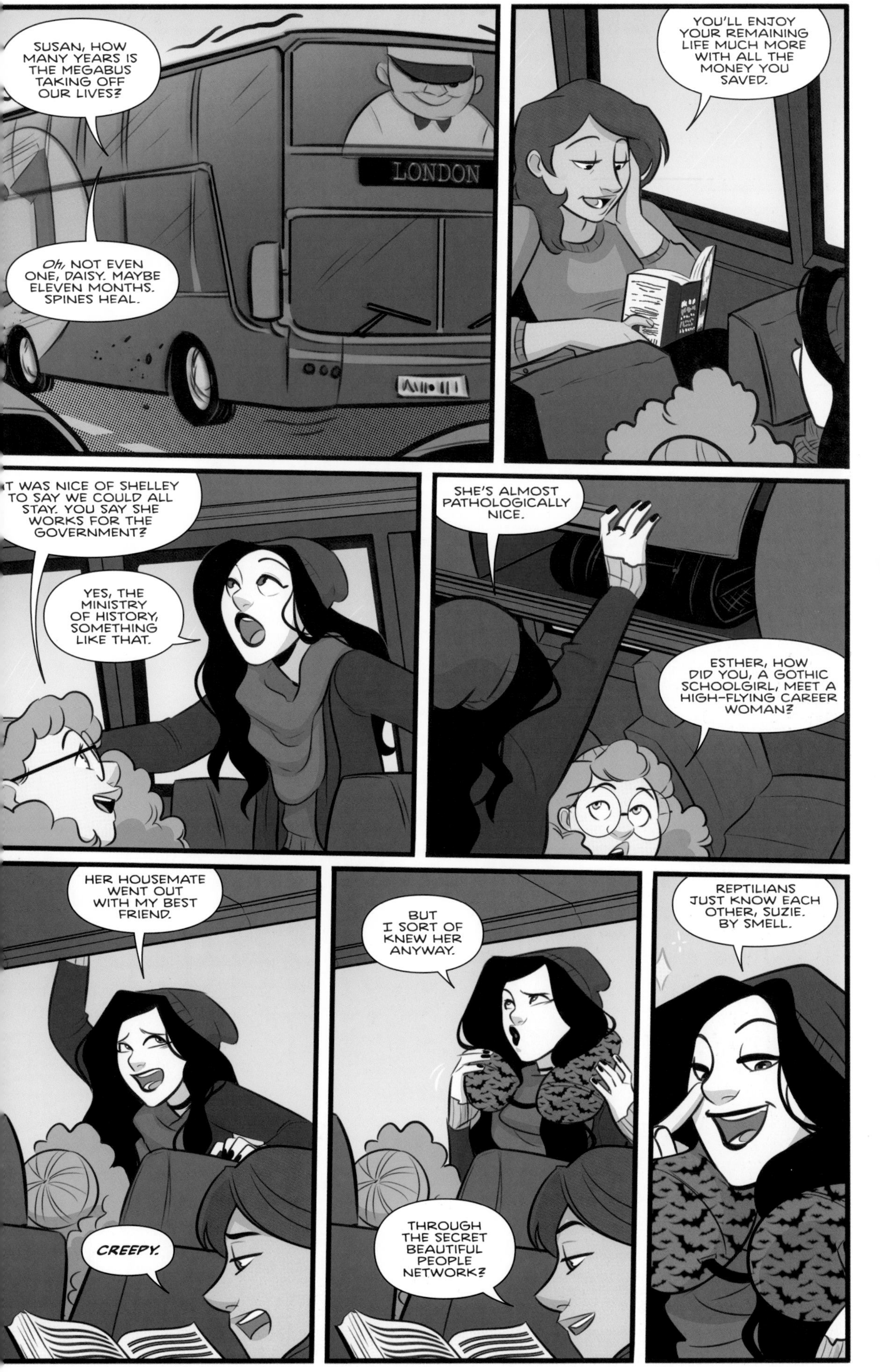

SUSAN, HOW MANY YEARS IS THE MEGABUS TAKING OFF OUR LIVES?
Oh, NOT EVEN ONE, DAISY. MAYBE ELEVEN MONTHS. SPINES HEAL.
LONDON
YOU'LL ENJOY YOUR REMAINING LIFE MUCH MORE WITH ALL THE MONEY YOU SAVED.
T WAS NICE OF SHELLEY TO SAY WE COULD ALL STAY. YOU SAY SHE WORKS FOR THE GOVERNMENT?
YES, THE MINISTRY OF HISTORY, SOMETHING LIKE THAT.
SHE'S ALMOST PATHOLOGICALLY NICE.
ESTHER, HOW DID YOU, A GOTHIC SCHOOLGIRL, MEET A HIGH-FLYING CAREER WOMAN?
HER HOUSEMATE WENT OUT WITH MY BEST FRIEND.
CREEPY.
BUT I SORT OF KNEW HER ANYWAY.
THROUGH THE SECRET BEAUTIFUL PEOPLE NETWORK?
REPTILIANS JUST KNOW EACH OTHER, SUZIE. BY SMELL.

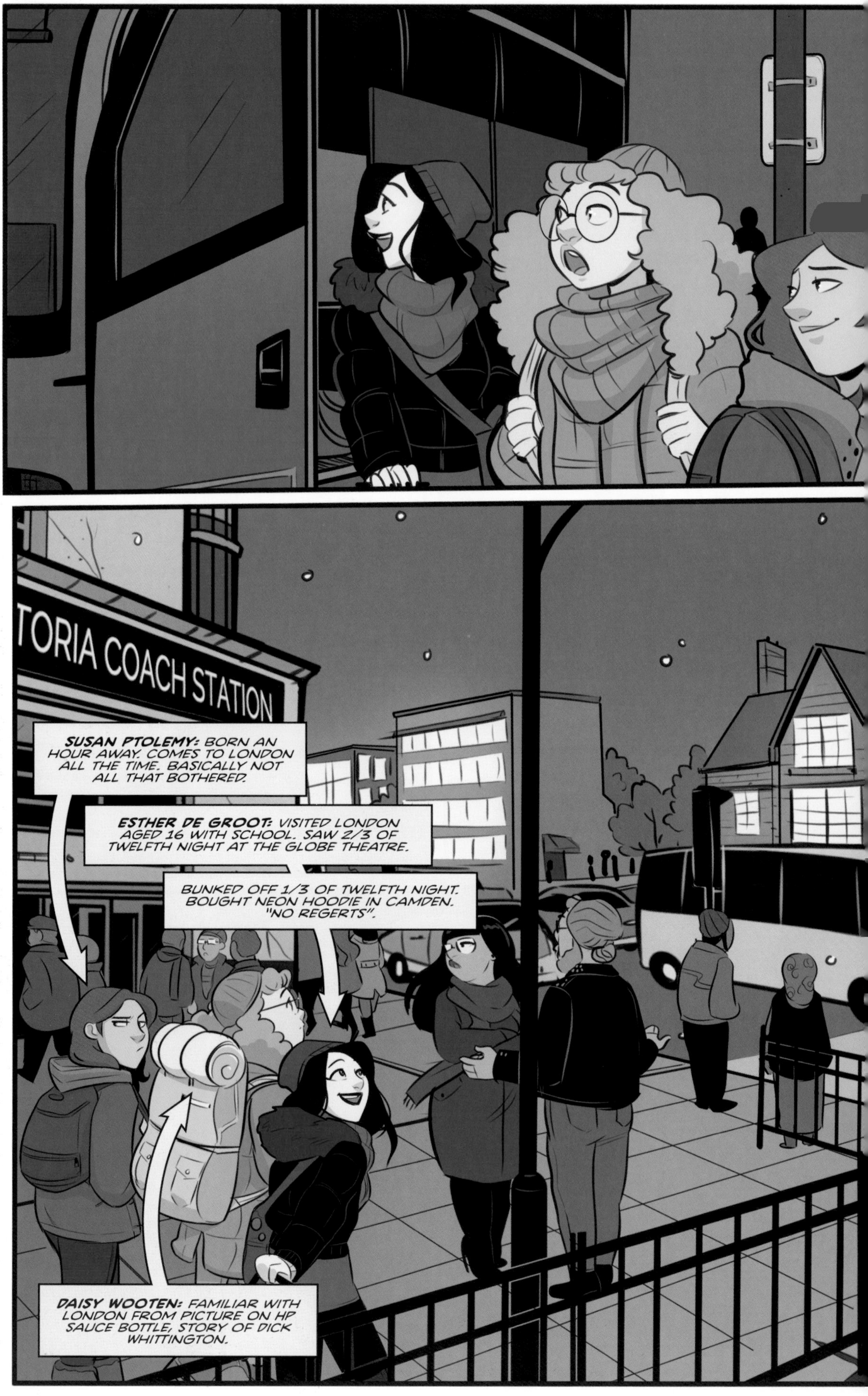
TORIA COACH STATION
SUSAN PTOLEMY: BORN AN HOUR AWAY. COMES TO LONDON ALL THE TIME. BASICALLY NOT ALL THAT BOTHERED.
ESTHER DE GROOT: VISITED LONDON AGED 16 WITH SCHOOL. SAW 2/3 OF TWELFTH NIGHT AT THE GLOBE THEATRE.
BUNKED OFF 1/3 OF TWELFTH NIGHT. BOUGHT NEON HOODIE IN CAMDEN. "NO REGERTS".
DAISY WOOTEN: FAMILIAR WITH LONDON FROM PICTURE ON HP SAUCE BOTTLE, STORY OF DICK WHITTINGTON.

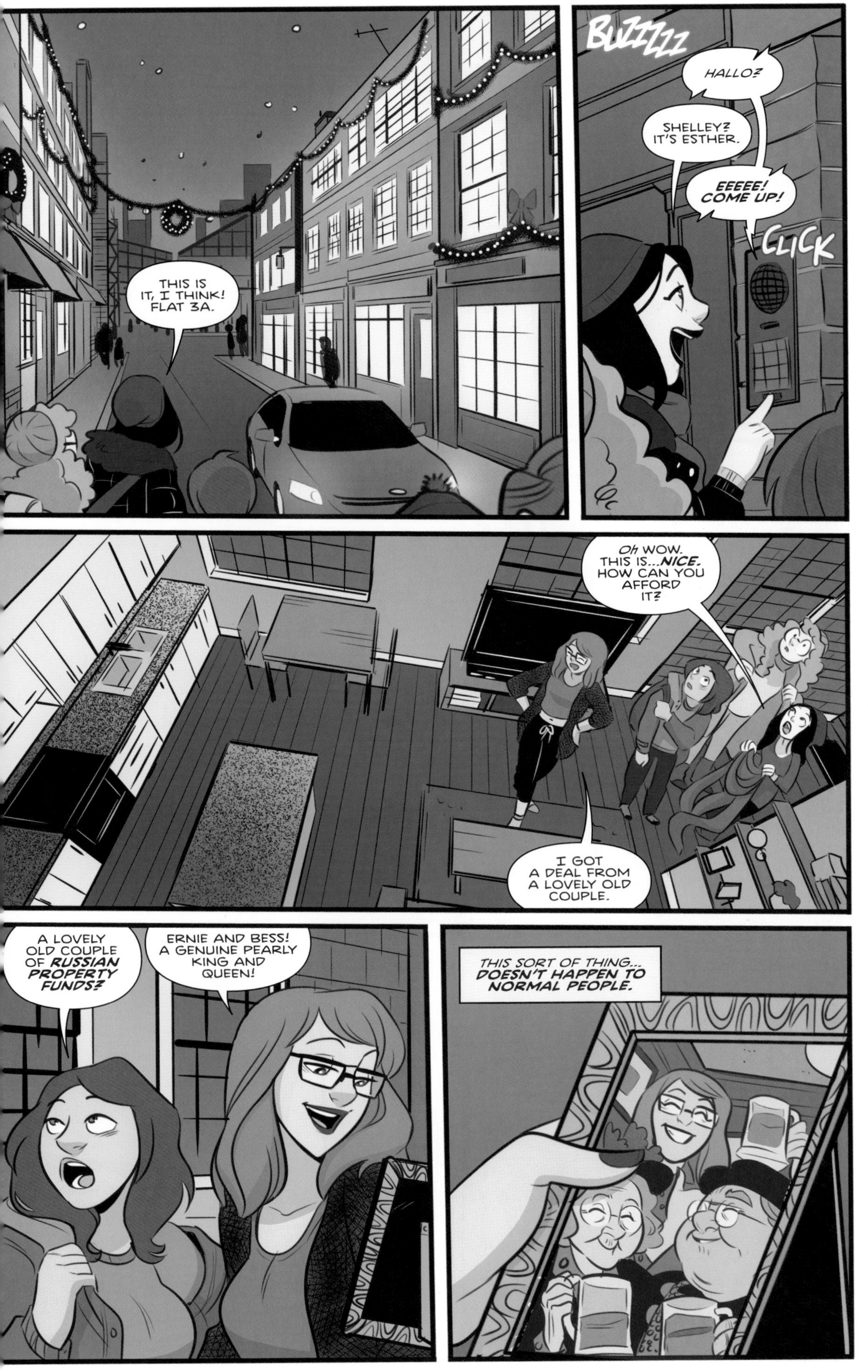
THIS IS IT, I THINK! FLAT 3A.
BUZZZZZ
HALLO?
SHELLEY? IT'S ESTHER.
EEEEE! COME UP!
CLICK
Oh WOW. THIS IS...NICE. HOW CAN YOU AFFORD IT?
I GOT A DEAL FROM A LOVELY OLD COUPLE.
A LOVELY OLD COUPLE OF RUSSIAN PROPERTY FUNDS?
ERNIE AND BESS! A GENUINE PEARLY KING AND QUEEN!
THIS SORT OF THING... DOESN'T HAPPEN TO NORMAL PEOPLE.

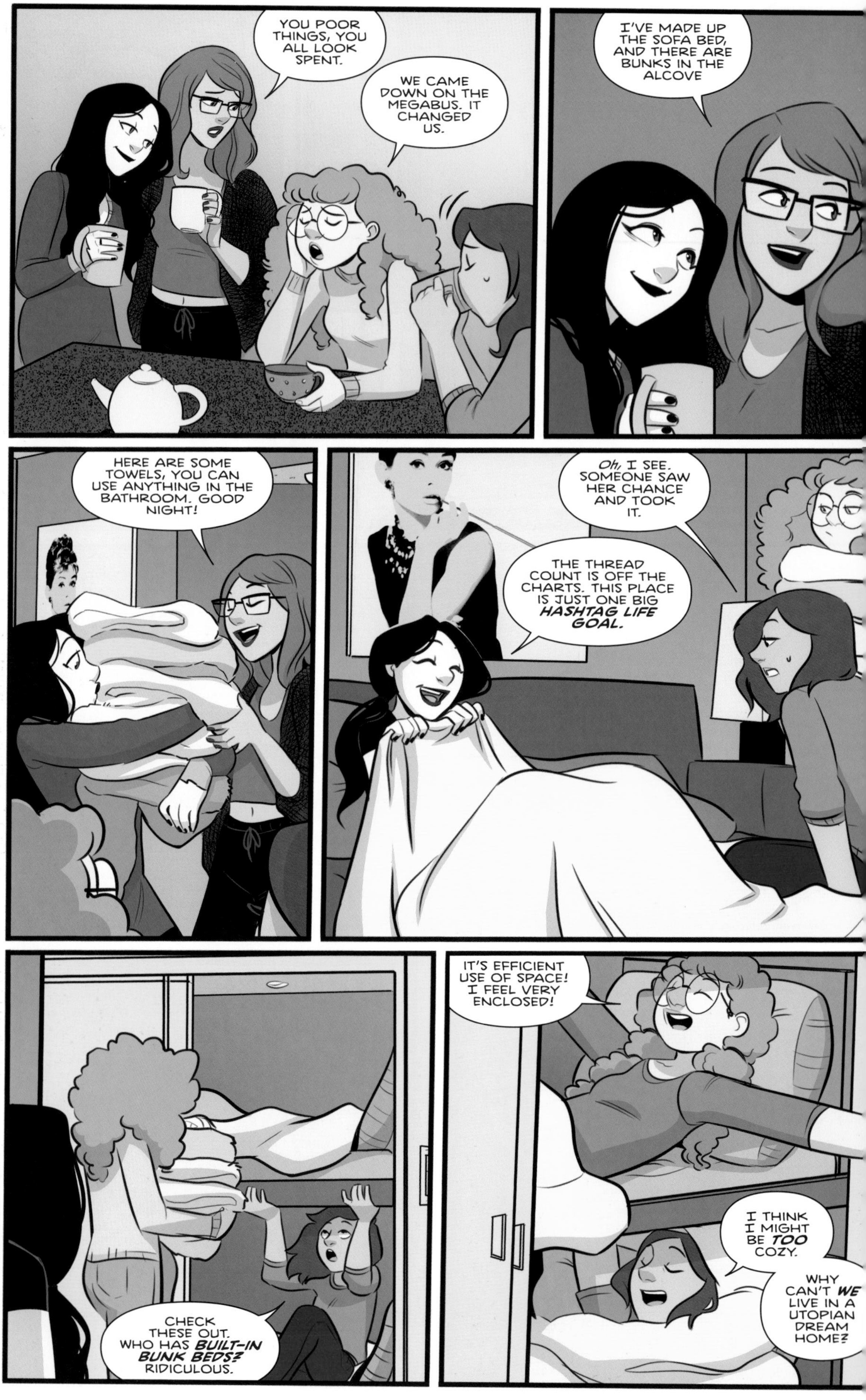
YOU POOR THINGS, YOU ALL LOOK SPENT.
WE CAME DOWN ON THE MEGABUS. IT CHANGED US.
I'VE MADE UP THE SOFA BED, AND THERE ARE BUNKS IN THE ALCOVE
HERE ARE SOME TOWELS, YOU CAN USE ANYTHING IN THE BATHROOM. GOOD NIGHT!
Oh, I SEE. SOMEONE SAW HER CHANCE AND TOOK IT.
THE THREAD COUNT IS OFF THE CHARTS. THIS PLACE IS JUST ONE BIG ***HASHTAG LIFE GOAL.***
CHECK THESE OUT. WHO HAS ***BUILT-IN BUNK BEDS?*** RIDICULOUS.
IT'S EFFICIENT USE OF SPACE! I FEEL VERY ENCLOSED!
I THINK I MIGHT BE ***TOO*** COZY.
WHY CAN'T ***WE*** LIVE IN A UTOPIAN DREAM HOME?

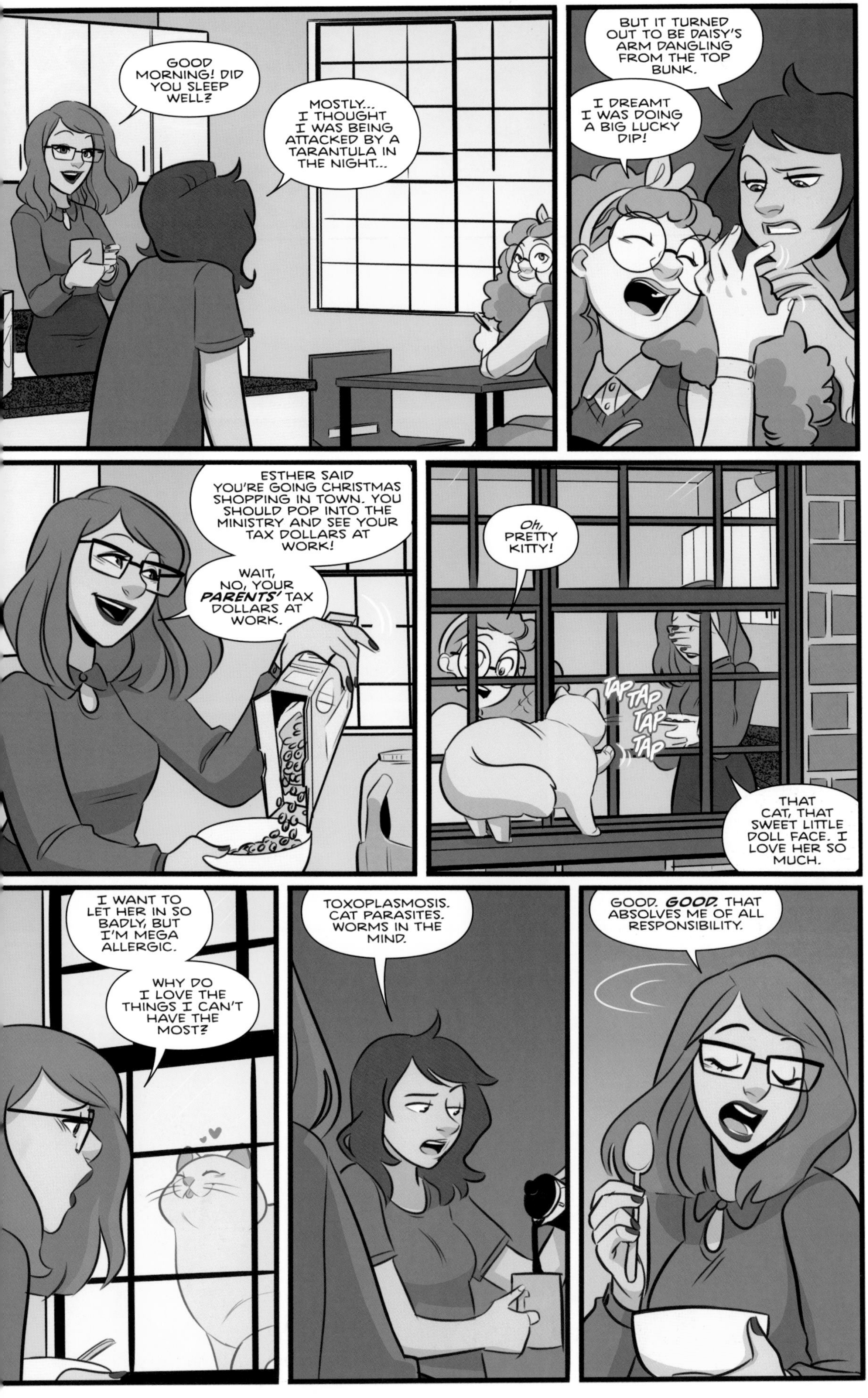
GOOD MORNING! DID YOU SLEEP WELL?
MOSTLY... I THOUGHT I WAS BEING ATTACKED BY A TARANTULA IN THE NIGHT...
BUT IT TURNED OUT TO BE DAISY'S ARM DANGLING FROM THE TOP BUNK.
I DREAMT I WAS DOING A BIG LUCKY DIP!
ESTHER SAID YOU'RE GOING CHRISTMAS SHOPPING IN TOWN. YOU SHOULD POP INTO THE MINISTRY AND SEE YOUR TAX DOLLARS AT WORK!
WAIT, NO, YOUR *PARENTS'* TAX DOLLARS AT WORK.
Oh, PRETTY KITTY!
TAP TAP TAP TAP
THAT CAT, THAT SWEET LITTLE DOLL FACE. I LOVE HER SO MUCH.
I WANT TO LET HER IN SO BADLY, BUT I'M MEGA ALLERGIC.
WHY DO I LOVE THE THINGS I CAN'T HAVE THE MOST?
TOXOPLASMOSIS. CAT PARASITES. WORMS IN THE MIND.
GOOD. *GOOD.* THAT ABSOLVES ME OF ALL RESPONSIBILITY.

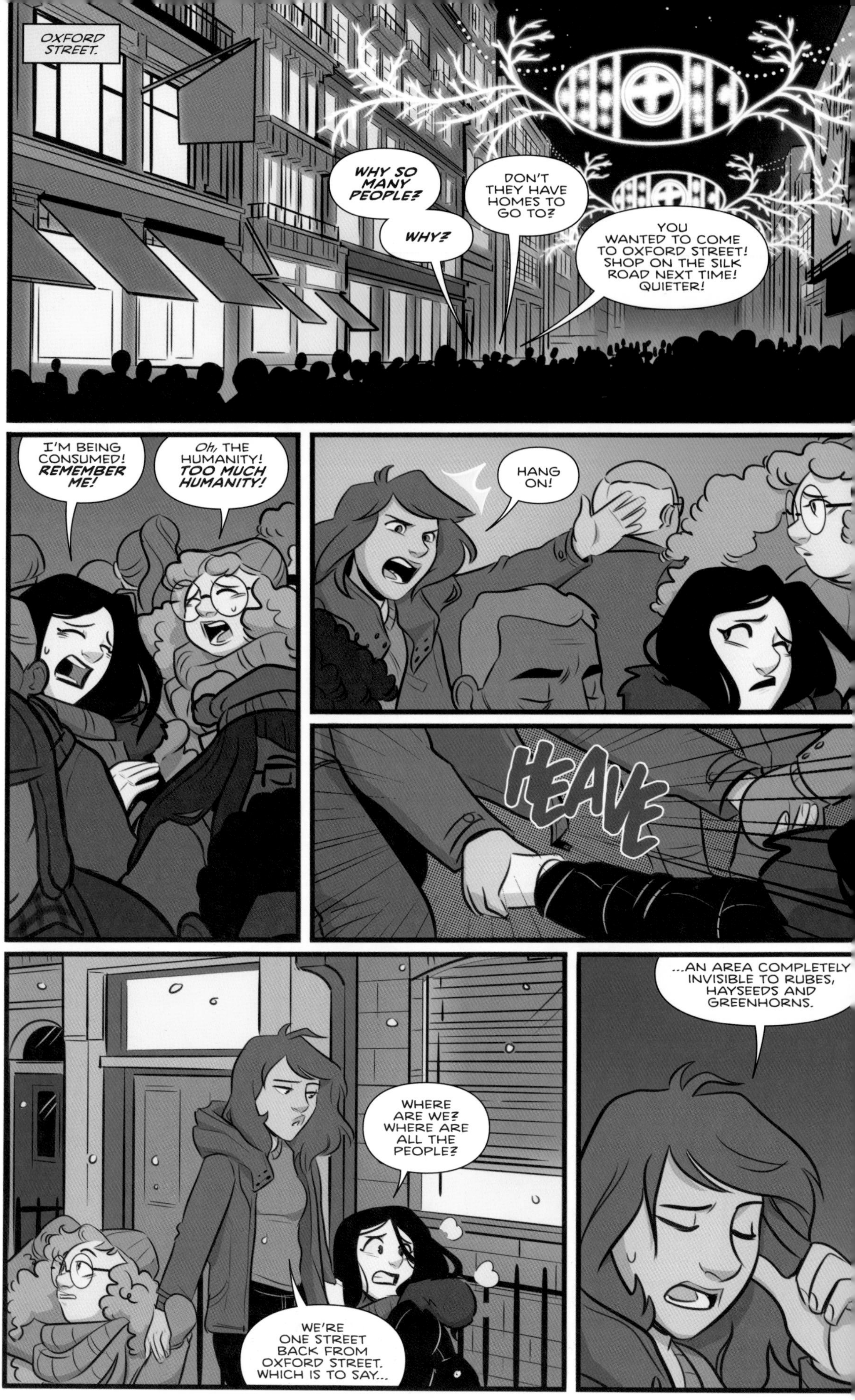
OXFORD STREET.
WHY SO MANY PEOPLE?
WHY?
DON'T THEY HAVE HOMES TO GO TO?
YOU WANTED TO COME TO OXFORD STREET! SHOP ON THE SILK ROAD NEXT TIME! QUIETER!
I'M BEING CONSUMED! REMEMBER ME!
Oh, THE HUMANITY! TOO MUCH HUMANITY!
HANG ON!
HEAVE
WHERE ARE WE? WHERE ARE ALL THE PEOPLE?
WE'RE ONE STREET BACK FROM OXFORD STREET. WHICH IS TO SAY...
...AN AREA COMPLETELY INVISIBLE TO RUBES, HAYSEEDS AND GREENHORNS.

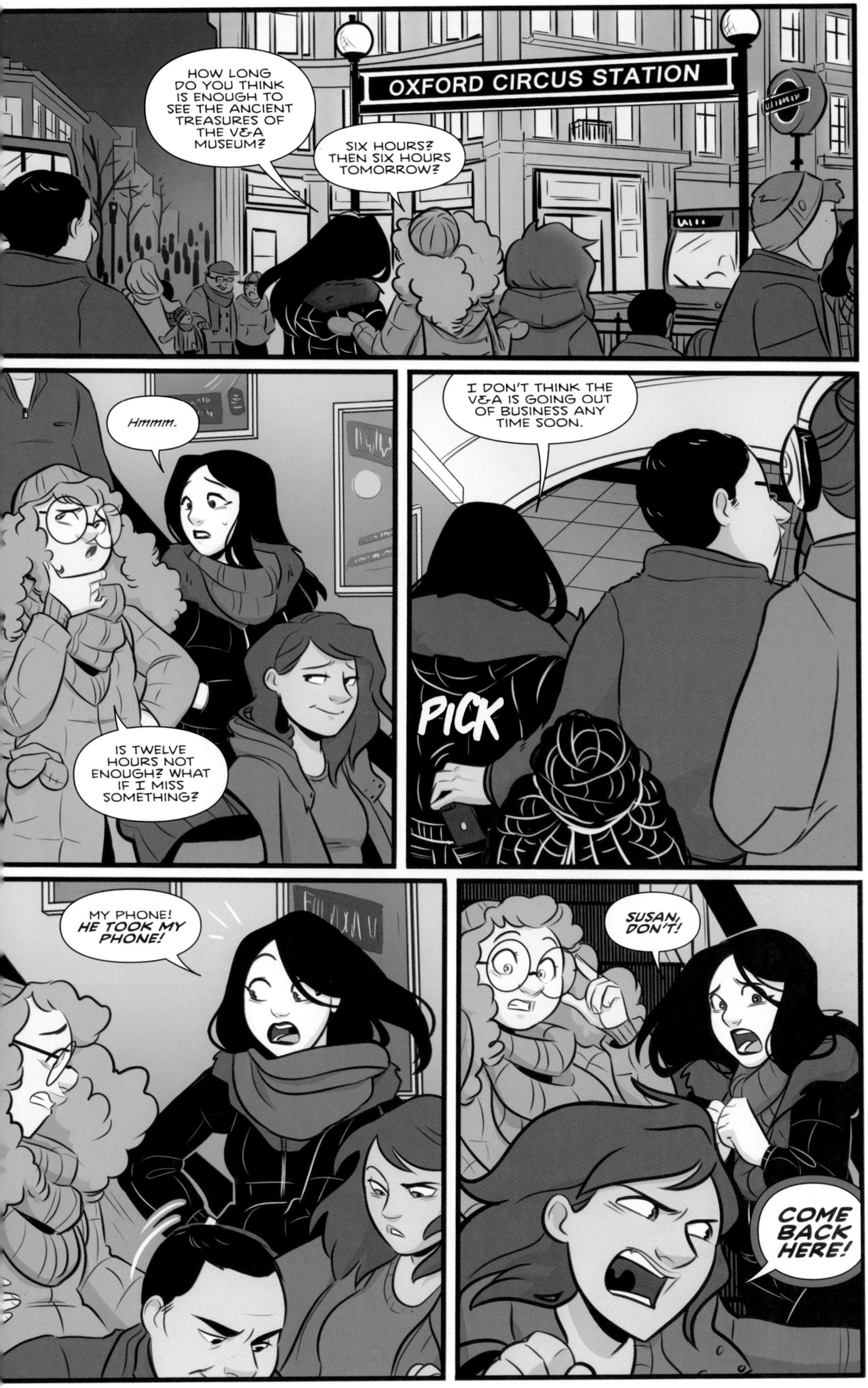
OXFORD CIRCUS STATION
HOW LONG DO YOU THINK IS ENOUGH TO SEE THE ANCIENT TREASURES OF THE V&A MUSEUM?
SIX HOURS? THEN SIX HOURS TOMORROW?
Hmmm.
IS TWELVE HOURS NOT ENOUGH? WHAT IF I MISS SOMETHING?
I DON'T THINK THE V&A IS GOING OUT OF BUSINESS ANY TIME SOON.
PICK
MY PHONE! HE TOOK MY PHONE!
SUSAN, DON'T!
COME BACK HERE!

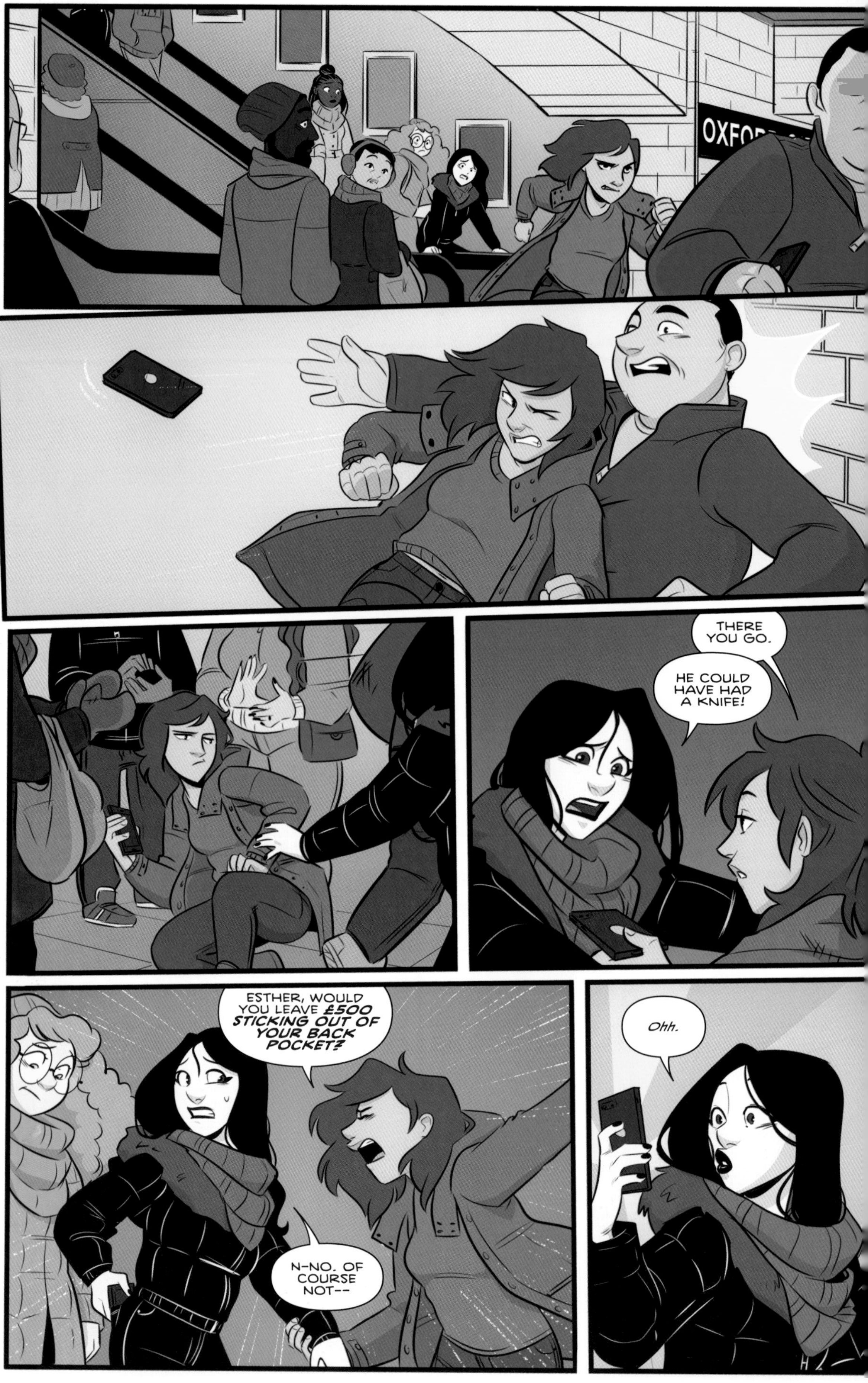
OXFOR
THERE YOU GO.
HE COULD HAVE HAD A KNIFE!
ESTHER, WOULD YOU LEAVE £500 STICKING OUT OF YOUR BACK POCKET?
N-NO. OF COURSE NOT--
Ohh.

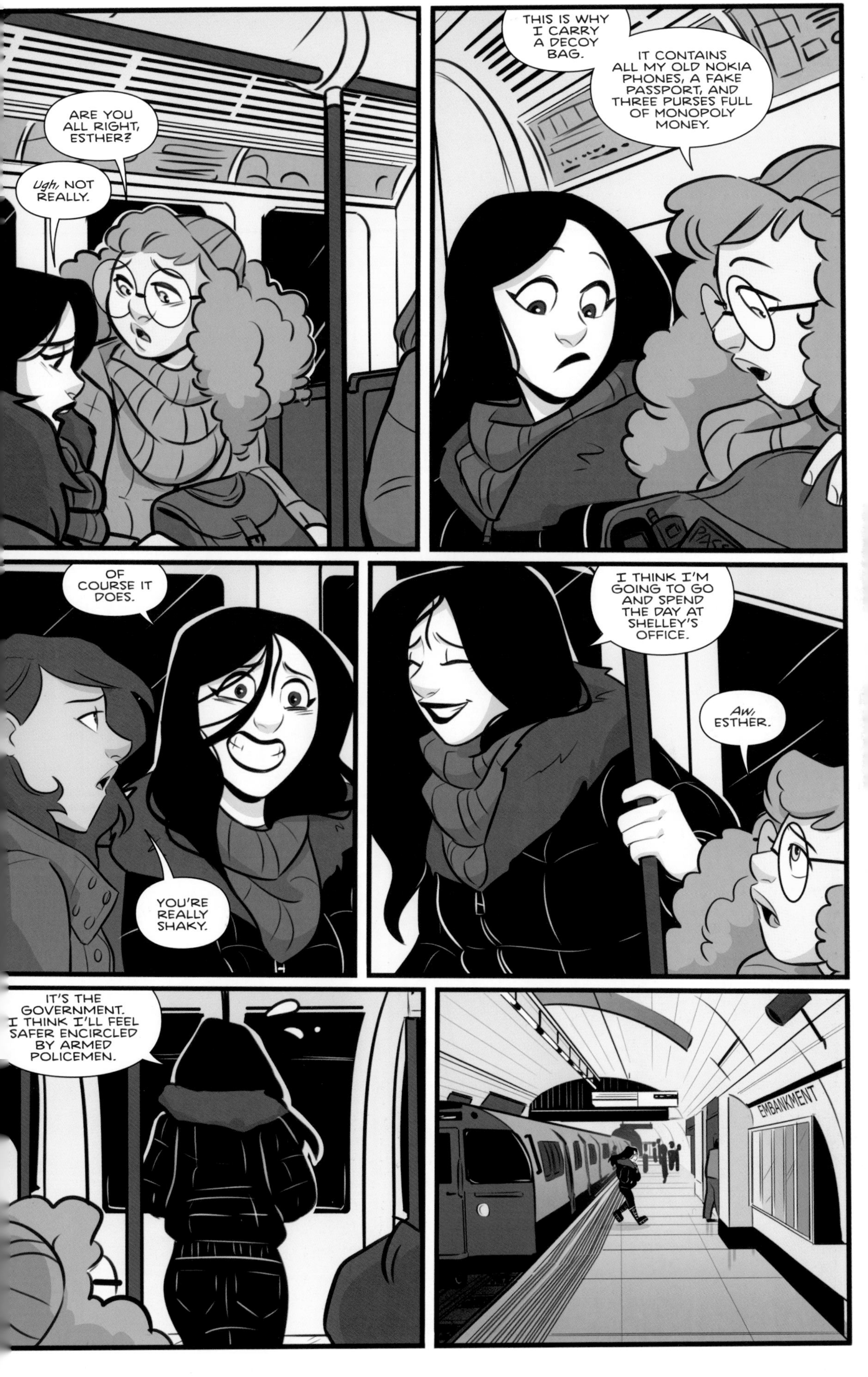
ARE YOU ALL RIGHT, ESTHER?
Ugh, NOT REALLY.
THIS IS WHY I CARRY A DECOY BAG.
IT CONTAINS ALL MY OLD NOKIA PHONES, A FAKE PASSPORT, AND THREE PURSES FULL OF MONOPOLY MONEY.
OF COURSE IT DOES.
YOU'RE REALLY SHAKY.
I THINK I'M GOING TO GO AND SPEND THE DAY AT SHELLEY'S OFFICE.
Aw, ESTHER.
IT'S THE GOVERNMENT. I THINK I'LL FEEL SAFER ENCIRCLED BY ARMED POLICEMEN.
EMBANKMENT

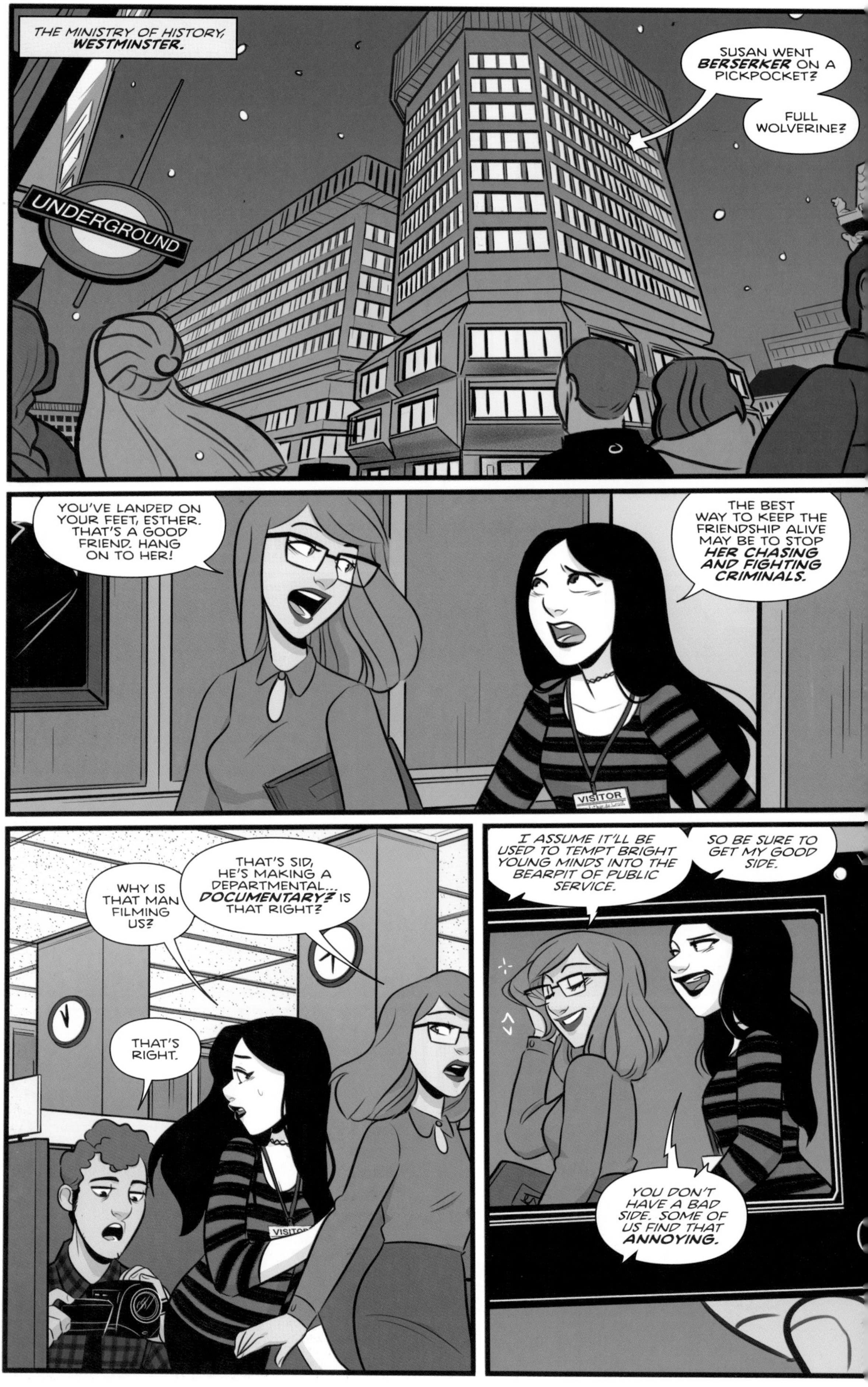
THE MINISTRY OF HISTORY, WESTMINSTER.
UNDERGROUND
SUSAN WENT BERSERKER ON A PICKPOCKET?
FULL WOLVERINE?
YOU'VE LANDED ON YOUR FEET, ESTHER. THAT'S A GOOD FRIEND. HANG ON TO HER!
THE BEST WAY TO KEEP THE FRIENDSHIP ALIVE MAY BE TO STOP HER CHASING AND FIGHTING CRIMINALS.
VISITOR
WHY IS THAT MAN FILMING US?
THAT'S SID, HE'S MAKING A DEPARTMENTAL... DOCUMENTARY? IS THAT RIGHT?
THAT'S RIGHT.
I ASSUME IT'LL BE USED TO TEMPT BRIGHT YOUNG MINDS INTO THE BEARPIT OF PUBLIC SERVICE.
SO BE SURE TO GET MY GOOD SIDE.
YOU DON'T HAVE A BAD SIDE. SOME OF US FIND THAT ANNOYING.

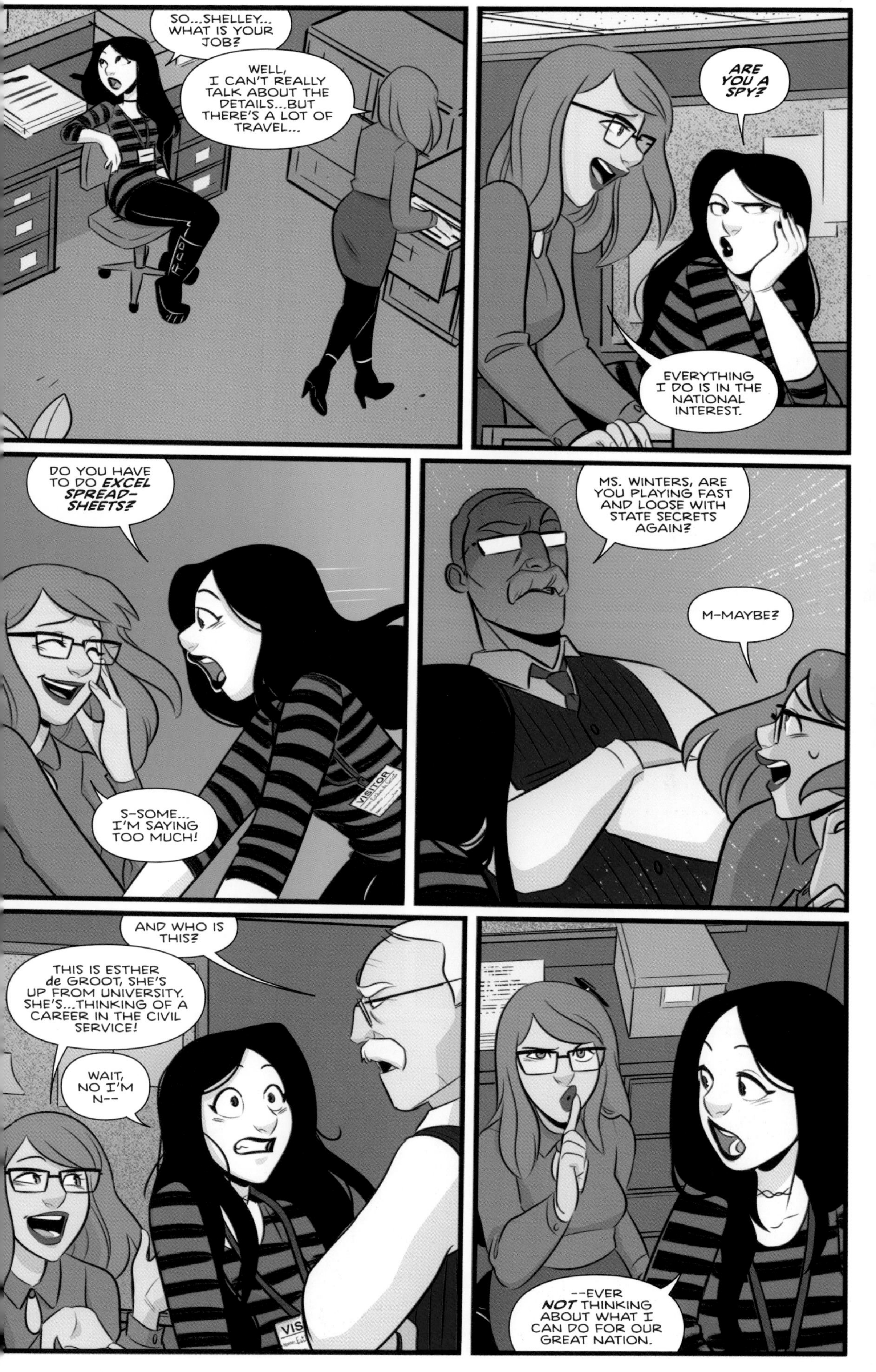
SO...SHELLEY... WHAT IS YOUR JOB?
WELL, I CAN'T REALLY TALK ABOUT THE DETAILS...BUT THERE'S A LOT OF TRAVEL...
ARE YOU A SPY?
EVERYTHING I DO IS IN THE NATIONAL INTEREST.
DO YOU HAVE TO DO EXCEL SPREAD-SHEETS?
S-SOME... I'M SAYING TOO MUCH!
MS. WINTERS, ARE YOU PLAYING FAST AND LOOSE WITH STATE SECRETS AGAIN?
M-MAYBE?
AND WHO IS THIS?
THIS IS ESTHER de GROOT, SHE'S UP FROM UNIVERSITY. SHE'S...THINKING OF A CAREER IN THE CIVIL SERVICE!
WAIT, NO I'M N--
--EVER NOT THINKING ABOUT WHAT I CAN DO FOR OUR GREAT NATION.

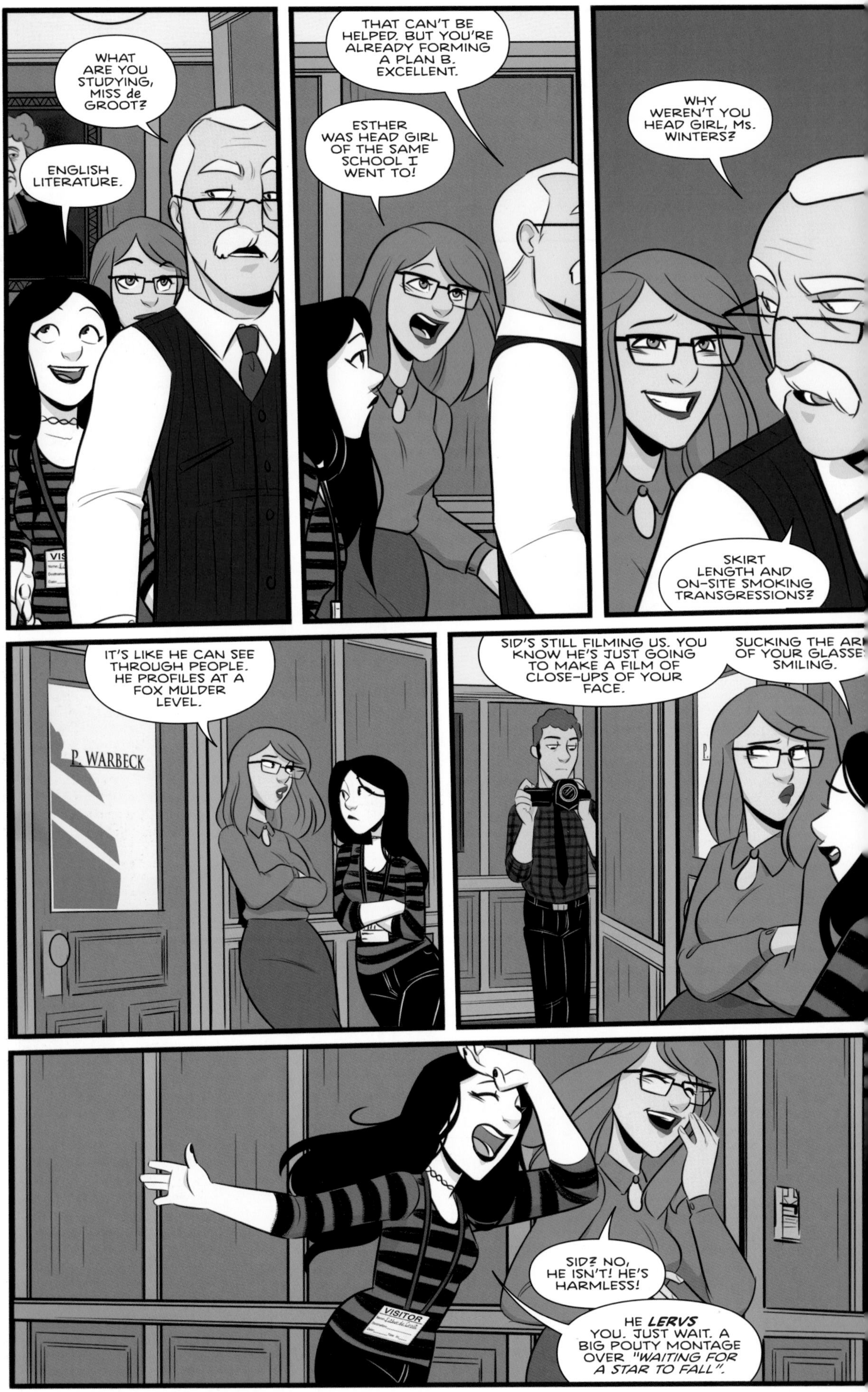
WHAT ARE YOU STUDYING, MISS de GROOT?
ENGLISH LITERATURE.
THAT CAN'T BE HELPED. BUT YOU'RE ALREADY FORMING A PLAN B. EXCELLENT.
ESTHER WAS HEAD GIRL OF THE SAME SCHOOL I WENT TO!
WHY WEREN'T YOU HEAD GIRL, Ms. WINTERS?
SKIRT LENGTH AND ON-SITE SMOKING TRANSGRESSIONS?
IT'S LIKE HE CAN SEE THROUGH PEOPLE. HE PROFILES AT A FOX MULDER LEVEL.
P. WARBECK
SID'S STILL FILMING US. YOU KNOW HE'S JUST GOING TO MAKE A FILM OF CLOSE-UPS OF YOUR FACE.
SUCKING THE AR
OF YOUR GLASSE
SMILING.
VISITOR
SID? NO, HE ISN'T! HE'S HARMLESS!
HE *LERVS* YOU. JUST WAIT. A BIG POUTY MONTAGE OVER *"WAITING FOR A STAR TO FALL"*.

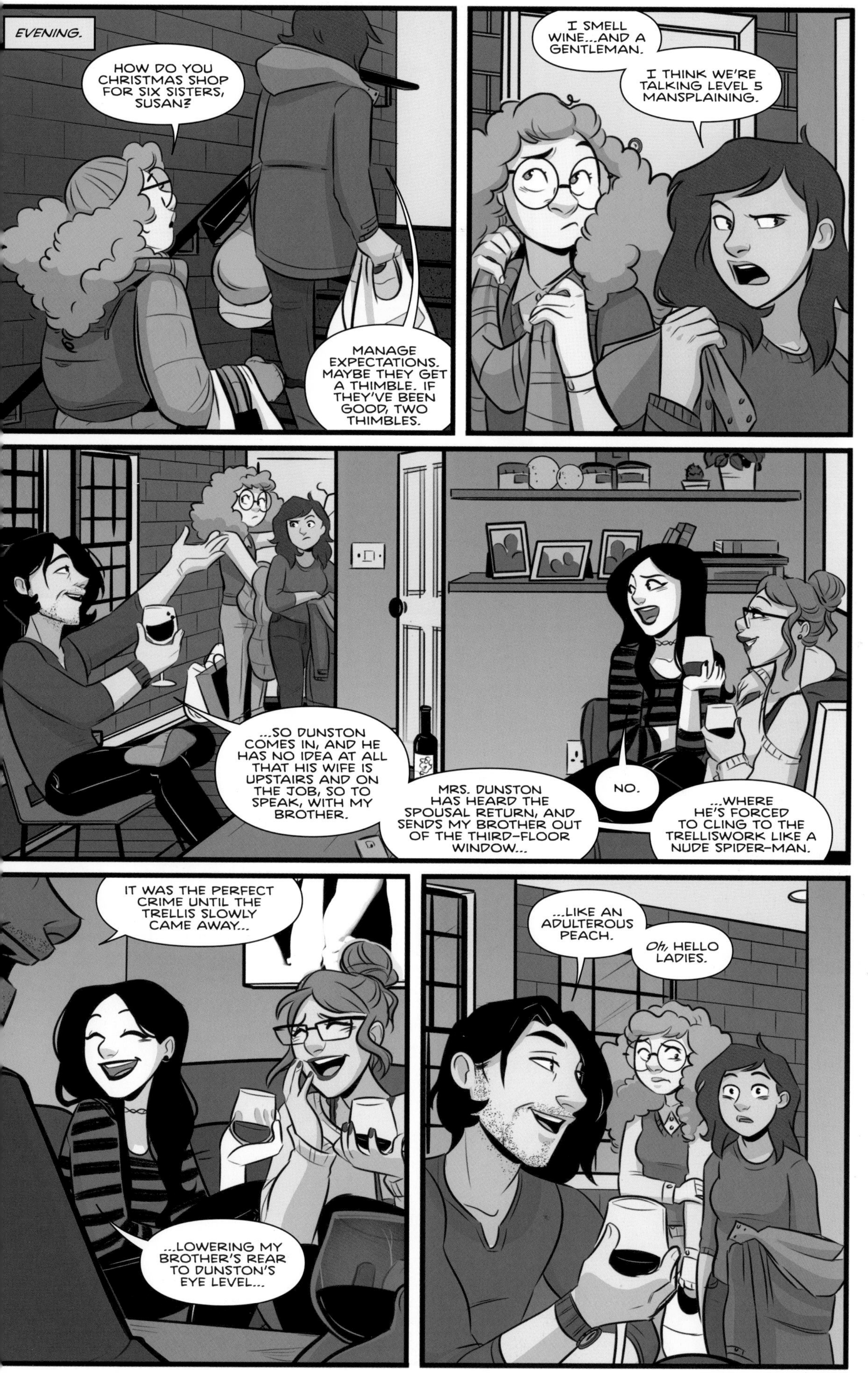
EVENING.
HOW DO YOU CHRISTMAS SHOP FOR SIX SISTERS, SUSAN?
MANAGE EXPECTATIONS. MAYBE THEY GET A THIMBLE. IF THEY'VE BEEN GOOD, TWO THIMBLES.
I SMELL WINE...AND A GENTLEMAN.
I THINK WE'RE TALKING LEVEL 5 MANSPLAINING.
...SO DUNSTON COMES IN, AND HE HAS NO IDEA AT ALL THAT HIS WIFE IS UPSTAIRS AND ON THE JOB, SO TO SPEAK, WITH MY BROTHER.
MRS. DUNSTON HAS HEARD THE SPOUSAL RETURN, AND SENDS MY BROTHER OUT OF THE THIRD-FLOOR WINDOW...
NO.
...WHERE HE'S FORCED TO CLING TO THE TRELLISWORK LIKE A NUDE SPIDER-MAN.
IT WAS THE PERFECT CRIME UNTIL THE TRELLIS SLOWLY CAME AWAY...
...LOWERING MY BROTHER'S REAR TO DUNSTON'S EYE LEVEL...
...LIKE AN ADULTEROUS PEACH.
Oh, HELLO LADIES.

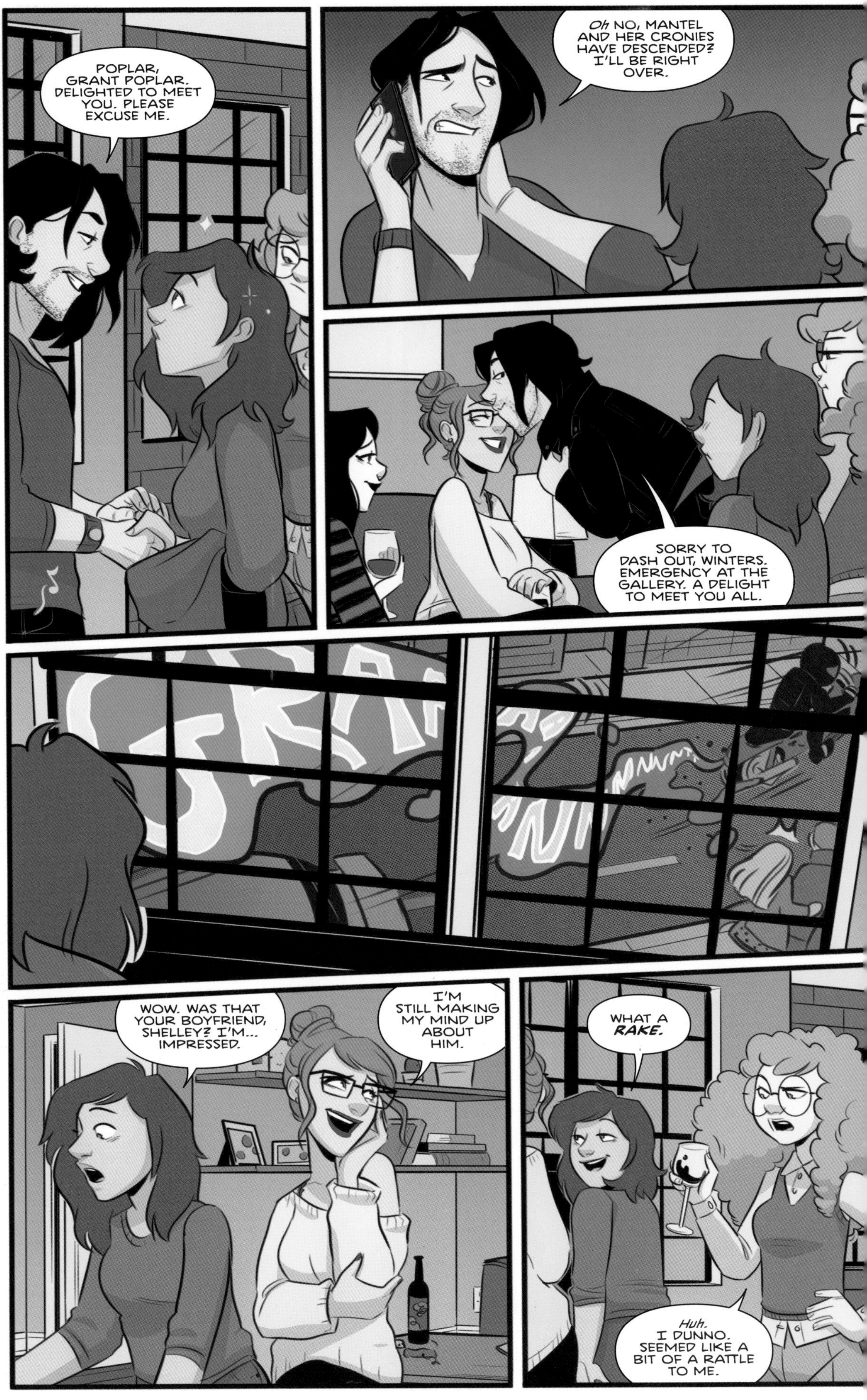
POPLAR, GRANT POPLAR. DELIGHTED TO MEET YOU. PLEASE EXCUSE ME.
Oh NO, MANTEL AND HER CRONIES HAVE DESCENDED? I'LL BE RIGHT OVER.
SORRY TO DASH OUT, WINTERS. EMERGENCY AT THE GALLERY. A DELIGHT TO MEET YOU ALL.
WOW. WAS THAT YOUR BOYFRIEND, SHELLEY? I'M... IMPRESSED.
I'M STILL MAKING MY MIND UP ABOUT HIM.
WHAT A ***RAKE.***
Huh. I DUNNO. SEEMED LIKE A BIT OF A RATTLE TO ME.

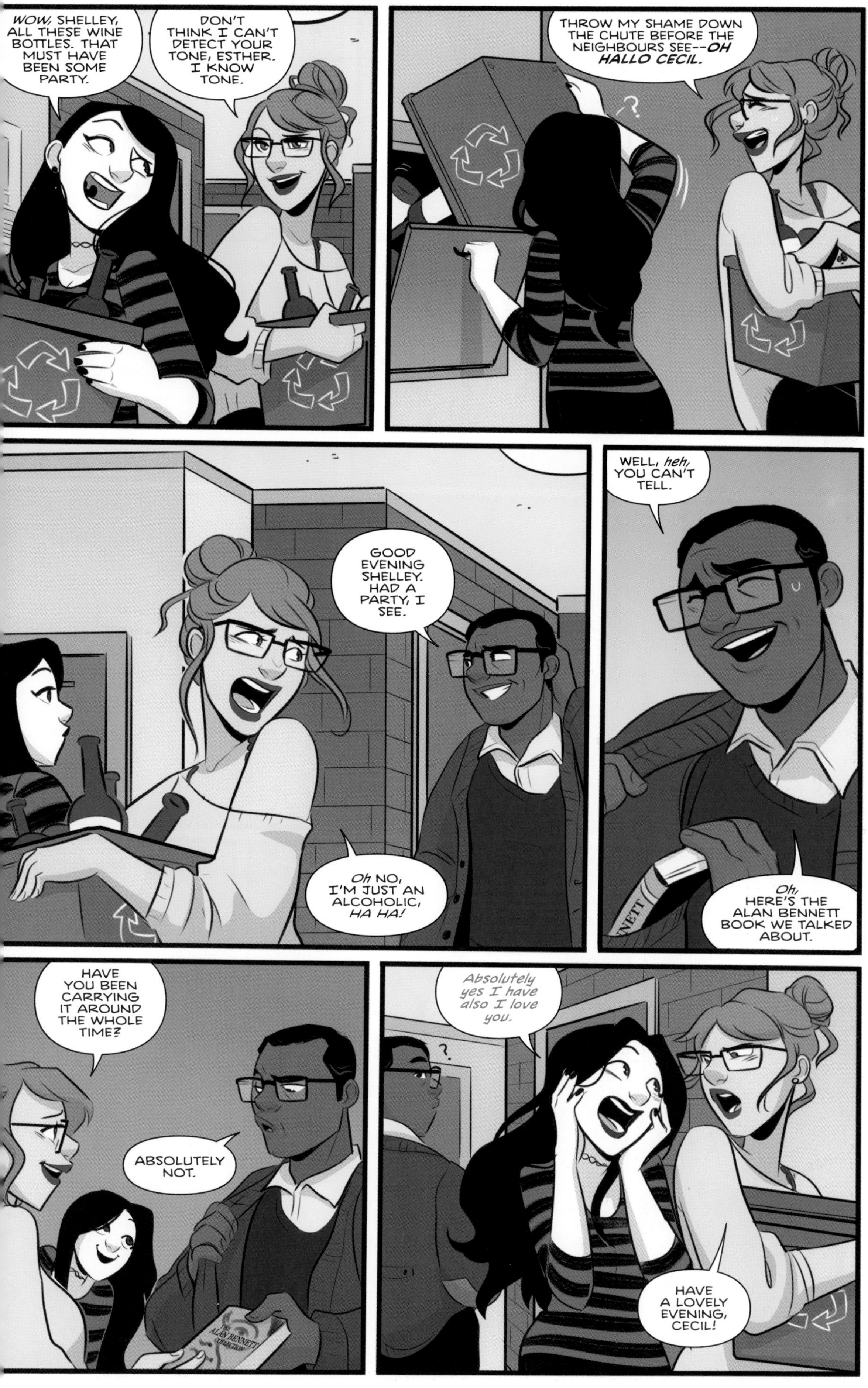
WOW, SHELLEY, ALL THESE WINE BOTTLES. THAT MUST HAVE BEEN SOME PARTY.
DON'T THINK I CAN'T DETECT YOUR TONE, ESTHER. I KNOW TONE.
THROW MY SHAME DOWN THE CHUTE BEFORE THE NEIGHBOURS SEE--OH HALLO CECIL.
?
GOOD EVENING SHELLEY. HAD A PARTY, I SEE.
Oh NO, I'M JUST AN ALCOHOLIC, HA HA!
WELL, heh, YOU CAN'T TELL.
Oh, HERE'S THE ALAN BENNETT BOOK WE TALKED ABOUT.
HAVE YOU BEEN CARRYING IT AROUND THE WHOLE TIME?
ABSOLUTELY NOT.
THE ALAN BENNETT COLLECTION
Absolutely yes I have also I love you.
?
HAVE A LOVELY EVENING, CECIL!

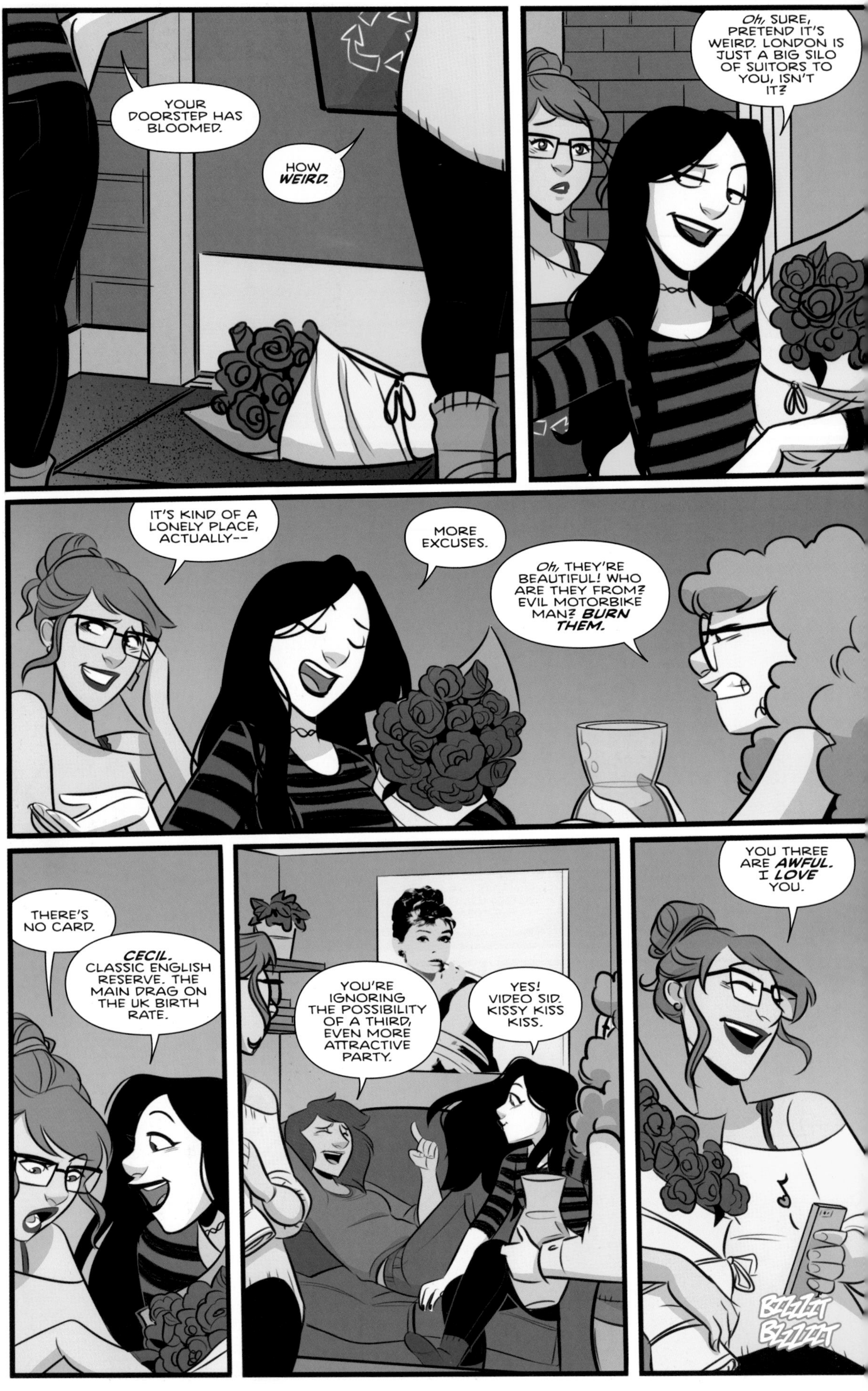
YOUR DOORSTEP HAS BLOOMED.
HOW *WEIRD.*
Oh, SURE, PRETEND IT'S WEIRD. LONDON IS JUST A BIG SILO OF SUITORS TO YOU, ISN'T IT?
IT'S KIND OF A LONELY PLACE, ACTUALLY--
MORE EXCUSES.
Oh, THEY'RE BEAUTIFUL! WHO ARE THEY FROM? EVIL MOTORBIKE MAN? ***BURN THEM.***
THERE'S NO CARD.
CECIL. CLASSIC ENGLISH RESERVE. THE MAIN DRAG ON THE UK BIRTH RATE.
YOU'RE IGNORING THE POSSIBILITY OF A THIRD, EVEN MORE ATTRACTIVE PARTY.
YES! VIDEO SID. KISSY KISS KISS.
YOU THREE ARE ***AWFUL.*** I ***LOVE*** YOU.
BZZZZT BZZZZT

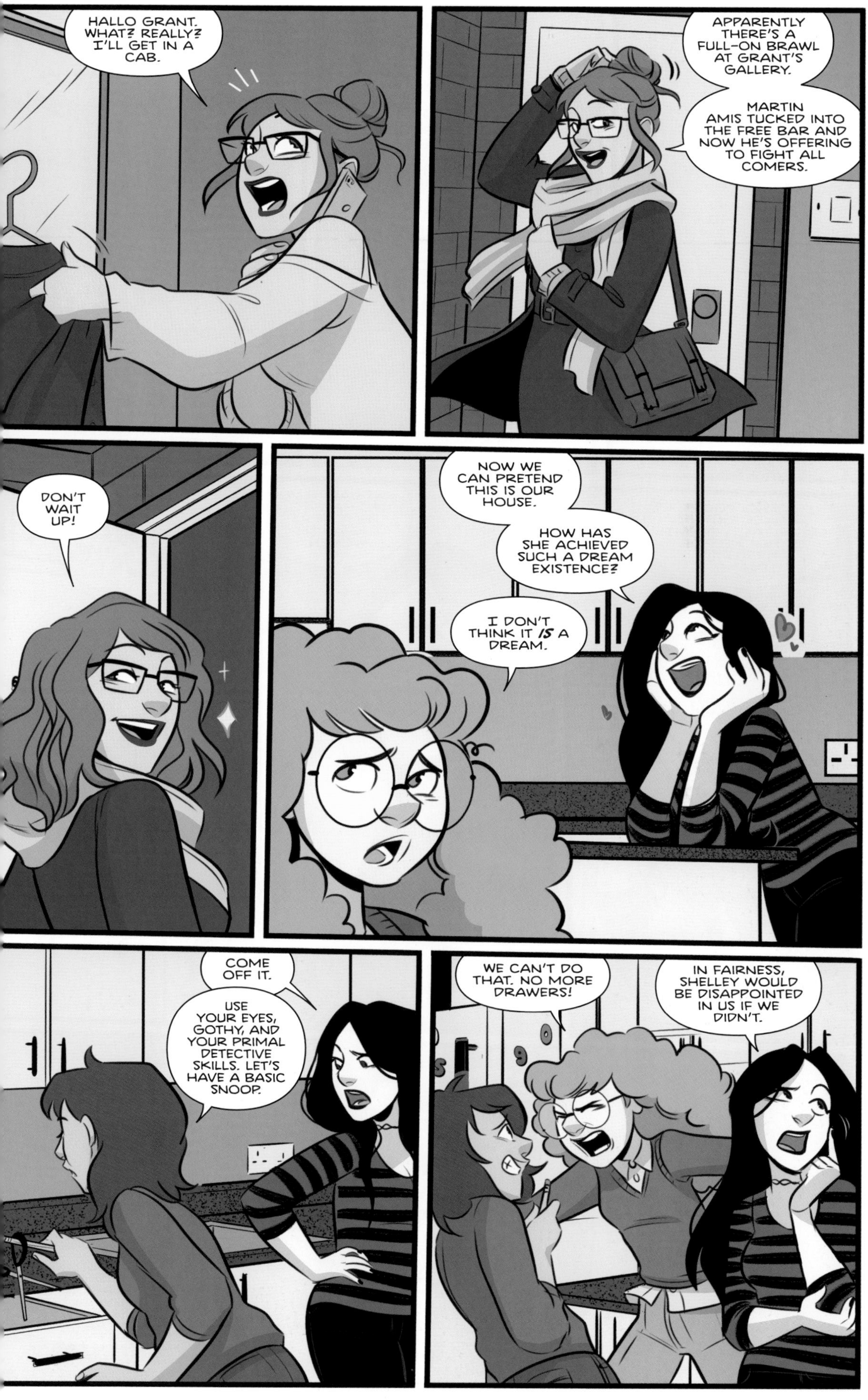
HALLO GRANT. WHAT? REALLY? I'LL GET IN A CAB.
APPARENTLY THERE'S A FULL-ON BRAWL AT GRANT'S GALLERY.
MARTIN AMIS TUCKED INTO THE FREE BAR AND NOW HE'S OFFERING TO FIGHT ALL COMERS.
DON'T WAIT UP!
NOW WE CAN PRETEND THIS IS OUR HOUSE.
HOW HAS SHE ACHIEVED SUCH A DREAM EXISTENCE?
I DON'T THINK IT *IS* A DREAM.
COME OFF IT.
USE YOUR EYES, GOTHY, AND YOUR PRIMAL DETECTIVE SKILLS. LET'S HAVE A BASIC SNOOP.
WE CAN'T DO THAT. NO MORE DRAWERS!
IN FAIRNESS, SHELLEY WOULD BE DISAPPOINTED IN US IF WE DIDN'T.

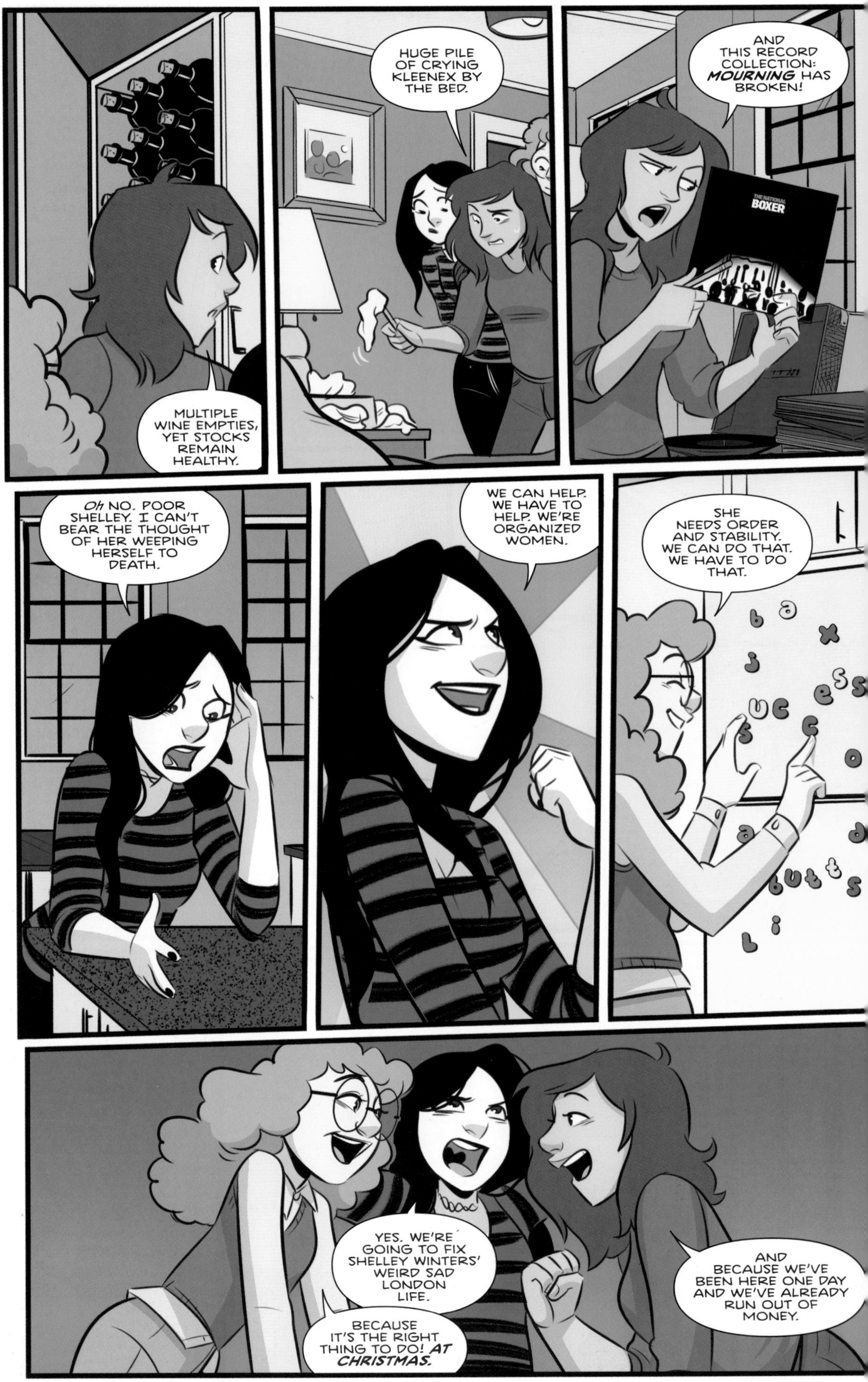
MULTIPLE WINE EMPTIES, YET STOCKS REMAIN HEALTHY.
HUGE PILE OF CRYING KLEENEX BY THE BED.
AND THIS RECORD COLLECTION: *MOURNING* HAS BROKEN!
THE NATIONAL BOXER
Oh NO. POOR SHELLEY. I CAN'T BEAR THE THOUGHT OF HER WEEPING HERSELF TO DEATH.
WE CAN HELP. WE HAVE TO HELP. WE'RE ORGANIZED WOMEN.
SHE NEEDS ORDER AND STABILITY. WE CAN DO THAT. WE HAVE TO DO THAT.
YES. WE'RE GOING TO FIX SHELLEY WINTERS' WEIRD SAD LONDON LIFE.
BECAUSE IT'S THE RIGHT THING TO DO! *AT CHRISTMAS.*
AND BECAUSE WE'VE BEEN HERE ONE DAY AND WE'VE ALREADY RUN OUT OF MONEY.

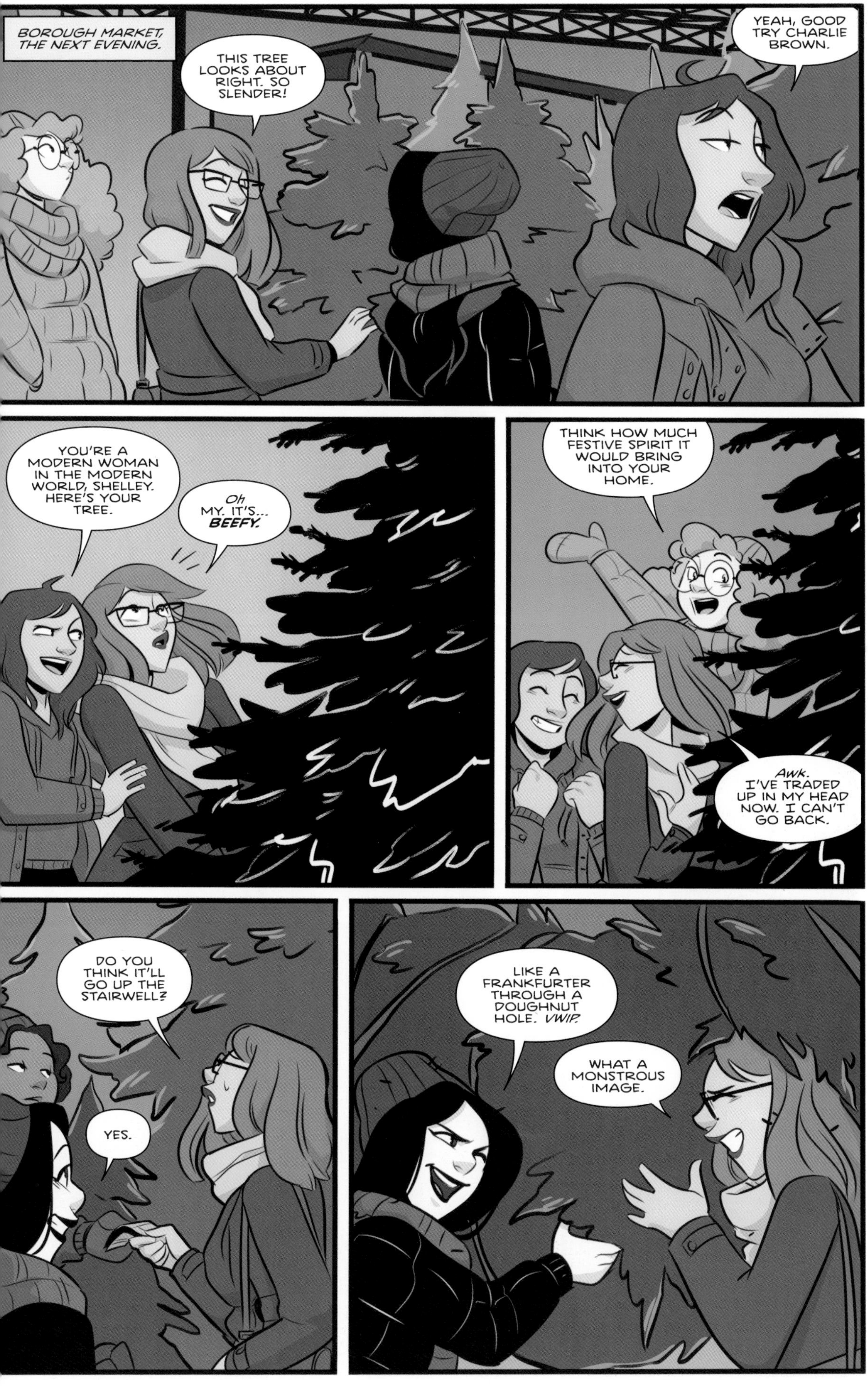
BOROUGH MARKET, THE NEXT EVENING.
THIS TREE LOOKS ABOUT RIGHT. SO SLENDER!
YEAH, GOOD TRY CHARLIE BROWN.
YOU'RE A MODERN WOMAN IN THE MODERN WORLD, SHELLEY. HERE'S YOUR TREE.
Oh MY. IT'S... BEEFY.
THINK HOW MUCH FESTIVE SPIRIT IT WOULD BRING INTO YOUR HOME.
Awk. I'VE TRADED UP IN MY HEAD NOW. I CAN'T GO BACK.
DO YOU THINK IT'LL GO UP THE STAIRWELL?
YES.
LIKE A FRANKFURTER THROUGH A DOUGHNUT HOLE. VWIP.
WHAT A MONSTROUS IMAGE.

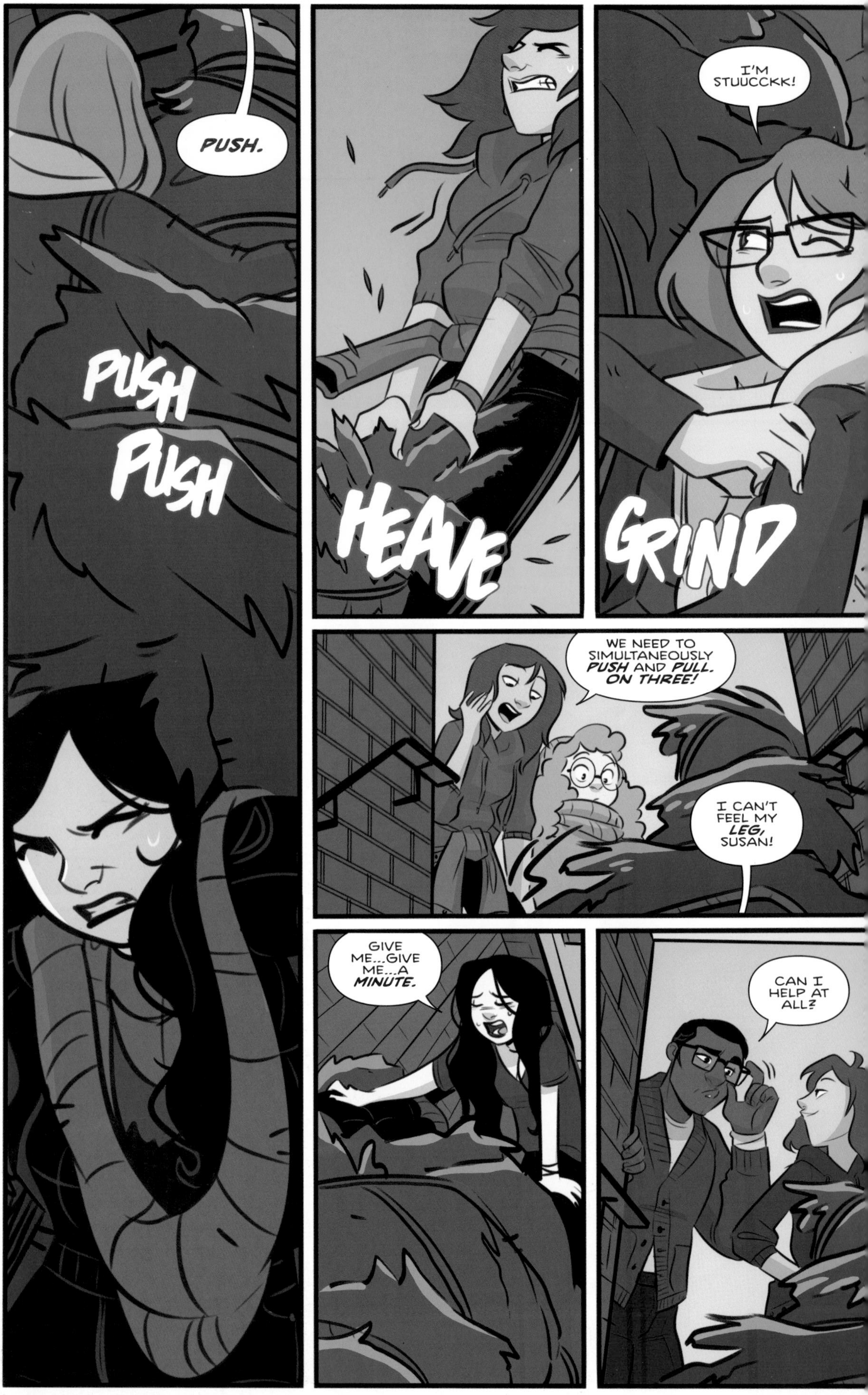
PUSH.
PUSH
PUSH
HEAVE
I'M STUUCCKK!
GRIND
WE NEED TO SIMULTANEOUSLY PUSH AND PULL. ON THREE!
I CAN'T FEEL MY LEG, SUSAN!
GIVE ME...GIVE ME...A MINUTE.
CAN I HELP AT ALL?

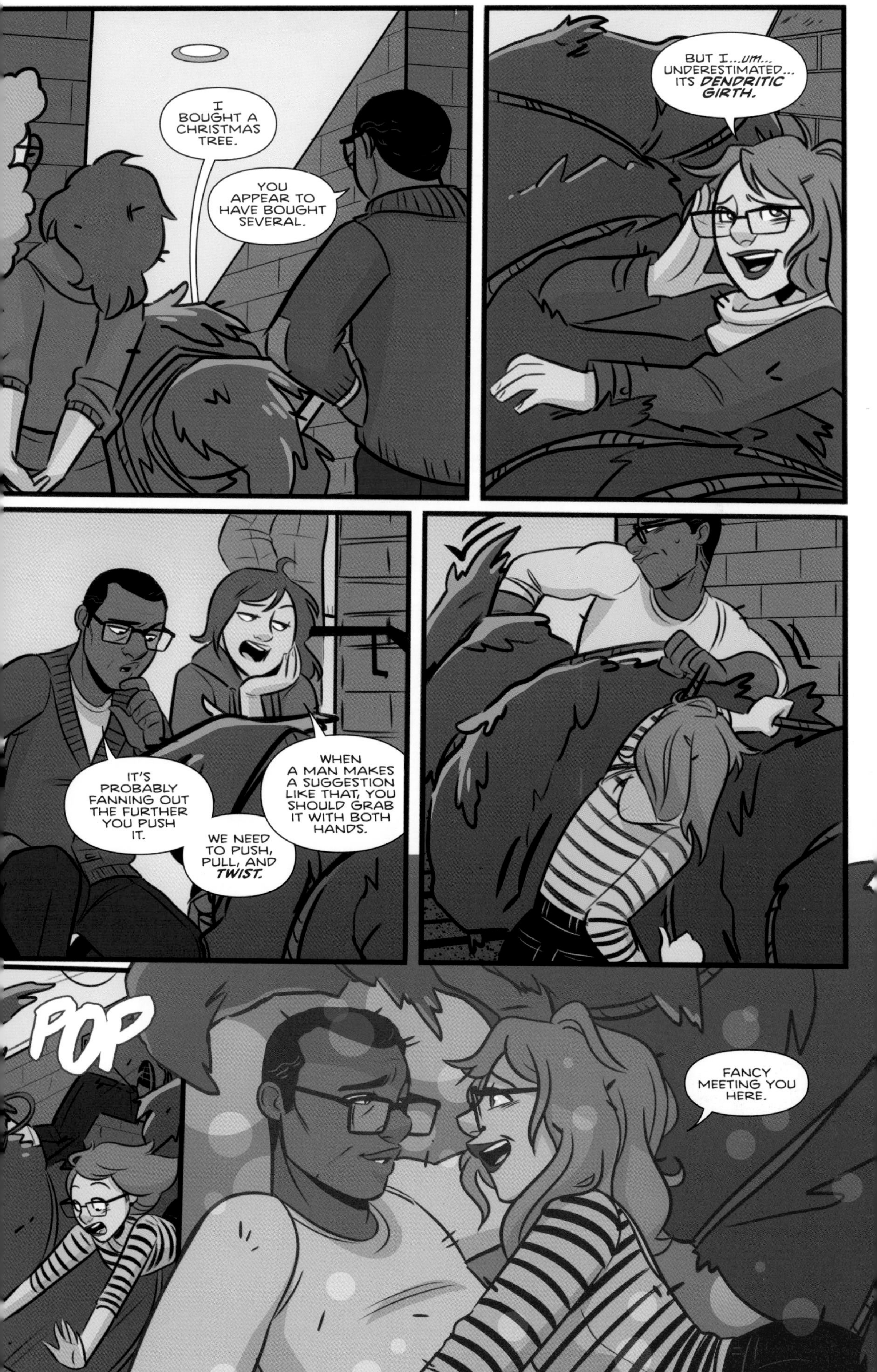
I BOUGHT A CHRISTMAS TREE.
YOU APPEAR TO HAVE BOUGHT SEVERAL.
BUT I...UM... UNDERESTIMATED... ITS DENDRITIC GIRTH.
IT'S PROBABLY FANNING OUT THE FURTHER YOU PUSH IT.
WE NEED TO PUSH, PULL, AND TWIST.
WHEN A MAN MAKES A SUGGESTION LIKE THAT, YOU SHOULD GRAB IT WITH BOTH HANDS.
POP
FANCY MEETING YOU HERE.

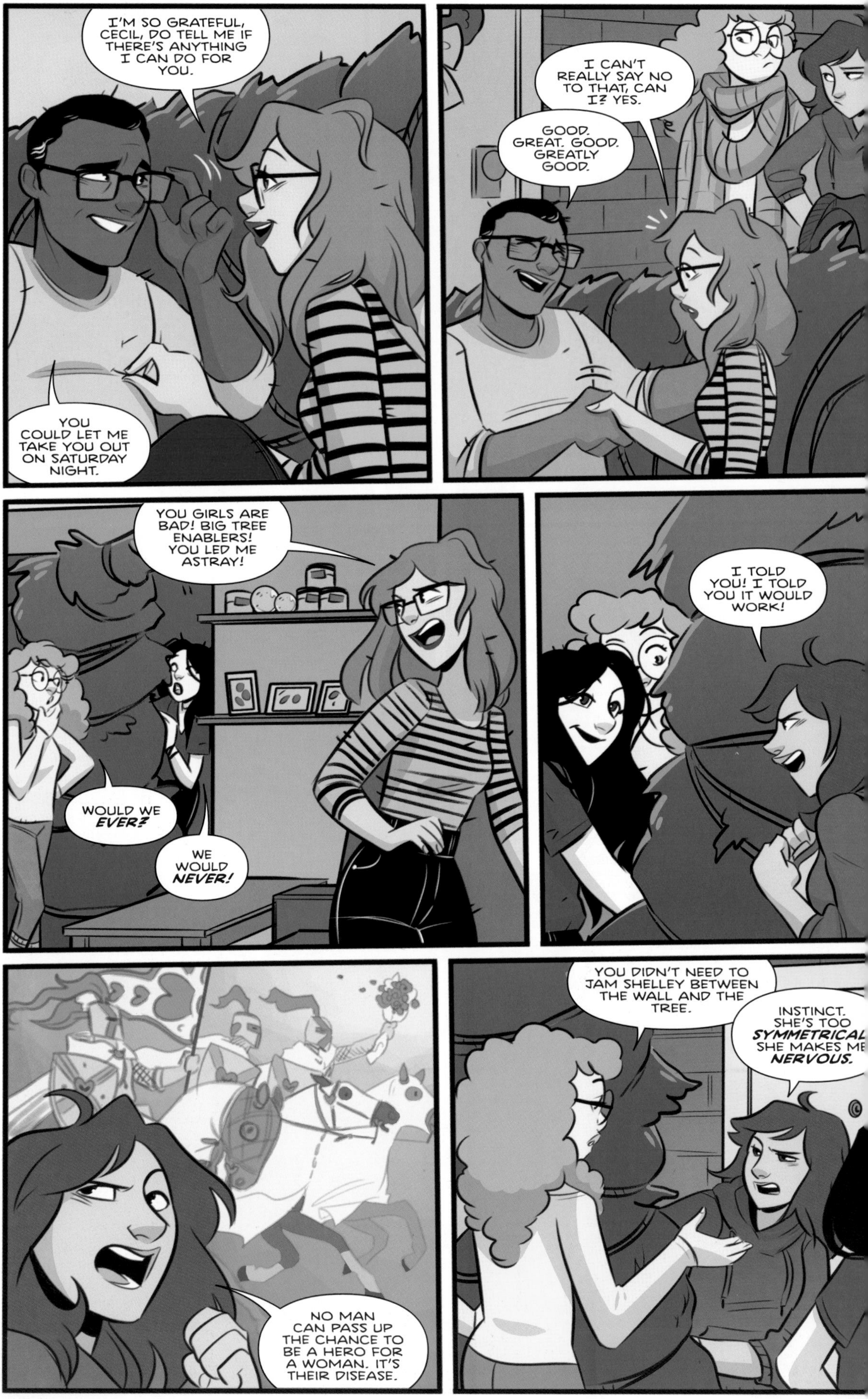

I'M SO GRATEFUL, CECIL, DO TELL ME IF THERE'S ANYTHING I CAN DO FOR YOU.
YOU COULD LET ME TAKE YOU OUT ON SATURDAY NIGHT.
I CAN'T REALLY SAY NO TO THAT, CAN I? YES.
GOOD. GREAT. GOOD. GREATLY GOOD.
YOU GIRLS ARE BAD! BIG TREE ENABLERS! YOU LED ME ASTRAY!
WOULD WE *EVER?*
WE WOULD *NEVER!*
I TOLD YOU! I TOLD YOU IT WOULD WORK!
NO MAN CAN PASS UP THE CHANCE TO BE A HERO FOR A WOMAN. IT'S THEIR DISEASE.
YOU DIDN'T NEED TO JAM SHELLEY BETWEEN THE WALL AND THE TREE.
INSTINCT. SHE'S TOO *SYMMETRICAL.* SHE MAKES ME *NERVOUS.*

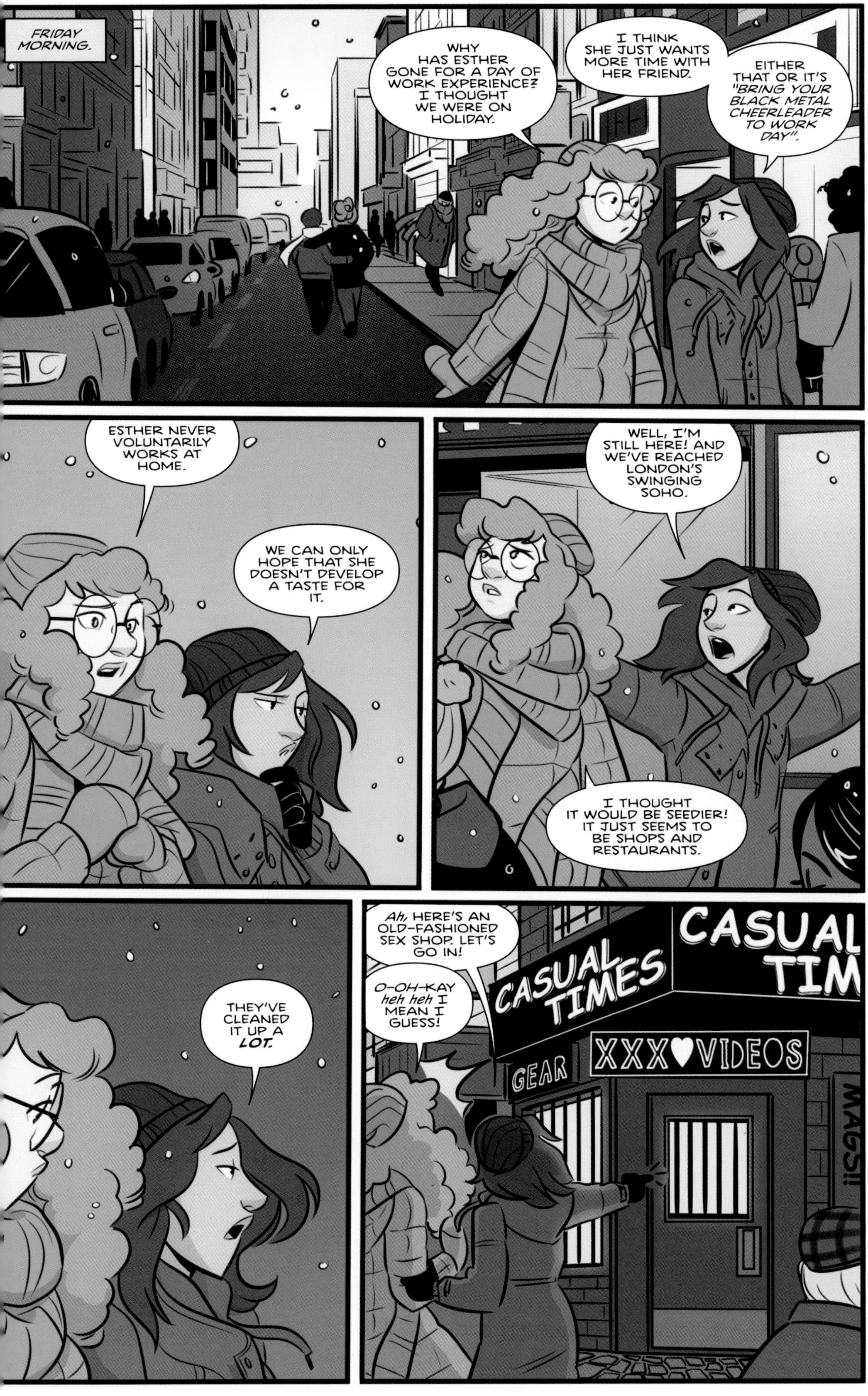
FRIDAY MORNING.
WHY HAS ESTHER GONE FOR A DAY OF WORK EXPERIENCE? I THOUGHT WE WERE ON HOLIDAY.
I THINK SHE JUST WANTS MORE TIME WITH HER FRIEND.
EITHER THAT OR IT'S "BRING YOUR BLACK METAL CHEERLEADER TO WORK DAY".
ESTHER NEVER VOLUNTARILY WORKS AT HOME.
WE CAN ONLY HOPE THAT SHE DOESN'T DEVELOP A TASTE FOR IT.
WELL, I'M STILL HERE! AND WE'VE REACHED LONDON'S SWINGING SOHO.
I THOUGHT IT WOULD BE SEEDIER! IT JUST SEEMS TO BE SHOPS AND RESTAURANTS.
THEY'VE CLEANED IT UP A *LOT.*
Ah, HERE'S AN OLD-FASHIONED SEX SHOP. LET'S GO IN!
O-OH-KAY *heh heh* I MEAN I GUESS!
CASUAL TIMES
CASUAL TIM
GEAR
XXX♥VIDEOS
MAGS!!

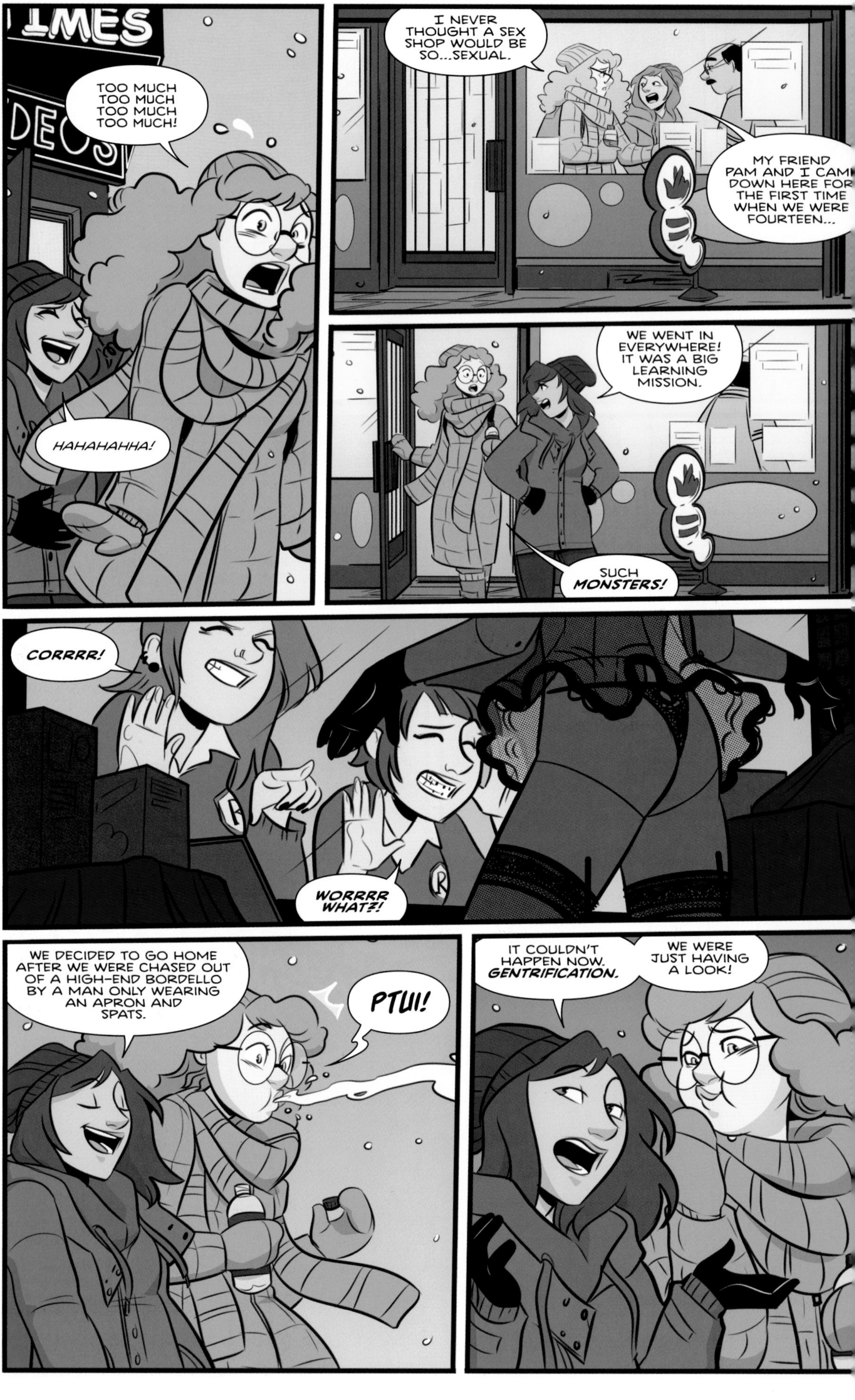
TIMES
DEOS
TOO MUCH TOO MUCH TOO MUCH TOO MUCH!
HAHAHAHHA!
I NEVER THOUGHT A SEX SHOP WOULD BE SO...SEXUAL.
MY FRIEND PAM AND I CAME DOWN HERE FOR THE FIRST TIME WHEN WE WERE FOURTEEN...
WE WENT IN EVERYWHERE! IT WAS A BIG LEARNING MISSION.
SUCH MONSTERS!
CORRRR!
WORRRR WHAT?!
WE DECIDED TO GO HOME AFTER WE WERE CHASED OUT OF A HIGH-END BORDELLO BY A MAN ONLY WEARING AN APRON AND SPATS.
PTUI!
IT COULDN'T HAPPEN NOW. GENTRIFICATION.
WE WERE JUST HAVING A LOOK!

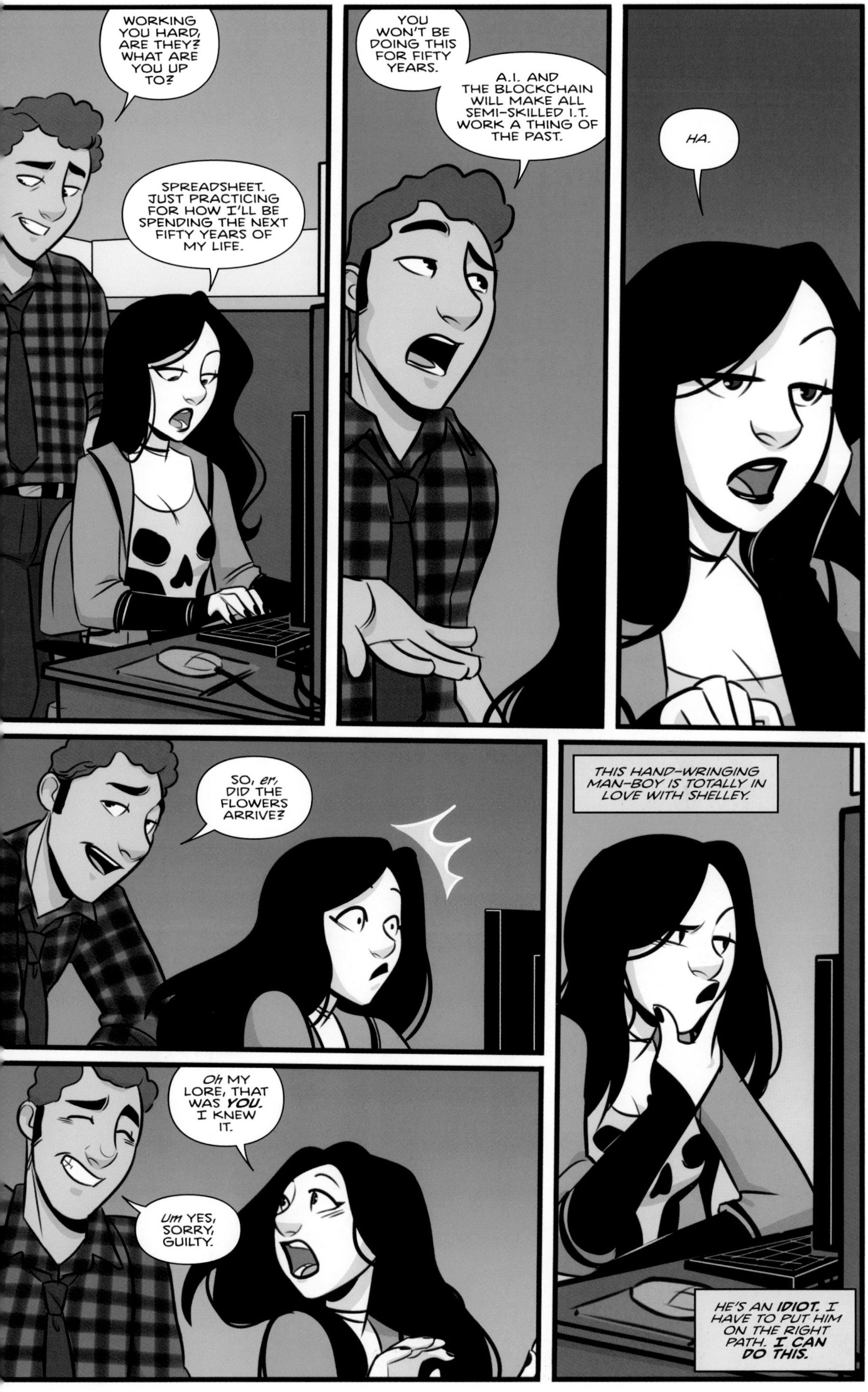
WORKING YOU HARD, ARE THEY? WHAT ARE YOU UP TO?
SPREADSHEET. JUST PRACTICING FOR HOW I'LL BE SPENDING THE NEXT FIFTY YEARS OF MY LIFE.
YOU WON'T BE DOING THIS FOR FIFTY YEARS.
A.I. AND THE BLOCKCHAIN WILL MAKE ALL SEMI-SKILLED I.T. WORK A THING OF THE PAST.
HA.
SO, *er*, DID THE FLOWERS ARRIVE?
Oh MY LORE, THAT WAS ***YOU.*** I KNEW IT.
Um YES, SORRY, GUILTY.
THIS HAND-WRINGING MAN-BOY IS TOTALLY IN LOVE WITH SHELLEY.
HE'S AN ***IDIOT.*** *I HAVE TO PUT HIM ON THE RIGHT PATH.* ***I CAN DO THIS.***

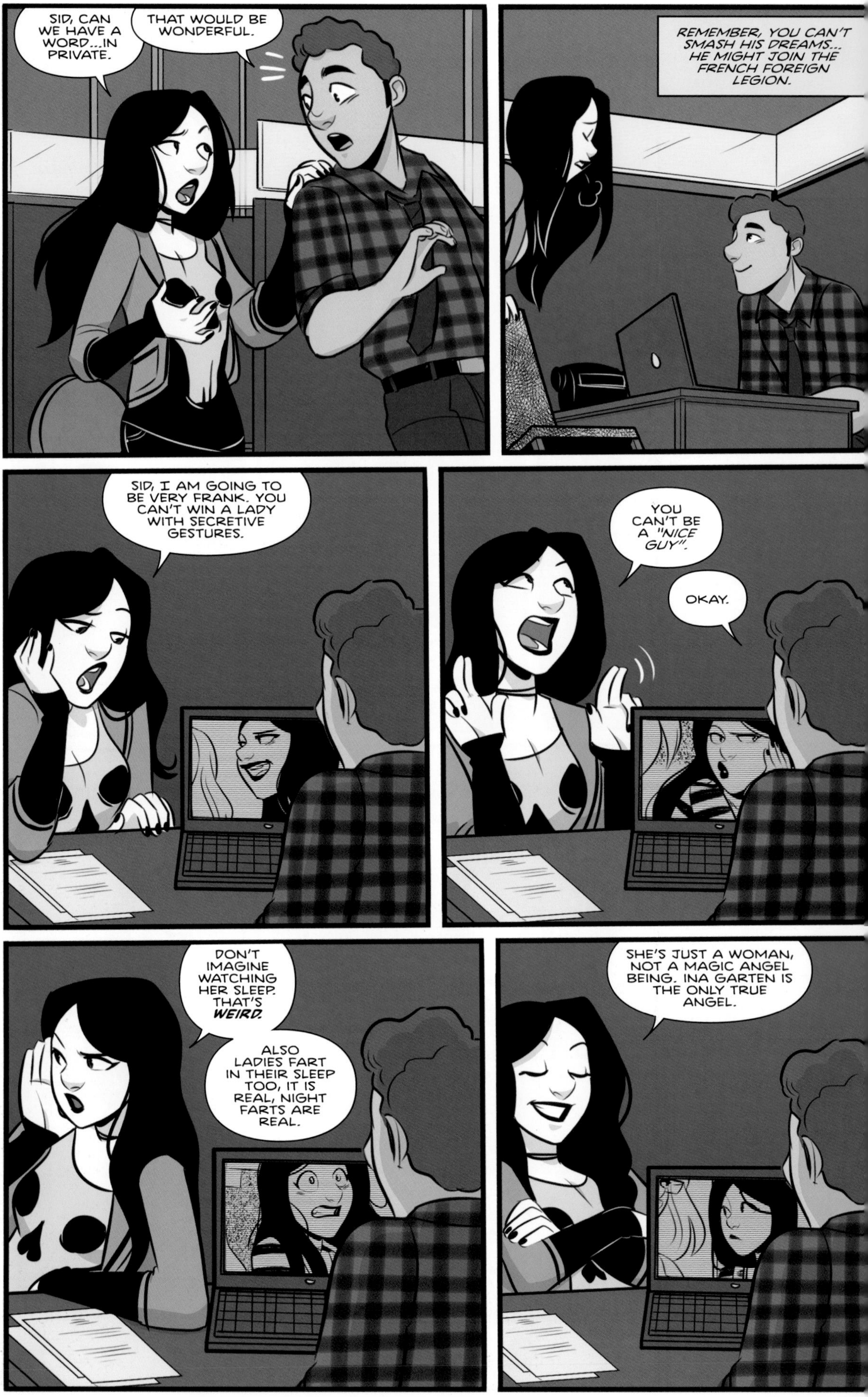
SID, CAN WE HAVE A WORD...IN PRIVATE.
THAT WOULD BE WONDERFUL.
REMEMBER, YOU CAN'T SMASH HIS DREAMS... HE MIGHT JOIN THE FRENCH FOREIGN LEGION.
SID, I AM GOING TO BE VERY FRANK. YOU CAN'T WIN A LADY WITH SECRETIVE GESTURES.
YOU CAN'T BE A "NICE GUY".
OKAY.
DON'T IMAGINE WATCHING HER SLEEP. THAT'S WEIRD.
ALSO LADIES FART IN THEIR SLEEP TOO, IT IS REAL, NIGHT FARTS ARE REAL.
SHE'S JUST A WOMAN, NOT A MAGIC ANGEL BEING. INA GARTEN IS THE ONLY TRUE ANGEL.

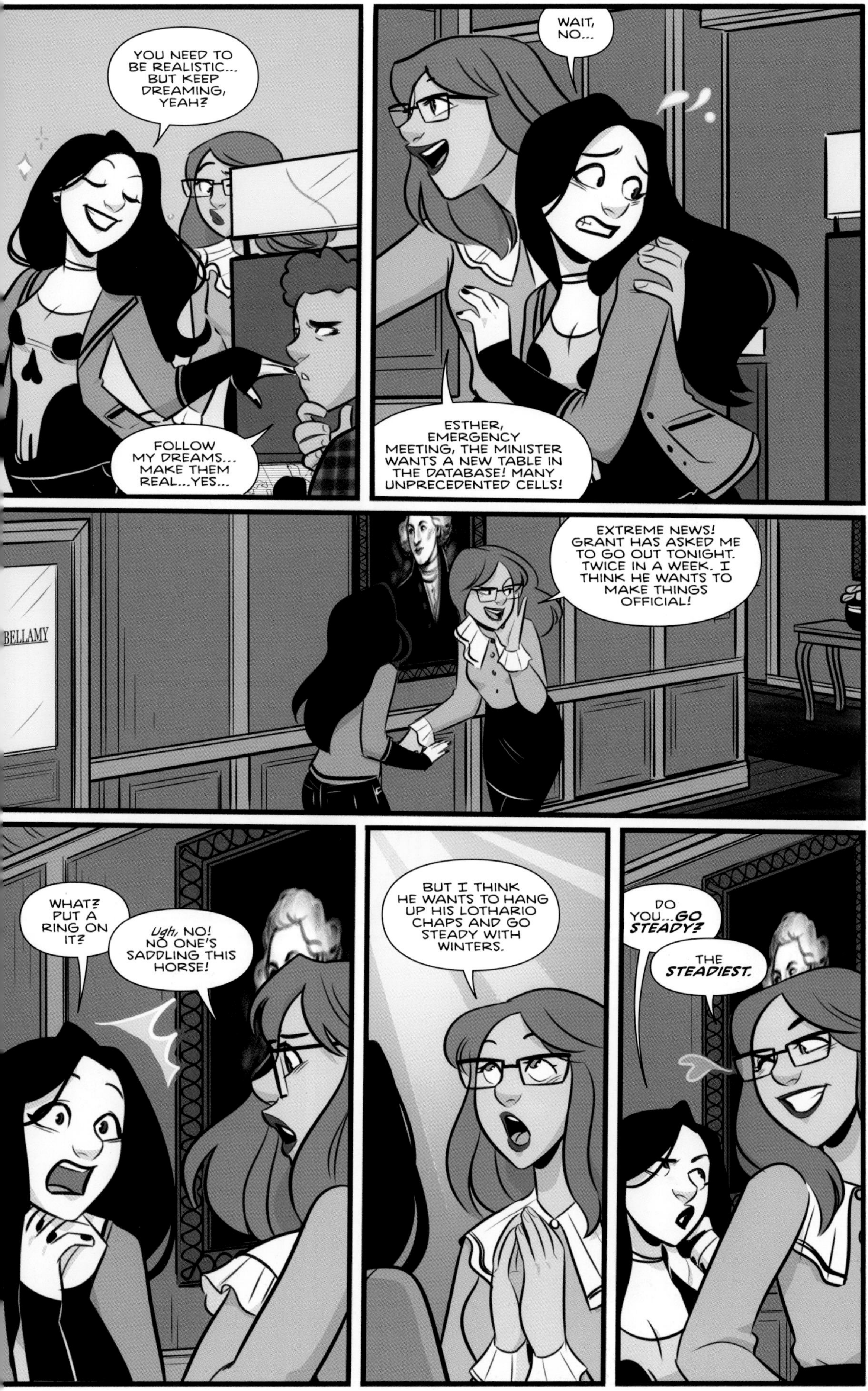
YOU NEED TO BE REALISTIC... BUT KEEP DREAMING, YEAH?
FOLLOW MY DREAMS... MAKE THEM REAL...YES...
WAIT, NO...
ESTHER, EMERGENCY MEETING, THE MINISTER WANTS A NEW TABLE IN THE DATABASE! MANY UNPRECEDENTED CELLS!
BELLAMY
EXTREME NEWS! GRANT HAS ASKED ME TO GO OUT TONIGHT. TWICE IN A WEEK. I THINK HE WANTS TO MAKE THINGS OFFICIAL!
WHAT? PUT A RING ON IT?
Ugh, NO! NO ONE'S SADDLING THIS HORSE!
BUT I THINK HE WANTS TO HANG UP HIS LOTHARIO CHAPS AND GO STEADY WITH WINTERS.
DO YOU...***GO STEADY?***
THE ***STEADIEST.***

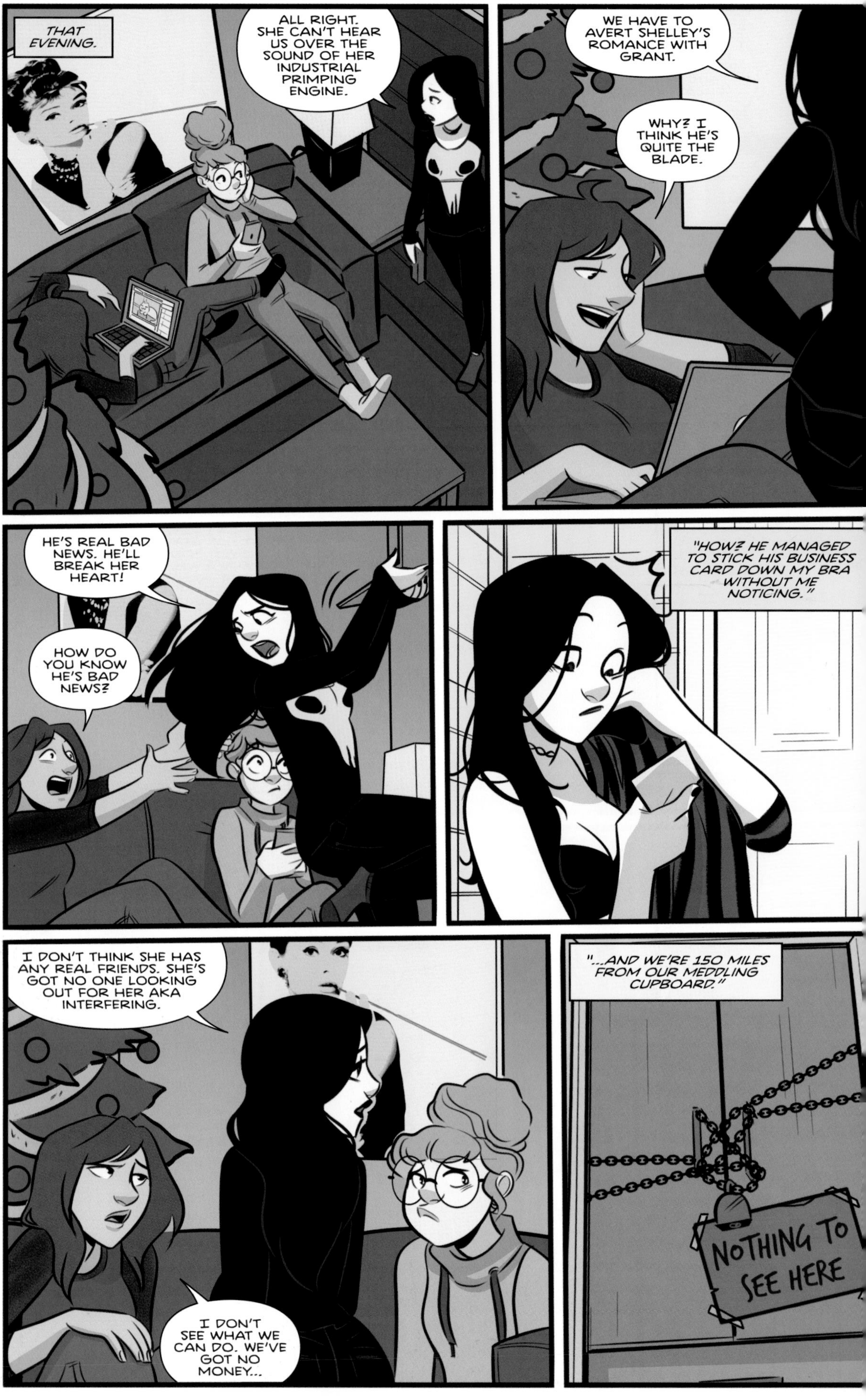
THAT EVENING.
ALL RIGHT. SHE CAN'T HEAR US OVER THE SOUND OF HER INDUSTRIAL PRIMPING ENGINE.
WE HAVE TO AVERT SHELLEY'S ROMANCE WITH GRANT.
WHY? I THINK HE'S QUITE THE BLADE.
HE'S REAL BAD NEWS. HE'LL BREAK HER HEART!
HOW DO YOU KNOW HE'S BAD NEWS?
"HOW? HE MANAGED TO STICK HIS BUSINESS CARD DOWN MY BRA WITHOUT ME NOTICING."
I DON'T THINK SHE HAS ANY REAL FRIENDS. SHE'S GOT NO ONE LOOKING OUT FOR HER AKA INTERFERING.
I DON'T SEE WHAT WE CAN DO. WE'VE GOT NO MONEY...
"...AND WE'RE 150 MILES FROM OUR MEDDLING CUPBOARD."
NOTHING TO SEE HERE

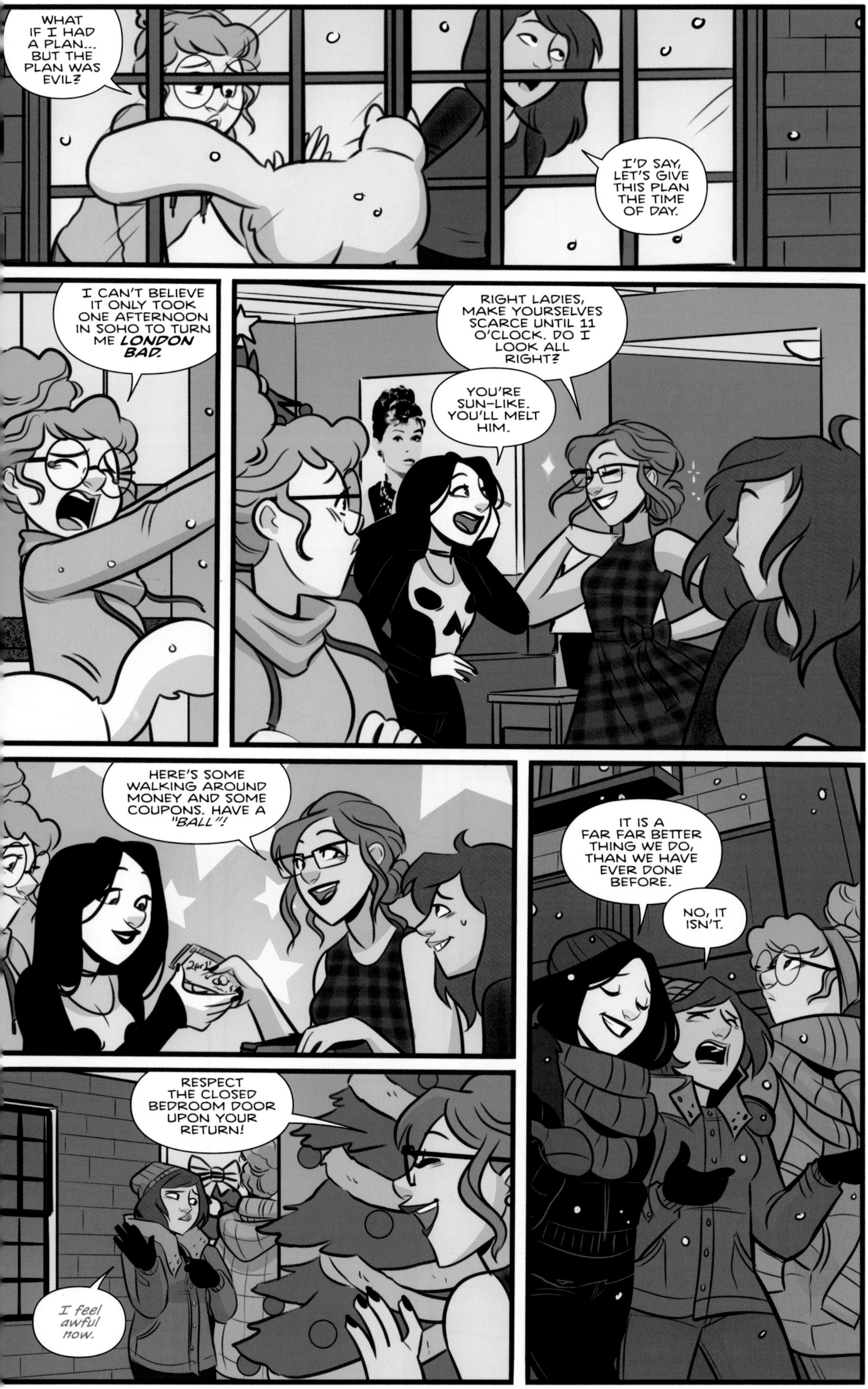

WHAT IF I HAD A PLAN... BUT THE PLAN WAS EVIL?
I'D SAY, LET'S GIVE THIS PLAN THE TIME OF DAY.
I CAN'T BELIEVE IT ONLY TOOK ONE AFTERNOON IN SOHO TO TURN ME LONDON BAD.
RIGHT LADIES, MAKE YOURSELVES SCARCE UNTIL 11 O'CLOCK. DO I LOOK ALL RIGHT?
YOU'RE SUN-LIKE. YOU'LL MELT HIM.
HERE'S SOME WALKING AROUND MONEY AND SOME COUPONS. HAVE A "BALL"!
IT IS A FAR FAR BETTER THING WE DO, THAN WE HAVE EVER DONE BEFORE.
NO, IT ISN'T.
RESPECT THE CLOSED BEDROOM DOOR UPON YOUR RETURN!
I feel awful now.

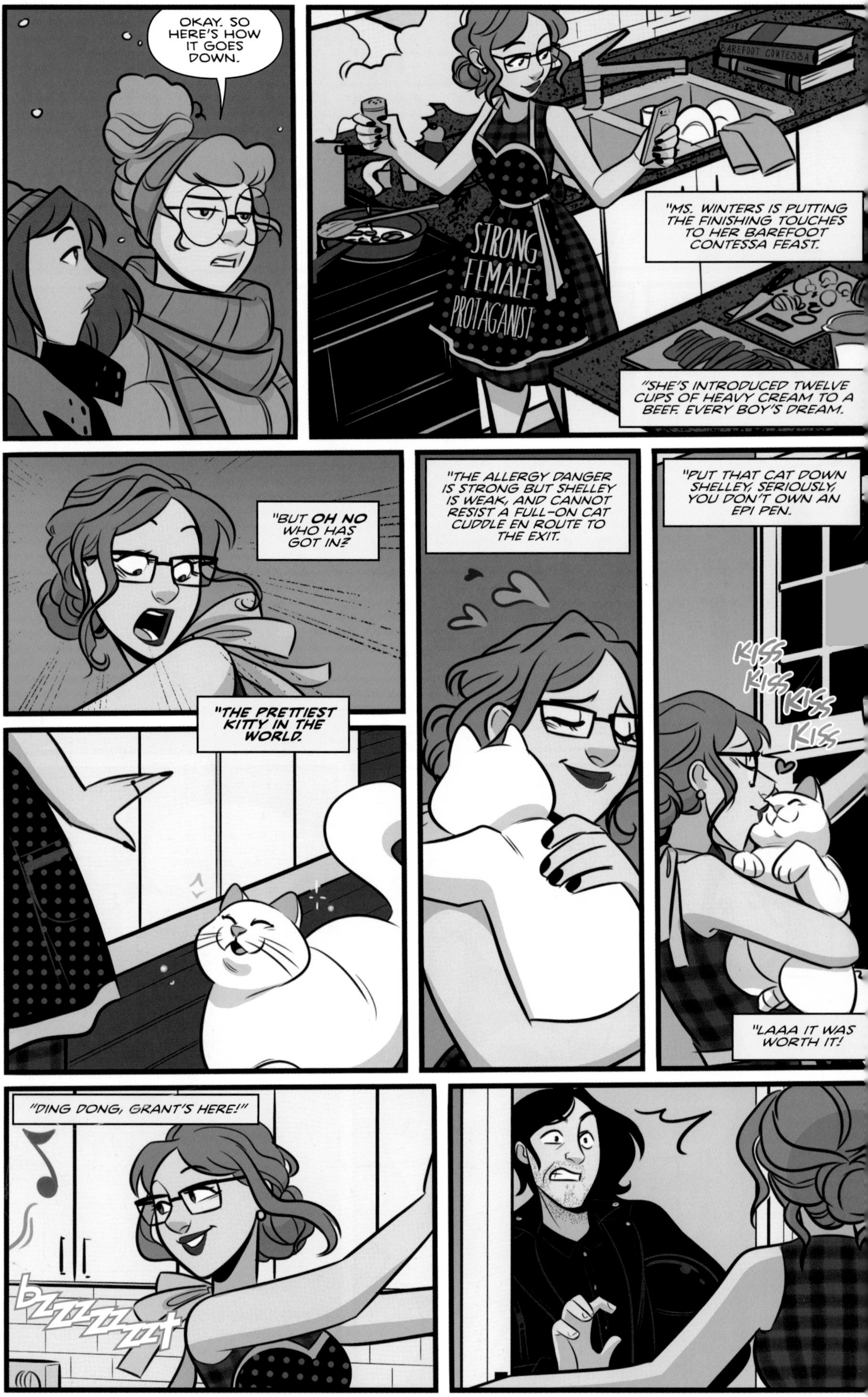
OKAY. SO HERE'S HOW IT GOES DOWN.
BAREFOOT CONTESSA
"MS. WINTERS IS PUTTING THE FINISHING TOUCHES TO HER BAREFOOT CONTESSA FEAST.
STRONG FEMALE PROTAGANIST
"SHE'S INTRODUCED TWELVE CUPS OF HEAVY CREAM TO A BEEF. EVERY BOY'S DREAM.
"BUT OH NO WHO HAS GOT IN?
"THE PRETTIEST KITTY IN THE WORLD.
"THE ALLERGY DANGER IS STRONG BUT SHELLEY IS WEAK, AND CANNOT RESIST A FULL-ON CAT CUDDLE EN ROUTE TO THE EXIT.
"PUT THAT CAT DOWN SHELLEY, SERIOUSLY, YOU DON'T OWN AN EPI PEN.
KISS KISS KISS KISS
"LAAA IT WAS WORTH IT!
"DING DONG, GRANT'S HERE!"
bzzzzzzzt

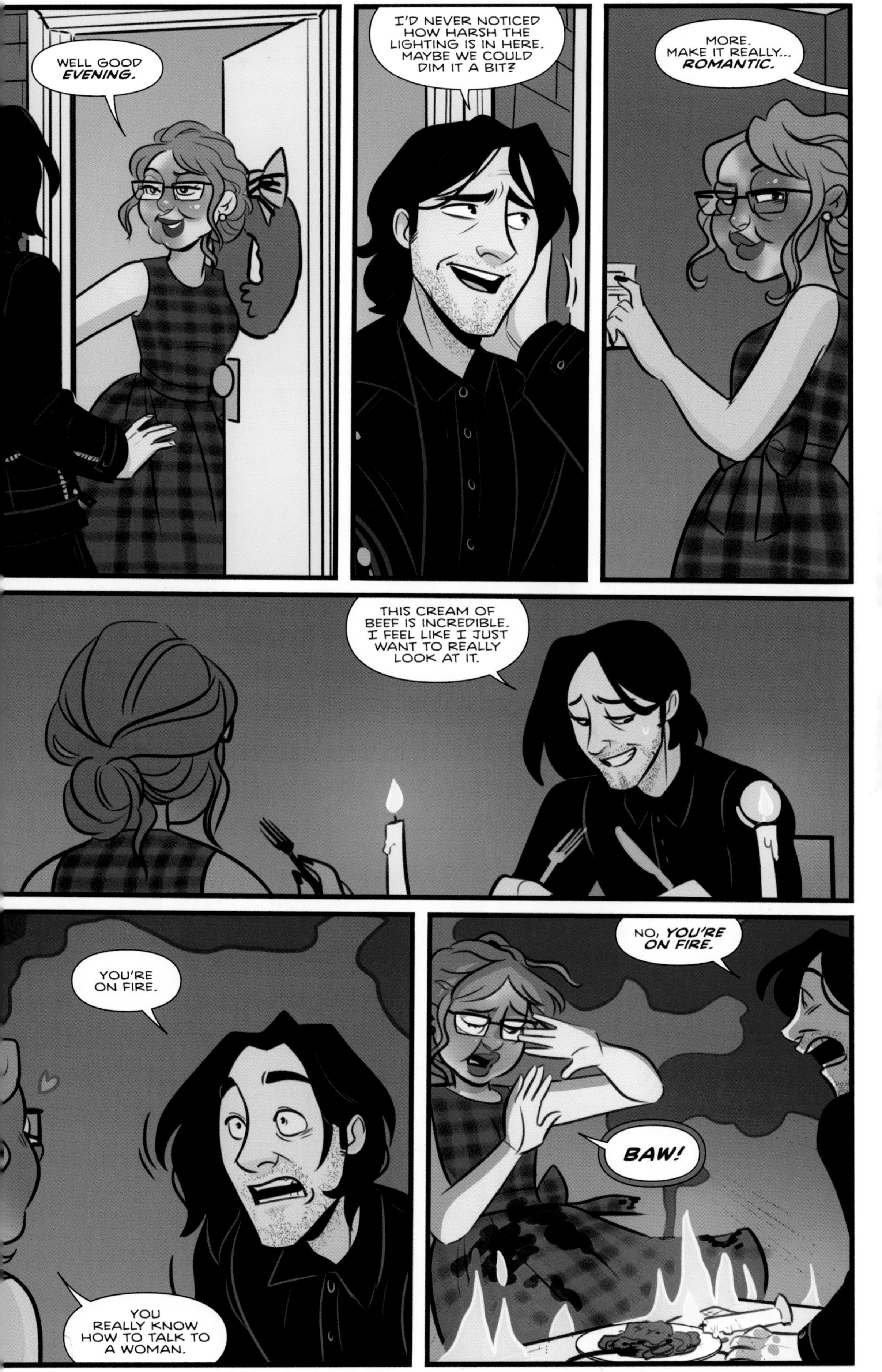
WELL GOOD *EVENING.*
I'D NEVER NOTICED HOW HARSH THE LIGHTING IS IN HERE. MAYBE WE COULD DIM IT A BIT?
MORE. MAKE IT REALLY... *ROMANTIC.*
THIS CREAM OF BEEF IS INCREDIBLE. I FEEL LIKE I JUST WANT TO REALLY LOOK AT IT.
YOU'RE ON FIRE.
YOU REALLY KNOW HOW TO TALK TO A WOMAN.
NO, *YOU'RE ON FIRE.*
BAW!

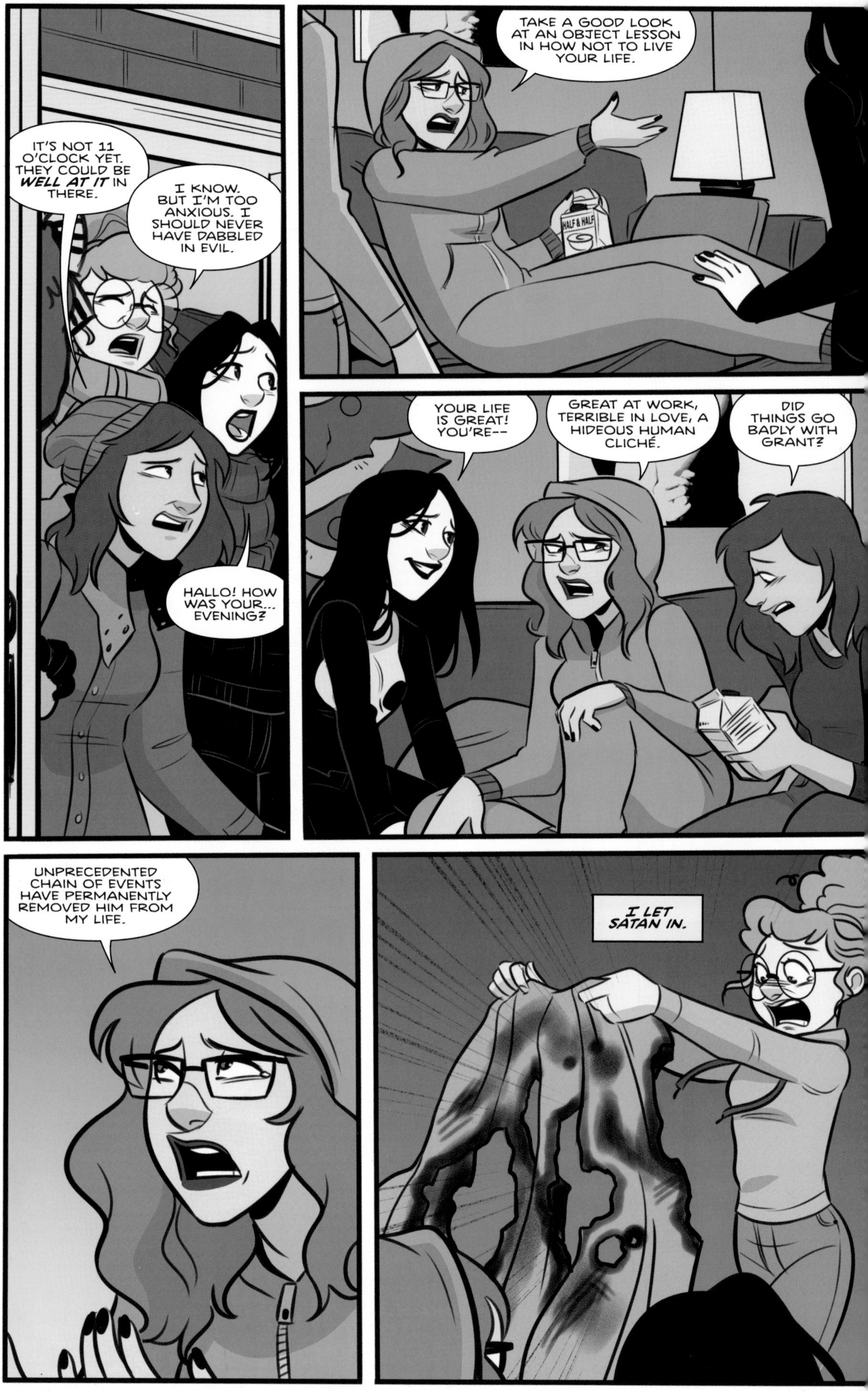
IT'S NOT 11 O'CLOCK YET. THEY COULD BE ***WELL AT IT*** IN THERE.
I KNOW. BUT I'M TOO ANXIOUS. I SHOULD NEVER HAVE DABBLED IN EVIL.
HALLO! HOW WAS YOUR... EVENING?
TAKE A GOOD LOOK AT AN OBJECT LESSON IN HOW NOT TO LIVE YOUR LIFE.
HALF & HALF
YOUR LIFE IS GREAT! YOU'RE--
GREAT AT WORK, TERRIBLE IN LOVE, A HIDEOUS HUMAN CLICHÉ.
DID THINGS GO BADLY WITH GRANT?
UNPRECEDENTED CHAIN OF EVENTS HAVE PERMANENTLY REMOVED HIM FROM MY LIFE.
I LET SATAN IN.

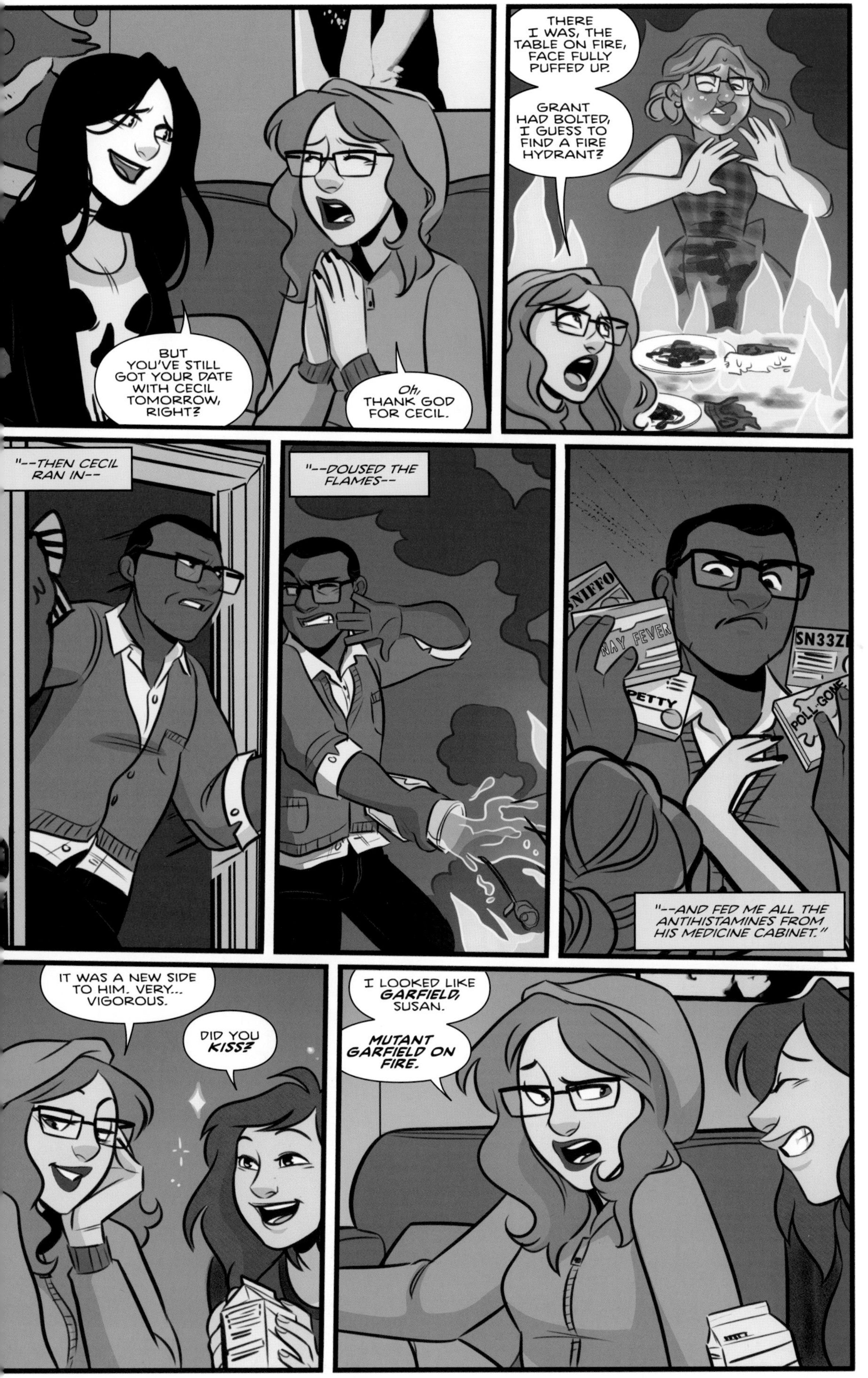
BUT YOU'VE STILL GOT YOUR DATE WITH CECIL TOMORROW, RIGHT?
OH, THANK GOD FOR CECIL.
THERE I WAS, THE TABLE ON FIRE, FACE FULLY PUFFED UP.
GRANT HAD BOLTED, I GUESS TO FIND A FIRE HYDRANT?
"--THEN CECIL RAN IN--
"--DOUSED THE FLAMES--
SNIFFO
HAY FEVER
PETTY
SN33Z
POLL-GONE
"--AND FED ME ALL THE ANTIHISTAMINES FROM HIS MEDICINE CABINET."
IT WAS A NEW SIDE TO HIM. VERY... VIGOROUS.
DID YOU *KISS?*
I LOOKED LIKE *GARFIELD,* SUSAN.
MUTANT GARFIELD ON FIRE.

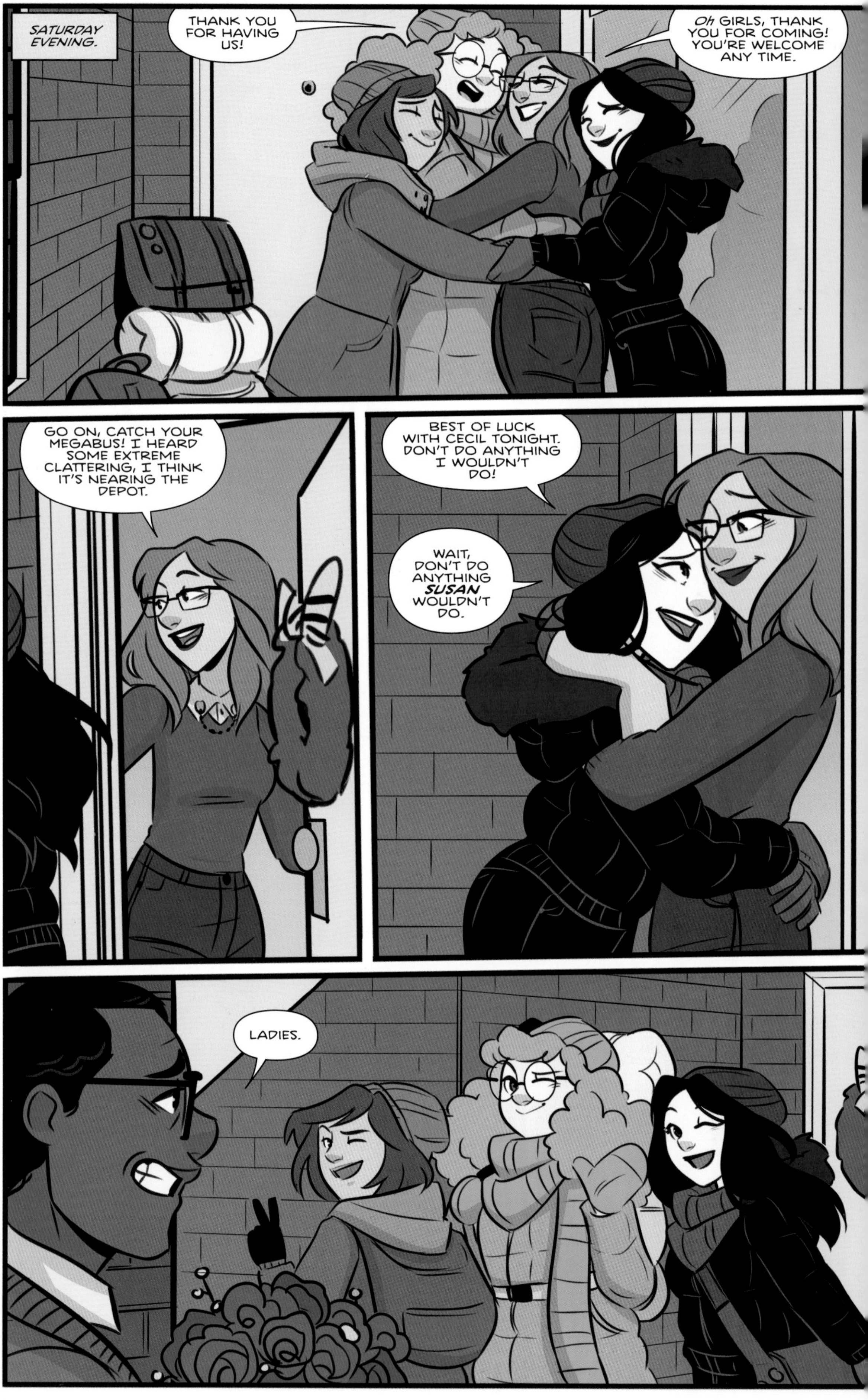
SATURDAY EVENING.
THANK YOU FOR HAVING US!
Oh GIRLS, THANK YOU FOR COMING! YOU'RE WELCOME ANY TIME.
GO ON, CATCH YOUR MEGABUS! I HEARD SOME EXTREME CLATTERING, I THINK IT'S NEARING THE DEPOT.
BEST OF LUCK WITH CECIL TONIGHT. DON'T DO ANYTHING I WOULDN'T DO!
WAIT, DON'T DO ANYTHING ***SUSAN*** WOULDN'T DO.
LADIES.

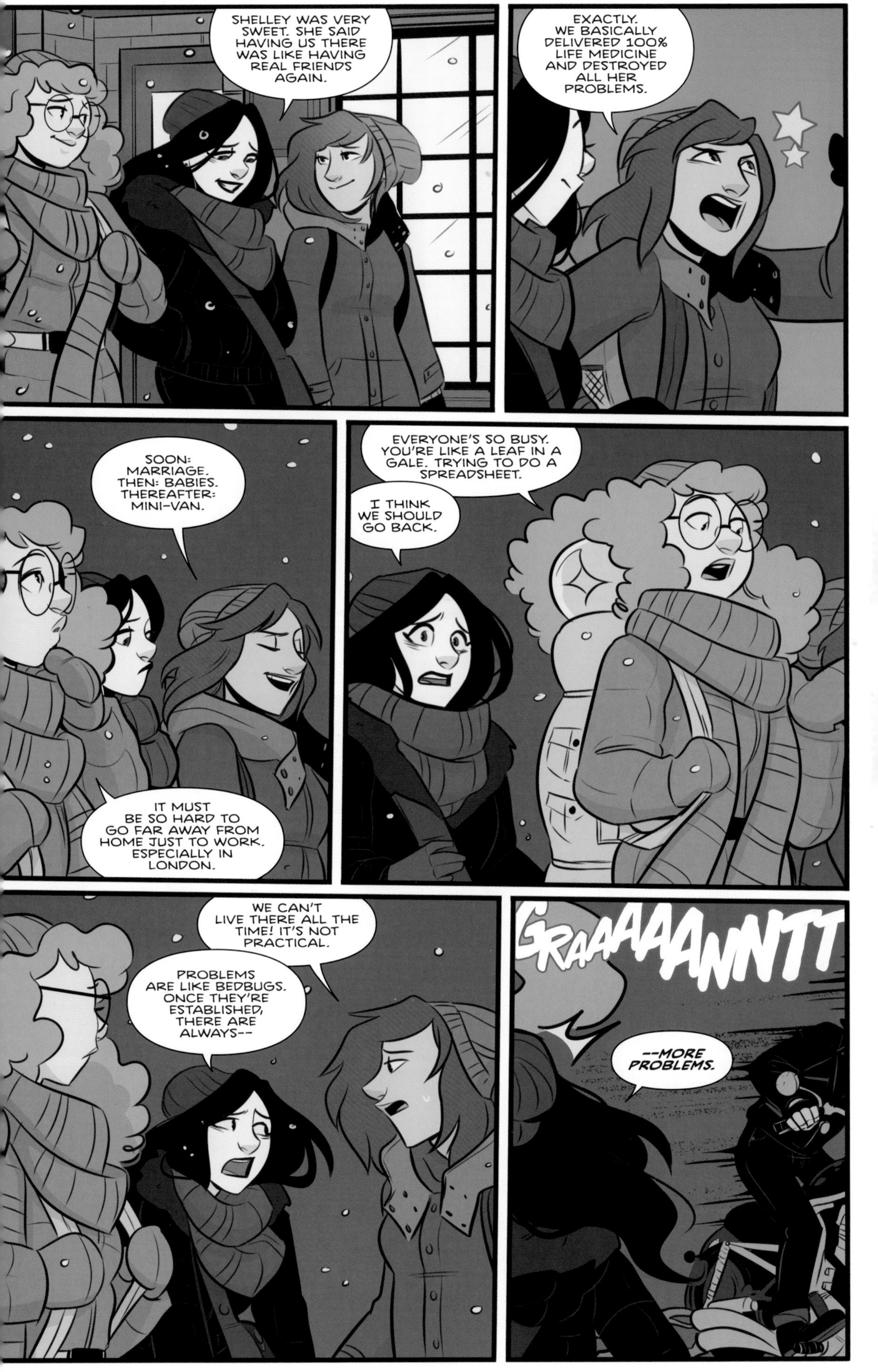

SHELLEY WAS VERY SWEET. SHE SAID HAVING US THERE WAS LIKE HAVING REAL FRIENDS AGAIN.
EXACTLY. WE BASICALLY DELIVERED 100% LIFE MEDICINE AND DESTROYED ALL HER PROBLEMS.
SOON: MARRIAGE. THEN: BABIES. THEREAFTER: MINI-VAN.
IT MUST BE SO HARD TO GO FAR AWAY FROM HOME JUST TO WORK. ESPECIALLY IN LONDON.
EVERYONE'S SO BUSY. YOU'RE LIKE A LEAF IN A GALE. TRYING TO DO A SPREADSHEET.
I THINK WE SHOULD GO BACK.
WE CAN'T LIVE THERE ALL THE TIME! IT'S NOT PRACTICAL.
PROBLEMS ARE LIKE BEDBUGS. ONCE THEY'RE ESTABLISHED, THERE ARE ALWAYS--
GRAAAAAANNNTT
--MORE PROBLEMS.

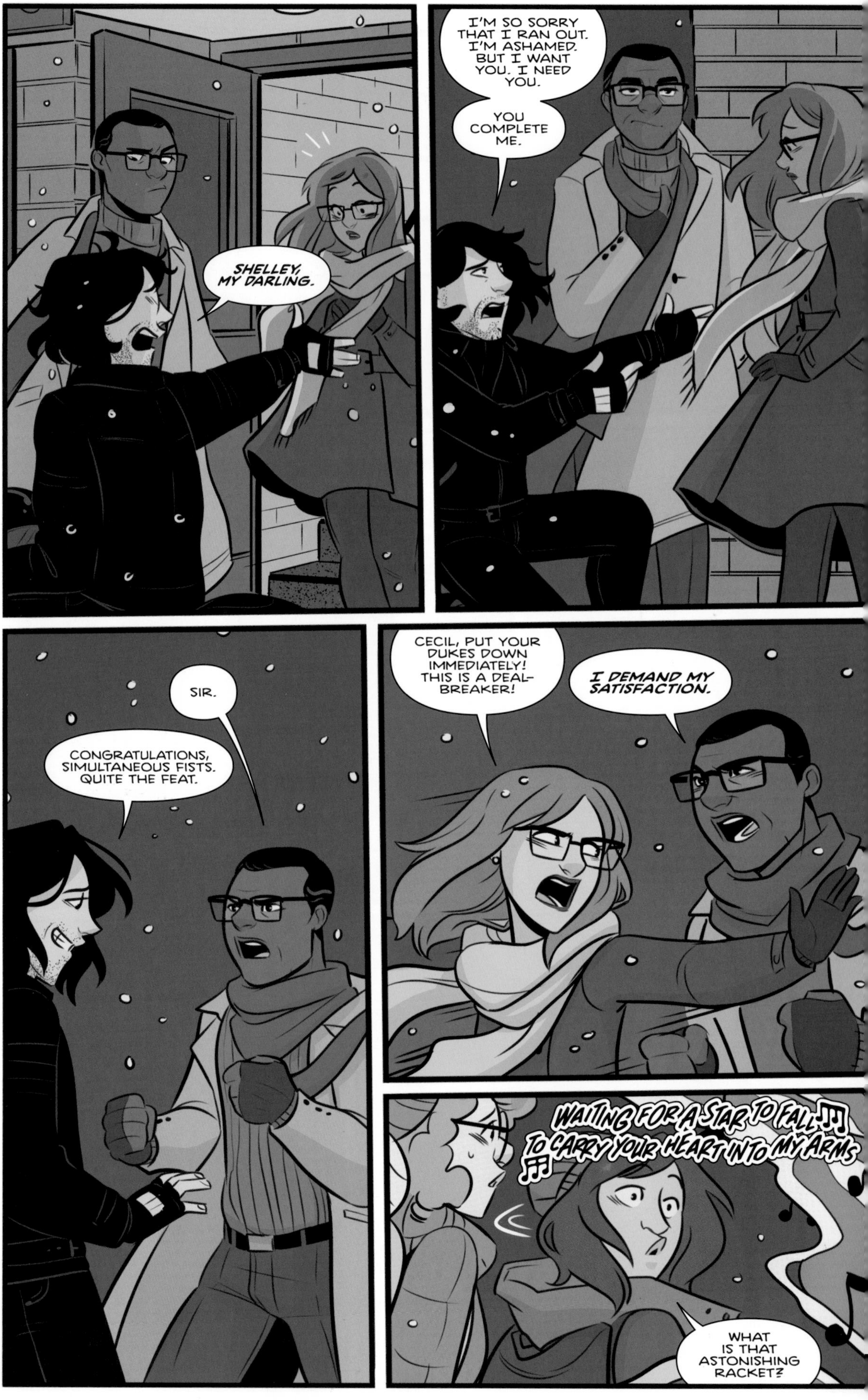
SHELLEY, MY DARLING.
I'M SO SORRY THAT I RAN OUT. I'M ASHAMED. BUT I WANT YOU. I NEED YOU.
YOU COMPLETE ME.
SIR.
CONGRATULATIONS, SIMULTANEOUS FISTS. QUITE THE FEAT.
CECIL, PUT YOUR DUKES DOWN IMMEDIATELY! THIS IS A DEAL-BREAKER!
I DEMAND MY SATISFACTION.
WAITING FOR A STAR TO FALL
TO CARRY YOUR HEART INTO MY ARMS
WHAT IS THAT ASTONISHING RACKET?

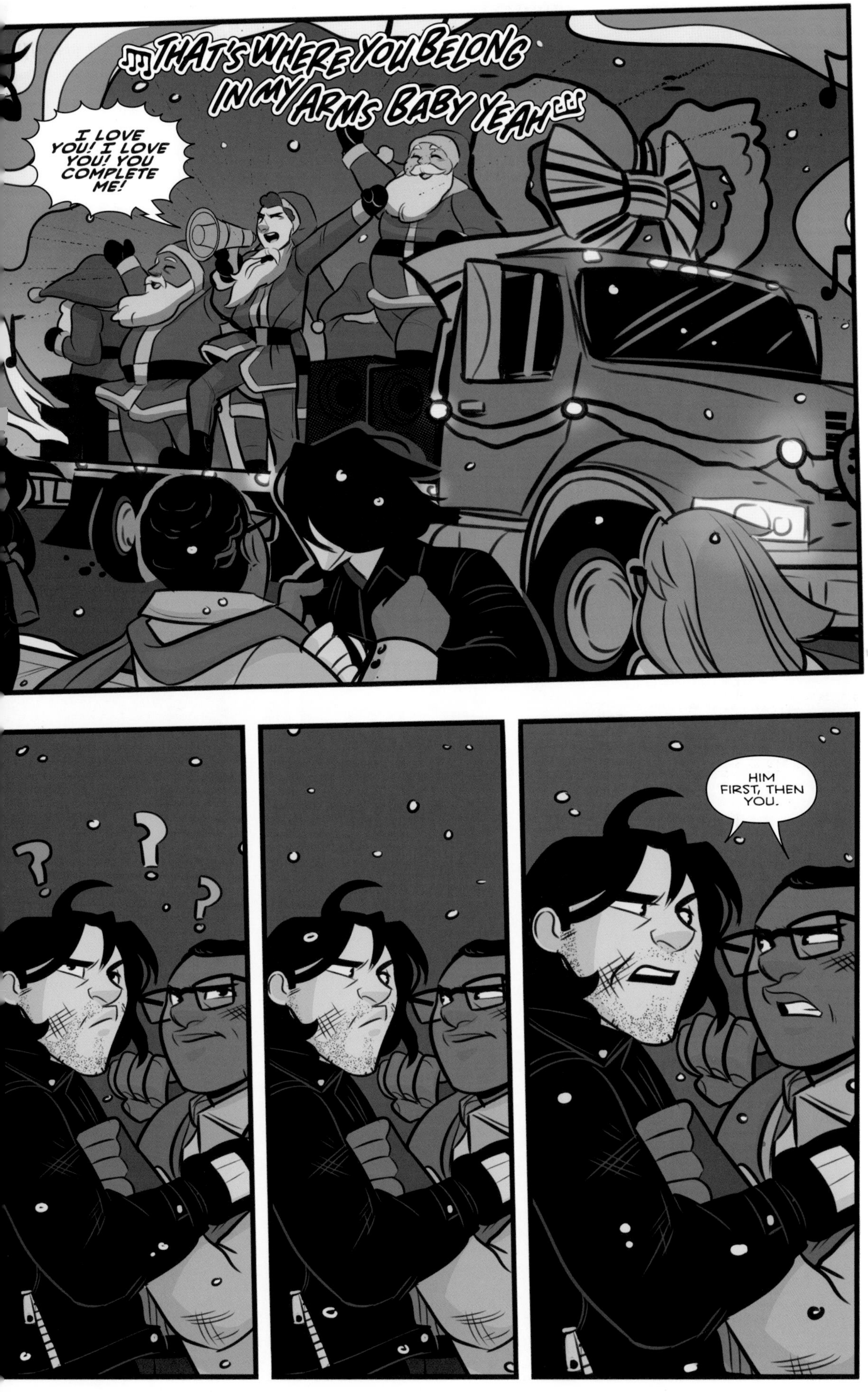

THAT'S WHERE YOU BELONG IN MY ARMS BABY YEAH
I LOVE YOU! I LOVE YOU! YOU COMPLETE ME!
?
?
?
HIM FIRST, THEN YOU.

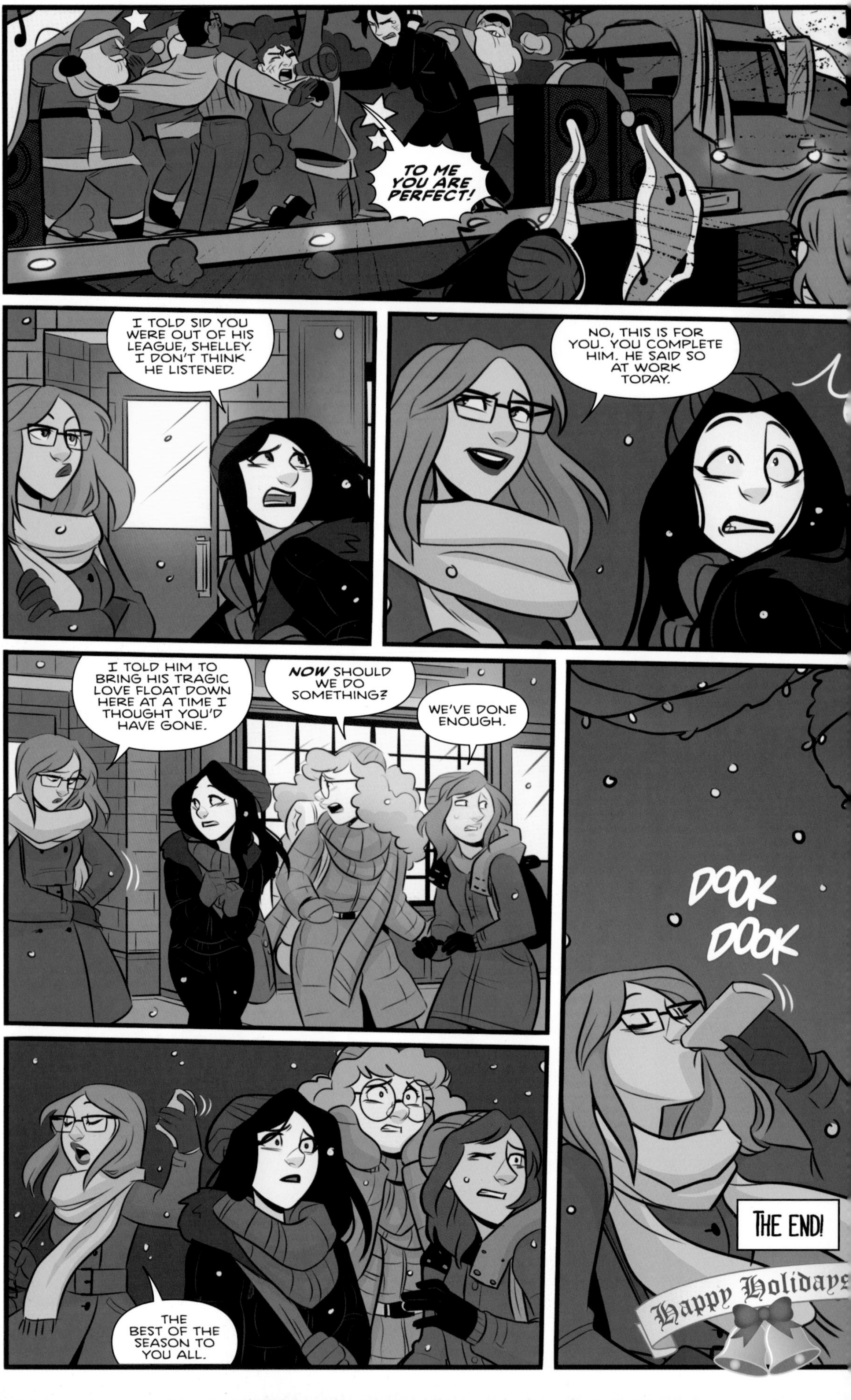
TO ME YOU ARE PERFECT!
I TOLD SID YOU WERE OUT OF HIS LEAGUE, SHELLEY. I DON'T THINK HE LISTENED.
NO, THIS IS FOR YOU. YOU COMPLETE HIM. HE SAID SO AT WORK TODAY.
I TOLD HIM TO BRING HIS TRAGIC LOVE FLOAT DOWN HERE AT A TIME I THOUGHT YOU'D HAVE GONE.
NOW SHOULD WE DO SOMETHING?
WE'VE DONE ENOUGH.
THE BEST OF THE SEASON TO YOU ALL.
DOOK DOOK
THE END!
Happy Holidays

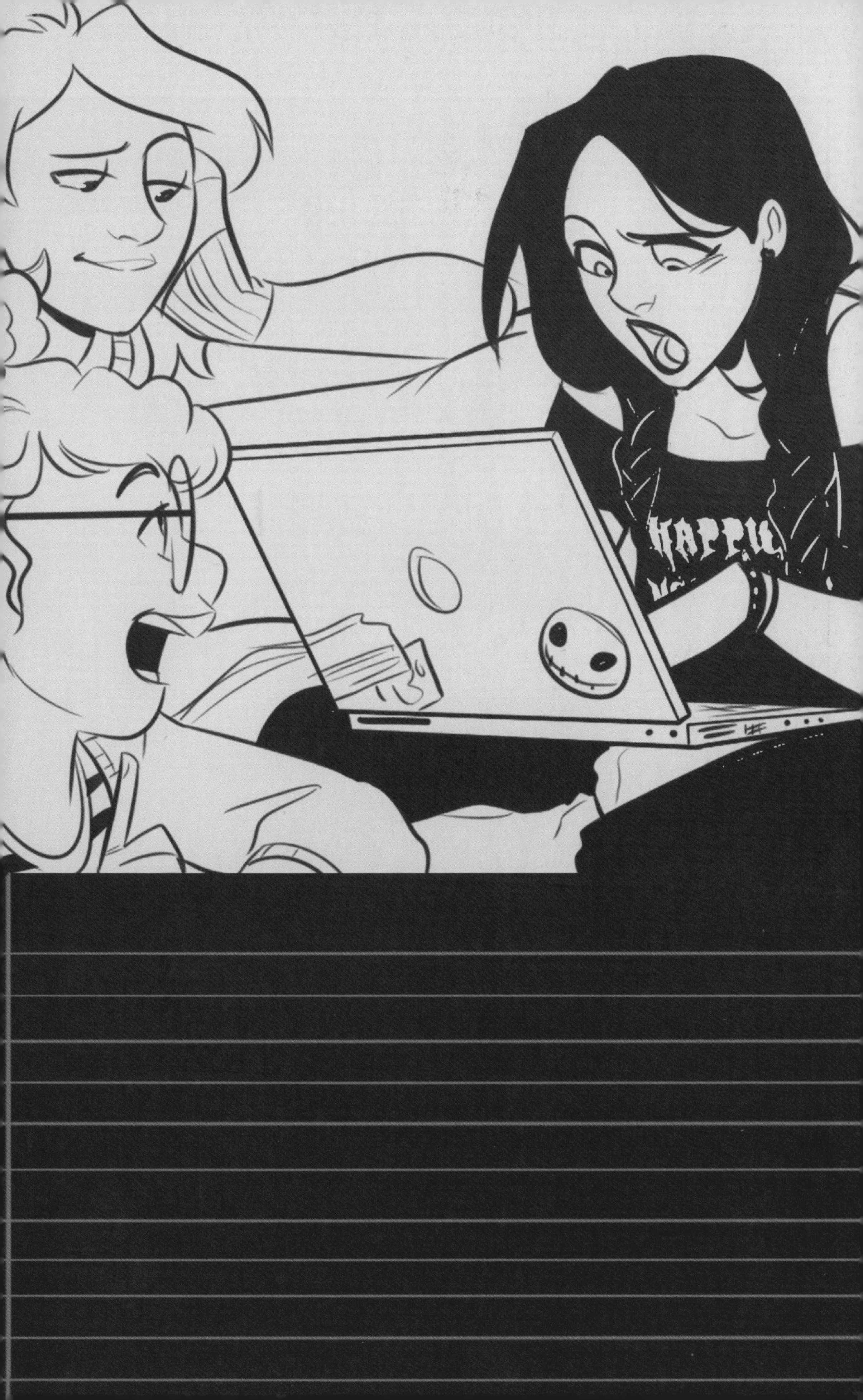

FRIDGE RAIDER BY JOHN ALLISON

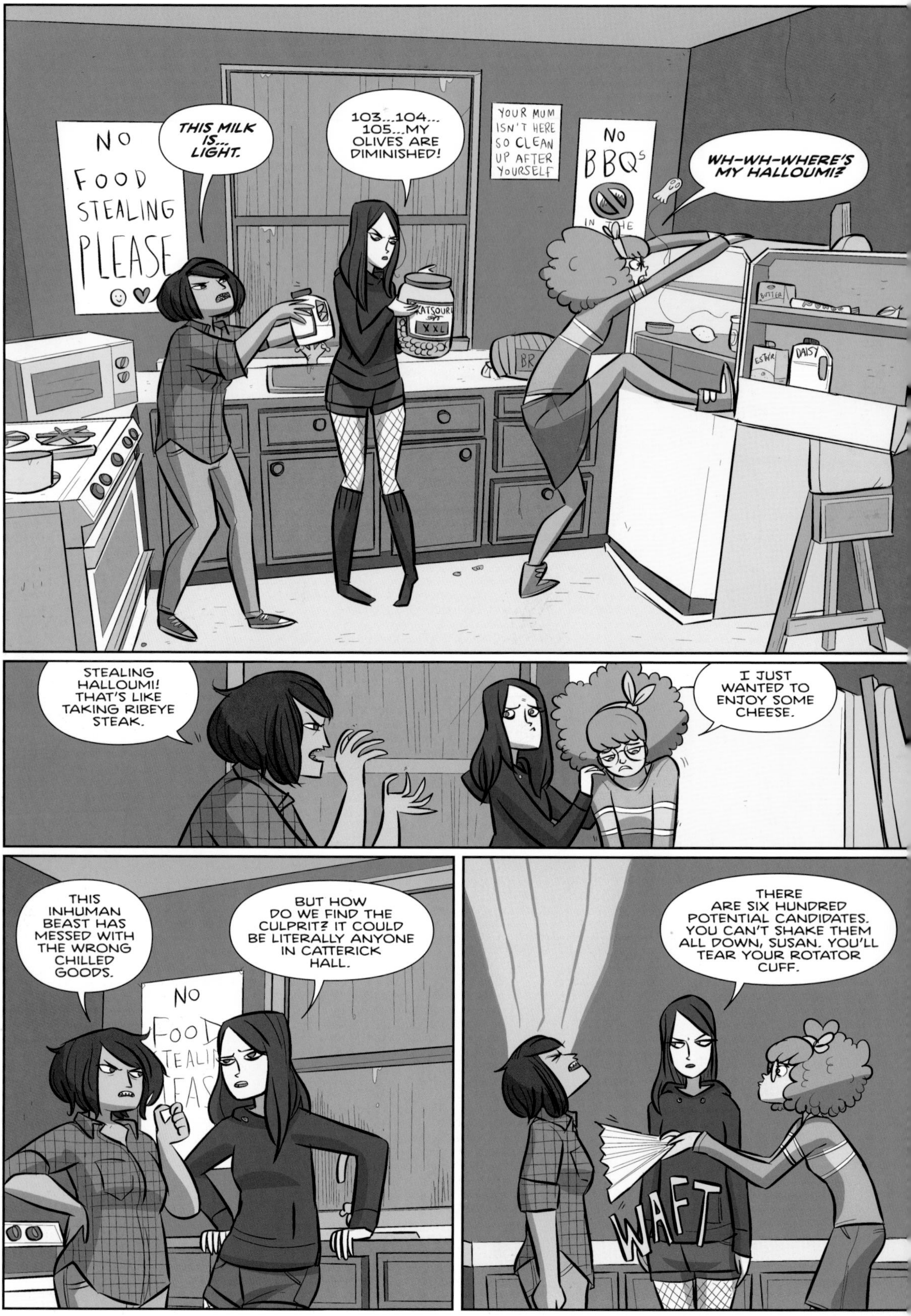
NO FOOD STEALING PLEASE
THIS MILK IS... LIGHT.
103...104... 105...MY OLIVES ARE DIMINISHED!
YOUR MUM ISN'T HERE SO CLEAN UP AFTER YOURSELF
WH-WH-WHERE'S MY HALLOUMI?
STEALING HALLOUMI! THAT'S LIKE TAKING RIBEYE STEAK.
I JUST WANTED TO ENJOY SOME CHEESE.
THIS INHUMAN BEAST HAS MESSED WITH THE WRONG CHILLED GOODS.
BUT HOW DO WE FIND THE CULPRIT? IT COULD BE LITERALLY ANYONE IN CATTERICK HALL.
THERE ARE SIX HUNDRED POTENTIAL CANDIDATES. YOU CAN'T SHAKE THEM ALL DOWN, SUSAN. YOU'LL TEAR YOUR ROTATOR CUFF.
WAFT

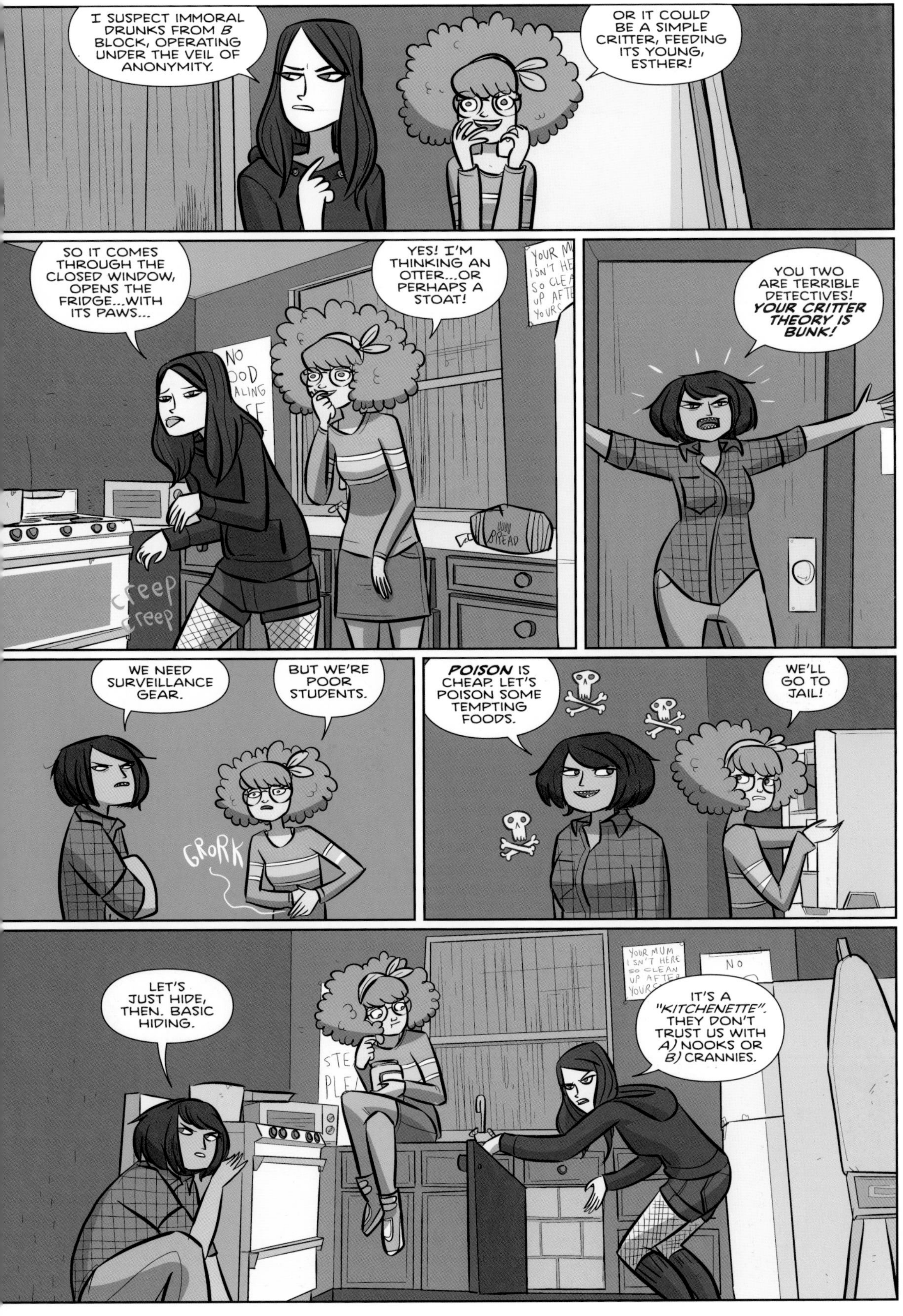
I SUSPECT IMMORAL DRUNKS FROM *B* BLOCK, OPERATING UNDER THE VEIL OF ANONYMITY.
OR IT COULD BE A SIMPLE CRITTER, FEEDING ITS YOUNG, ESTHER!
SO IT COMES THROUGH THE CLOSED WINDOW, OPENS THE FRIDGE...WITH ITS PAWS...
YES! I'M THINKING AN OTTER...OR PERHAPS A STOAT!
BREAD
creep creep
YOU TWO ARE TERRIBLE DETECTIVES! ***YOUR CRITTER THEORY IS BUNK!***
WE NEED SURVEILLANCE GEAR.
BUT WE'RE POOR STUDENTS.
GRORK
POISON IS CHEAP. LET'S POISON SOME TEMPTING FOODS.
WE'LL GO TO JAIL!
LET'S JUST HIDE, THEN. BASIC HIDING.
IT'S A *"KITCHENETTE"*. THEY DON'T TRUST US WITH *A)* NOOKS OR *B)* CRANNIES.

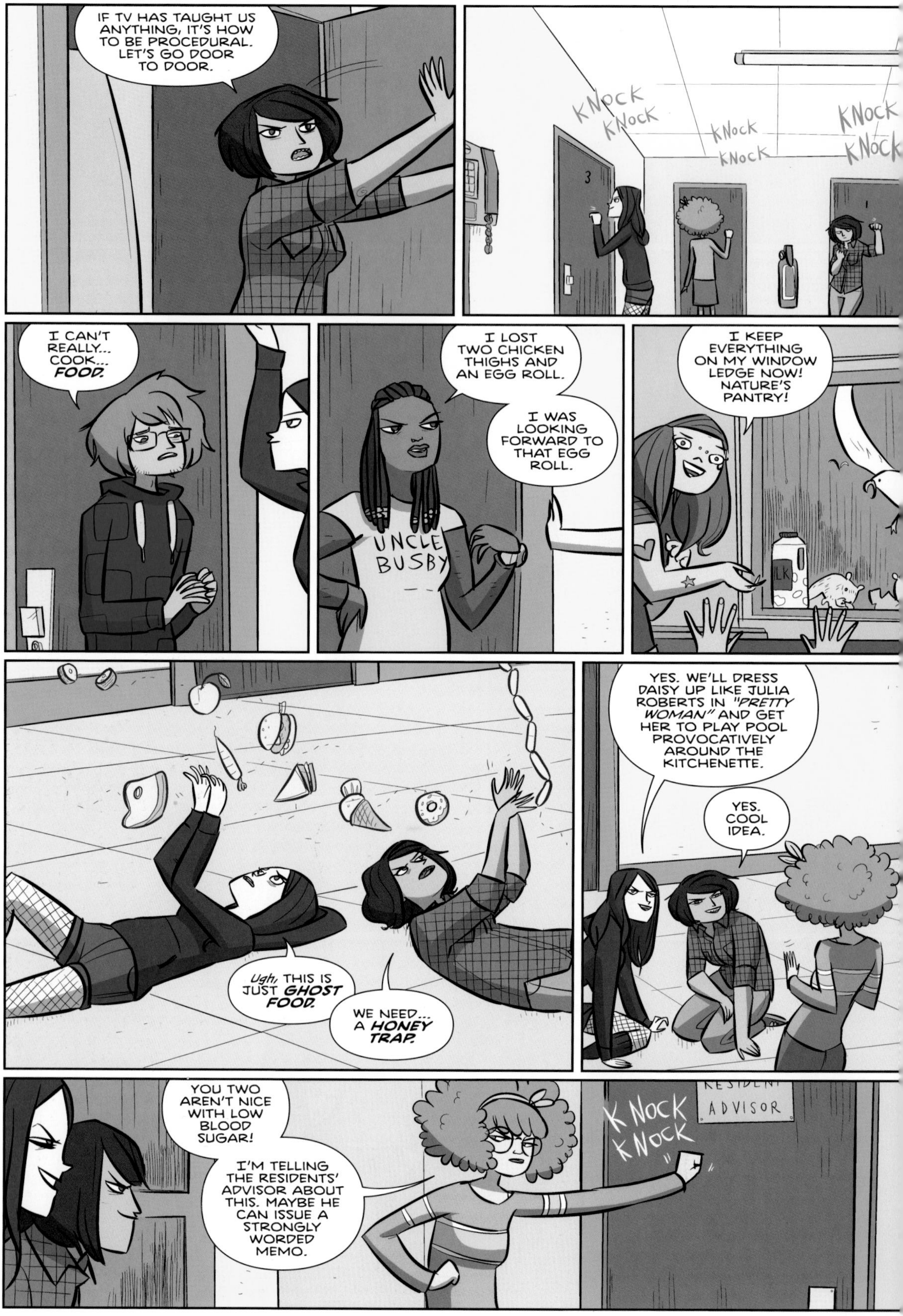
IF TV HAS TAUGHT US ANYTHING, IT'S HOW TO BE PROCEDURAL. LET'S GO DOOR TO DOOR.
KNOCK KNOCK
KNOCK KNOCK
KNOCK KNOCK
3
I CAN'T REALLY... COOK... FOOD.
I LOST TWO CHICKEN THIGHS AND AN EGG ROLL.
I WAS LOOKING FORWARD TO THAT EGG ROLL.
UNCLE BUSBY
I KEEP EVERYTHING ON MY WINDOW LEDGE NOW! NATURE'S PANTRY!
Ugh, THIS IS JUST GHOST FOOD.
WE NEED... A HONEY TRAP.
YES. WE'LL DRESS DAISY UP LIKE JULIA ROBERTS IN "PRETTY WOMAN" AND GET HER TO PLAY POOL PROVOCATIVELY AROUND THE KITCHENETTE.
YES. COOL IDEA.
YOU TWO AREN'T NICE WITH LOW BLOOD SUGAR!
I'M TELLING THE RESIDENTS' ADVISOR ABOUT THIS. MAYBE HE CAN ISSUE A STRONGLY WORDED MEMO.
ADVISOR
KNOCK KNOCK

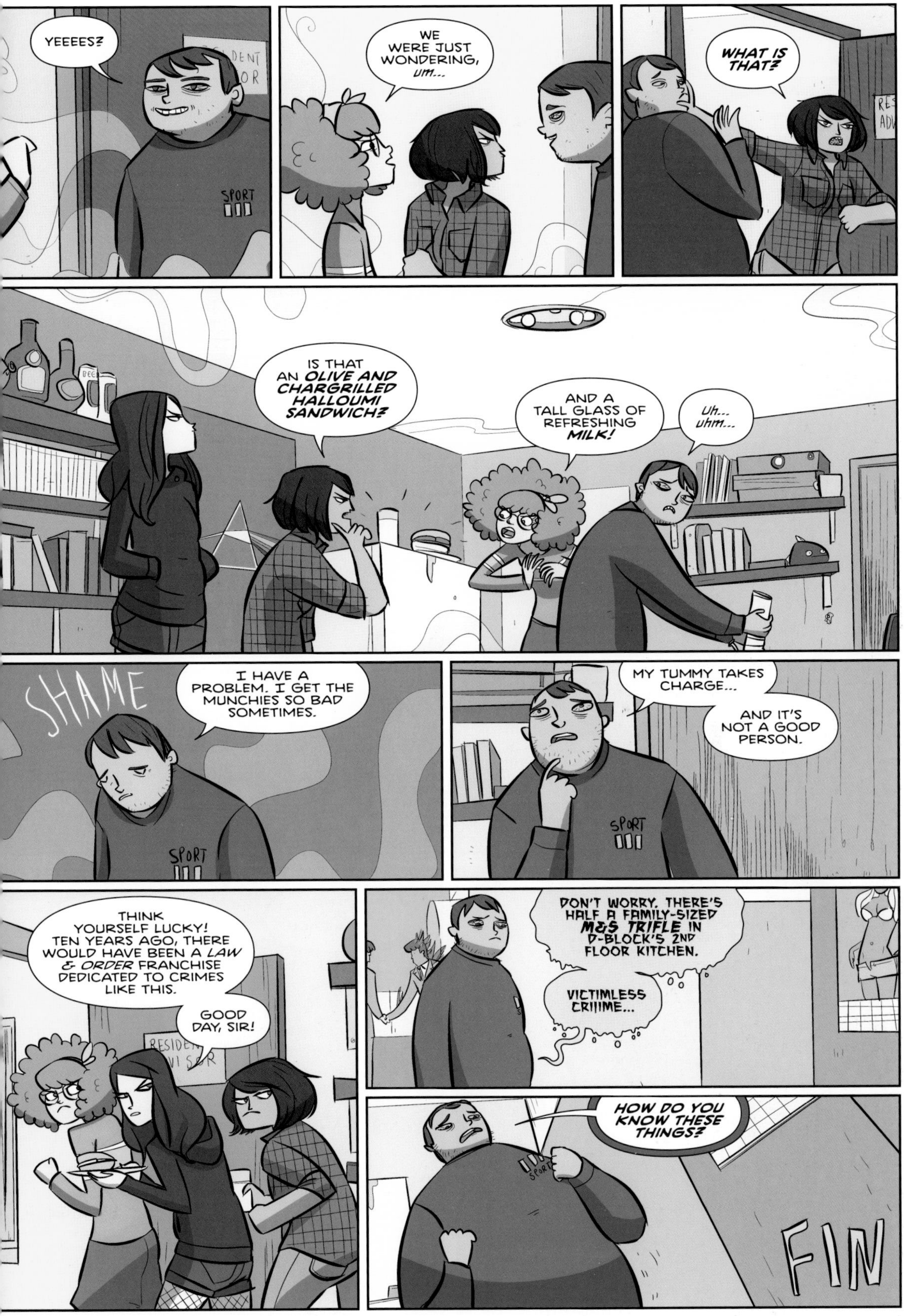
YEEEES?
WE WERE JUST WONDERING, UM...
WHAT IS THAT?
IS THAT AN OLIVE AND CHARGRILLED HALLOUMI SANDWICH?
AND A TALL GLASS OF REFRESHING MILK!
Uh... uhm...
SHAME
I HAVE A PROBLEM. I GET THE MUNCHIES SO BAD SOMETIMES.
MY TUMMY TAKES CHARGE...
AND IT'S NOT A GOOD PERSON.
THINK YOURSELF LUCKY! TEN YEARS AGO, THERE WOULD HAVE BEEN A LAW & ORDER FRANCHISE DEDICATED TO CRIMES LIKE THIS.
GOOD DAY, SIR!
DON'T WORRY. THERE'S HALF A FAMILY-SIZED M&S TRIFLE IN D-BLOCK'S 2ND FLOOR KITCHEN.
VICTIMLESS CRIIIME...
HOW DO YOU KNOW THESE THINGS?
FIN

MUSIC IS IMPORTANT BY JOHN ALLISON

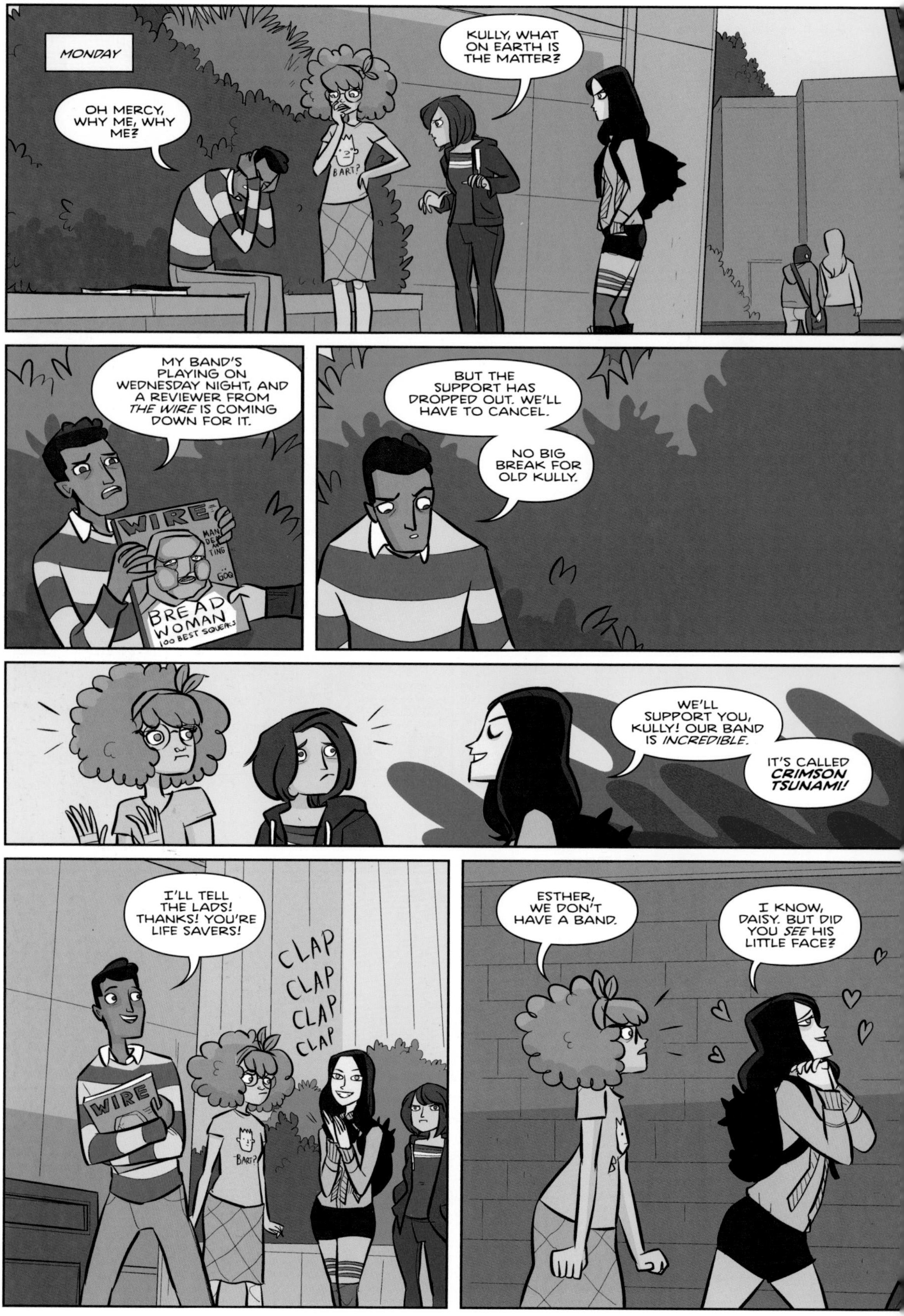
MONDAY
OH MERCY, WHY ME, WHY ME?
KULLY, WHAT ON EARTH IS THE MATTER?
MY BAND'S PLAYING ON WEDNESDAY NIGHT, AND A REVIEWER FROM THE WIRE IS COMING DOWN FOR IT.
WIRE
BREAD WOMAN
100 BEST SQUEAKS
BUT THE SUPPORT HAS DROPPED OUT. WE'LL HAVE TO CANCEL.
NO BIG BREAK FOR OLD KULLY.
WE'LL SUPPORT YOU, KULLY! OUR BAND IS INCREDIBLE.
IT'S CALLED CRIMSON TSUNAMI!
I'LL TELL THE LADS! THANKS! YOU'RE LIFE SAVERS!
CLAP CLAP CLAP CLAP
WIRE
ESTHER, WE DON'T HAVE A BAND.
I KNOW, DAISY. BUT DID YOU SEE HIS LITTLE FACE?

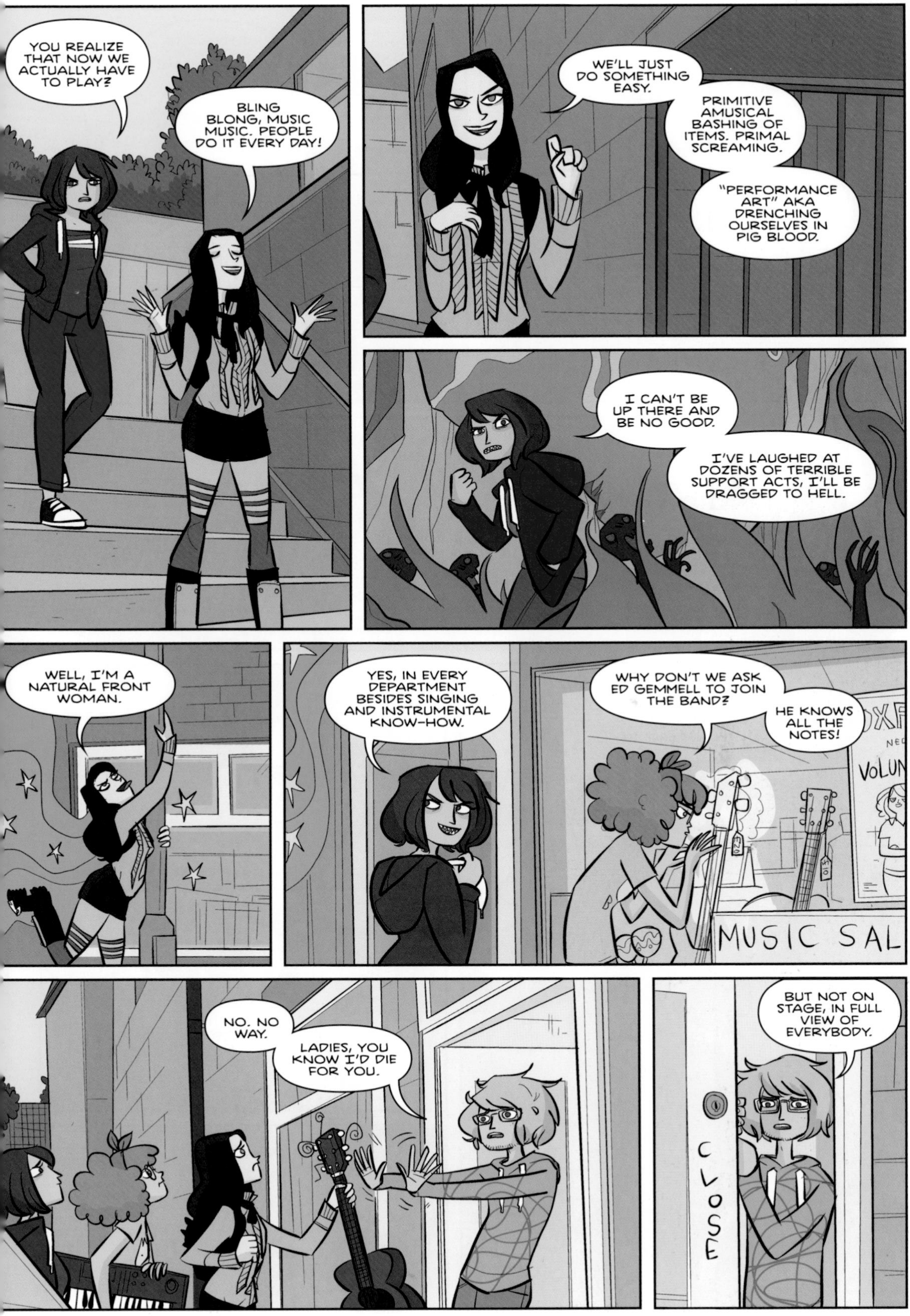
YOU REALIZE THAT NOW WE ACTUALLY HAVE TO PLAY?
BLING BLONG, MUSIC MUSIC. PEOPLE DO IT EVERY DAY!
WE'LL JUST DO SOMETHING EASY.
PRIMITIVE AMUSICAL BASHING OF ITEMS. PRIMAL SCREAMING.
"PERFORMANCE ART" AKA DRENCHING OURSELVES IN PIG BLOOD.
I CAN'T BE UP THERE AND BE NO GOOD.
I'VE LAUGHED AT DOZENS OF TERRIBLE SUPPORT ACTS, I'LL BE DRAGGED TO HELL.
WELL, I'M A NATURAL FRONT WOMAN.
YES, IN EVERY DEPARTMENT BESIDES SINGING AND INSTRUMENTAL KNOW-HOW.
WHY DON'T WE ASK ED GEMMELL TO JOIN THE BAND?
HE KNOWS ALL THE NOTES!
MUSIC SAL
NO. NO WAY.
LADIES, YOU KNOW I'D DIE FOR YOU.
CLOSE
BUT NOT ON STAGE, IN FULL VIEW OF EVERYBODY.

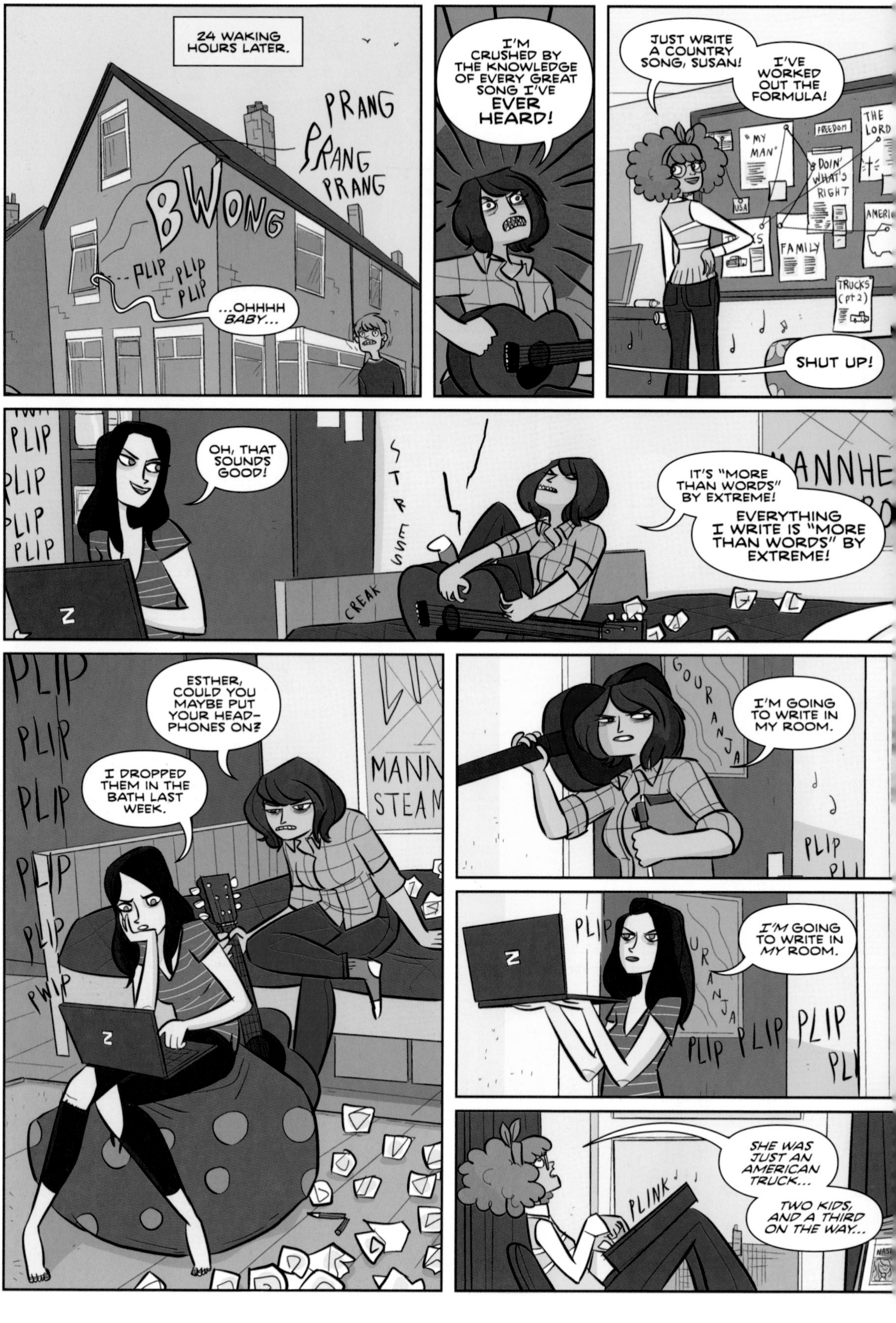
24 WAKING HOURS LATER.
PRANG
PRANG
PRANG
PRANG
BWONG
PLIP PLIP PLIP
...OHHHH BABY...
I'M CRUSHED BY THE KNOWLEDGE OF EVERY GREAT SONG I'VE EVER HEARD!
JUST WRITE A COUNTRY SONG, SUSAN!
I'VE WORKED OUT THE FORMULA!
"MY MAN"
FREEDOM
THE LORD
DOIN' WHAT'S RIGHT
USA
FAMILY
TRUCKS (pt 2)
SHUT UP!
PLIP
PLIP
PLIP
PLIP
OH, THAT SOUNDS GOOD!
STRESS
CREAK
IT'S "MORE THAN WORDS" BY EXTREME!
EVERYTHING I WRITE IS "MORE THAN WORDS" BY EXTREME!
ESTHER, COULD YOU MAYBE PUT YOUR HEAD-PHONES ON?
I DROPPED THEM IN THE BATH LAST WEEK.
PLIP
PLIP
PLIP
PLIP
PLIP
PWIP
GOURANJA
I'M GOING TO WRITE IN MY ROOM.
PLIP
I'M GOING TO WRITE IN MY ROOM.
PLIP
PLIP PLIP PLIP
SHE WAS JUST AN AMERICAN TRUCK...
TWO KIDS, AND A THIRD ON THE WAY...
PLINK

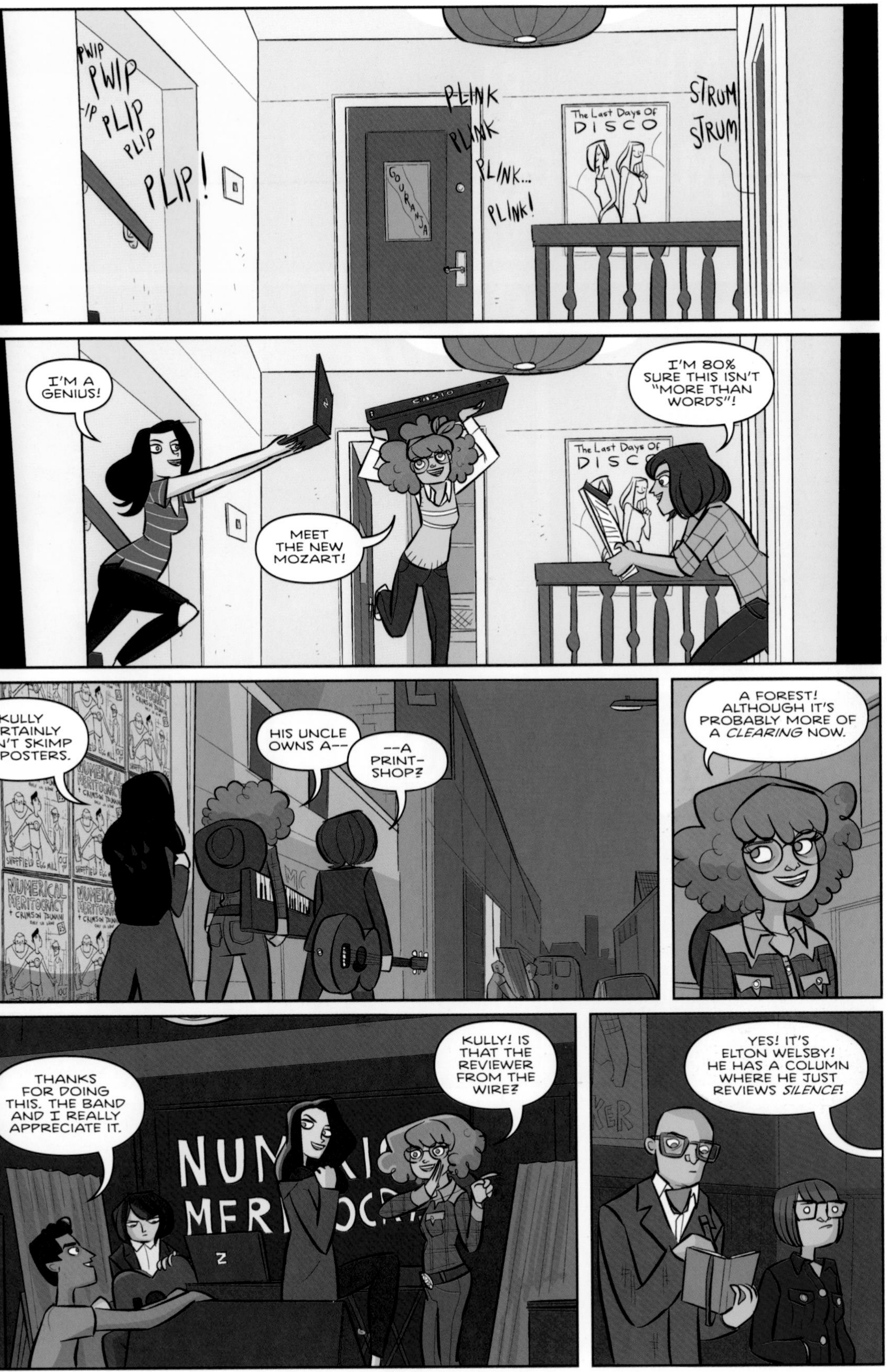
PWIP
PWIP
-IP PLIP
PLIP
PLIP!
PLINK
PLINK
PLINK...
PLINK!
The Last Days Of DISCO
STRUM
STRUM
GOURANJA
I'M A GENIUS!
MEET THE NEW MOZART!
CASIO
I'M 80% SURE THIS ISN'T "MORE THAN WORDS"!
The Last Days Of DISCO
KULLY CERTAINLY DIDN'T SKIMP ON POSTERS.
HIS UNCLE OWNS A--
--A PRINT-SHOP?
NUMERICAL MERITOCRACY
+ CRIMSON TSUNAMI
A FOREST! ALTHOUGH IT'S PROBABLY MORE OF A *CLEARING* NOW.
THANKS FOR DOING THIS. THE BAND AND I REALLY APPRECIATE IT.
KULLY! IS THAT THE REVIEWER FROM THE WIRE?
YES! IT'S ELTON WELSBY! HE HAS A COLUMN WHERE HE JUST REVIEWS *SILENCE*!

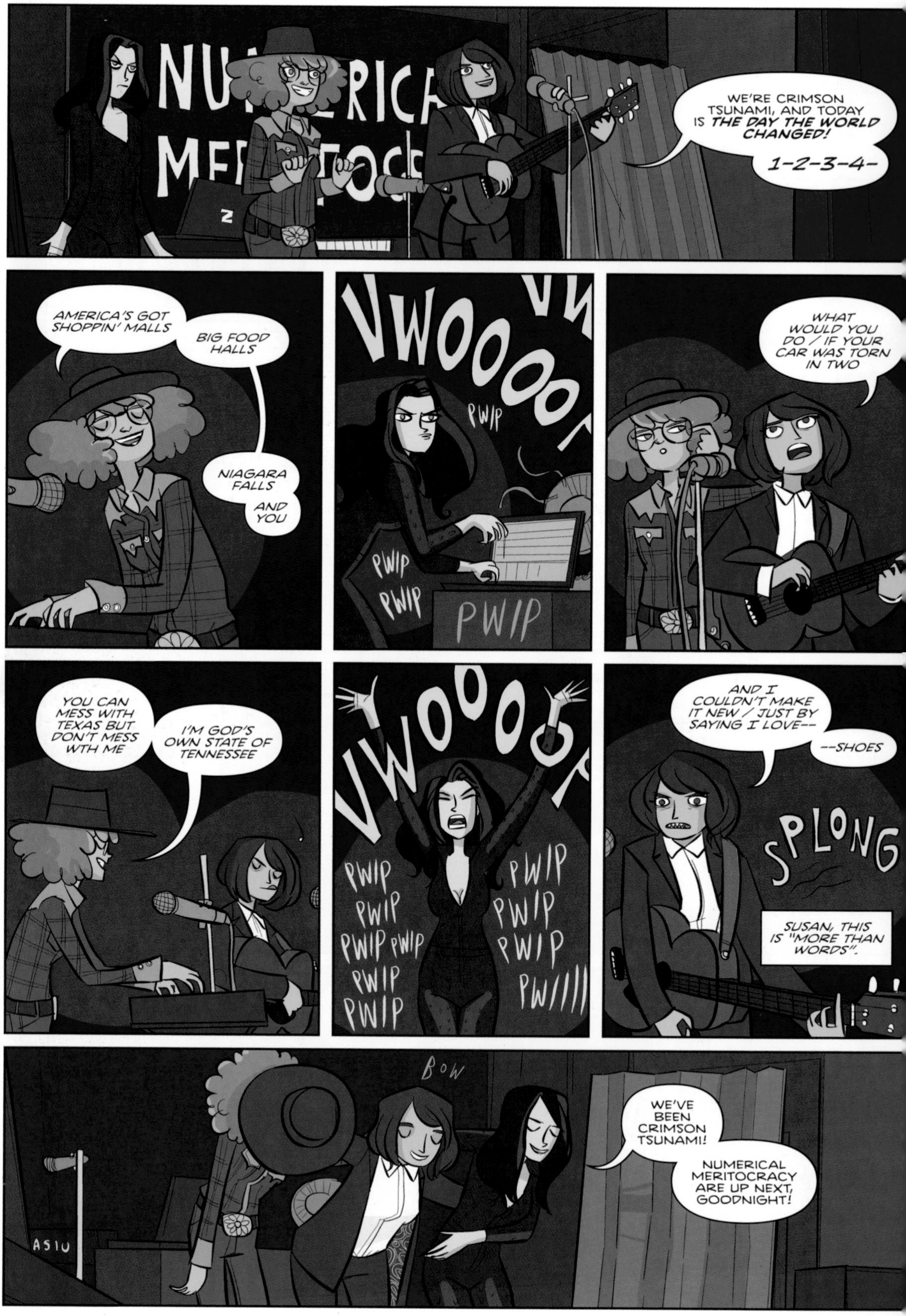
NU ERICA
ME OC
WE'RE CRIMSON TSUNAMI, AND TODAY IS ***THE DAY THE WORLD CHANGED!***
1-2-3-4-
AMERICA'S GOT SHOPPIN' MALLS
BIG FOOD HALLS
NIAGARA FALLS
AND YOU
VWOOOOR
PWIP
PWIP
PWIP
PWIP
WHAT WOULD YOU DO / IF YOUR CAR WAS TORN IN TWO
YOU CAN MESS WITH TEXAS BUT DON'T MESS WTH ME
I'M GOD'S OWN STATE OF TENNESSEE
VWOOOOR
PWIP
PWIP
PWIP PWIP
PWIP
PWIP
PWIP
PWIP
PWIP
PWIIII
AND I COULDN'T MAKE IT NEW / JUST BY SAYING I LOVE--
--SHOES
SPLONG
SUSAN, THIS IS "MORE THAN WORDS".
BOW
WE'VE BEEN CRIMSON TSUNAMI!
NUMERICAL MERITOCRACY ARE UP NEXT, GOODNIGHT!
ASIU

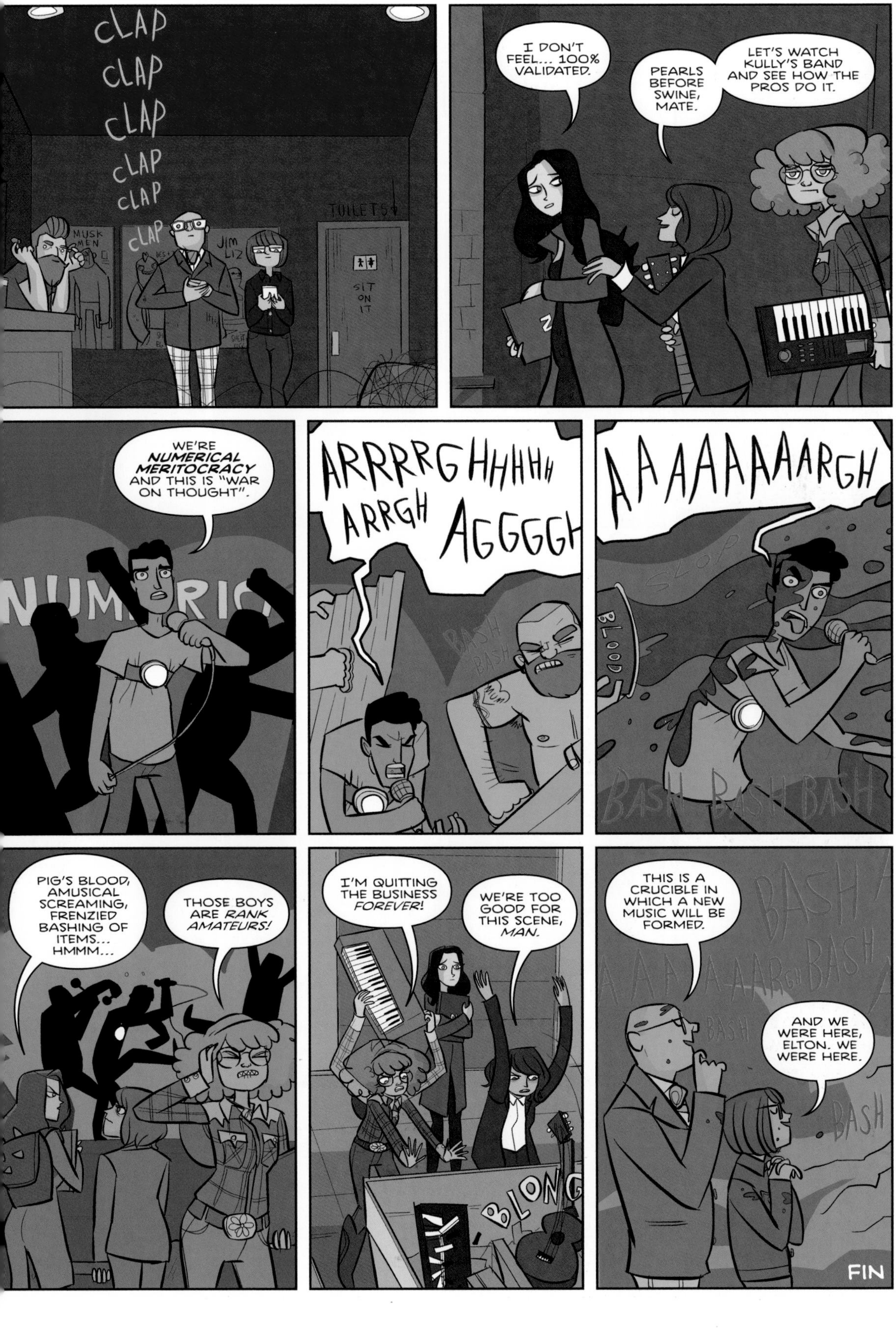
CLAP
CLAP
CLAP
CLAP
CLAP
CLAP
MUSK MEN
JIM LIZ
TOILETS
SIT ON IT
I DON'T FEEL... 100% VALIDATED.
PEARLS BEFORE SWINE, MATE.
LET'S WATCH KULLY'S BAND AND SEE HOW THE PROS DO IT.
WE'RE ***NUMERICAL MERITOCRACY*** AND THIS IS "WAR ON THOUGHT".
ARRRRGHHHHH
ARRGH
AGGGGH
BASH
BASH
AAAAAAAARGH
SLOP
BLOOD
BASH BASH BASH
PIG'S BLOOD, AMUSICAL SCREAMING, FRENZIED BASHING OF ITEMS... HMMM...
THOSE BOYS ARE *RANK AMATEURS!*
I'M QUITTING THE BUSINESS *FOREVER!*
WE'RE TOO GOOD FOR THIS SCENE, *MAN.*
BLONG
THIS IS A CRUCIBLE IN WHICH A NEW MUSIC WILL BE FORMED.
AND WE WERE HERE, ELTON. WE WERE HERE.
BASH
BASH
BASH
FIN

DISCOVER THE MYSTERY OF HISTORY, (OR AT LEAST SHELLEY'S VERY EXCITING AND NOT AT ALL PAPERWORK-BASED JOB AT THE MINISTRY OF IT), IN THIS SPECIAL SHORT...

DESTROY HISTORY! BY JOHN ALLISON

My baby takes the morning TRAIN
It is environ-mentally responsible
He works from nine to five and THEN
Yes now you are intrigued
He takes another *home again*
I mean what else is he going to do
To find me waiting for him.
WITH A GUN.
Good morning!
MINISTRY of HISTORY

Babs, I have been here for a month.
When will I learn the SECRETS of the Ministry of History?
FRENCH REVOLUTION (THE)
Secrets dear? What a treasure you are.
BABS!
This *secret panel* is hanging off and I can hear beeping!
I think that's the furnace timer.
BIP Beep Beep
Back to work.
Mr. Robespierre, you can't have a reign of terror wearing *candystripes*.
PAT PAT

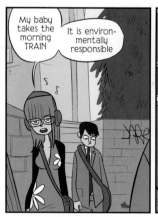

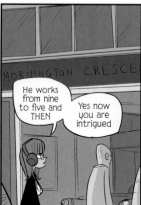

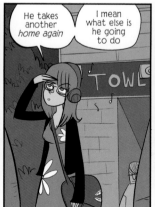

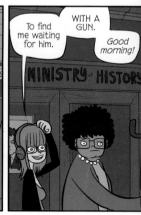

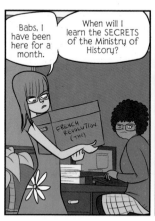

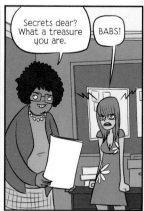

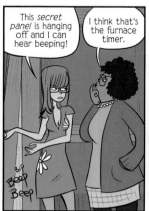

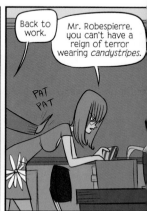

Congratulations, Shelley, you've passed your one-month probationary period.

You will now be allowed access to the secrets of the Ministry of History.

YESSS SECRETS YESSSSS.

Now, this contract just confirms that on leaving the Ministry...

I'LL SIGN IT, I LOVE SECRETS!

...all your memories of your time here will be wiped.

You have an old pro's way with an ellipsis, Mr. Warbeck.

The Ministry Of History is dedicated to maintaining the "flow" of history, Ms. Winters.

CLICK

Human memory is fallible, and so are events. Things fall out of order! We refer to this as "future creep".

This is bananas. It sounds made up.

In this facility, we return people and places to their correct order.

That's why you're here.

I assume I do this with a drone. Or nanobots!

Controlled from a remote, extremely comfortable location.

CHUNK
WHIRRRRRRR

Fixing history sounds blue collar! And *I've passed the civil service exam!*

Shelley, you were specially selected for this job.

Here is your Nemulon unit. Don't lose it.

Just what I've always wanted. *In a way?*

Barbara will take you through the technicalities.

Babs, there's been a terrible mistake.

We'll get you started with a level one event. Nothing too tricky.

And they gave you a Nemulon-9. Good, no one's exploded using one of those yet.

What the Dickens do I do with a Viking helmet with headlamps?

It's biometric. Put your palm on the top.

Okay...

BWAAAK!

It's a cybernetic demonoid!

A STEAM-PUNK NIGHT-MARE!!

This must be the "unflappability" you talked about in your interview.

Bash its nut in with a stapler, Babs! Then we can throw its brain in the River Thames!

I see, so this abomination is going to help me...right the wrongs of history.

Who designs these awful things?

Better. Much better.

How do you tell if history has gone wrong anyway? Wouldn't we just think it had *always been that way*?

The Ministry keeps an indestructible record.

History started going wrong after you invented these things, didn't it? DIDN'T IT?

YOU ARE SO BUSTED, BABS.

So Shelley, are you ready for your first historical rectification?

No! I've had no training!

PLONK

In fact, I'm not sure this is what I want to do with my li-

PUSH

-fe.

Oh CHIP-STICKS.

History! History! I'm in history! What do I do?

It's history with houses! Houses and cars!

I can work with this!

DUST

History with judgemental staring!

Am I showing too much leg for the era??

I don't want to scandalise people with my gams!

SORRY ABOUT MY EROTIC KNEES!

NOT ACTUALLY SORRY!

Now what do I do?

THE YEAR IS 1941.

TUG

Ahh! Time ghosts!! Help me, time ghosts!

YOU HAVE 72 HOURS TO ENGAGE HEDY LAMARR IN THE WAR EFFORT.

Nemulon!! I forgot you were on top of my head.

So I need to get old Hedy in the USO show?

Singing a patriotic song with Mister WC Fields?

YOUR CURRENT SUCCESS PROJECTION IS 4.8%.

If you can't be inconspicu-ous, you could at least be *encouraging.*

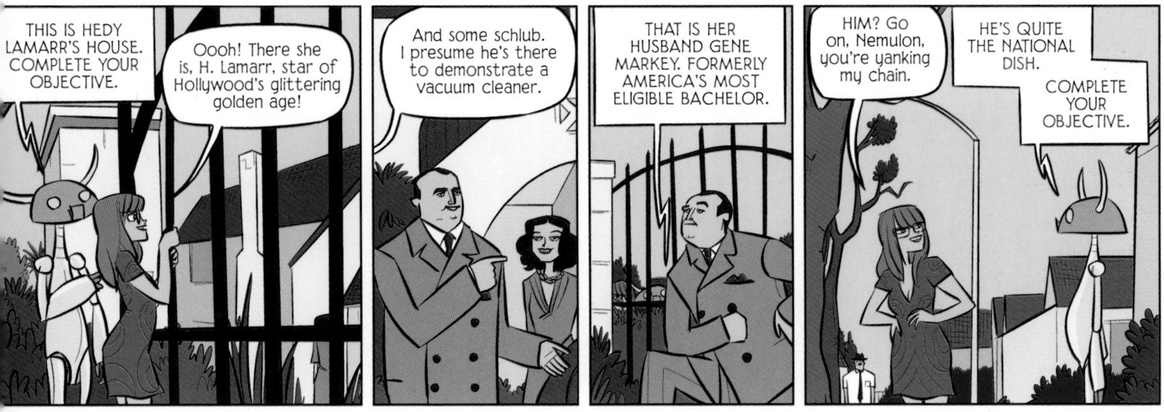
THIS IS HEDY LAMARR'S HOUSE. COMPLETE YOUR OBJECTIVE.
Oooh! There she is, H. Lamarr, star of Hollywood's glittering golden age!
And some schlub. I presume he's there to demonstrate a vacuum cleaner.
THAT IS HER HUSBAND GENE MARKEY. FORMERLY AMERICA'S MOST ELIGIBLE BACHELOR.
HIM? Go on, Nemulon, you're yanking my chain.
HE'S QUITE THE NATIONAL DISH.
COMPLETE YOUR OBJECTIVE.

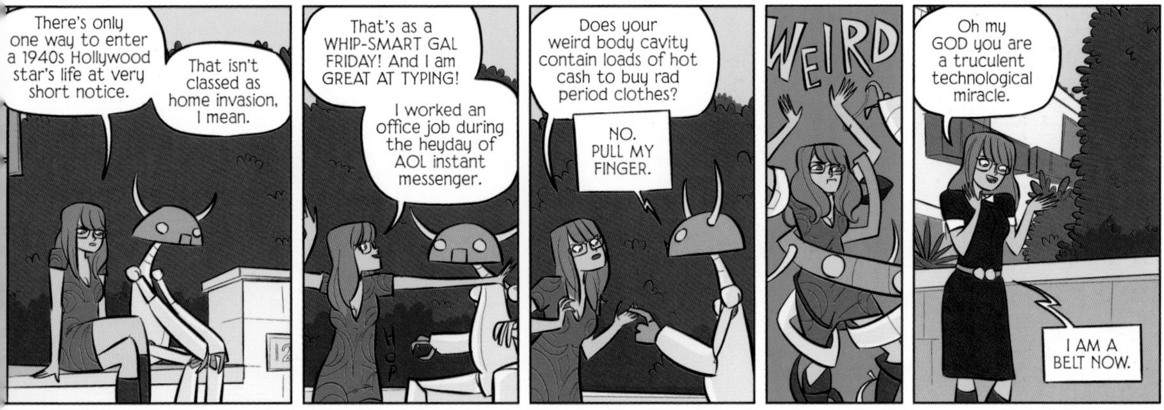
There's only one way to enter a 1940s Hollywood star's life at very short notice.
That isn't classed as home invasion, I mean.
That's as a WHIP-SMART GAL FRIDAY! And I am GREAT AT TYPING!
I worked an office job during the heyday of AOL instant messenger.
HOP
Does your weird body cavity contain loads of hot cash to buy rad period clothes?
NO. PULL MY FINGER.
WEIRD
Oh my GOD you are a truculent technological miracle.
I AM A BELT NOW.

Good MAWNING Ms. Lamarr, the studio sent me over.

Well I didn't ask for anybody.

Well Mr. Mayer was under the impression that you required an assistant.

Well I require nothing of the sort, Miss...?

Schrift, Shirley Schrift.

Well I shall have to telephone Mr. Mayer and ask him to take you back.

TROT TROT

Well you see the MGM lion is loose again, Ms. Lamarr, so I wouldn't bother him now.

WELL!

Now Ms. Schrift, you may set up your work here. There is only one rule in this house.

Make use of any of the facilities. Food, drink, whatever you like.

If you want to try on my beautiful clothes while we're out and parade around like a jackass, feel free.

I *applaud.*

There is one thing in this house you keep your hands off: MY GENE MARKEY.

There's not a girl doesn't blow her wig around him, and it's easy to see why.

So, if you feel at all goofy, *take a bromide.*

Cigarette, Ms. Schrift?
No, thank you.
I see, old fashioned gal, eh?
FLICK
No, I would love to smoke all those lovely cigarettes.
But it's very addictive and gives you the canker.
Well I never heard such a thing.
The Surgeon General says it strengthens lungs, teeth and bones.
TYPE
TYPE
TYPE
Mr. Markey, it's a tiny dirty bonfire you suck into your body.
So it is!

Miss Schrift, this memo is slapdash and ackadaisical! What does "open bracket dash colon" mean?
I'm sorry, Ms. Lamarr, I know it's bad. I was... distracted.
Mr. Markey told me at least forty incredible anecdotes. He's a hurricane of chat.
Hm. Yes he is. Well, wear earmuffs in future.
Are you engaged this evening? We're attending a party at a neighbor's house. He's an *endocrinologist*.
Oh yes?
I'm going to see if he can do something about my jugs.

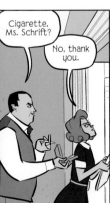

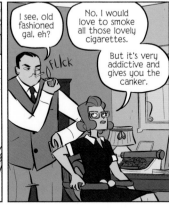

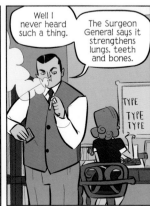

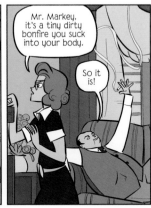

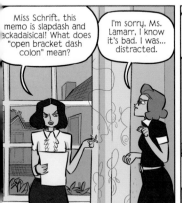

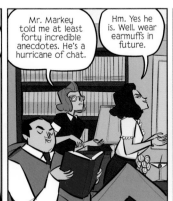

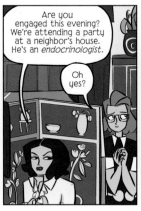

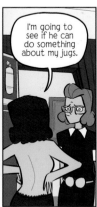

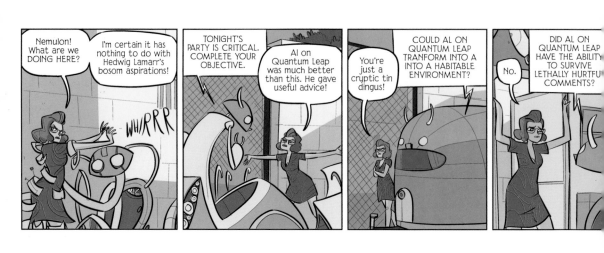

Nemulon! What are we DOING HERE?

I'm certain it has nothing to do with Hedwig Lamarr's bosom aspirations!

WHIRRR

TONIGHT'S PARTY IS CRITICAL. COMPLETE YOUR OBJECTIVE.

Al on Quantum Leap was much better than this. He gave useful advice!

You're just a cryptic tin dingus!

COULD AL ON QUANTUM LEAP TRANFORM INTO A INTO A HABITABLE ENVIRONMENT?

No.

DID AL ON QUANTUM LEAP HAVE THE ABILITY TO SURVIVE LETHALLY HURTFU COMMENTS?

...and I believe that, having studied his charts in Esquire magazine...

...George Antheil is the nation's foremost expert on *glands*.

He's also the "bad boy of music", Miss Schrift.

WHAT.

Oh, he causes riots!

He pointed an airplane propellor at a New York audience.

And he has a boxer's nose! BAFF!

He sounds like exactly the sort of man I would trust with my anatomy.

Though not...*in a medical sense.*

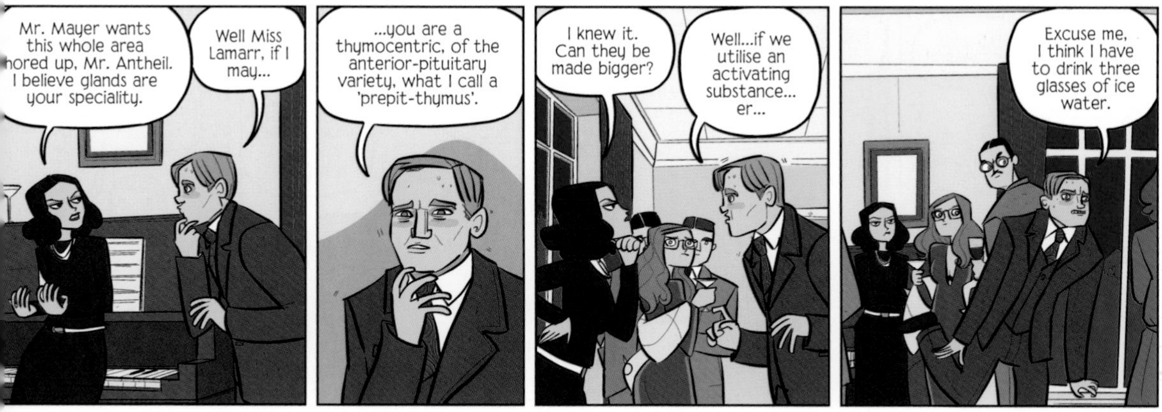
Mr. Mayer wants this whole area hored up, Mr. Antheil. I believe glands are your speciality.
Well Miss Lamarr, if I may...
...you are a thymocentric, of the anterior-pituitary variety, what I call a 'prepit-thymus'.
I knew it. Can they be made bigger?
Well...if we utilise an activating substance... er...
Excuse me, I think I have to drink three glasses of ice water.

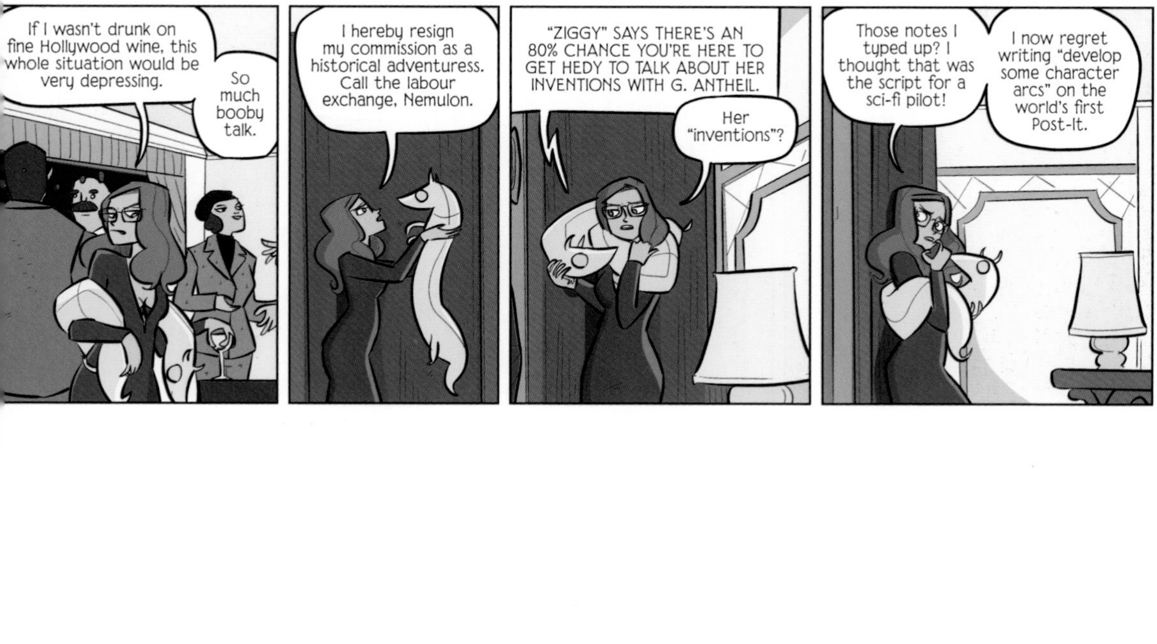
If I wasn't drunk on fine Hollywood wine, this whole situation would be very depressing.
So much booby talk.
I hereby resign my commission as a historical adventuress. Call the labour exchange, Nemulon.
"ZIGGY" SAYS THERE'S AN 80% CHANCE YOU'RE HERE TO GET HEDY TO TALK ABOUT HER INVENTIONS WITH G. ANTHEIL.
Her "inventions"?
Those notes I typed up? I thought that was the script for a sci-fi pilot!
I now regret writing "develop some character arcs" on the world's first Post-It.

Mr. Antheil, can I show you some-thing?
MORE... ICE WATER.
This...is the KEYTAR!
it is the most advanced musical instrument ever invented and VERY AVANT-GARDE.
WHIP
BIP BOP BOOP
All you have to do to own this incredible dream device...
YES?
...is get Hedy Lamarr off the subject of her frankly extra-order rack.
Talk about the war. She's war potty.
I think it worked.
THIS IS THE MOST SENSUAL NIGHT OF HIS LIFE.

Hedy and Antheil have been in there talking about torpedoes for hours, Miss Schrift.
It's getting me interested in the war. I'm a patriot too, after all.
WRITE WRITE
Maybe it's time for me to re-enlist, be... an admiral or something similar.
Well I think that's just a capital idea.
We'll use your player piano rolls, George, we'll change the frequencies. Short bursts!
Will you need anything else today, Miss Lamarr?
Just a medal for being brilliant.

So do the army use Hedy's piano-roll frequency-hopping torpedo machine to win WWII?

NO, THEY THINK SHE'S A NUISANCE.

BUT SHE SELLS A LOT OF WAR BONDS BY REPEATEDLY KISSING A SAILOR.

Oh. Blugh.

AND HER IDEA FORMS THE BASIS OF WIFI. IT'S TOTALLY BOSS.

She freed the world from the tyranny of ETHERNET CABLE!

So much better!

Do you have an ethernet port, Nemulon?

YES. AND FIREWIRE 400. AND A PARALLEL INTERFACE.

Right, I've mailed back Hedy's fancy dress. Am I done now?

YOUR MISSION IS 100% COMPLETE.

How do I get home?

FALL BACK-WARDS.

What?

TRUST ME.

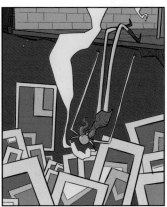

Did I do it, Babs? Did I rectify the past?

It seems like...some-how...you did. Now let's see. Your *timestream entropy level* was 94%.

That's pretty good, right? Pretty good for a beginner?

We'd be looking for about 1-3%.

What does that mean?

Well Shelley, imagine that you'd managed to knock a whole house down...

...and the roof somehow was still floating in mid-air.

FIN

DISCOVER
ALL THE HITS

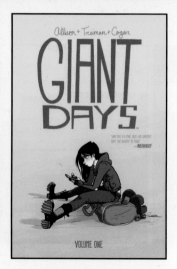

Lumberjanes
Noelle Stevenson, Shannon Watters, Grace Ellis, Brooklyn Allen, and Others
Volume 1: Beware the Kitten Holy
ISBN: 978-1-60886-687-8 | $14.99 US
Volume 2: Friendship to the Max
ISBN: 978-1-60886-737-0 | $14.99 US
Volume 3: A Terrible Plan
ISBN: 978-1-60886-803-2 | $14.99 US
Volume 4: Out of Time
ISBN: 978-1-60886-860-5 | $14.99 US
Volume 5: Band Together
ISBN: 978-1-60886-919-0 | $14.99 US

Giant Days
John Allison, Lissa Treiman, Max Sarin
Volume 1
ISBN: 978-1-60886-789-9 | $9.99 US
Volume 2
ISBN: 978-1-60886-804-9 | $14.99 US
Volume 3
ISBN: 978-1-60886-851-3 | $14.99 US

Jonesy
Sam Humphries, Caitlin Rose Boyle
Volume 1
ISBN: 978-1-60886-883-4 | $9.99 US
Volume 2
ISBN: 978-1-60886-999-2 | $14.99 US

Slam!
Pamela Ribon, Veronica Fish, Brittany Peer
Volume 1
ISBN: 978-1-68415-004-5 | $14.99 US

Goldie Vance
Hope Larson, Brittney Williams
Volume 1
ISBN: 978-1-60886-898-8 | $9.99 US
Volume 2
ISBN: 978-1-60886-974-9 | $14.99 US

The Backstagers
James Tynion IV, Rian Sygh
Volume 1
ISBN: 978-1-60886-993-0 | $14.99 US

Tyson Hesse's Diesel: Ignition
Tyson Hesse
ISBN: 978-1-60886-907-7 | $14.99 US

Coady & The Creepies
Liz Prince, Amanda Kirk, Hannah Fisher
ISBN: 978-1-68415-029-8 | $14.99 US

BOOM! BOX™

AVAILABLE AT YOUR LOCAL COMICS SHOP AND BOOKSTORE
To find a comics shop in your area, call 1-888-266-4226
WWW.BOOM-STUDIOS.COM

All works © their respective creators. BOOM! Box and the BOOM! Box logo are trademarks of Boom Entertainment, Inc. All rights reserved.